To Ela,

Best wishes!
Michael Babbish
-2016

The Rabbit-Man

by

Michael Babbish

DORRANCE
PUBLISHING CO
EST. 1920
PITTSBURGH, PENNSYLVANIA 15238

The contents of this work, including, but not limited to, the accuracy of events, people, and places depicted; opinions expressed; permission to use previously published materials included; and any advice given or actions advocated are solely the responsibility of the author, who assumes all liability for said work and indemnifies the publisher against any claims stemming from publication of the work.

Cover art by David N. Corrado

Dorrance Publishing Co
585 Alpha Drive
Pittsburgh, PA 15238
Visit our website at *www.dorrancebookstore.com*

ISBN: 978-1-4809-2458-1
eISBN: 978-1-4809-2228-0

For Josie Ana

Chapter One

Trouble in the Garden

The Rabbit-Man thought he was going to have an overall pleasant day after waking on the morning of the most fateful day of his life. It seemed as ordinary as any other. He woke up in his home in the Diamond Mine on the outskirts of Lady Easter's Garden. He lived a simple and content life in that place, assisting the gracious lady with the maintenance of her fair home, and he had many pleasant friends to help him in his work, which was not too strenuous but did not leave him idle either. Such work was always the best kind, and often it was found in the Bastions of the world. There was no obvious reason that the Rabbit-Man should expect to have anything but another ordinary day in his usual routine. But then again, some strange things were happening in the Garden as of late.

As Steven Tolibus Ranger (birth name of the Rabbit-Man that he rarely used, often shortened to S.T. Ranger on the few occasions he did) popped out of his rabbit hole that led into the depths of the Diamond Mine, the sky was overcast and the air was slightly cool, but not uncomfortable. Some might call the day a little gloomy, but the Rabbit-Man would not have said so; the weather that day was agreeable to him. He was already dressed. Putting on his rabbit outfit was something he did every single day after waking up, and so he no longer even consciously thought about doing it. Everybody in the Bastion of Lady Easter's Garden wore animal suits, because that was the proper form. Nobody could reside in a Bastion without one, except a leader of the Bastion like Lady Easter. If you asked any of the residents why this was the case, they would think it odd you were even asking. That was just the way things were. People in the Bastions wore their animal suits, and that was that. Nobody ever questioned it, why would they? It was not the least bit necessary to question or even think about such things. That was the attitude in the Bastions, and the Lady's Garden was no exception. Many might think this is very unbecoming of people to do such a thing without thinking about it, but those who say so would not understand what Bastion-life was like.

The Rabbit-Man did have an understanding of Bastion-life, and he found it very good. Lady Easter treated him very well, as she did all of those in her care. The kind Lady's job was becoming more difficult in recent months though, and the stress of maintaining the Bastion she hosted was becoming more obvious. The Rabbit-Man noticed this, and like any good resident of the Garden, he increased his efforts in his work. Still, something seemed strange in the Garden. The Rabbit-Man tried not to think about it very much, because such thoughts were likely to become very painful, and he spent most of his life coaching himself *not* to think of such things.

This day, however, dark thoughts of trouble in the Garden were not on the Rabbit-Man's mind. Going out for a nice stroll was what he felt inclined to do that day, before getting some of his work done. This seemed well enough so he set out. The suit he wore was made of a fine quality that made its exterior have a similar texture to rabbit fur. His suit was one of the better ones, but not so great that it made him look indistinguishable from an ordinary rabbit. No, suits like that were very hard to come by, and those who did often kept to themselves. The Rabbit-Man's suit was brown, and covered most of his body from his shoulders to his ankles. He wore it overtop his regular human clothes, because it was a light and flexible material. His blue shirt and yellow tie could be seen out of the v-shaped cleft in his rabbit suit at the chest, but other than that no human attire could be seen. He had five-fingered gloves over his hands and booties shaped like rabbit feet. Despite this slight discrepancy in the hands, it was still obviously a rabbit suit. No reasonable person could have doubted it. On his head was a cap that fit snugly on his head just over his ears and from this there were two long brown rabbit ears which were arguably the most definitive aspect of his suit. Second to these ears would have been the white fluffy bunny tail on his posterior. His face was mostly uncovered except for a little rabbit snout and two protruding teeth strapped overtop his nose. This helped him nibble away at vegetables quickly, as all rabbits do. Simply put, there was no better way to describe him than to say he was a Rabbit-Man; *the* Rabbit-Man, in fact.

So along he went in his rabbit suit to enjoy fresh air and the beginning of a new day in the Bastion known as the Garden. His role was especially important at that time, because Lady Easter went away on a temporary leave of absence. She put him and several of the other inhabitants in charge of keeping the Garden at peace. The Rabbit-Man was honored to be charged with this task, but a tiny little seed of anxiety was also planted inside of him upon receiving it. This was because keeping peace in the Garden was not as easy as it had been in previous years. It was not incredibly difficult, but more and more things were happening in the Garden that should not have been, and deep in the back of his mind, the Rabbit-Man suspected why. He would not consciously acknowledge these suspicions if he could help it; and every time they crept into his mind he ardently stifled them quickly, before such dark thoughts could cause him any kind of mental pain.

The Rabbit-Man did what he had to for the sake of maintaining his own peace of mind and personal happiness. Nevertheless, the history of the Garden and its relevance to the strange occurrences within the Garden recently were not negated because of his efforts. Many years ago, before the Rabbit-Man was even born, there was a brief period in the Garden known as the Dark Spell. Lady Easter told the inhabitants of her Bastion that such a thing had occurred, but she was very sparing of details and dismissed the questions of her subjects when they asked her about it. Eventually the inhabitants understood that it was a subject not to be discussed, but there was something the Lady made perfectly clear: the Dark Spell was something she did not want to have happen again. It never did, and Lady Easter swore it never would. The Rabbit-Man knew something about the Dark Spell that most of the other residents did not, however. He was aware that this terrible period involved some kind of foreign entity, some person or creature that did not belong, making its way into the Garden. This was the kind of thing that was *never* supposed to happen in a Bastion. On the few dreadful occasions when the boundaries of a Bastion were breached, it resulted in the destruction of the place, and left it nothing but a faint memory. This did not happen to Lady Easter's Garden after the Dark Spell luckily. She had some kind of power to dispel darkness and evil from her domain, which is why she was in charge of the Bastion. Some way or another Lady Easter sent the intruder away, but the breach in the boundary still let occasional foes into the Bastion who had to be dealt with quickly. This was taken care of by Lady Easter's appointed Protectorates, who were able to dispel the foes quickly and efficiently, and often times without the inhabitants even being aware of the occurrence until after the fact. Thus, despite those few lingering aftereffects of the Dark Spell, life was still very good in the Garden.

The Rabbit-Man was not a Protectorate, but he still had many important functions in the Garden, especially now during the Lady's temporary absence. Not surprisingly, it was the carrot field that he was in charge of, but he helped with the cabbages and potatoes too. He would make his usual rounds to those sections of the garden after his walk. He was feeling energetic as usual and wanted to dispense some of his energy with a walk to Madam Duckly's lake. He could meditate to himself on his way there, as he always liked to do during walks. If he was lucky, Madame Duckly might have an extra biscuit or two left after feeding her ducklings that she would share with him. Biscuits! Now there was a pleasant little thought that the Rabbit-Man enjoyed entertaining his mind with.

Along he went toward the lake until on his way he spotted something peculiar. A headpiece was lying on the ground, and the Rabbit-Man knew immediately that it was part of somebody's suit. He picked it up and discovered that it was a black head cap, with the only opening being the face. Two black antennae extended from the top of the cap. The Rabbit-Man knew who this belonged to; it was the cap of Bumbleman, one of the most industrious and responsible inhabitants of the Garden. Bumbleman was a Protectorate and wore the suit of a bee, and it would be very unlike him to leave one of his caps lying about. Some of the younger inhabitants did such things, but Bumbleman would certainly not have.

"What does this mean?" the Rabbit-Man asked himself as a slight little pang of apprehension rose in his belly. He sensed another one of those unpleasant thoughts rising in his mind, and instantly he forced it out. Of course there was some very rational explanation for this. Even the best inhabitants lose things every now and then, or maybe a little child mistakenly got hold of one of the Protectorate's caps and dropped it. The Rabbit-Man had no idea where Bumbleman would be at the moment, but he knew Madam Duckly was good friends with him and could return the cap when she saw the bee-man next. So he continued along, sure not to let any bad ideas enter into his mind. He had no time for distress caused by such things.

The Rabbit-Man was a well-meaning and true-hearted fellow, as just about all inhabitants of the Garden were, but he did not do himself any favors by suppressing negative thoughts from his mind. This method of his was understandable considering his situation, but that is not to say it was good or effective for a long term. The truth was, as the Rabbit-Man would soon find out, that there were many unpleasant things he would have to deal with, and his discovery of Bumbleman's cap was only the beginning.

The Rabbit-Man could no longer dismiss the notion that something was wrong as he came closer to the lake. He heard unusual sounds coming from that direction; sounds he did not hear before. His premonitions could no longer be rushed away by willful thinking when he saw something that terrified him. Two large dark-feathered wings were flapping in the distance, and they were directly above Madam Duckly's lake. Reality, as if with a cold steel scythe, cut through the Rabbit-Man's barricade of imagined relief as he realized the strange sounds were combined with the cries of children. Consternation gripped the Rabbit-Man immediately, and for a very foul moment he was overcome with terror. He saw no sign of Madam Duckly anywhere, and feared for the worst. Despite being afraid, the Rabbit-Man ran closer to the lake and huddled behind a large rock near the trunk of a tree. From here he had a much better view of what was happening.

The dark wings belonged to a massive bird of prey; the kind spoke of only in discussions, but never seen. The Rabbit-Man always understood they were out there in the world, but he never imagined he would ever see one in the Garden. He was ignorant of the exact type of bird this newfound enemy was, but that mattered little. It was large and hungry, and that was all the quivering Rabbit-Man needed to know. The little ducklings, all of them young children in tiny duck suits, were huddled at the edge of the pond. They were holding onto each other, their terrified red faces were crying. The older ones tried to comfort the little ones, but were so frightened themselves they could not offer much. The Rabbit-Man was made sick by what he saw– this was the type of thing that was never ever supposed to enter the Garden, or any of the Bastions for that matter. This was genuine fear he witnessed among the duckling-suited children. Actual mortal terror suffered from the threat of a great foe. Worst of all, it was terror in the hearts of those who could not defend themselves. It was not supposed to be, not ever. It was not *right*. Still, it was so. What could possibly be done? Just like the children, so many of the adults in the Garden could not defend themselves either. It was the worst of situations. Sometimes in such cases, however, hope blooms in people like a flower amid wreckage.

"This is not good at all!" the Rabbit-Man said as despair took a tightening grip on him. "How can this be? Where did this evil bird come from? How could this happen here and now? Why, why, *why*? I can't bear to see this. Those are Madam Duckly's children! They are *only children*! This just can't be!" Hot tears ran down the Rabbit-Man's face as he sat shaking. He wanted so desperately, more than anything, to help those little ducklings on the edge of the pond, but he did not have the skill to confront that terrible bird. If he drew attention to himself, he would surely die, and then the fiend would just turn its attention back to the little ducklings anyway. Any effort on his part would only postpone the inevitable. For the first time in his life, the Rabbit-Man was overwhelmed by an intense feeling of bitterness and hatred; a feeling of disgust that he could not be rid of, and would linger with him for a long time.

But just then he observed something. One of the bird's large wings moved aside and the Rabbit-Man noticed that there was someone struggling in the talons of the gigantic bird. He recognized the victim in the bird's grasp as Bumbleman. The Protectorate's cap was off and blood was dripping from a large cut on the busty man's forehead. His bee wings were bent and mangled and his stinger was broken. This increased the Rabbit-Man's sorrow very much. Poor Bumbleman, who was always so helpful to everyone he encountered in the Garden. He was a large man, but his presence always made others feel safe rather than intimidated. Now he was all but broken and defeated – almost dead, murdered by the talons of an intruder that had no business being there. This was too much for the Rabbit-Man; he had to do something, but what?

He knew he was unable to fight the bird, but if he could only sneak over to the edge of the pond, he might be able to gather the smallest ducklings together and flee with the others close to him. If the bird saw them, they would all be doomed, but if Bumbleman could distract the bird long enough he might be able to get them away. The Rabbit-Man, still incredibly frightened, decided it best not to over-think the situation. With the cap firmly in his gloved hands, he dashed out from behind the rock and tree and made his way to the other end of the lake as stealthily as he could.

"I sure hope I can do this," he thought as he ran around the water's edge. "If there is anything I ever wanted, it would be to get these duckling-kids out of here." So he went as quickly as he could, each second seemed like an hour or more. Fighting with all of his might, he tried not to let the internal panic and fear within him seize control of his thinking. He made his way to where the frightened duckling-children were and gestured to the oldest among them.

"Come here, follow me!" the Rabbit-Man urged, trying not to let his voice get the attention of the large dark brown bird. The confused ducklings, about nine of them were there, gained enough of their senses to realize a friend was near. Courage and desire to flee from the predator overcame their fear and they made their way toward the Rabbit-Man. As they were all gathered around him, he directed them away from the lake. He had no idea where he was going to take them, but he knew they needed to leave where they were. Again, the idea of a second Dark Spell entered the Rabbit-Man's troubled mind, but he shooed it away and focused on getting the duckling-children to safety.

"This way!" he instructed them. "Be quick, but stay together. You are all doing very well, but we must keep moving." The Rabbit-Man was touched by how orderly the children moved along despite their obvious fear. Some of them were still crying, and others had dried tears on their face. One of the older children, probably only eight years old, was carrying a weeping toddler on his back. The smaller child's hood had fallen back, exposing a tuft of light brown hair and leaving only the little duck-bill on his frightened face. The Rabbit-Man saw the older boy was struggling, so he went and took the younger child onto his own back. The Rabbit-Man was not an athlete, but he was in good enough shape to carry the toddler and move quickly. As he did, however, he heard a blood-curdling screech from the predatory bird behind him. In a moment of horror he looked back and saw the enormous eyes of the brown bird looking directly at him. There was no longer any sign of Bumbleman, but the blood dripping from the great bird's beak made it clear the stout Protectorate had lost the struggle. Just as the bird spread its ominous brown wings, a large pink rope that resembled a whip shot out of the lake and wrapped around the bird's ankle. Then out came a giant frog, an inhabitant of the lake who was known as Marshy. He was a friend of the Rabbit-Man and Madam Duckly, and now he made an effort to help his friends flee from this wretched intruder. It was Marshy's tongue wrapped around the bird's ankle, and as it rose higher the giant frog was pulled farther out of the water. He gestured with a finned hand for the Rabbit-Man to flee. Again the man in the rabbit suit led the children farther away from the lake.

Marshy did not last long against the great bird, however. As the bird's sharp beak thrust downward the massive frog's moist body was torn asunder in only a fleeting moment. The Rabbit-Man glanced back once to see the worst of this, and the pain that shot like an arrow through him was almost unbearable. If not for his determination to help the duckling-children he may have broken down in despair. He hoped that none of the children saw the poor frog's fate, but they seemed to be running along and he assumed none of them noticed.

"Two of our own have died already," the Rabbit-Man thought with remorse. "How can this be? What is going on here?" After Marshy's demise it
seemed clear the great bird would descend upon them, but there was one last
ally that lived in the water that would come to their aid. After swallowing the
final remains of the frog it devoured, the bird felt a sharp pain on his other
ankle. This time it was not a tongue but a reptilian mouth biting into it. The
head of a turtle and the front part of his shell were out of the water, and his
weight kept the predator from flying higher into the air.

The shrill cries of the bird made the children tremble with fright, but the
Rabbit-Man urged them along. A final glance back showed him the delay that
would save their lives. The turtle was Troy Dow, one of the oldest inhabitants
of the lake. As the Rabbit-Man ran along after the children, he sent one final
desperate wish out to the struggling turtle, and hoped he would not meet the
same fate as Bumbleman and Marshy. Although he was heavy, the great bird
was able to pull Troy Dow out of the water and onto the land beside the lake.
The turtle was fortunate to land on his stomach. As the bird of prey descended
on his newly arrived foe, Troy Dow gave him a broad grin before slipping his
head and appendages into his hard shell. The bird violently bit and slashed
and thrashed at the shell, but to no avail. Troy Dow was safely in his shell, and
the distraction to the great bird allowed the Rabbit-Man to slip away into a
grove about a mile away from the lake.

The grove had a little canopy shelter in it that the Rabbit-Man gathered
the duckling-children into. They were still frightened, but some were relieved
they were away from the danger. Although he tried not to show it, the Rabbit-
Man was still very frightened and confused himself. He had no idea how the
predator entered the Garden or where he should bring the ducklings. He did
not know what happened to Madam Duckly, but feared the worst. Just as he decided he should bring them into his home, he saw in the distance an icon which
made hope immediately blossom in him. A large golden model of the number
one was drifting by from behind a shrubbery, and the Rabbit-Man knew what
that meant. It was the logo atop the vehicle of Mister One, a friend of Lady
Easter who came from one of the Metroscape regions. Mr. One supplied the
Protectorates with the weapons they used to guard the Bastion, and if there was
anybody that could help defend the children against a predator it would be him.
Despite his tendency to occasionally refer to himself in the third person and his
fondness for weaponry, Mr. One was an old friend of the Rabbit-Man. S.T.
Ranger never knew a more reliable and trustworthy individual than good old

Mr. One.

"Come along children, follow me!" the Rabbit-Man said to the duckling-kids. "We must get to that vehicle with the number one over there." The children obeyed and followed the Rabbit-Man in an orderly line, just as they used to follow their now-absent teacher Madame Duckly. Sure enough, from behind a hill emerged Mister One's large weapon van with his arsenal inside. It was not moving along very fast; it seemed like Mr. One was aware something was amiss in the Garden and was proceeding with caution. The Rabbit-Man waved his arms wildly until the van slowed to a stop. Mr. One then stepped out of the vehicle to greet the Rabbit-Man and the ducklings. He was a tall man with a stern head, atop which was a large brown hat with the golden number one logo on it and light brown close-trimmed facial hair. He never wore an animal suit, and ignored the mandate that one do so in a Bastion. In fact, Mr. One ignored many of the rules that were in place from the Caretaking Body, but always managed to evade the severe penalties for doing so. It was known by some that Mr. One was once appointed to be a member of the mysterious governmental group, but ended up having differences with them and lived on the fly ever since.

"Mr. One, I am so glad you are here!" the Rabbit-Man exclaimed. "You could not have appeared at a better time. A terrible bird has gotten into our Garden, and I have no idea how. It would have devoured all these children if I didn't lead them away. Our friends from the lake distracted the bird and we got away, but it is still out there. What's happening? Can you use one of those long metal firearms of yours to defeat this enemy?"

"I have no idea what's happening, Rabbit-Man," Mr. One replied. "But you're right; it seems I'm needed here. Mr. One never leaves his friends in need! I can definitely take down a bird, even a large one, with some of the equipment I have. Mr. One's way is a sure way to get rid of enemies quick, make no mistake about it. And that's why all the enemies of Mr. One can't get me. They try to slow me down and ruin me. Always trying to grind Mr. One to dust they are, but they don't know who they're dealing with! That nasty bird is going to learn the hard way that you don't mess with the friends of Mr. One! But I'm certain this bird isn't the only enemy here. I saw some other dark creature flying through the air earlier. It had wings, but I don't think it was a bird. It was gone in an instant, but the look of it was enough to put me on my guard. It's very dangerous here."

"What about these children?" the Rabbit-Man asked. "I can take them to my home, unless they will be safer with you. I don't know what happened to their caretaker, but I don't even like to think about it. Bumbleman and Marshy the frog have already fallen to the enemy."

"Mommy was chasing away another bad guy when the bird came," one of the ducklings said. "But then she never came back."

"The equipment in my van is secured, and there is enough space back there for these children, but not much more," said Mr. One. "I can take them to safety in The One Van. Rabbit-Man, I'll need you to find any others and gather them together at Lady Easter's palace. That will provide a refuge until we can figure out what to do, but be careful. We know there are other enemies around."

"Thank you, Mr. One," said the Rabbit-Man. "I'll make it there as soon as I can." He then helped Mr. One gather the children into the back of the vehicle. They bid each other farewell. But before Mr. One drove off he said to the Rabbit-Man, "I'm glad I'm here to help you all in the Garden. Whatever happens, remember this: You're an old friend of mine, Rabbit-Man. It pays to be a friend of the first, the only, number one, Mr. One!" Then he drove off.

The Rabbit-Man decided he should head to his home to gather a few essential supplies, and then find any friends he could and go to Lady Easter's palace. He never made it there, though. As he set out and ran toward the Diamond Mine he noticed something strange in the air. A faint blue haze appeared and permeated everywhere around him. He had no idea what this was, but the more he moved along the thicker and darker the blue haze became. It was not mist, because it could not be felt on the skin, and it was more than a mere light. Whatever it was, the Rabbit-Man dreaded seeing it, and wanted it to go away. A few glimmers of blue light simmered here and there, and then were gone without a trace.

"What is this?" the Rabbit-Man asked himself. Before he could think about it long, he saw a shadowy figure coming toward him in the distance. The figure seemed to be human, but had two large dark bat-like wings on its back. The Rabbit-Man knew that nobody in the Garden wore a suit like that, and he recalled what Mr. One told him about the winged creature he saw earlier in the day. As the figure approached the Rabbit-Man could tell it was a very large person, and he noticed two unnatural glowing yellow eyes on its face. He froze dead in his tracks. The blue haze now grew so much that it seemed like a thick shadow covering everything around him. Still there were faint twinkles of blue light flashing here and there, and still the figure walked on. Then, in an instant, faster than the blinking of a rabbit's eye, all else was blocked out by an enormous , hideous grinning blue face that was immediately in front of him. This face had bulging yellow eyes with tiny black pupils, a skeleton-like nose of two narrow holes, and a lipless mouth curved into a hellish smile lined with sharp jagged teeth. The Rabbit-Man screamed as this awful face appeared before him in a flash, and stepped backwards away from it. That face – the terrible face he would never, ever forget – just gazed at him with its infernal grin. As he stepped back, the ground beneath the Rabbit-Man's booties gave way and he stepped off into a hole in the ground that was certainly not there before. He fell backwards through the hole and screamed. Up above him was that horrible face, grinning down at him and laughing at him in his fright. The blue haze was all around him as he fell, farther and farther down. The fall never seemed to end. The blue demon-face remained above him and eventually he heard high, blood-chilling laughter all around him. The laugh matched the face in wretchedness, and the Rabbit-Man wished he would die rather than hear and see this monstrosity a moment longer. Then finally, the haze cleared and the face vanished as quickly as it appeared. The Rabbit-Man hit the ground with a thud and lay on a grey dusty surface that he knew was not part of Lady Easter's Garden. He knew he was far from the Bastion where he lived, and dread would have taken him if not for the shock and pain that racked him. The Rabbit-Man had fallen.

Chapter Two
After the Fall

The Rabbit-Man was somewhat hurt by the fall, but more confused than anything. He tried to get up and could not. The best he could do for himself was squirm on the dusty ground for a moment before he turned over onto his belly. He looked over and saw the roots of a massive tree beside him. Then, very faintly at first, he heard the same laughter that plagued him while he was falling. Only now it was a deeper, heavier voice laughing. Still, the Rabbit-Man somehow instinctively knew it was coming from the same foul source. He managed to prop himself onto his hands and knees, and looked over his shoulder. That same large dark winged figure was hovering in the air. The Rabbit-Man tried to get away, but only fell forward as his face landed into the dusty ground. The laughter then grew far louder. The fallen Rabbit-Man became increasingly desperate to get away from this foul thing near him, but lacked the strength to move. He put his arms forward and pulled himself along on his stomach as best he could. He was not going fast at all, and more resembled a snail than a rabbit in his movement. Still, he forced himself onward and made some progress. He felt hot and heavy air blowing onto his back, so he looked over his shoulder again and once more saw that terrible face with the yellow eyes and awful teeth. Now his adrenaline allowed him to prop himself back onto his hands and knees and crawl forward. He moved along like this for a length of time that was a mystery to him ever after, trying to flee the blue demonic face. He went as far as he could before he slipped and fell forward again, his face landing into the grey dust on the ground. He lifted his head and again pulled himself forward, all the while feeling the hot air on his back. His vision blurred, but as it did he saw something surrounding him – something he desperately hoped would save him from this pestilent face, laughter and breath. He could not see the specific direction it came from, but the weakened Rabbit-Man noticed a type of calming light surrounding his body. This welcome new light countered the horrid grey-blue haze emitted by the dark figure, and it warmed and comforted him. He sensed a voice deep in his consciousness whisper gently, "Don't worry, you're going to be alright." and for some inexplicable reason the Rabbit-Man believed this when he heard it in his mind. He thought he could hear a guttural voice from above him, presumably that of the manifest horror that frightened him, say "That could be a problem, I'll need to get rid of that," but the Rabbit-Man didn't care. The glow of light that enveloped him gave him comfort, and a very brief and fleeting image of a happy smiling face within the glow flashed vibrantly in his mind and was gone in an instant. The comforting glow of light vanished along with it, but that brief moment of comfort gave the rabbit-suited man laying prone on the ground enough reassurance to help him remain calm. It also must have sent some kind of message to the dark creature because it did nothing to him at that time. The Rabbit-Man did not even remember the incident until something reminded him of it later.

The Rabbit-Man, still laying flat on his stomach, reached out his right hand, as if making a somber plea for this blessed sensation to return. His vision blurred and then darkened as his face fell onto the ground along with his hand, and he lay unconscious. The winged figure then flew off into the sky, which was now a hue of slate grey. It would not be very long until the Rabbit-Man encountered this considerable foe again, but for the time being he was safe from it. When the Rabbit-Man eventually woke, he did not know what happened to him.

Sometime later, S.T. Ranger woke up sore and aching. He had a bad feeling in his stomach and felt a dizzy sensation in his head. He opened his eyes and blinked several times, trying to take in the features of the environment around him. It was a very barren place and appeared tired and old, like land that had seen far too much activity over the millenniums and had grown weary of it. It was a stark contrast to the blessed Garden Bastion he was used to. The ground, though covered in a layer of grey sandy dust, was very hard. It was nighttime; the sky was cloudy and no stars were visible. The air was crisp and the Rabbit-Man shivered a bit. He looked up and noticed he was beside a very tall tree. Upon seeing this, he vaguely remembered his fall, the hideous demonic face, and even faintly remembered the comforting glow that saved him. None of these were present now, however. No soothing light, no blue haze or laughter, only this solitary tree. He was surprised anything could grow in such a place as this, but there seemed to be no other life apart from this one tree. He craned his neck and looked farther up but still could not see the top of it. It then dawned on him in an unsettling rush of realization that the top of this massive tree is where he fell from.

"How can I even hope to get back up there?" the Rabbit-Man asked himself. The tree was so high, and the branches did not even start protruding from the sides until far up on the trunk. Still, he made several efforts to climb up the tree, but slid down every time. At last he sat down on one of the roots bulging from the ground. He hoped that the duckling-children were alright, but was comforted knowing he left them in the protection of Mr. One. The feeling in his stomach grew worse as he contemplated his situation. He had fallen from his well-loved home in Lady Easter's Garden and had no idea how to get back there. With growing anxiety, he wondered if he had the survival skills and instinct necessary to make it in this chilled and desolate world he had fallen into. He had heard of people leaving their Bastions before, but never thought he would do so himself.

"Is this what it's like for everyone who leaves a Bastion?" he asked himself. "It's no wonder few folk ever venture away at all. I heard that these places can make one go insane upon entering them; I feel a little bit like I am going insane." He did not have much time to consider this however, because as he gazed at the high tree he heard a scratching noise not far from him. He looked off into the gloomy distance and noticed two bright, leering eyes similar to the demonic ones he saw before. These were different, but still looked frightening, like two great orbs of hateful fire, and they were fixed directly upon him. They were surrounded by long black lashes and in this horrifying instant the Rabbit-Man also observed the other features of this newly arrived creature. Sharp yellow teeth like short dangerous swords lined a mouth dripping with saliva and a wiggling purple, vein-riddled tongue spread out of it. A curled snout was above the awful mouth, and the Rabbit-Man recognized the awful creature to be a massive, grey-haired hungry wolf. Such creatures of the wild were fearsome enough, but this one was larger and his features more grotesque than any other. The luckless Rabbit-Man had only seen images of wolves within the safety of Lady Easter's Garden. He believed this fearsome wolf to be a Grandie – exceptionally large animals of prey that were alleged to live in lands outside of the Bastions. He thought the massive bird that entered Lady Easter's Garden must have been the same thing. "I always doubted whether Grandies were real or not," the Rabbit-Man thought, "I never imagined I would ever see one. What has happened to cause all this?"

The quivering yelp he would have let out was stifled in his throat. After a fleeting moment of immersion in fear, the Rabbit-Man's survival instinct returned to him as he turned and fled from the wolf. He was a fast runner compared to other inhabitants of the Garden, but he knew he could not possibly outrun this Grandie wolf. Still, he knew he had to at least try.

There was no place to hide because the land around him was so completely sparse. No brushes or shrubs to hide in were to be found, and there were no holes in this hard ground beneath its dusty surface. The hope for the Rabbit-Man came when he found a massive rock to hide behind. He knew this would most likely do little good, and the wolf would surely find him, but he was steadily running out of breath and he could not see any other possible way to avoid the predator. He heard a guttural growling sound behind him as he quivered behind the rock, and it was getting closer. In the second before the wolf would have reached the rock and found him, a blackbird descended onto the rock he was hiding behind. It had strange white eyes, and plucked a black feather from one of its wings and let it fall before the trembling Rabbit-Man.

"Use this," he heard a voice say. "It will make you like a shadow, and disguise you from the wolf's gaze and smell." The bird then flew away, leaving the Rabbit-Man alone with the feather. He picked it up and held it close to his chest. Sure enough, the frightful wolf leaped over the rock and stared directly in the Rabbit-Man's direction. The fiend's face was contorted into an insane grin. The wolf let out another guttural sound that sounded like devilish laughter.

"Where did you go, little rabbit?" the wolf growled, evidently not able to see his prey and also confirming to the Rabbit-Man that Grandies also had the ability for speech. "I don't know how you got away from me. Most can never hope to flee my pursuit, but mark my words little rabbit: I will remember you. I remember everyone I meet. You can only postpone your doom. Someday, somewhere, maybe even years from now, I will find you. When I do, you will wish you had never been born as I tear you apart and devour your carcass. It will be pain like you never thought possible. It's going to happen little rabbit.

I will get you." The wolf looked around, still unable to see his prey, and then spoke again in the Rabbit-Man's general direction. "I get them all in the end." The wolf then stalked off, eventually increasing his pace into a swift run until the Rabbit-Man could not see him anymore. The Rabbit-Man was greatly disturbed by the wolf's presence, but also very relieved to see him gone. He wondered where the strange blackbird went, and would very much have liked to thank him. Since there was no sign of anyone else nearby, he crept out from behind the rock and moved along. He opened his hand and noticed the black feather had vanished. "What is going on?" he thought anxiously as he continued along with caution. In a matter of only a few hours, he had gone from having a comfortable and content life, to being in a strange lonesome place and having encountered very threatening enemies. What happened, the Rabbit-Man wondered, to have caused all of this upheaval? What in all the name of creation went wrong? He pondered this, understanding deep in his mind that they were incredibly difficult questions to answer. Even deeper in his mind, possibly at the source of his growing fear and anxiety, he wondered if they were questions that had any answers to be found.

If there was ever a bad first impression, the Rabbit-Man experienced it when he entered this new strange and dark world he was unfamiliar with. Worse yet, the large wolf set a terror in his mind he was unsure how to cope with. What troubled him most was the final message the fiend left him before it stalked off, "I get them all in the end..." The words lingered in his mind like a poisonous, pervasive mist. In a way, that last phrase of the wolf affected the frightened Rabbit-Man the same way the strange blue haze had.

"He gets them all..." the Rabbit-Man thought to himself. "Who does he mean when he says 'them,' and how many of 'them' are there for him to get? Just what exactly *happened* to me?" he thought in distress. The trouble on his mind only grew as he then thought, "What will happen to me?" He never knew how long he sat by that rock, considering his situation with mixed feelings involving confusion, doubt, fear, and a faint but firmly present curiosity. He then heard the voice of that strange blackbird speaking again, "He will be back soon. For goodness' sake, stop sitting around wallowing and stewing. Get out of here, or you will be dead!" So the Rabbit-Man started walking forward, entirely unsure of where he was going. He quickened his pace as his fear increased. He did not wish to have the burning eyes of the wolf upon him again. He continued along the hard, dust-covered ground until his eye sighted a figure in the distance. He discovered it was a person sitting on the ground, holding something he could not see clearly. The figure did not appear threatening. Excited to see someone else in this desolate world, he moved swiftly toward the person.

The Rabbit-Man then found a young woman holding an infant in her arms. She looked disheveled but still attractive, with dark brown hair flowing over her shoulders and back. It was unruly, but this made her look more beautiful and even erotic. The Rabbit-Man's soul was stirred instantly upon viewing the young lady, although he was deeply concerned to see such a fine-looking woman with her child in a place like this. This helped him, because he temporarily forgot his own troubles for a moment, and instead felt an arcane instinct to aid her. "Could she have come from a Bastion as well?" The Rabbit-Man thought, "She doesn't have an animal suit, so she cannot be from Lady Easter's Garden. Still, I wonder where she is from, and where she is going."

The woman looked at the Rabbit-Man as he approached her. She did not seem in any way surprised by his rabbit suit. At first her face was solemn and she appeared quite unhappy. When she smiled at the Rabbit-Man, he could tell she had to force it, although he still appreciated the gesture. He wanted very much to get her away from this lonesome place, and his fear gave way to eagerness while he was in her presence. She appeared to be alone, and in his enthusiasm the Rabbit-Man concluded it would only be logical if they both helped each other in this unwelcoming environment. He had no friends in this strange land, and had already encountered one enemy. Clad in a rabbit suit though he was, he figured the woman would be much better off with an ally like him than none at all.

"Hello," the Rabbit-Man said. "How did you and your child end up in a place like this? It's very dangerous here. I've only been here a short while and I just narrowly escaped an encounter with a terrible wolf. Do you have any-where else to go?"

"I've been here a while," the woman replied. "I am trying to find a place for my son and me to go. We've been estranged from Main City, the Met-roscape we came from. It's a long story; all I can say is that I am unable to take care of both me and my baby, so I would have had to forfeit both of us to Mr. Spiderhat. He is in charge of the Grand Coliseum, the greatest spectacle in all of Main City. The only way I could have avoided going there is if we paid Spi-derhat off with some cabbage, but we don't have any, so I ran away."

"I'm afraid I don't understand what you're talking about," the Rabbit-Man said, though he was sympathetic to her situation. He did not know what the

Grand Coliseum or this 'cabbage' was, but he understood all too well what being alone in this dreadful world entailed. "I am very new to this place. I fell from Lady Easter's Garden, and what I suspected seems to be true: I'm in the vicinity of a Metroscape. Main City is the one, as you just said. I know the odds of a person from a Bastion making it in a Metroscape are slim, but I am going to do the best I can. I have some talents. Hopefully they will get me by until I find a way to get back to the Garden. I am very pleased I met you, though. I am S.T. Ranger, the Rabbit-Man, one of the caretakers in Lady Easter's Garden. Please tell me your name. Perhaps we may help each other." The woman smiled faintly at the Rabbit-Man, but the sadness he saw in her expression haunted him for a while afterward, and he became disheartened.

"My name is Pertho, and your offer is kind, but there is nothing you can do to help me. You seem like a really nice person, Rabbit-Man, but you are doomed. We both are. Those like us simply don't make it in a place like this. Without any cabbage, we are powerless, and it's only a matter of time until someone comes and devours us."

"Pertho, what do you mean? I always knew the Metroscapes were very cutthroat places, but surely people cannot just go around murdering others without some kind of penalty. Who can do something like that? Murder the mother of a child without any remorse." Then the Rabbit-Man immediately thought of the foul wolf he encountered and knew the answer to his own question. Horror now overwhelmed him even more than it had before. Pertho must have noticed this in his expression.

"You have seen one of the Grandies, haven't you?" she asked. "They are very large and hungry animals, and also very treacherous. Those of us who stray from our safety zones are their nourishment. The Guard Dogs keep the cabbage from them, and thus they prey on whoever they can. I really wish you could help me Rabbit-Man, but I doubt you'll even be able to save yourself."

Before the Rabbit-Man could reply to this, he noticed something on its way toward them. It was not the Grandie wolf he recently met. Instead, this was a large metallic vehicle riding along. The driver halted the vehicle near Pertho and the Rabbit-Man. A tall man in a fly suit stepped out and looked at them. Pertho gazed up at him as he approached her. He paid no attention to the Rabbit-Man.

"Strays!" the fly-man said as he leered at the young woman. "What have you got?" Pertho, with a desperate look in her eyes the Rabbit-Man despised, knelt in front of the fly-man and held her child up to him. The fly-man took it into in his arms, and then looked down at her. He undoubtedly sensed something in Pertho's attitude that indicated to him he could control her. "You need a sanctuary?" he asked her.

"Yes please," she responded, almost as if she were begging him.

"You're coming with me, get in!" he exclaimed. The Rabbit-Man could not watch this and do nothing. He did not like the look of this fly-man one bit, or that of his little driver, who wore a cap over his head that covered his eyes. The Rabbit-Man approached the fly-man.

"What is going on here?" he asked. "Where are you taking this woman? She and her child are in need, and it looks to me like you intend to take advantage of their unfortunate situation. Who are you, and what are you after?"

The fly-man opened the door to his vehicle, handed the child to Pertho as she stepped inside. He then pulled a thick club from the vehicle and waylaid the Rabbit-Man across the head with it so suddenly the Rabbit-Man fell to the ground dazed. The carriage was gone before he could regain his senses. When his vision cleared he stood up. No sign of the vehicle or Pertho remained. Feeling utterly miserable, he continued along. He still had no clear direction, but at least he had more information. Before he could encounter more danger, he decided he ought to try and get to Main City. He had no idea what waited for him there, but come whatever may, he would find his way back to the Garden or go down trying.

What the Rabbit-Man did not understand was that the man in the fly outfit was actually a Morphie. This was something similar to a Grandie, but quite different in that Morphies had the physical characteristics of both humans and the animals of which they resembled. These individuals become so intrinsically connected with their animal costume that it becomes part of their physical body and it is permanently attached. They then become a type of animal-person rather than just a person in an animal suit. Morphies were not uncommon in Main City and the surrounding areas, but ordinary humans and Grandies were more numerous. The fly-man was a well-known Morphie in Main City known as Buzzy Hopedasher, who worked for Mr. Spiderhat.

The Rabbit-Man would learn more about Morphies and Grandies in the near future, but until then he continued onward, disgusted and disappointed that Pertho would favor a vile man in a fly suit with poor manners over him. Again this was evidence of the Rabbit-Man's unfortunate ignorance of the Metroscape areas and the way they operated. Because Buzzy Hopedasher was a Morphie, he had some distinctive characteristics of that insect. For example, flies are attracted to and consume dung. This makes them essential to decomposition in the natural world. Buzzy Hopedasher, although not attracted to dung, had a constant habit of collecting other people's garbage whenever he came across it. If someone were throwing something away, the fly-man would snatch it up and find some kind of use for it. In this way, he was similar to an actual fly in that he collected waste. He was not the most appealing of companions, but Pertho saw that he at least had a place in the society of Main City, and thus she would be more protected in his care than she would with the idealistic but powerless Rabbit-Man, who had no practical skills to be applied in Main City, or any Metroscape for that matter.

The fly-man's resemblance to the insect enabled him to detect certain aspects of luckless Pertho's psyche that the Rabbit-Man and other people could not. He sensed that somebody in need was nearby, and when somebody is in need (the more dire the better) they can be taken advantage of. This was another of Buzzy Hopedasher's areas of expertise – exploiting the weaknesses of others. Pertho had essentially become the "waste product" of Main City after she and her child were cast away. Keeping true to his fly-like nature, the fly-man made his way over to her as quick as he could and snatched her away. What added to his success, however, was Pertho's attitude toward herself. Because she believed she and her child were doomed to be wastrels, they became that. Her belief that such a condition was inevitable is what made her the target for the fly-man, and thus he got what he wanted.

"I hope you'll be alright Pertho." the Rabbit-Man thought as he continued along. Although greatly troubled by the young lady's speedy surrender to the fly-man, he could not help but keep warm feelings for her. "Well, whatever happens to Pertho and her baby, I need to find a place to settle before I make my return to the Garden. I will not do much good for anyone unless I can take care of myself."

It was not long before Main City was in sight. Tall grey buildings could be seen in the distance. Eventually a black road formed on the ground leading in the direction of the city. The Rabbit-Man continued along this road and walked toward the buildings. A small, quivering sense of fear rose in his stomach as he approached. It was a Metroscape after all. He had never been to one before. Folk who lived in Bastions seldom went into the Metroscapes, and when they did they were usually accompanied by some kind of Protectorate, and usually with a specific destination and business in mind. The Rabbit-Man had neither of these, but continued along because he had no other choice.

"Well," he said to himself after letting out a sigh, "here I go."

Chapter Three
The Coveted Cabbage

So the Rabbit-Man went on, toward Main City where he hoped he could find a way to return home. His enthusiasm and determination soon gave way to hunger and anxiety as the mental precursors to discouragement and despair began to form in his mind. The city did not appear to be very far away when he first viewed it, but as he walked on he became more famished and fatigued. He moved forward though, until he made his way to the outskirts of the city.

It had no main gate, but only a massive sign that read Main City in vibrant red letters painted on a grey backdrop. There was a hard paved road extending throughout the areas around the buildings on either side. They were very plain-looking structures, but the dusty-grey hues combined with their height gave the buildings an ominous presence. The Rabbit-Man felt intimidated viewing these structures, as they were very foreign to him. He had only ever seen the likes of them in books and the videos that he saw in the Garden. Places like Main City and other Metroscapes seemed fascinating to the Rabbit-Man when he saw them in the videos he watched with his friends, but now that he was away from his Bastion, he did not like the atmosphere. He saw some people milling between the buildings and crossing the street. He also saw occasional vehicles passing by, similar to those that the fly-man rode.

As he walked deeper into the city, the Rabbit-Man saw a man walking down the road toward him. The man wore stained overalls and a tight-fitting cotton cap on his head. Although he knew animal suits were optional in the Metroscapes, the Rabbit-Man could not help but be surprised at seeing someone not wearing one. He never thought he would see the day when he was outside a Bastion and interacting with people in a Metroscape. He always regarded the Suitless as a different breed of people remote from his sphere of existence, yet here he was in the presence of one.

"Excuse me sir," the Rabbit-Man said to the man. "I'm new to this place and I don't know where to find food or a place to stay. I'm trying to get back to my home in Lady Easter's Garden. I had an accident that left me far away from there; it's difficult to explain, really. If you could please tell me what I need to do I would appreciate it."

"You're lucky you ran into me before anyone else, newcomer," the man said in a weary but not unfriendly voice. "We've been seeing a lot of those lately. What you need to do first is register yourself here in the city. The office is just down the road further. You can't do anything here without doing that. They'll set you up with an Identity Card and a work assignment, and then you'll be in a better way soon. If you're new I assume you don't have any of the Coveted Cabbage. That's gonna have to change if you hope to survive here at all."

"Thank you," the Rabbit-Man answered. "I'll be sure to do this registration. But please tell me, I heard of this Coveted Cabbage you speak of, and I can tell it's very essential to the operation here in the city, but I'm afraid I still don't exactly know what it is. Can you explain more about this?"

The man's mouth made a half-smile and he looked at the Rabbit-Man with an expression of combined pity and amusement. It left his face quickly, but the Rabbit-Man noticed it, and he felt his sense of anxiety grow. It was now more obvious to him that he knew nothing about where he was, and would have much difficulty in the future unless he learned the operations of Main City quickly. He was also aware of how much trust he was putting in this stranger, revealing his vulnerability through the questions he asked. The man in overalls did not seem like a threat, but he wondered what would have resulted if he met the fly-man alone and asked him the same things. The idea made him shudder inside.

"Look fellow," the man said, placing a hand on the Rabbit-Man's shoulder. "I'm going to try and make this as simple for you as possible. The Coveted Cabbage is *everything* here in Main City. You cannot do anything without it, and you can never get enough of it. It is the most essential facet of life here. Whatever you knew in this garden you came from, just forget about it. From now on, your only concern better be the Coveted Cabbage and how to get some of it. Many people here, a lot of them animal-folks like you, work tirelessly and rigorously to get even just a little bit of it. It is well kept and guarded by Grandies known as the Guard Dogs. Fellow, please tell me you know what Grandies are."

"I certainly do," the Rabbit-Man said and gulped, thinking back on the wolf Grandie he encountered. "I was already chased by a wolf in the clearing outside this place."

"Oh yes, Wolfsnare the Terrible. We all know about him around here, but luckily he doesn't come into Main City very often. He tore up a good many folks in the Grand Coliseum though. I'm surprised you got away from him. Maybe you're fitter than you seem to be. If you think he's bad though, you better not cross the vicious Guard Dogs – they can tear someone ten times the size of you to pieces. I've seen them do it before. Many people in this city despise them, with good reason, but very few would dare to cross them. I would stay away from them if I were you."

"I'll keep that in mind. Thank you for the information sir. What is your name?"

"I'm Dale Apple. Most people just call me Ap, and who might you be?"

"I'm the Rabbit-Man, and it's a pleasure to meet you, Ap. You are more approachable than some others I met so far. I suppose you wouldn't happen to know how to get back to Lady Easter's Garden, would you?"

"I'm afraid I've never heard of the place. I can tell you that you'll have a very hard time getting out of Main City without a Pass. That's a special certification you can purchase with enough Cabbage. It's quite costly though, so you may want to work on getting more of that Cabbage as soon as possible."

"Thank you for all your help, Ap." said the Rabbit-Man. "I am going to find this registration building. Maybe I'll see you again sometime."

"I hope so, Rabbit-Man. Best of luck to you." Ap and the Rabbit-Man shook hands and each continued on their way. The Rabbit-Man walked onward, passing many buildings until he came to the one with Registration labeled above its door. He walked inside and went to the desk. Sitting behind it was a very fat woman wearing a bonnet with a daisy on top of it. She looked very comical, but the few other individuals milling around in the office seemed not to notice at all. She looked up from the book she was reading as the Rabbit-Man approached the desk. She looked at him grumpily as if he was disturbing her. The Rabbit-Man guessed he probably was, but because his registration was essential he knew he had to.

"Hello, I would like to register in Main City," he told the woman. She leaned forward and opened a drawer in her desk, and then pulled out a clip-board with papers on it, and handed this to the Rabbit-Man.

"Fill these out then bring 'em back to me," she said apathetically. "We'll get your blood sample then one of our agents will get you some kind of work."

"Thanks," the Rabbit-Man said as he took the clipboard. He found a chair in the office and then sat down to fill out the papers he was given. The first page asked general information: his name, where he came from before entering Main City, why he came to Main City, how much Cabbage he had, what type of animal suit he wore, if any. He wrote all this then flipped the page over. The next page asked many odd questions he did not understand: had he ever ingested or smoked marijuana, how often did he drink to intoxication, did he use cocaine, did he use acid, what was his annual income, did he ever file for Special Training (he thought this was an especially vague question, but his an-swer was still no), did he have a Pass (this question interested him, because this is what he wanted to pursue because he thought it would help him get back to the Garden). He finished these questions and continued to the third page, which asked a series of personal questions. Again he thought many of these were odd, but filled them out nonetheless. It was essential to getting reg-istered and pursuing the Coveted Cabbage, after all. The total application was nine pages long, and after he completed it the Rabbit-Man was hungry and irritated. He handed the clipboard back to the woman with the daisy bonnet.

"Have a seat and an agent will be with you shortly," she said, so the Rabbit-Man sat and waited. It was not long before a tall thin man entered the office. He had dark hair that was balding and wore a suit with a tie, but no animal costume.

"Hello, sir," the man said with a smile. "Welcome to registration. Have you had any food recently?"

"Hello and thank you," the Rabbit-Man answered, excited by this last question. "No, I haven't. If you have something to offer I'd be very grateful."

"You must be starving," the man replied. "Most newcomers are. Some poor chaps are nearly dead when they come in here. You seem to be in mod-erately fine condition though." The man in the suit was very amicable, and led the Rabbit-Man into a room behind the main office. In the room there was a mirror, and when the Rabbit-Man saw himself he was surprised. His suit was dirty and he looked more frayed than he ever saw himself before. If he looked better than most that arrived for registration, he understood that the condition of most newcomers must have been quite severe.

"Please have a seat," the suited man said. "I'll have a meal sent into you soon."

"Thank you very much, sir," The Rabbit-Man said with sincerity. He began to feel better than he had the past several hours. At last he had met some kind individuals and would be given a meal. The woman in the front office indicated they would give him some kind of work, which he was sure would allow him to collect some of the Coveted Cabbage. With that, he may be able to purchase the Pass Ap mentioned and be on his way back to Lady Easter's Garden. Perhaps his visit to the Metroscape would not be so bad. So long as he avoided conflict with the Guard Dogs, he may get back home soon enough. It might be an interesting story to tell everyone back home, he thought.

As he waited for his meal and pondered his return to the Garden, however, he knew there were many questions that would need to be answered. What happened that caused him to fall? How did that Grandie bird gain entrance to the Garden? And who was that shadowy figure that produced that awful blue aura and dreadful face and laughter? He knew there was trouble in his home and wanted very much to help resolve it. He needed to find a way out of Main City if he wished to do that, though. Still, after he returned to the Garden, he would make an effort to contact Mr. One and assure the safety of his home in order to prevent another breach.

As he was thinking of this, a woman in a blue outfit entered the room with a tray and a meal of roast beef, potatoes, and peas. The Rabbit-Man thanked her with sincerity before he indulged in his meal. After he finished, he felt quite content sitting in his seat waiting for the suited man to return. The woman had already left, and he burped as he sat and thought further of how he could eventually leave Main City. Other thoughts crept into his mind as he was left on his own, however. What if something went terribly wrong in the Garden? Something that not even Lady Easter or Mr. One could resolve? Such a scenario would be disastrous, but even worse would be if such a thing had already occurred and he did not even know about it. What if he obtained this Pass in order to get home, only to find that there was no home to go back to? The Rabbit-Man forced these ideas out of his head as quickly as he could. Of course he would make it back to his Garden. Certainly that bird that tried to prey on Madame Duckly's children would not be a match for Mr. One, the arms master that supplied the Protectorates with their weapons. "One day I'll make it back there." he thought to himself. "I'll get there soon enough…I hope."

Then another man entered the room. It was not the suited man that brought him there. This was a large burly man with a bright red hardhat on his head and overalls that were far more heavily stained than the ones Ap wore. The man's red face was covered with soot, and he had a piercing bitter gaze in his eyes. The Rabbit-Man was startled to see such a man in the office building, but then again this strange new world was very full of surprises.

"Okay, pal," the man said in a grizzly voice. "You've had your free food, and you're registered. I have to take you to get your blood test and a picture and then you can come to work with me. The room's down the hall. Let's go." The man turned and exited the room and the Rabbit-Man followed. He brought him to another room with a large padded chair and a table. Another woman in a blue suit sat at the table and greeted the Rabbit-Man with a smile.

"Please sit down and we can get started. This won't take long," she said. The Rabbit-Man did as he was bid and sat at the table. The woman produced a strange tool and asked the Rabbit-Man to remove his glove and hold out his finger. He did so, and then she placed the tool on the tip of his finger. A small blade clipped his finger and the tool sucked some blood from the cut. The woman left this tool on there for a moment and then removed it. The Rabbit-Man had no idea how much of his blood the small device took from him, and he had no idea at all why this was necessary, but he did not ask. He did not wish to make himself appear foolish and vulnerable in front of these strangers, especially not in front of the grizzly man. When this was finished the woman placed a little bandage over the Rabbit-Man's finger and he placed his glove back on.

"Now all we need is a picture and we'll be done," the large man grunted and led the Rabbit-Man out of the room. This time they walked farther down the hallway and turned a corner. The man brought the Rabbit-Man to another door but did not enter it. "You go inside and I'll wait here. Get your picture then come on out and we'll be movin' on." The Rabbit-Man did so. He entered the room, though nobody was inside. There was a big blue panel on the wall to his left, and a camera on his right.

"Please stand before the blue board facing the camera," a voice told him through a speaker above the blue board. He did so, and the camera snapped a picture of him. "Please remove your cap and facial piece." the voice said. The Rabbit-Man did this also, and another picture was taken. "Thank you, your Registered Identity Card will be available at the front desk. Keep it in a safe place and do not lose it. A replacement card costs twelve Cabbage leaves. Thank you, you may now go."

The Rabbit-Man exited the room and met the grizzly man again. They proceeded back the way they came and went into the front office. "Get your card, then come on," the man growled. The Rabbit-Man went to the front desk and was given his card by the woman with the bonnet. It had his name and both images that were taken. "Let's go," the large man said and walked out of the room. The Rabbit-Man followed him back into the streets of Main City.

They walked on, past more of the dust-colored buildings until they arrived at a large cinder block structure. The large grizzly man led the Rabbit-Man inside, and they immediately ascended a flight of stairs. The top of this led to a hallway that contained very small rooms on either side. As they walked down the hall the Rabbit-Man saw many of the occupants of these rooms, and almost all of them were doing the same thing – they were looking intently at the screens that were installed in the walls of their room. Some of these people were dressed in ordinary, nondescript clothing while others wore animal suits. But they all were watching their screens. Whether nibbling on a small morsel of food or just lounging on a small chair that each room included, they all were focused on that screen. The Rabbit-Man found this strange, because when he lived in the Garden watching a movie was a pleasant activity that folks did occasionally. These people in the rooms, however, seemed to be completely enthralled in their viewing. The Rabbit-Man wondered what could have been showing on the screens to keep the attention of so many people at once. He did not have much time to consider this, however, because the large man stopped and the Rabbit-Man nearly walked into his wide back.

"This is your container," the large man said, pointing to the room he stopped before. "Swipe your card in the slot of the door and you can enter. It's number Ten Twenty-two, so don't forget it. When your alarm goes off in the morning, come down to the basement for seven in the morning and I'll show you your work. My name's Barface. See you then."

Barface then turned and walked away before the Rabbit-Man could reply. He stepped into the room after Barface was out of sight and closed the door behind him. The room was small and sparse. It contained a bed at the far end, a chair and a little table on a side of the room. To the immediate right of the door, there was a screen set up on the wall. A tiny clock was beside the bed indicating it was five minutes past seven in the evening. The Rabbit-Man sat down on his chair at the small table. It was lightly padded but comfortable enough. He saw on the table a remote controller for the screen. He used this to turn it on, and hoped that he could find more information about Main City and how he could return to the Garden by viewing it. He soon discovered the screens in all Main City were operated by a system known as the TeleWeb, often called the T-Web. The screens in the Garden had had a system like this, but it wasn't nearly as widely used as the T-Web of Main City. The first broadcast the Rabbit-Man viewed on the screen involved a suited man and woman speaking directly at the viewer, with images appearing behind them. It was a Main City newsreel. The woman was speaking to the viewer about a resident of Main City that had been arrested by the Main Patrol and turned over to the Guard Dogs for some kind of crime he had committed. The Rabbit-Man's heart sank as he heard mention of the Guard Dogs, as he recalled Ap telling him about how they were even more fearsome than Wolfsnare the Terrible.

"The man in question is one Tim Berry," the woman said as a picture of a frightened-looking young man with disheveled hair appeared behind her. "He was seen two days ago wearing a red suit and calling himself Old Nick. It is unclear where he discovered this name or the character associated with it. However, upon further investigation it was discovered that the reference was part of the Old Focus which, as most residents know, is a collection of old superstitions and beliefs that have been outlawed in order to preserve peace and equality in Main City. Tim Berry said he did not know his outfit was part of the Old Focus and was only trying to have some fun. Authorities say this is no excuse, and Berry has been turned over to the Guard Dogs for punishment. The chief of the Main Patrol commented on the Tim Berry affair." At this point the screen showed a man in a black padded suit holding a black baton. He had large black glasses on his face and his hair was shaved very close to his head. The Rabbit-Man correctly assumed this was the chief of the Main Patrol the woman had indicated.

"We have a zero tolerance policy here in Main City for celebrating anything recorded in the Old Focus, which the Old Nick myth certainly is." The Main Patrol chief, named Boss Barns, said to a woman interviewing him. "This particular legend is one of the more arcane ones, and most folks probably don't know much about it, but it is our duty to keep it that way. Everything listed in the Old Focus is there for a reason. These old legends and superstitions have been used by bad people in the past to inflict oppression on others, and that's why the Caretaking Body has put an end to it. Anyone caught violating the ban on the Old Focus will be punished accordingly, as this Tim Berry will surely be."

The Rabbit-Man was somewhat confused by this statement from Chief Barns, but he now understood that this Old Focus and all it entailed was something to beware of. He had never heard of the legend about Old Nick in a red suit, but whoever that might have been he was certainly an unpopular outlaw in this Metroscape. The scene on the screen then shifted again and it now showed one of the Guard Dogs. It was an exceptionally large Grandie dog (even bigger than Wolfsnare, the Rabbit-Man guessed) with a black coat and red eyes. Its most fearsome characteristic was its large sharp teeth. The Rabbit-Man's heart sank even further as he viewed this monstrosity. Even on a screen it was frightening to look at. Tim Berry was curled up weeping on the ground before the Grandie dog-monster. The Rabbit-Man felt overwhelming pity and sorrow for the helpless man, whose only crime was to absent-mindedly wear the costume of a banned character. The Rabbit-Man's dismay was furthered when he noticed there were many other people, most in animal costumes, looking down upon Tim Berry and cheering the Guard Dog on. Did they really believe that Tim Berry was a threat and the Guard Dog was protecting them from him? He understood this was what the scene implied, but the Rabbit-Man could not believe that the spectators of this torment could actually believe that. "They are making themselves believe it," the Rabbit-Man thought. "They cheer this monster on in the hope that he will not turn his attention to destroying them. What kind of a city is this place? I really need to get some of that Coveted Cabbage so I can make it back to Lady Easter's Garden as soon as I possibly can."

The image on the screen shifted back to the man and woman in suits before Tim Berry's fate could be viewed. The man then began speaking of another topic, but the Rabbit-Man was not paying attention even though he was looking at the screen. His mind continued with its maelstrom of ideas, some good but most bad. He then realized how exhausted he was and decided to go to bed for the night, and hoped he could find out more about how he could return to the Garden the following day.

He fell asleep soon after going to bed. He was troubled by unpleasant dreams that night. The hideous face and the blue aura appeared to him, and the mouth on the face opened, chased him, and tried to engulf him in its sharp jagged teeth. He ran away but could not see anything in front of him. Finally he tripped, and before hitting the ground was startled awake. His clock indicated it was five minutes past three in the morning. The Rabbit-Man understood that he did not know what to expect at his work assignment tomorrow and that a decent night's rest would do him good. He was relieved that the haunting image of the face was gone, but was still troubled that he woke in his container. He hoped the entire experience after falling from the tree was all just a bad dream, but such was not the case. He knew he could not keep on letting his anxiety get the better of him, so he tried to think of a way to get himself back to sleep.

As he lay on the small bed in his container, he tried to think back on his life in the Diamond Mine in Lady Easter's Garden, and detach the sad feelings of separation that accompanied them. He made his best effort to recall his fondest memories from the Garden as he experienced them at the time. He remembered his walks with Lady Easter, visiting her at her palace on fair-weather days. He remembered the feasts he would attend on special occasions where his friends would gather for camaraderie and merry-making. Planting flowers with his friends and helping the other inhabitants of the Garden harvest their vegetables. Such was the life he once knew. "I'll have it back," he told himself in his mind. "I'll find a way to get back there again."

Despite his best efforts to prevent his sense of longing from getting the better of him, the pain of his loss overwhelmed him. He knew that even if he returned to Lady Easter's Garden things would never be the same again. He knew that the invasion of the Grandie bird and the other monster was the beginning of an irreversible change for the worse. He had heard when he was younger that many Metroscapes were actually once Bastions that had been overwhelmed by bad creatures. Is that what was happening to his beloved Garden; the place that was his happy home? He knew what the recent occurrences there indicated, and even if the Garden did not become a Metroscape it would surely never be as peaceful as it once was. Then he could not contain his grief anymore, and hot tears filled his eyes and streamed down his face. He turned onto his stomach and buried his face in his pillow and poured his bitter remorse and sadness into it. It was soaked by the time he was through, but no other residents in the building heard him. After he let his emotions out he felt better. Again he thought back on the Garden and all he knew there, and this time the memories were comforting and relaxing. As his mind relaxed he once more felt the presence of the peaceful glow that came to him after his fall and recalled the smiling, child-like face among the light. This comforted him and calmed his nerves. And then he fell back to a more peaceful sleep.

•   •   •

The alarm made a loud and unpleasant buzzing noise at six in the morning the following day, and at first the Rabbit-Man struggled with how to turn it off. When he was awake, he went to the tiny bathroom at the far end of his room and washed up, then put his Rabbit-suit back on. He remembered he was to meet Barface in the basement that morning, so after he was dressed he left his room with his card and descended the stairs. He saw there were signs along the building indicating the path to the basement, and the Rabbit-Man followed these until he went through a large set of rusted double-doors with peeling red paint. Inside there were many other people milling around, some of whom wore animal suits and some who did not. The Rabbit-Man made his way through the crowd until he spotted Barface. He approached the grizzly man who looked exactly as he had the previous day.

"You take one of the shovels and go to area Thirty-two," Barface barked at him. "The area supervisor will tell you what to do." The Rabbit-Man then shuffled further through the crowd over to a series of wooden barrels that contained shovels. Some of them appeared to be in very poor condition. He grabbed one that seemed slightly better than the rest then tried to find his way over to area Thirty-two. The entire workplace was a very vast basement beneath the building where the containers were, and each work area was a large square region with a sign and a number hanging above it. The Rabbit-Man made his way through to the area with the sign Thirty-two above it and walked into the square, outlined in red tape on the gritty ground. A tall man wearing an animal suit (the Rabbit-Man could not tell if it was a rat or a ferret) was standing in the area.

"Hello," the Rabbit-Man said to the rodent-man. "Are you the area supervisor? Barface told me to come to this area."

"Yeah, I am," the rodent-man replied in a hoarse voice. "You must be one of the newbies. I see you already have a shovel. Start digging in the region. Dig about three feet, and if you find any gold or silver or copper, place it in the bucket here." He indicated a rusty metal bucket near the edge of the red square. "If you don't find anything after three feet, put the dirt back and move to a different spot. Keep doing that 'til the bucket's full then come find me. Got it?"

"Yes," the Rabbit-Man replied before the rodent-man walked away. He looked at the ground and realized the entire workplace must have been dug out beneath the building. He did not find this work to be unbearable. After all, he had dug holes while planting in the Garden before. The dirt was tougher than in the Garden, but not unmanageable. He started digging a hole where he was, and did not find anything. The first couple of hours in the day went by quickly and the Rabbit-Man did not mind the work much. However, as the day went on it grew very monotonous as such work always does. By the time he dug two holes and found nothing, he moved onto his third hole. He then started to realize how hungry he was, especially because he had no breakfast. He wondered if he would ever get a break. He started to become tired and angry. He kept telling himself that this was necessary to return to the Garden, and that idea helped him get through it. After three hours, the rodent-man came back to him.

"You got fifteen minutes," the supervisor told him. "Be back here after that."

"Thank you," the Rabbit-Man said. He put his shovel down and made his way back toward the front of the workplace. There was a kiosk distributing food that was densely populated. The Rabbit-Man waited for what seemed like an eternity before he made it to the counter. A man in a lobster-suit asked for his card. When the Rabbit-Man presented it he was handed a biscuit and a small bottle filled with water. He consumed these hastily and then headed back to his work station because his time was almost up. He picked up his shovel and continued to work. He got one other fifteen minute break after another three hours working, and then went home three hours after that. He left the basement at fifteen minutes past four in the afternoon. He only produced three pieces of copper from digging holes he eventually lost count of. The rodent-man took his bucket away after telling him he can go at the end of the day. The Rabbit-Man was very tired after this, and could not wait to get back to his chair in his container.

When he returned to his container, he washed himself in the small bathroom and then turned on the screen. This time he changed the station to a show called the Grand Coliseum, broadcasted from Main City. The host of this show was a Grandie spider wearing a black top hat called Mr. Spiderhat. The Rabbit-Man remembered Pertho mentioning him. The show involved an arena where two contestants, or teams of contestants, fought against one another before a live audience. In this episode, a man in a yellow cat suit was facing a man in a black cloak. The cloaked man was using some type of pyrotechnic device to blast flames at the cat-man, whose gloves with sharp claws seemed to do him little good. The audience was enthralled by the display, and many of the viewers cheered loudly at the spectacle. The Rabbit-Man thought the odds were uneven in this contest, and thought the idea of the show was somewhat obscene. Still, it kept his attention and he watched the contest to the end. Eventually the cloaked man threw an exploding ball at the cat-man's head, which struck him and left him unconscious. The contest was ended after that, and a thin man in a red shirt entered and raised the hand of the cloaked man. The cat-man was taken away by the Grand Coliseum's crew. It was unclear whether the cat-man was dead, and the thing the Rabbit-Man found most disturbing was that nobody seemed to care at all.

"And so we have a victor!" the jovial voice of Mr. Spiderhat said. The voice seemed unfitting for a Grandie spider. "Spectro has succeeded yet again. If he keeps this up, he might be a contender for the championship. Stay tuned for more exciting contests in the Grand Coliseum!" When Spiderhat said the title of his show, his voice echoed and the show's signature tune played. The Rabbit-Man then turned off the screen and decided to find dinner.

He left the container building and wandered through the streets of Main City until he came upon a small eatery three blocks down. He went inside and saw a long counter and an assortment of tables. The place was not very busy; two people sat at the long counter and only a few of the tables were occupied. The Rabbit-Man sat in one of the elevated chairs before the counter not far from the door. A fat man in a raccoon costume approached and handed him a menu.

"Howdy bud," he said. "My name's Snoop, just give me a shout whenever you decide what you're having." The Rabbit-Man thanked Snoop and looked at the menu. He was accustomed to having a mostly vegetarian diet when he lived in the Garden and rarely ate meat. He did not recognize most of the foods listed on Snoop's menu, but fortunately for him there were descriptions beneath many of the items. He decided to order a salad with vegetables and nuts. This dinner more resembled those he had in the Garden more than any of the other choices. After only a few minutes Snoop brought him his salad with a glass of juice and asked for his card. The Rabbit-Man presented this to the raccoon-man who then swiped it through a small device he pulled from his pocket. "Thank you," he told the Rabbit-Man. "If you need anything, give me a shout."

The Rabbit-Man finished his meal quickly; he was very hungry after the full workday and then grew tired after eating. He asked Snoop where he could buy his own food and other supplies because he had nothing in his container. The raccoon-man directed him to a building called the All-Mart several blocks away. The Rabbit-Man thanked him again and then left for the All-Mart. His experience there was not very long. The outside of the building looked as nondescript as the others, and inside there were many people milling around through the various isles of the store. As soon as he walked in, a very ancient-looking man in a worn-out snail suit asked to see his card. The Rabbit-Man presented this to him, and the old snail-man slid it through a machine beside him.

"You only have the value of two Cabbage leaves left on your card," the man told him in a raspy voice. "Be careful what you spend."

"Thanks," the Rabbit-Man said, and then proceeded into the store. The shelves were not heavily stocked, and the Rabbit-Man was surprised to see that the boxes of many of the items were very dirty. The small amounts of produce and other foods that were available did not look very appealing. After milling through these isles for several minutes, the Rabbit-Man eventually purchased a small case of crackers, two small bags of raisins, and a little container of water. He brought these to one of the counters at the front of the store to pay for the items. The clerk, wearing ordinary clothes (the Rabbit-Man was still getting used to seeing this), passed them before the price scanner and then asked for his card. When he passed the card before the machine he told the Rabbit-Man, "Your purchase costs four leaves of Cabbage and you have only two remaining on your card. I can place an advance-transfer on it if you want."

"What is that?" the Rabbit-Man asked.

"When you work again and earn the value of more Cabbage on your card, the registration system will automatically pay off the rest of what you owe. It has to be paid back within a week or they'll come looking for you." the clerk said. The Rabbit-Man did not know who "they" were, but he needed the items to have in his house so he agreed to the advance-transfer.

"Be sure to keep better track how much value is on your card," the clerk told him.

"How do I do that?" the Rabbit-Man asked. The clerk looked at him with an irritated expression.

"I can tell you're new," he said. "You can keep track of all that on the T-Web screen wherever you live. Ask someone else how to figure it out."

The Rabbit-Man left the All-Mart with a bad feeling. He only worked a single day and already he had a small debt. It dawned on him that obtaining this Coveted Cabbage in order to get a Pass would be very difficult. This made sense to him, as he thought of it more while walking home. Main City seemed like a very abysmal place to be – how else would the people who ran the city be able to keep anybody here if getting away was easy? That thought brought another question into his mind – who *did* run Main City? Who were the Guard Dogs and the Main Patrol working for? Perhaps if he found these individuals he could explain to them his situation and negotiate a way to return to his home. Then a strong premonition told him that would most likely not work. The Rabbit-Man was naïve in many ways, but even he understood the nature of most people. He went back to his container building, placed his groceries in a small compartment drawer, and then turned on the T-Web Screen. He found a button on the controller labeled 'personal info' and pressed it. The screen then brought up the images that appeared on his card. He could use other buttons to scroll a red arrow icon to various locations on the screen. He found a location labeled Cabbage and pressed the 'select' button. A small box then appeared on the screen with red letters inside it that read '-2.' He correctly assumed that this indicated the two Cabbage leaves he owed to the All-Mart that would automatically be withdrawn from his Identity Card.

"This city has all of my information recorded in their system," he thought to himself. "Worse yet, I do not even get to physically hold the Cabbage that I've earned, it is simply applied to my card. Maybe I should find a way to get the Cabbage I've earned and buy the Pass with that?" The question did not seem very relevant to his present circumstances, because he knew he did not have any Cabbage at the moment, and the Pass would most likely be very expensive.

He watched another contest in the Grand Coliseum, but turned his screen off before it was over. He went to bed feeling uneasy that night, and simply hoped that something better would happen in the near future that could help him better his predicament. He may have had difficulty falling asleep if he had not been so exhausted after the busy day. Fortunately, no dreams of the horrible face and the dreadful blueness that accompanied it troubled him that night.

Chapter Four
The Hero That Never Was

The following day the nasty alarm woke the Rabbit-Man again. He repeated the same routine as the previous day, only this time he had some crackers and raisins for breakfast. The second workday went better than the first. The Rabbit-Man was assigned to work at area thirty-two again, but this time there was a man in a blue jay suit working with him. His coworker introduced himself as Phil Blue. The Rabbit-Man talked with Phil throughout the workday, and came to better understand the operations of both his workplace and Main City. He enjoyed working with Phil and it made the day go by better and easier. Between the two of them, they uncovered six pieces of copper and one small piece of silver. Phil told him that the rodent-man supervisor's name was Archo, and most of the workers did not like him. He was known to assign people he disliked to exceptionally difficult workplaces, and would punish them if their turnout was not adequate. Phil advised the Rabbit-Man to stay clear of Archo and avoid getting on his bad side. This information did not surprise the Rabbit-Man; many people in Main City seemed very unfriendly. The entire atmosphere had a sordid and unwelcoming feel.

After lunch, in the second half of the day, the Rabbit-Man told Phil more about himself. He briefly described his life in Lady Easter's Garden and how he recently fell out of his Bastion. Phil was shocked to hear of his encounter with Wolfsnare the Terrible, and empathized with the Rabbit-Man and his experience with Pertho.

"You're lucky to even be alive," Phil told him. "Most folks who cross the path of Wolfsnare are goners. I have no idea who that blackbird could have been, but he certainly did you a favor that day. I knew a guy once that was killed by that Grandie wolf. He was a zebra-man that liked to wander off. One day he went outside the borders of the city believing he could find some staircase into a Bastion. The rumor was bogus, but this guy believed it for some reason. He left and didn't even make it ten miles before Wolfsnare ate him up. I heard about it on my T-Web screen a few days later. I wasn't that close to him, but he was a nice enough fellow. Bad things happen to people often enough around here, but if you go off on your own like that guy did, you're very likely doomed." This made the Rabbit-Man think to ask Phil about the question that concerned him most.

"Phil, to the best of your knowledge, do you know if there is any way to make it into a Bastion from here? Do you think there is any chance I can get back to my home? From what I understand it is very difficult, nearly impossible it seems, to get out of this city and find a better life. Is there any way to do it?"

"Well, I know there are ways to do it because other people have before. Some people do manage to get a Pass and move on to live in a Bastion somewhere. That doesn't happen very often though, because Passes are so expensive. Some people struggle their whole lives to move on and never do, while others either get the Pass or just leave into the unknown. Many of these, like that zebra guy, are killed by a type of predator and we eventually hear about it on the news, but there are others who leave and seem to get away unharmed. They take their cards with them, and the card will indicate in the city's records when a person has died, but there is never anything else recorded about them. It is a mystery what happens to them. But be very careful about talking about this subject, Rabbit-Man, because it can be a sensitive issue in some places. The Caretaking Body is not fond of people concerning themselves with leaving Main City, or any Metroscape. They like having control, as you can tell. And when someone escapes their control with no consequence, they are very unhappy about it. As you know, it's best not to draw too much negative attention to yourself, and talking about a thing like that will. Pursuing a Pass is considered acceptable, but anything else is almost considered as bad as discussing the Old Focus."

Between his conversations with Phil and what he saw on the screen in his container, the Rabbit-Man understood the Caretaking Body as the group that controlled the Coveted Cabbage and the affairs of Main City. However, he still had no idea who they were, and figured it was best not to inquire about it. When the workday finally ended he said goodbye to Phil and went back to his container. Phil lived at the other end of the building. The Rabbit-Man felt better than he did the previous day. Again he went to the eatery and had a similar dinner to his previous one. That evening he turned on his screen to see what would be showing. He recalled Phil mentioning a personal station and meant to ask him what this was. The first thing he came upon that caught his interest was a documentary about one of the contestants in the Grand Coliseum. The Rabbit-Man decided to watch this. The Grand Coliseum, despite its gruesome nature, had caught his attention in the past few days. A woman was narrating the program, and telling the audience about the competitors that gained the status of Hero in the Coliseum by earning the continued approval of both Mr. Spiderhat and the audience, a difficult feat to achieve according to the narrator.

"As most viewers know, Mr. Spiderhat is a true innovative genius in regard to entertainment and his most successful concept is the widely popular show broadcast from the Grand Coliseum," the woman's voice said as an image of Mr. Spiderhat appeared on the T-Web screen. "Although the charismatic Grandie finds various ways to keep his audience engaged in his program, his opinion of who the ideal Hero would be often conflicts with that of the viewers. This generally results in Mr. Spiderhat's choice competing against the favorite of the audience. Mr. Spiderhat rarely interferes with the competitions, and so this dynamic often makes for suspenseful spectacles. But there is one instance that long-time viewers of the Grand Coliseum show may recall that does not fit into this common routine.

"Kroscar Hunderbar, a name still familiar to many Grand Coliseum fans, had much potential to become the Hero of the Grand Coliseum when he first emerged in the battle arena several years ago." At this point the screen showed a fit young man with a dog mask on his face wearing black shorts with red suspenders and large leather boots. He had gloves on his hands that had wolf claws on them, and he stood in the center of the battleground of the Grand Coliseum, being cheered on by the audience.

"Kroscar was trained by White Top, the great eagle Morphie that is to this day one of the best known of all Grand Coliseum Champions." The screen then showed a tall muscular man with the head of a bald eagle and massive wings. As the narrator mentioned, he was a Morphie, a person that possessed both animal and human physical traits. "The upcoming star seemed within reach of obtaining the Hero status and the prize every competitor hopes to win – the Grand Coliseum Championship. The Sun Crown, symbol of the Championship, retired along with White Top when nobody could win it from him. Mr. Spiderhat introduced the Silver Star Trophy as a replacement symbol for the Championship.

"Then on one special night, Mr. Spiderhat announced that the former glorious champion, White Top, would return to the Grand Coliseum with the Sun Crown and defend his title once more. This sent a buzz throughout the entire viewership of the show and all of the Metrocapes that featured the show. Everyone believed the talented Kroscar would ascend to challenge his former trainer and obtain the Championship and the Sun Crown. Suddenly and unexpectedly, to the dismay of all, the great Champion White Top collapsed and died in the midst of one of the Grand Coliseum's shows. Everyone was devastated, and Mr. Spiderhat's popular show began to fall into decline. The entrepreneur would not go down so easily, however, and he decided to have a contest for the Sun Crown and the coveted Championship that White Top left behind.

"Kroscar Hunderbar had some continued success, but his popularity in the Coliseum began to weaken. He never did manage to obtain Hero status, and signs of his despair started to show through on the program." The screen then showed an image of Kroscar pounding his fists on the floor of the battleground. He dug through the mat and into the ground beneath with his claws, lifted and handful of dirt, and tossed it forcefully at Mr. Spiderhat, who was sitting in his usual spot above the outskirts of the battleground in the rafters of the structure. The narrator described how this occurrence made Kroscar unpopular with both Spiderhat and the audience, eliminating his chance to gain the Hero status.

"Just as Mr. Spiderhat's show and Kroscar's career seemed to be on the point of failure, a new competitor emerged that wowed the audience and Mr. Spiderhat alike. Eagle Top, the son of the great Champion White Top, made his debut in the Grand Coliseum and wasted no time in calling Kroscar Hunderbar out. Within weeks, Eagle Top made the Hero status to the delight of all – except Kroscar, who became his most fierce rival. At last, Mr. Spiderhat arranged a match between the two competitors with the Sun Crown and the Grand Coliseum Championship as the prize. This was the match that elevated the Grand Coliseum show to the top program on all T-Web stations. The competition was intense, but in the end Eagle Top won a distinct victory over his rival, to the delight of the adoring public everywhere. Kroscar retired from the Grand Coliseum soon after and has not appeared on any programs since. The Hero of the Grand Coliseum still maintains his Championship to this day. Stay tuned while we interview the Morphie that has captivated the minds and hearts of viewers." As the narrator said this last part, the screen showed Eagle Top flying high into the air in the Coliseum with Kroscar gripped firmly in his arms. He then slammed the dog-man into the floor of the arena. His hand was raised by the red-shirted referee as he stood above Kroscar.

The Rabbit-Man was intrigued by this history of the Grand Coliseum and Mr. Spiderhat's popular show. He heard Eagle Top mentioned on the show before, but did not see him in action yet. Before the interview with Eagle Top started, however, the screen showed another scene from the match. The image made the Rabbit-Man's heart skip a beat. In the scene Kroscar made ready to leap at Eagle Top. He had his claws poised and leaned down, preparing to pounce. Then faintly in the background – so faint that one could easily have missed it – there was an image in the audience the Rabbit-Man recognized instantly. It was the face he saw before falling down from the Garden. The features of the face were slightly different this time; the eyes were not as large and the teeth were not as jagged. It looked more like a blue skull with glowing yellow eyes and curved horns on the forehead. Despite these minor differences, the Rabbit-Man recognized the face as the very same one. He also noticed that something resembling a long blue tail stretched out from an unseen source and wrapped itself around Kroscar's ankle before he could pounce. The Rabbit-Man noticed that it distracted Kroscar and then Eagle Top struck him hard on the head. Most viewers may have missed the tail and would have just thought that Eagle Top's attack stopped Kroscar from leaping. The Rabbit-Man knew what he saw, however, and fell back in his chair as that sickly feeling of fear boiled up in his stomach again. Who was that foul creature with that terrible face? Was that blue tail part of the same being? Did this thing that had somehow entered the Garden also interfere in this match at the Grand Coliseum? Such were the thoughts pulsing through the Rabbit-Man's mind. He suspected it was a possibility, and figured that he was not the only person this foul entity troubled – whatever it was.

His sense of fear eventually gave way to confusion as he thought of this strange creature further. What made this bizarre entity so terrifying to the Rabbit-Man was his inability to identify what exactly it was, or who it was. He pieced together all of the details he could remember: first, there was the tall shadowy figure with wings. This was the same image Mr. One noticed before he went into the Garden that fateful day. There was also the blue aura that permeated the entire atmosphere before the Rabbit-Man fell. It was not quite a mist, but something more than simply a color. The Rabbit-Man could not have described it well. The face was the worst part of the strange being; and second to that was the laughter. As he thought back on these things, the Rabbit-Man remembered them very vividly. The memories were far too poignant in his mind for him to be comfortable. It seemed that when he thought back on this terror, it would appear to him again any moment. As hostile as Main City seemed to be, the Rabbit-Man believed he could be at least minimally content there if he did not have to encounter that awful blue enemy again or Wolfsnare the Terrible.

The interview with the Grand Coliseum Champion Eagle Top was under way on the screen, but the Rabbit-Man hardly paid any attention to it. He was too shaken by the image he saw in the scene from the contest. Then he wondered if this blue laughing oddity had some type of grudge against the would-be Hero of the Grand Coliseum Kroscar Hunderbar. If the Rabbit-Man was correct in that the blue tail was related to the foul face, it certainly had cost Kroscar the contest and prevented him from fulfilling his dream. Were there others out there that this thing pursued and tormented?

"I need to find out what that thing was," the Rabbit-Man thought to himself. "It caused me to fall out of the Garden, and may do the same to others if it is not stopped. But what *is* it? It can't be a Morphie, the thing didn't even resemble an animal. It didn't resemble anything. I wonder if Phil or Snoop would know anything about it. Perhaps I should ask around." But then a disturbing idea occurred to the Rabbit-Man. A disembodied blue light, an odd face that spontaneously appears from nowhere and a large unidentifiable Morphie all seemed to be qualities that could be categorized in the forbidden Old Focus of the Metroscapes. If this thing was something that was in the Old Focus and the Rabbit-Man started asking about it, he knew he might suffer a fate similar to that of luckless Tim Berry. "So much danger is in this place." he said solemnly to himself. It was not long before he turned off his T-Web screen and went to bed. The following two weeks were quite unpleasant for him.

The buzzer sounded the following day to begin another long shift of toil in the underground mine below the container building. Eventually, the days tended to all blur into one endless stream of monotonous digging. The Rabbit-Man did not work with Phil again, and had only seen the blue jay-suited man in passing one day. One good thing was that Archo, the rodent-man supervisor, did not trouble him at all. For some reason he stayed away from the Rabbit-Man, who noticed him heckling other workers in the mine on several occasions. He discovered that the schedule of the mine ran for six days in the week, with the sixth day possibly being a half-day if the bosses let the workers leave. The Rabbit-Man's routine became going home to watch his T-Web screen, and he usually watched an episode of Mr. Spiderhat's Grand Coliseum if it was on. Spectro, the black-robed man the Rabbit-Man saw the first time he watched the show, was now a contender for Eagle Top's Championship. The Rabbit-Man knew that it would be a long time before he could save enough Cabbage "value" on his card to obtain a Pass, and so he decided that the best way to cope with the daily monotony of his existence in the Main City Mine would be to set other goals for himself in the meantime. The next thing he wanted to do was learn how to interact with the T-Web screen in his room and establish his own personal station, as Phil mentioned he had done. He did not see Phil often anymore and usually worked by himself in the recent weeks. Still, he decided to ask about how to get a personal station when he worked with another approachable coworker.

His opportunity to get this knowledge came during his third week in the mine (weeks in Main City ran Day One to Day Seven, with Day Seven being the only certain day off). One trait of the Rabbit-Man that aided him much was his ability to learn things quickly, even if sometimes the hard way. He was working in station nine alongside a man in a grey cat suit named Peace Shadow. The Rabbit-Man had a pleasant conversation with him as they dug their holes; Peace was a fan of the Grand Coliseum show as well. When the Rabbit-Man brought the subject of the T-Web screen in his container up, his coworker seemed quite enthusiastic about telling him how to set up his own station.

"It's very easy, actually," said Peace. "All you do is press the 'search' button on the remote controller, and then enter the phrase 'share,' the screen will then give you the steps to access its information and enter information of your own that other sharers have entered. You can really find out a lot of information, some things you would never have thought you could find. It is allegedly not monitored by The Caretaking Body, but most folks know better than to believe that. But even if they are monitoring it, there's so much information on the personal stations that even a skilled T-Web expert would have difficulty sifting through it all. Still, it's a good idea to be careful what you put on there. Just use common sense and you'll be fine."

"Thanks," the Rabbit-Man answered. "I'll try that. But you know; I've also heard there are other stations that are not as readily accessible as the others. Some call them underground stations. Is there any truth in this?"

"Oh yeah, there sure is," Shadow said. "There are more underground stations than anyone can count, but to be honest with you most of them don't really contain anything worthwhile. Most people use them to find some music or other entertainment. Some academic information can be found on them that the regular stations may not have. Just be careful though; many stations contain information regarding things listed in the Old Focus. Lots of folks access this material often, and it's nearly impossible for anyone to keep track of. If you are caught, though, it would not end well." The Rabbit-Man understood Peace's last statement, and he also guessed that this was how Tim Berry came upon the character of Old Nick which got him into trouble. He was intrigued by the notion of these underground channels, however, and very much anticipated exploring them further.

That night after work, the Rabbit-Man went into his container and began sleuthing through stations on his screen. He followed Peace's advice and established his own personal station, which turned out to be easy to do after all. Once he did this, he used the button pad to search for more information. One of the first topics he researched in the extensive database of the T-Web was the career of Kroscar Hunderbar and his history in the Grand Coliseum. He found the scenes from the documentary he viewed previously that week available to watch again, and also saw a story clip written about two years ago regarding Kroscar's infamous battle with Eagle Top for the Grand Coliseum Championship. The Rabbit-Man eagerly selected this article using his controller, hoping that he could find information on the strange blue tail that tripped the dog-man and cost him the contest.

"Perhaps Kroscar Hunderbar knows of this terrible being that chased me from my Garden," the Rabbit-Man thought to himself as he selected the article. "If there are others in this city who know what that thing is, maybe they can help me understand how to get away from it. Then after I get back home I will know how to keep it away; I'll make sure it doesn't trouble me or anyone else again. What was that tail that tripped Kroscar? I really hope this article offers some answers."

The Rabbit-Man read the article, and to his disappointment it mentioned nothing of Kroscar being tripped. In fact, the brief synopsis of the contest did not even mention that there was any outside interference whatsoever. It simply told of how Eagle Top defeated Kroscar and obtained the Sun Crown that represented the Grand Coliseum Championship. No mention of a long tail slithering into the battleground and tripping Kroscar. When the Rabbit-Man thought back on it, the trip he saw was very brief, and he understood that some viewers may have missed it. He knew he saw it though, and wondered if the writer of the article missed it. Something seemed very out of place in regard to this strange blue character, even in a place as wayward as Main City. It just did not seem to fit, and the Rabbit-Man knew there was something very dark behind this formidable creature. He was determined to understand what it was, and so he continued searching through T-Web stations. Further information about Kroscar Hunderbar told of other contests he competed in, but made no mention of any enemy interfering in the contest with Eagle Top. Eventually the Rabbit-Man became tired with searching for that night, and turned the screen off and went to bed. He was not troubled by bad dreams that night. He planned on doing more searching the next day.

Chapter Five
The Knowledge Forbidden

The next day was even worse for the Rabbit-Man, as his work became increasingly difficult and his opportunity of escaping Main City and returning to his beloved Garden seemed more distant each passing day. The only thing that gave him any motivation and sense of morale was the screen in his container. Each night after washing up and eating a small dinner he plopped himself back into his little chair and began plugging away at the remote controller, trying desperately to find more information about the scary blue foe whose identity was so elusive. He researched Eagle Top and his career in the hope of discovering any friends he may have that would have helped him against Kroscar. Eagle Top was on very good terms with Mr. Spiderhat and had very many fans and supporters, but none of whom resembled that horrid person he recognized in the audience as he viewed the scene of the famous Grand Coliseum Championship contest.

He also tried to research Lady Easter and her Garden, in the hope of finding news of what was occurring in his home. He found nothing except basic information explaining that Lady Easter presided over a Bastion to the north of Main City. The article he found mentioned that there was a period in the history of the Garden known as the Dark Spell in which the security was threatened. The Rabbit-Man knew about this, and the only further information that the article gave was that the Garden came through the Dark Spell and was restored. It told him nothing he did not already know. He also researched ways to get into a Bastion from a Metroscape, but again the only information he found involved the Pass as the way to do this.

"This tool seems to contain such a vast amount of information," the Rabbit-Man thought. "Yet when I try to find something I really need to know it seems to offer almost nothing at all. It's a wealth of shows and games and other such things, but is very lacking in useful resources. I wonder if I'm doing something wrong. Peace Shadow seemed to know a lot about these systems, but I haven't seen him lately. So many people use this system, and it can't all be tracked by the Caretaking Body. I wonder if any of the other users have dared to post secrets that could help get out of this trap of life in this city. I wonder who else is out there and trying to get out."

The next day at work was exceptionally egregious for the Rabbit-Man. He was working alongside two large men in bullfrog suits and their job was to stand before a long trough and pick the pieces of gold and silver from among the copper. Both of the other men stunk horribly, and their speech was so slurred the Rabbit-Man could hardly understand what they were saying. This particular function at his workplace was not paid by the hour as digging was, but rather by the amount of "product" (being gold and silver) that a worker produced. These were few and far between amid the slew of coal pouring down the trough. The arms of the bullfrog-men were longer than his and they were taller so they stood higher above the trough. Whenever a glittering chunk made its way down the trough, one of the other large workers would snatch it away before the Rabbit-Man could. Many of them he could hardly even reach. In a few instances, one of the large bullfrog-men elbowed the Rabbit-Man or shoved him aside in order to get the sought-after piece that slid down. This aggravated the Rabbit-Man, but he tolerated it for the first half of the day. When the Rabbit-Man began to show even the slightest sign of discontent it made the wretched day even worse. The bullfrog-men were simpletons that had so little pleasure in their lives that they amused themselves whatever way they could. They harassed the Rabbit-Man and laughed at him – and snickered more gaily the more miserable he became.

When he finally got his fifteen minute lunch break, the tormented and frustrated Rabbit-Man quickly ate a small burrito and drank his bottle of water and considered what he should do. He would not get paid very much for the day if he kept on like this. He knew he could ask Archo for a change of assignment, but the rodent-man supervisor was unapproachable on a regular basis and he seemed in a very foul mood this week. Sometimes if a worker approached Archo when he was in a bad mood it would result in them getting a worse assignment as well as a firm whack with Archo's club. The Rabbit-Man decided it might be best to stay put rather than invoke the ire of the supervisor and risk worsening his situation.

After lunch, his situation worsened anyway. The bullfrog-men were even more aggressive after lunch, and the Rabbit-Man was getting no gold or silver from the trough. After being elbowed by one of the coworkers so hard he was knocked to the ground, he decided enough was enough and left his station to find Archo. He could not deal with the bullfrog-men any longer. He went to the front of the mine where the rodent-man's station was and saw Archo sitting at his desk. The Rabbit-Man approached and the supervisor looked at him with a sour expression.

"I am having too much difficulty at my current station," the Rabbit-Man said. "These other men are insufferable. I can't get any work done with their antics. If I could please have a different assignment for the day, or the same assignment with different coworkers, it would be greatly appreciated. Is there anything you can do?"

"Can't get your work done?" Archo barked. "What good are you people? Well, I know how those two frog buttholes can be, so I can see where you're coming from, rabbit. Come with me." He got up from his desk and walked off. The Rabbit-Man followed, slightly relieved that Archo did not explode on him as he was known to do with other workers. The rodent-man led him to a far corner of the mine lined with tables. Two sheep-women were kneeling and cleaning the legs of the tables with rags. They both winced and turned their heads down the moment Archo entered the area. He led the Rabbit-Man to an unlabelled door that was shut near the tables. Before the elevated door were three steps.

"This leads up to the bosses' containers, y'understand?" said Archo; the Rabbit-Man nodded. "I need these steps nice and clean, 'cause when the bosses come they ain't gonna be happy if their steps ain't clean. Get to it, rabbit!" The Rabbit-Man looked around, and then he asked Archo, "Are there anymore rags and buckets of water?"

Archo looked over his shoulder then back at the Rabbit-Man. "We're outta rags, bunny-cup." he said before he grabbed the small rabbit snout strapped to the Rabbit-Man's face. He pulled it forward and let it snap back. The Rabbit-Man let out a cry of surprise as his snout hit his face hard. It was completely unprecedented to touch another person's suit in the Garden, so

51

the Rabbit-Man was startled even though he knew full well he was no longer in the Garden. Archo then said to him, "Looks like ya gotta use that pretty little snout o' yours to clean 'em off. Ya didn't want to do your last assignment – had difficulty workin', ya did. Ya shoulda been happy ya had a good job! Now you're gonna do this, and you better do it well or there'll be a good deal of disciplinin' for ya. I want to see ya doin' it. Get over there and do it now!"

The Rabbit-Man simply stood there in shock for a moment, unable to believe what the supervisor was telling him to do. The sheep-women kept their faces very low as they scrubbed away feverishly at the table legs, as if desperately hoping Archo would not look at them again. Before the Rabbit-Man even knew what happened, he was knocked to the ground by a cruel hard slap from the rodent-man. "Ya have about two seconds to get back ta work, or you'll be out on your ass with a Penalty attached to your card. Clean those fuckin' steps or I'll clean that gay little bunny tail on your ass with my boots! Do it *now*!"

The Rabbit-Man understood what the consequences of a Penalty were – it basically blacklisted anyone in Main City and prevented them from getting work, and hence prevented them from getting Cabbage as well. "If I don't do this, I may never get back home." The Rabbit-Man thought. Overwhelmed by shame and degradation he crawled to the steps and pushed his snout onto the bottom one. He moved it back and forth, in an effort to polish the step. As he did so, Archo walked up and kicked him firmly on his butt, causing him to bang his face hard on the solid step. The Rabbit-Man lay cringing on the ground as Archo let out venomous laughter that sounded like the death squeal of a rat being dismembered. The Rabbit-Man's nose was bleeding beneath the snout, so he removed the face-piece and pinched his nostrils. He could not help it when the tears began to flow down his face and his body began trembling. This made Archo laugh even more, and soon the Rabbit-Man's feeling of shame gave way to a boiling bitter anger that remained with him for the rest of his stay in Main City, and even beyond. How could this be happening? How could he have gone from a well-meaning and dutiful inhabitant of the Garden to this? He could not see it where he was, but if he looked over, the Rabbit-Man would have seen a tear falling down the face of one of the sheep-women too. They felt for him, but they dared not say a single thing. That was life in Main City, alright. That was life in a Metroscape.

It was just too much for him, and as he lay on the ground crying, racked with rage he could not channel anywhere, the door above the steps swung open and Archo stopped laughing instantly. The Rabbit-Man crawled off to the side and sat on the ground, trying to dry his tears and stop the nosebleed. He had never been more humiliated in all his life. From the doorway emerged a tall fat man in a dark blue suit without any kind of animal costume. He was followed by two large, very muscular men with shaven heads and a dark mask over their nose and mouths. They wore only loincloths and brown strapped sandals. Each held a clubs in their hands. Archo stood frozen with a gaping mouth and eyes wide when the man in the suit emerged.

"What the hell's goin' on in this damn mine, you shriveled old rodent carcass?" the man asked. "We are down on product more than we've been in months, and nobody's doin' a damn thing about it! And those Mad Dogs keep causin' trouble! If they ever get near this place, it's going to be your ass that gets fried for it Archo! You understand me?" The man then walked over to Archo and grabbed him by the collar of his shirt, pulling him up to his tiptoes. He peered at the rodent-man, and for a fleeting moment the Rabbit-Man actually feared for Archo despite the humiliation he just suffered.

The man in the suit dropped Archo and walked back into the door he came out of. Now it was Archo lying on the floor cringing and weeping. The Rabbit-Man noticed that the rodent-man's tears were genuine – he was actually crying even harder than the Rabbit-Man was. In a flash of epiphany, the Rabbit-Man realized that the torment he went through each day at work, especially today, was not really the fault of Archo or the other coworkers. Although he disliked many of them, the Rabbit-Man knew that the cycle of misery that life in a Metroscape entailed was actually driven by those who controlled the city rather than those who functioned within it. The man in the blue suit must have been one of the more influential individuals in Main City, and the Rabbit-Man's mind filled with loathing as he reflected on the fat man he just saw. His nosebleed stopped, so he got up and walked over to Archo and extended a hand to him. Archo took it and the Rabbit-Man helped him get to his feet. The rodent man wiped his eyes and turned away, leaving the Rabbit-Man and the two sheep women where they were without saying a single word.

The Rabbit-Man was eventually given another digging assignment by Barface for the remainder of the day; this time without any coworkers. The Rabbit-Man never saw Archo again after that day, and would occasionally wonder with mixed feelings what happened to him. He went home and did his usual ritual of perusing through shows and articles on his screen. His mood that night was a kind of numbed misery – a feeling he was beginning to grow used to. The humiliation and rage he felt at what Archo did to him that day never truly subsided, but instead simply went dormant in his psyche. He did not know if it was possible for anyone to ever get over treatment such as that, and in his conscious mind he really did not care. The wrongness of the entire episode troubled him – just as the wrongness of Main City as a whole troubled him.

The weeks never got any better after that awful day. Each work week went by longer and longer. Each day he felt more and more wretched; his hopes of gaining enough Cabbage to purchase a Pass and return home grew thinner and thinner. The screen gave his mind less and less stimulation as he watched the programs it featured every night. He was sickened by his life and his daily routine, and the sense of entrapment grew more intense with each monotonous day that crawled agonizingly by. He never would be able to recall exactly when, but one day it all just came to be too much for him. Pass or no Pass; Garden or no Garden – the miserable life he lived in Main City was not worth living. He decided he had to – for the sake of his own sanity – do something to gain more excitement and stimulation for himself, and he had to do it soon.

After another exceptionally egregious day at work (it was a Day Six that the crew was required to work extra), he went home and began surfing through information on his screen. Fully understanding but no longer caring about the severity of what he was doing, the Rabbit-Man decided to research some of the Old Focus on his screen. He knew how vast the wealth of knowledge was in the T-Web and also knew that the Caretaking Body could not possibly regulate all of it. So, he figured he would just have a look. If he was caught, that would be unfortunate, but he figured even being devoured by the Guard Dogs would be preferable to another day in his monotonous life of useless toil. For several months now he had been working in the mine, and had not even fifty leaves of Cabbage "value" attached to his card. A Pass was at least one hundred thousand leaves of Cabbage, and often even more than that depending on how the market changed. He was resentful that he had never even seen a single leaf of The Coveted Cabbage in all his time in Main City; he simply used the "value" affiliated with his card to do all his business.

His research into the Old Focus was entertaining. He discovered an assortment of things he never knew before. He came upon an article about Old Nick – who was allegedly a figurehead for a strange ritual from the Arcane Days (meaning the time before the Caretaking Body was established) that involved a tree people grew in their homes that bore gifts. According to the article, Old Nick would travel to homes every winter and water the tree, giving it the ability to produce valuable items for the household overnight.

"Of course, such superstition is preposterous," the article said, "as there is no evidence whatsoever that such a tree ever even existed. Thus, the character of Old Nick was added to the Old Focus in an effort to discourage false hope among citizens of the Metroscapes." The Rabbit-Man could not understand why people would believe a tree could do such a thing. "Fruit is the finest gift a tree could give anyway." he thought to himself. "And why bring it into the home? How is it supposed to grow indoors?" The entire tale seemed odd, as so many aspects of the Old Focus did, but the Rabbit-Man also could not understand what harm could be done by such tales. They were fantastical sure enough, but the idea that a man suffered severe punishment (possibly death?) for merely mentioning the story filled the Rabbit-Man with dread, and only increased his growing distrust of the Caretaking Body. He read on, but found little else of interest.

Two days later, it was Day One of the week, he was back at his screen as surely as the Sun rose in the morning (not that it mattered much to him, as he was in the mine all day long). That day he found something particularly interesting during his research. He came upon an old documentary that had not been broadcast on any of the primary stations in several years. It was about a band of men bedecked in strange-looking dog suits known as the Mad Dogs. A male voice was narrating the segment, referring to the group as a "deadly subversive gang, bent on disrupting the order of Main City and stealing the Coveted Cabbage." This was something new to the Rabbit-Man, and he was excited at the thought of any kind of group having the audacity to challenge the Guard Dogs and make an attempt to steal the Coveted Cabbage. The narrator of the documentary told how the group recruited prospective members and had them prove their worth by doing something subversive. "These could range from killing an agent of the Caretaking Body to simply vandalizing a building. A prospect of the Mad Dogs is willing to risk his freedom, reputation, and even his life to prove himself. It is generally believed that anyone willing to be a prospective member of this vicious gang is so ill in the mind that they cannot be redeemed. If they are ever caught, they are treated the same way as an actual member – they are executed by the Guard Dogs. No allowance can be made for such blatant disrespect, and none shall be."

"Hmm interesting," the Rabbit-Man thought as he watched. "So the Mad Dogs are a dog-suited gang that oppose the Guard Dogs of the Caretaking Body. These people have some nerve to challenge Grandies, let alone the Guard Dogs themselves. It seems all of Main City has already gone to the dogs- whether they be guards or mad!"

The scene on the documentary then changed to a woman in a sheep suit very much like the ones the women at his workplace were wearing the day the Rabbit-Man was insulted by Archo. Upon looking closer, he was surprised that it *was* one of those women. She was weeping and speaking to an unseen interviewer, "I never thought my son could descend to such a level." she sobbed, "As soon as I found out I had to report him. I hated having to do it. That damn gang should be ashamed of themselves… for the things… for the…" the sheep-woman's voice was breaking up as her weeping became heavier. "For the things they do to our families and friends!" her crying now gave way to a burst of angry shouting. "Damn them! Who do they think they are, anyway? Trying to steal Cabbage as the rest of us work tirelessly to earn it! Damn them all! I did *not* kill my son; he was my baby! The Guard Dogs didn't either! It was *them*! That damn gang and all the others like them! They killed my boy, and I hope they are all ruined because of it!" The scene then changed to a still image of the leader of the Mad Dogs Tribe, as they called themselves. His name was Rip A. Sunder, and his outfit was that of a gruesome dog, with a leather jacket that had spikes over the shoulders. He had a vicious dog's snout strapped to his face and his eyes were yellowed. He wore a cap with spikes atop his head over matted long brown hair. On his torso he wore a ragged vest and on his hands were gloves with large black claws more like a wolf's than a dog's. He also had black pants and high boots which ended below his knees. The Rabbit-Man hardly saw anyone so vicious-looking in all of Main City. The documentary went on to describe Rip A. Sunder as one of the most wanted men in all Main City. It went on to describe the methods the Mad Dogs used to evade the Guard Dogs and the other agents of the Caretaking Body. The screen displayed an image of a silver rocket with the shape of a devil's head at the front. "These fire-horses are the method of transportation that the gang uses, and it is still unclear where or how the vagabonds came to possess these vehicles. They travel faster than any other vehicles known to the Metroscapes, but as far as anyone can tell they cannot ascend into the air."

The Rabbit-Man was fascinated and also disturbed by what he learned about the Mad Dog Tribe. One the one hand, he was repulsed by the idea that a gang would disrupt already-struggling families in an effort to gain what so many other people were already working for. On the other hand, however, he understood full well why they would want to steal the Coveted Cabbage. It was very difficult to obtain. He believed the narrator of the documentary when he said the Mad Dogs were dangerous, and from the image he saw of their leader Rip A. Sunder they looked it. There was one detail in the documentary that triggered something else in the Rabbit-Man's mind. He recalled the devilish head that adorned the front of the "fire-horse" vehicles that the Mad Dogs rode, and he was reminded of the demonic entity whose image haunted him ever since he fell from the Garden.

"Hmmm, I wonder if I could find anything out about that," the Rabbit-Man thought. His feelings were a mix of enthusiasm and fear. He desperately wanted to understand more about this dreaded thing that haunted his mind and memory, but was also afraid of it. Still, he *had* to know. A very strong intuition told him that this creature was intricately connected to his fall from the Garden, and may also be essential to discovering how he could return there. He entered the phrase "devil face" into the screen from the controller, but this did not bring any results, except that he learned both devils and demons were listed as elements within the Old Focus, a fact he knew he would do well to remember. It did not stop him from searching though. Other phrases like "fire-horse face," "demon tail," and "laughing demon" did not produce anything he believed was affiliated with the demented enemy he encountered. He wished he could find something more, but decided he researched enough for the night. "If I keep going like this, I might get into trouble. I best be getting to bed for the evening." He did so, but he had unpleasant dreams that night. He dreamt of the face on the Mad Dogs' "fire-horse" turning blue and laughing at him. It chased him and he ran away. To his dismay, he then realized he was running into the open mouth of one of the Guard Dogs. He woke in fright, but was relieved his nightmare was over – for now, anyway. He got out of bed and took a sip of water. He had less than two hours before he had to wake up for work. He could not get back to sleep when he tried. The following day would be difficult, as usual. Though he did not know it at the time, a bit of luck was coming his way.

Chapter Six

Hard News and Strange Luck

The Rabbit-Man thought much about the Mad Dog Tribe the next day, and then remembered where he heard of them before – the fat man in the suit had mentioned them to Archo as he was scolding him. As the Rabbit-Man recalled, the man seemed concerned that the Mad Dog Tribe would interfere with business in the Main City Mine. He concluded that the Mad Dogs were still very active in Main City. Not only were they active, they were the foremost threat to the Caretaking Body within Main City. There were other groups like them that wished to obtain the Coveted Cabbage, but none were as organized or as influential as the Mad Dog Tribe. The next several days, when he went to his container after work, the Rabbit-Man researched the Mad Dog Tribe on his T-Web screen. To his surprise, information on the group was sparse, and most of what he found only reaffirmed what he already heard in the documentary. He wondered if the Caretaking Body made an effort to suppress the dissemination of information regarding this outlaw group, or if the Mad Dogs themselves tried to keep such information away from the public eye. Perhaps it was either, or maybe even both. Whatever the reason, he could not find much information about them.

The workweek crept agonizingly by as they always did, but it was on Day Six, after another extra long day in the mine, that the Rabbit-Man had a very significant meeting. He was in the habit of making himself a quick dinner after getting home from work and beginning his activity on the T-Web. This night, however, he decided to go into Snoop's eatery and treat himself to a dinner. As he walked into the place, he saw a man sitting at one of the tables that he thought he recognized. Upon observing the man further, the Rabbit-Man noticed a small emblem on the man's vest that he instantly recognized – it was a small gold icon of the number one. The Rabbit-Man then knew who the man was immediately. It was Mr. One, the merchant that travelled to the Garden and provided the Protectorates their defensive weapons. The Rabbit-Man was extremely excited to meet an old and dear friend and someone that was familiar with his home. He walked over to the table where Mr. One was sitting.

"I don't believe it, Mr. One!" the Rabbit-Man said. "How are you? I'm so glad I found you here! So much has happened since I was chased out of the Garden. You were there that day, so please tell me everything that happened."

"Well, imagine that!" Mr. One said with a smile. "It's the Rabbit-Man! I thought you were dead. When you didn't meet me at Lady Easter's palace I feared for the worst. I'm really sorry to say it my friend, but many of your peers didn't make it out of the Garden alive." The Rabbit-Man's heart sank, but still he needed to ask the questions that were troubling him for the past several weeks. Whatever news he may hear, at least now he would get some answers.

"Mr. One, what happened at the Garden?" the Rabbit-Man asked after sitting down at the table. "Is there any chance I can return there? Can you help me get back there?" Mr. One's eyes darkened and the expression on his face told the Rabbit-Man that something severe had indeed occurred in his beloved Garden. It seemed his darkest fears may have come true after all.

"Look Rabbit-Man," Mr. One began, "I'm not sure how to say this, but... well, your Garden is gone. I'm afraid the entire Bastion was destroyed. I don't know what happened to Lady Easter- she never did return. Now there's nothing for her to return to. I was getting ready to retire from all this travelling and live there with you folks, but that's not going to happen now. I guess Mr. One must remain on the fly. Rabbit-Man, I'm really sorry to have to tell you this, but there's nothing we can do now. He destroyed everything when he arrived... I never encountered anyone like him before."

"Who destroyed everything?" the Rabbit-Man asked. His entire body seemed numb. He wished firmly but fruitlessly that what he was hearing was false – but in his mind he knew it had to be true. "Who was it that invaded the Garden and destroyed it?"

"It was The Blue Demon." Mr. One replied. "I heard of him before, but I never really believed such a thing existed. Believe me Rabbit-Man, he does;

the Blue Demon is very real. I saw him face to face. I tried to shoot him with one of my firearms, but the shots seemed to pass right through him. He blew this strange blue mist out of his mouth that surrounded me. Before I knew what was happening, I was falling. I woke up, I have no idea how much later, and The One Van was near me. I was near this city –definitely not where I wanted to be – and The One Van was ruined. But before that happened I brought those ducklings to Easter's palace. A Protectorate who used to work in another Bastion, Christie Starlight, took them away to safety. I'm not sure where, because the demon was approaching and I turned back to drive him off. The children were safe though, as far as I know. Christie Starlight's background is a mystery, but she has great and vast powers that betray her lovely appearance. The children were in good hands with her. As for the rest of the Garden – most of it was set ablaze in a dark blue fire unlike any I have ever seen. The entire experience was surreal, and I have no idea what happened, but there is no way the Garden could have survived it. The thing that bothers me most about it was how quickly it spread, and how it seemed to just appear out of nowhere."

"I know this Blue Demon you're talking about," the Rabbit-Man replied. "I'm sure he is part of the Old Focus in this city, so we better be careful who we discuss this near. I saw him as well. He has a horrible face and the most wretched laughter I ever heard. He caused me to fall from the Garden, but I just can't figure out *what* he is. He can't be a Grandie or a Morphie, they resemble animals and he's just ... well, he's just this weird *thing*. I don't even know what to call it."

"He's a demon," Mr. One replied; the expression on his face grew even grimmer. "The Caretaking Body refuses to acknowledge the existence of such, and most citizens of these Metroscapes cannot even see them, but they are real. Only folks like you and me, Rabbit-Man, who have lived in the Bastions and have helped care for them, can see the demons in our midst. I have had experiences with them before, but I don't want to get into all that now. We have a serious problem in this Blue Demon, but I can't figure out what the solution is. If I can't destroy him with my firearms, I have no idea what I can do to stop him."

"I know, I've often wondered what I can do to keep away from him. He has been in this city before. I've seen him in a scene from one of the contests in the Grand Coliseum. He interfered in the famous match between Eagle Top and Kroscar Hunderbar. I have no idea why, but when I saw the scene I was sure it was him – The Blue Demon. I think he can alter his appearance, but still; for some reason, I know him when I see him. I can't stand it. This is all wrong, Mr. One! How did this all happen? Just what exactly went wrong, and how?"

"I wish I could answer that for you, Rabbit-Man, I really do," Mr. One replied. The Rabbit-Man had his dinner with Mr. One that evening, and they agreed to keep in close contact. They were two lone friends in a hostile land; although an unfortunate situation to be in, such is what gives a real bond of friendship its essence and makes it stronger. It helped both of them immensely, the Rabbit-Man especially. He was devastated to hear that he no longer had a Garden to return to. Nevertheless, he and Mr. One established a common goal among the two of them – get out of Main City as soon as possible. Mr. One explained how the Blue Demon sent him sailing out of the Garden, even though he somehow survived the fall. They also discussed Christie Starlight, whom the Rabbit-Man heard of in his browsing sessions on his T-Web screen. She was a powerful Protectorate and a star among both the Metroscapes and Bastions. She made efforts to help people as much as she could, believing that the world could be made better through kind acts. Through this activity and her vibrant music videos she gained the title "The Dream Queen." Her music was very popular, and made her a beloved icon among many people. Mr. One believed the duckling children would have been in good hands with her. Although the Caretaking Body secretly abhorred people like Christie Starlight, they did not impede her work because it was not overtly against their power, and because it fostered hope among the citizens. The Rabbit-Man discussed this and other things with Mr. One as the evening grew late.

They bid each other farewell that evening and agreed to meet the following day, which the Rabbit-Man had free of work. Before they parted, Mr. One left the Rabbit-Man with a final warning: "I am not very popular in this city. I have enemies in the Caretaking Body, and they've been after me for a while. Always trying to drag Mr. One down they are, but they haven't got me yet. Mr. One won't be taken by the likes of them that easily. So far the Caretaking Body has not shown that they know of my whereabouts, and there are others that are not fond of me here. It would be a good idea to not mention your association with me to anyone you do not trust. Take care Rabbit-Man, I'll see you tomorrow."

Although he was very upset to hear the news of his Garden, the Rabbit-Man also felt reinvigorated after meeting an old friend and finally discovering more about the enemy that haunted him. His main focus for the rest of that evening and the following day was to learn as much about the Blue Demon as he could. As soon as he was back in his container, he was searching through information on the T-Web in the hope of discovering more. He entered the phrase "The Blue Demon" into his screen via his button pad to see what he could find. An article about the demonic creature appeared on the screen. It read:

The Blue Demon
by M. J. Brungis

The Blue Demon, originally known by the name Vulgar Squalor, is a person entered in the Old Focus and is a very controversial figure in most Metroscape areas. It is widely believed that The Blue Demon is a mythical entity created by disenfranchised citizens to rationalize their failures in life and blame their situation on an external entity. This coincides with the legal definition of a demon purported by the laws of the Caretaking Body. As with all laws regarding the Old Focus, it is illegal to dispute such facts, and transgression of this mandate can result in severe punishment.

According to legends, The Blue Demon is an enigmatic character that preys on individuals who are idealistic, but have little practical sense. The most common victims are people who hail from a Bastion, but have ended up in a Metroscape. Because the lifestyles of these two living environments are so vastly different, some believe that the Blue Demon is a symptom of insanity caused by the stress of the transition from living in a Bastion to living in a Metroscape. Although acknowledgement of the Blue Demon as a real entity is illegal, the consistency among eye-witness accounts who claim to have seen the creature is striking. For generations those who claim to have seen the Blue Demon say his most common form is a tall, dark figure with large wings and curved horns upon his forehead. However, most of the accounts also say that he can alter his appearance, and that he can also show only certain features of himself at any given time. The secret to this, some researchers say, is the strange blue aura emitted when the Blue Demon is near. This bizarre characteristic – which has never been satisfactorily determined as a light, a mist, or both – is commonly seen when the Blue Demon is near.

The most notable researcher in the Blue Demon phenomenon is one Tom Oddberry, who eventually died under mysterious circumstances and was found outside the Butterchunk Pub in Main City. This event gave rise to a new interest in the Blue Demon, but also caused the Caretaking Body to become stricter in enforcing the ban on the topic. Nevertheless, there are numerous individuals that claim the creature is real and has done them harm in the past. Perhaps only time will tell if the Blue Demon is real or fictitious, but as of now the character is still listed in the Old Focus and legally defined as a fantastical character that can be used by outlaws for dangerous purposes.

When the Rabbit-Man was finished with this article, he researched both the author of the article, M.J. Brungis, and the researcher the article named, Tom Oddberry. He discovered that M.J. Brungis was eventually arrested and turned over to the Guard Dogs after his writings about the Blue Demon and other topics in the Old Focus were discovered. As the article mentioned, it is unclear what caused the death of Tom Oddberry, but the Rabbit-Man learned that he was wanted by the Caretaking Body for several months before his death. "I wonder how he evaded them for all those months." the Rabbit-Man thought. It was becoming clear to him that despite the control the Caretaking Body held over Main City, they were definitely not all-knowing. They could not regulate everything on the T-Web and there were some people – like the Mad Dog Tribe and, for a brief time, Tom Oddberry who could avoid their wrath. The Rabbit-Man understood that the Coveted Cabbage was a highly desired commodity in Main City, but he also could not understand why these elusive individuals would not try to find a way out of the city if they were able to avoid the authorities. He considered these ideas as he searched for more information about the Blue Demon. The article by M.J. Brungis was the best he was able to find that day, and he could not find any video scenes that involved the Blue Demon other than the Grand Coliseum Championship match he already saw.

The following day the Rabbit-Man was greatly anticipating his meeting with Mr. One. He wanted to discuss with him the information he discovered on the T-Web the previous day. Now that he knew about the Blue Demon, he had a renewed sense of purpose which helped to counter some of the internal turmoil he was suffering after learning of the demise of the Garden. The despair that existed in his mind was steadily replaced by determination to learn all he can about the Blue Demon, and also to escape Main City along with Mr. One – his only friend that remained from his old home. The Rabbit-Man left his container and went down the grey streets of Main City toward a coffee shop called Alp's. This was where he arranged to meet Mr. One for the day. The inside of Alp's was slightly dingy, but the woman in a ladybug costume at the counter was pleasant enough. The Rabbit-Man bought himself a little cup of coffee and sat at a table in a wooden seat. As he waited for Mr. One to arrive, he tried not to think of the troubles that may possibly be awaiting him that week in the mine.

When Mr. One arrived, his face appeared greyer and his eyes more tired than the previous evening. The Rabbit-Man could tell he was a changed man since he parted ways with him in the Garden. He figured life in Main City would wear down anybody. He himself became more tired and shabby-looking in his time in the city, but he still did not look as bad as Mr. One did today.

"I have some bad news, Rabbit-Man." said Mr. One as he sat at the table. "The Caretaking Body has heard rumors of my presence in Main City and they know about my trading of defensive weaponry with the Bastions. They don't like people like me being in their city; they don't hate me as much as they do gangs like the Mad Dogs, but if any of the Main Patrol finds me they'll turn me over to the Guard Dogs. I may have to go into hiding for a while. I'm not sure where, but I'll get in contact with you whatever way I can. I might have to flee the city and meet some relatives of mine in Libiscape – a Metroscape not too far from here. I'll be on the lookout for the Blue Demon and let you know if I learn anything else. Just be careful and don't tell anybody you know me. These two meetings we've had already might have been risky enough. Just be careful, Rabbit-Man."

The Rabbit-Man understood what Mr. One was saying and told him about what he learned about the Blue Demon the night before. He was unhappy about having to part from his old friend again so soon after reuniting with him, but he knew there was nothing else he could do. Life in Main City had many limitations.

"I hope you'll be alright, Mr. One," the Rabbit-Man told him. "I wish there was more I could do to help you, but I'm not in a good situation myself. I haven't received any negative attention from any of the authorities so far, but with the research I've been doing it might be more difficult for me to maintain that. So far there have been no penalties for what I've been doing, and I don't think the Caretaking Body is aware of what I'm up to. Still, we both have to be on our guard."

Mr. One agreed with the Rabbit-Man's final comment before hastily leaving the small lounge. He was wearing sunglasses and a hat with a wide brim to conceal his identity from others in the city, and he no longer wore the golden number one icon on his shirt. The Rabbit-Man was nervous but still resolute in his intentions to learn more of the Blue Demon and his role in the matters of Main City and elsewhere. The Rabbit-Man decided that if he could not return to the Garden he knew and loved, he would at least try to get out of Main City and find another Bastion to live in. He accepted the difficult reality that a Pass was practically impossible for him to get in his present situation. He barely earned enough Cabbage from the work he did to support himself. Still, at least he had the T-Web screen in his container, and could use it to learn what he could.

The evening of Day Seven of that week brought another unsettling event to the Rabbit-Man. As he turned on his screen upon arriving in his container, the station featured a news program warning the audience of newfound "enemies of the peace," as the Caretaking Body called them. Featured on the program was Mr. One, as a male voice described the Rabbit-Man's friend with obvious bitter hostility. "The long-dreaded firearms dealer known as Mr. One is believed to be abroad in Main City. As most viewers know, he is a highly dangerous criminal that has been a threat to the peace and harmony of Main City for several years. Mr. One was absent from Main City for a period of time, where he was known to have provided firearms illegally to various Bastions. Anyone with any information on Mr. One and his whereabouts is expected to promptly report to the Main Patrol or the Guard Dogs. Failure to do so will result in punitive action." The ire of the Rabbit-Man rose to a height not reached since he was insulted by Archo at work. The Rabbit-Man knew Mr. One for many years, and knew full well that his longtime friend was not a harmful threat in any way. The overt contradictions that defined Main City were difficult enough to live with, but seeing one of these overt lies painted on his last remaining friend was just too much for the Rabbit-Man. He angrily turned the screen off and began slamming his fists onto his bed. He feared for his friend, and was very concerned that a terrible fate may befall Mr. One, leaving him helpless and alone in Main City once more. What troubled him most was his inability to be able to *do* anything about all the things that upset him in Main City. He could not change his work routine, he could not change his living quarters, he could not help his friend who was in danger, he could not return to his home, and he could not find anything regarding the whereabouts of Lady Easter – who he greatly missed. The Rabbit-Man was ready to snap, but of course he could not even do that. To let out some frustration, he decided to leave his container and go for a walk.

When he was outside walking along the streets, his mind was ablaze with thoughts and emotions. Nobody said anything to him, and this was a good thing because if they had he would have had an erratic reaction that would have drawn suspicion upon him. So he simply walked onward, going nowhere in particular. He did not keep track of how many blocks he passed as he went along. Without fully realizing it, he was walking toward the center of Main City – where the post of the Guard Dogs was located. He never went there, partly because he had no reason to and partly because he disliked travelling through Main City. Looking at the dismal imagery and feeling the atmosphere that pervaded the city had a tendency to get his spirits even lower than they often were in his new life as a miner. The center of the city was a massive clearing, although there was usually much activity there. This was mainly because the great bowl filled with the Coveted Cabbage was also at the post of the Guard Dogs. Many people hustled and bustled in this area in the hope of obtaining some of those leaves. The Rabbit-Man was soon to see the heart of Main City, and doing so would verify beyond any doubt the dreadful contempt he felt toward the place. So many people milled through the Guard Post – either to exchange the value on their cards for actual Cabbage leaves (a process that was actually quite difficult, even though the cardholder technically earned the value and had the rights to the requested leaves) or possibly try to earn some from those who had access to it.

After walking for a while and passing an unknown distance, the Rabbit-Man finally entered the clearing. The first thing he saw in Main City's center was a very bizarre scene, and one he knew he would not encounter in the Garden. A man dressed in a tiger outfit was dragging three people along behind him. These three were crawling because each of them was wearing a set of cuffs on their ankles with a short chain between them. There were two women and a man. One woman wore a red outfit with a mask that looked like a skull on her face; the other woman wore a dark purple cat suit; the man wore almost nothing except brown shorts and a skull mask similar to the woman's on his face.

"Come on fools, off to the Coliseum we go," the tiger-man said to the three miserable people he was dragging along. As he passed the Rabbit-Man, the tiger-man gave him a lustful gaze before moving along. "Maybe you'll get into ol' Spiderhat's web if you're lucky!" the tiger-man said before laughing outrageously. It seemed like his comment was sarcastic. The Rabbit-Man was startled to see such a sight, and could have only imagined what must have been happening to the three luckless people. He moved forward, and then immediately noticed the great post of the Guard Dogs before him. Even at a distance the Guard Dogs were massive; much larger than any Grandie the Rabbit-Man had ever seen. Wolfsnare the Terrible was huge, but even he was dwarfed by these monstrosities. There was one large black dog at the forefront, with several other oversized canines around him that were not as large as him but still gigantic. The Rabbit-Man recognized the front dog as the one Tim Berry was cowering before in the brief scene he saw on his screen. He noticed that the mouths of the other Guard Dogs were disproportionally larger on their faces, and they had far more teeth than natural dogs would have had. Even the larger dogs that roamed in Lady Easter's Garden would have appeared tiny compared to them. The Rabbit-Man's heart filled with dread upon viewing the massive creatures. He desperately hoped that Mr. One could make it to safety and avoid having to confront these horrific beings. While viewing them the Rabbit-Man understood how the Caretaking Body had such firm control on Main City and all Metroscapes. Anyone who had control of such creatures would be essentially unstoppable.

As he continued observing, the Rabbit-Man looked above the group of Guard Dogs and saw the life source and also the greatest cause of pain and torment in Main City – a giant bowl filled with the shiny green leaves of the Coveted Cabbage. The leaves seemed to emanate a greenish-yellow glow, and for a moment as he looked at it the Rabbit-Man's eyes were fixed upon the Cabbage. His mouth was watering and his brow began to sweat as he peered at it. He shook his head and the sensations stopped, but he was still slightly unsettled by the feeling. "What is this Coveted Cabbage made of?" he thought to himself. It did indeed have a strong appeal, but the Rabbit-Man knew the trouble it caused and made a decision not to let it sway him from his ultimate goals.

He looked around to see all of the other people in the clearing. There was an assortment of people with and without animal suits, Morphies, and Grandies. Individuals of various appearances and sizes permeated the clearing around the Guard Post and the Coveted Cabbage, but none were as large as the Guard Dogs. Many of the smaller people in the area appeared frightened. The Rabbit-Man noticed that whenever someone looked at the Cabbage they were entranced by it, even if only for a temporary moment, as he was when he looked at it. He could not think of any rational explanation for why this happened, but he concluded that it was to do with the essence of the Cabbage itself – whatever those strange leaves happened to be made of. He also observed something else that piqued his curiosity; if someone – be it a Grandie, Morphie, or ordinary person – looked at the enthralling Cabbage and then immediately met the gaze of one of the Guard Dogs, their face was contorted into a fearful expression and their head was turned downward for a moment. Just as the Coveted Cabbage had a hypnotic affect on one viewing it, the Rabbit-Man concluded, a look into the eyes of a Guard Dog instilled terror into the viewer. This dynamic of longing and fear in such close conjunction in the minds of the Main City residents made this center clearing a wearisome place to be – and the Rabbit-Man soon discovered why.

As he walked slowly into the clearing, he saw many of the people there getting into arguments with each other. Some of these actually escalated into brawls and violent outbursts. He noticed a man in a bear costume standing with his eyes transfixed on the Cabbage. He did this until another man, not wearing any suit but just a tattered shirt and brown shorts, bumped into him. The bear-man turned around and raised a gloved hand with claws on it, and bore it down on the other man. This left a large scar on the other man's face; the bleeding man then ran away out of the clearing. A similar thing occurred not far away between two female Morphies – one with a fox's head, tail and hands and the other with some characteristics of a chimpanzee. The fox-woman snarled and bit at the neck of the chimp-woman, who screeched in fright and tried to beat her attacker away. This conflict ended abruptly, however, when one of the Guard Dogs let out a shrill bark at both of the Morphie women. They immediately ceased fighting and slowly walked away from each other with their heads down.

"The Cabbage brings out very erratic behavior from these people," the Rabbit-Man thought to himself. "They will destroy one another if they had the chance. That Cabbage casts a kind of spell on them that brings out the worst in them. These Guard Dogs have absolute control over everybody else, though. One single bark from that Guard Dog caused those two Morphies to stop their fight. Do any of these people really believe they are going to get any of that Cabbage? What exactly are they trying to accomplish, anyway?" These were good questions that raced through the Rabbit-Man's head. He noticed that none of the Cabbage left the great bowl above the heads of the Guard Dogs, and yet this did not stop any of the people present from gazing at it or getting into fights with each other over it. It was just sitting there – emitting its gold aura; driving all those in the clearing mad.

As the Rabbit-Man looked around more, he noticed another strange individual standing among the people in the clearing. This was a fat man in a pink pig suit. He wore overalls and a tight cap with pointed ears on his head, and a snout strapped to his face. He held a white paper in his hand and was addressing a crowd of people. The Rabbit-Man could not understand what he was saying, but it caught his attention when the pig-man left his crowd and walked over toward the large Guard Dog in the forefront of them all. The massive canine gazed down at the little fat man standing before him. The pig-man did not seem troubled by the Guard Dog's stare, but rather showed the paper he was holding. The Rabbit-Man watched with curiosity as the pig-man spoke to the enormous fiend. The Guard Dog's eyes narrowed and he lowered his head toward the paper the pig-man held. The Grandie then breathed onto the paper, which caught on fire in the pig-man's hand and was incinerated quickly.

"The Guard Dog just burned that paper with his breath!" the Rabbit-Man thought. "Just what in all creation *are* these things?" The pig-man winced in pain and quickly hopped away from the Guard Dog with a grimace on his face and tears welling in his beady eyes. The crowd he was talking to were now laughing at him and someone threw a glob of what appeared to be mud at him. "They didn't just do that, did they?" thought the Rabbit-Man as he was becoming more surprised and disturbed by what he was seeing in this clearing. By now tears were streaming down the pig-man's eyes and he ran from the abusive crowd. He stopped abruptly before the Rabbit-Man and looked at him.

"I think I know who you are," the miserable pig-man said. "I've seen you around. Oh yes, I remember where I saw you. You're that fellow that's friends with that terrible madman Mr. One!" Fear surged into the Rabbit-Man's brain and his stomach tightened. He had a strong survival instinct, though, and made his best effort to remain calm. "What are you talking about?" the Rabbit-Man asked. "I've never even seen you before. How can you know anything about who I associate with? I've never even seen this Mr. One you speak of. Go away and bother someone else you fat old fool!" Again the crowd that the pig-man was speaking to laughed at him. Looking closer, the Rabbit-Man was sure that it was in fact dung on the side of the pig-man's face.

"That old pig is a liar!" shouted a young man from the crowd. "He accuses everybody of everything. He got Tim Berry in trouble just a few weeks ago for wearing a suit that his pink ass sold to him! Don't listen to him, fellow, he's nothin' but a low-life goon."

"Yeah, so go away you low-life goon and leave me alone!" the Rabbit-Man said, trying to keep on the defensive. If his friendship to Mr. One was discovered right here before the Guard Dogs, he figured he was doomed. It seemed this pig-man was quite unpopular with the crowd, so the Rabbit-Man knew he must use this to his advantage. The pig-man turned around and ran back toward the Guard Dogs. He fell onto his hands and knees before them crying. "That man in the rabbit suit is an enemy!" he shrieked at the Guard Dog that just burned his paper. "I've seen him with Mr. One, the lunatic that is on the loose. He must be taken for questioning. I swear I'm not making this up! I swear it!"

The crowd gasped at hearing this. It was common knowledge in Main City that lying to the Guard Dogs was a severe offense. The Rabbit-Man did not know what the pig-man's paper was, but he guessed it had something to do with obtaining Cabbage. This obviously had not worked as the pig-man expected. Then the Rabbit-Man thought there must be a reward for supplying information about Mr. One and other enemies of the Caretaking Body to the Guard Dogs. The Rabbit-Man's instincts told him that the pig-man was acting fast in a final bid to possibly win some Cabbage from the massive hounds. The problem was that the Rabbit-Man actually did meet with Mr. One recently and was friends with him. If this was discovered, he would be in serious trouble. If he could think on his feet and convince the others he was innocent, he might have a chance to survive. Before he could say anything else, the front Guard Dog spoke to the pig-man in a deep growling voice that made all the others quaver. Some of the people trembled at hearing it. The Rabbit-Man made no outside sign of his fear, but a cold sweat formed on his brow.

"If this is another ploy to get some of the Cabbage, Marvin Pinkbelly, I will see to it that you go directly to the Panel for judgment!" the Guard Dog said as the pig-man quivered on the ground. "If there is proof this man is an ally to Mr. One you had better provide it within twenty-four hours. If you cannot do this, you shall go to the penitentiary, do you understand?"

"Yes sir, I do indeed!" squeaked Marvin Pinkbelly. He then crawled away from the Guard Dogs, and slowly got to his feet before he reached the Rabbit-Man again.

"I'll expose you, you loathsome scum!" he scowled at the Rabbit-Man.

"The only thing you're going to expose is how much of a slandering, dithering fool you are, little pig!" the Rabbit-Man answered. "Now get away from me before I smear more dung on that nasty little face of yours!" The Rabbit-Man raised his hand and Marvin Pinkbelly fell backward. Yet again the crowd bellowed laughter at him. The pig-man scrambled to his feet and ran off, away from the clearing. The Rabbit-Man would not have done such a thing to anyone, not even a foul fellow like this pig-man. Still, his threat seemed to endear him to the laughing crowd. They seemed just as unsavory as Marvin himself, but a simple Rabbit-Man needed to get by somehow. Before he realized it, two men from the Main Patrol wearing black helmets, black shades, red shirts, and brown pants had seized him by the arms and bound his wrists behind his back in cuffs. They led him foreword before the Guard Dogs, and one of them struck the backs of his knees with a baton, forcing him onto them. He looked up at the largest of the Guard Dogs and gulped.

"Who are you?" the Guard Dog asked. The Rabbit-Man was submerged in a sea of fear as the Grandie spoke to him, but he tried his best to conceal it. Before the Rabbit-Man could answer, one of the Patrolmen placed a hand into his pocket and pulled out his registration card. He then held it up to the Guard Dog, who leaned forward and sniffed it. By doing this, the massive hound seemed to somehow absorb some information the card contained. The Rabbit-Man did not understand how this could be, but there was much he did not understand in Main City.

"This is it," he thought. "I'm done for. If he knows what I've been researching on the TeleWeb I'll be punished for sure. I can't believe this." Unbeknownst to the Rabbit-Man, the Guard Dog could have discovered everything he did on his T-Web screen by sniffing the card, but the Guard Dog did not bother to do so. He simply checked to see if the Rabbit-Man had any offenses connected to his card, which he did not.

"Well Rabbit-Man," the Guard Dog said. "It seems you have no record of bad behavior, so unless Marvin Pinkbelly can prove something against you, you are free to go. If he is wrongfully accusing you, it will be he that suffers our wrath. Let him go." The Patrolmen then removed the cuffs from the Rabbit-Man's wrists and helped him to his feet. He then turned and walked away from the Guard Dogs as quickly as possible. He intended to leave the clearing and never return to it again. Before he could get away, however, another strange thing happened at the Guard Post.

A very young man in a bird suit flew through the air with wings he had attached to his arms and a feather-tail attached to his legs. At first glance, one might have thought he was a Morphie, but he was actually just a young man, nearly a boy, in one of the best animal suits the Rabbit-Man had ever seen. With suddenness like lightning, he flew through the air and landed directly into the bowl of Cabbage atop the Guard Dogs, who were temporarily distracted watching the Rabbit-Man. He grabbed two fistfuls of Cabbage and flew off as quickly as he came. A deafening roar came from the combined barks of the Guard dogs that knocked everyone else off their feet. The largest Guard Dog leapt to the top of the bowl and emitted thunderous barks from his snapping jaws. It was too late, however, because the thief was gone. Someone had achieved the unthinkable and managed to steal some of the Coveted Cabbage. Complete chaos ensued as panic gripped those gathered in the clearing and the Guard Dogs raged in anger and embarrassment. A few of them even caught some of the people up in their jaws and devoured them whole.

The Rabbit-Man saw his opportunity to flee from the madness and took it. He ran out of the clearing as fast as he could and did not look back. He slowed to a brisk pace as he was farther away from it and in the streets of Main City again. He was out of breath when he returned to his container and collapsed on his bed, hardly able to believe his luck. He was clear of the Guard Dogs for the moment, but his fate would be determined by whether or not Marvin Pinkbelly could prove his affiliation with Mr. One. To his surprise, he did not feel fear of what might happen to him if his recent activities were discovered. He felt relief – relief at being away from the Guard Dogs. For now, at least.

Chapter Seven
The Great White Calling

The Rabbit-Man was not sure what to expect after the wild events of the previous day, but for some reason he had a very strong feeling that something regarding his present situation was changing. It was a good feeling, and even though it was not entirely in his conscious mind his intuition did not fail him often. The weeks and weeks of consistent and unchangeable misery that so far characterized his time in Main City had taken their toll on his mind and spirit, which was once strong and vibrant but now felt shaken by the onset of despair. He made himself a small breakfast meal and went into the main lobby of the building where a coffee machine was located. He helped himself to a hot cup before moving down toward the rusty red door leading to the mine which he had come to dread the sight of. That day, however, his dread was not so great. He was apprehensive about whether or not the pig-man Marvin Pinkbelly would be able to turn him in to the Guard Dogs, but even this he considered with apprehension rather than outright fear. As he made his way down toward the door, his feeling of intuition grew stronger. As he looked at the red door to the mine he felt a type of calm resolve overwhelm him, although he had no idea why. When he went through the door and into his workplace, he learned that his feeling was correct. Something had indeed changed in the Main City Mine.

The other workers were all standing in an assorted crowd exchanging confused looks when the Rabbit-Man stepped inside. Rather than milling around the place like they usually did, they were waiting to hear some type of announcement. At last Barface, the man that brought the Rabbit-Man to the mine on his first day of the work assignment, appeared and stood before the crowd. All the workers grew silent as he stood on top of a platform before them.

"As of this moment, the Main City Mine is officially out of commission until further notice," Barface announced. "The owners of the mine have decided to invest their efforts into other endeavors, and whether or not the mine will be reopened is yet to be determined. For now, every one of you is advised to go back to your containers and do not return to the mine. Find other work if you can, and if you cannot, go to the registration office and they will help place you into a different workplace. Now, everyone get out of here!"

At first there was a buzzing hum as the workers exchanged confused comments. Many of them left the area through the large red door. Some of them looked distraught, some glad, and most were indifferent. The Rabbit-Man felt relieved as he turned around and walked out of the mine. He was unsure of how he would gain any more Cabbage value on his card, but the thought of not having to return to the mine again was pleasing to him. He made his way up the stairs he had just descended and went back into his container. He thought the abrupt closing of the mine was very peculiar, and wondered if the previous day's events at the Guard Post had any effect on it. He turned on his T-Web screen to find out, and sure enough the first program on the station was a news story discussing the Cabbage theft of the previous day. A female voice was narrating as a scene of the Guard Dogs barking wildly atop the bowl of Cabbage was shown on the screen. The Rabbit-Man had learned that small, floating one-eyed worms travelled through the air to observe the scenes that were shown on the T-Web's stations. These worms were tiny cameras that recorded scenes at any newsworthy events and brought it to the T-Web broadcasters. The imagery they collected was then disseminated among the various stations. At least one of the flying worms must have been present at the Guard Post yesterday, though the Rabbit-Man did not notice any when he was there. He noticed they did not capture any imagery of the bird-man as he stole the Cabbage; the only scenes showed the Guard Dogs barking after him as he flew swiftly away.

The Rabbit-Man wondered if he would see any footage of himself on the program or if it would acknowledge him as the cause of distraction that turned the Guard Dogs away from the Cabbage for the brief time it took the thief to steal some of it. There was none. Instead, the entire program consisted of information about the man in the bird-suit and strongly urged all citizens of Main City to report any and all information concerning him to the Guard Dogs. The young man's name was Sig Calcium, and the tone of urgency in the woman narrator's voice was unlike any the Rabbit-Man heard before. He knew this indicated the severity of Sig Calcium's offense, and also the ire of the Caretaking Body and the Guard Dogs at having been robbed of their dear Coveted Cabbage. This was obviously no small affair in the Metroscape of Main City.

"The suit that the burglar used to smuggle the Coveted Cabbage and make such a swift getaway is unlike any known in Main City," the narrator said as a tiny image of Sig Calcium flying off into the distance appeared on the screen. "It is believed that the suit must have been manufactured by the wanted arms dealer Mr. One, and had been created with the purpose of robbing the authorities and citizens of Main City of the Cabbage that should rightfully be theirs. The Guard Dogs have confirmed that Sig Calcium's punishment shall be severe when he is caught, and have offered rewards to anyone who can provide any valuable information to the Guard Dogs or the Main Patrol. The highest of these rewards is ten thousand leaves of Cabbage for Sig Calcium, dead or alive but preferably alive. Actual Cabbage leaves will be given to anyone able to bring this villain to the authorities. A reward has also been offered for Mr. One, who is suspected of aiding in the theft. The details of this reward have not yet been disclosed, but the Guard Dogs have made it clear that if anyone can bring both of these wanted criminals to the authorities they will be greatly compensated for their efforts.

"Mr. One, I hope you're alright," the Rabbit-Man thought to himself. He was relieved to be free of the mine, and he was even pleased to see that Sig Calcium managed to steal some of the Coveted Cabbage and get away with it so far. To the Rabbit-Man, it showed that somebody was able to break the monopoly that the Caretaking Body and the Guard Dogs held on Main City. Simply seeing someone able to defy them, even for a brief moment, was liberating to him, and he was happy he was able to see it in person. Still, he was also very concerned for Mr. One. He knew his longtime friend had made it safely out of difficult situations before; his escape from the Garden before it was destroyed was a recent example of his capabilities. The Rabbit-Man still could not help but worry for him despite this.

Almost as if in response to his thoughts, a firm knock sounded on the door to the Rabbit-Man's container. Fearful for a moment, but knowing there was nothing he could do, he got out of his chair and opened the door. Standing outside was a Patrolman wearing the typical black helmet and glasses along with the red shirt and brown pants. He could not tell if this was one of the Patrolmen he encountered the previous day or not. The Patrolman was holding a bundle beneath his right arm and his face was as expressionless as all Patrolmen's faces were.

"Good day to you Mr. Ranger," the visitor said. "It is known to us that immediately before yesterday's egregious theft at the Guard Post you were accused by one Marvin Pinkbelly of having an association with the wanted criminal Mr. One. We have given Mr. Pinkbelly ample time to provide clear evidence of this alleged wrongdoing on your part. He has failed to deliver what was requested of him, and thus he has been taken into custody for false accusation and lying to the Guard Dogs. As you are the victim of Mr. Pinkbelly's actions we are bestowing his valuables onto you, which we have confiscated from him today. Do with them as you will. Good day, Rabbit-Man." The Patrolman then handed the Rabbit-Man the bundle he was carrying and walked away. The Rabbit-Man closed the door and brought the bundle to his bed. He recalled the Guard Dogs giving Marvin Pinkbelly twenty-four hours to provide evidence, the entirety of which had not yet passed. The Rabbit-Man was relieved that the pig-man's effort to condemn him had backfired as he hoped it would.

The Rabbit-Man was met with one of his greatest surprises yet when he opened the bundle, and even more surprising was that this surprise happened to be a good one. When he poured out the contents of the bundle a few pieces of paper fell onto the bed along with two photographs and another smaller bundle that contained a large amount of leaves of the Coveted Cabbage. As it lay on his bed the bundle of leaves emitted the same greenish-yellow aura that those in the bowl did at the Guard Post. The Rabbit-Man could hardly believe what he was seeing. The bundle was held tightly together by a single string. The Rabbit-Man untied this and a plethora of leaves came loose and poured out onto his bed. It was an amazing sight. He marveled as he considered just what exactly he would do with all of this Cabbage – and then the idea occurred to him. The Pass to exit Main City could be purchased with Cabbage leaves.

"This is my chance to get out of here!" the Rabbit-Man thought. "If I get The Pass I can use it as my ticket out of this place forever. I doubt Marvin Pinkbelly realized how much of a favor he was doing me by voicing his accusation before the Guard Dogs, but it sure has benefitted me now." The Rabbit-Man considered the harsh irony of his situation for a moment. Marvin's accusation had been correct, but because he lacked the proof to verify it he was penalized as a slanderer and a liar. The Rabbit-Man shuddered to think what the pig-man's fate would be, but he rationalized that he would be better off not knowing. When the Main Patrol seized Marvin's valuables, this bundle of Cabbage must have been among them. Now the Cabbage was in the Rabbit-Man's possession, and he intended to use it to gain the freedom he had longed for since arriving in Main City.

The Rabbit-Man also thought about Mr. One, who was now in grave danger. He wished he could aid his friend, but without any way to contact him Mr. One was beyond his reach. So long as he was out of the reach of the Guard Dogs too, he would be alright. The Rabbit-Man knew Mr. One was capable of taking care of himself, but his next thought was where he must go to get the Pass. He decided to count how many leaves of Cabbage he had, and then he would set out on his mission to find a Pass. He sat in his room counting, and when he was through he had about ten-thousand leaves for himself. "I can hardly believe this! Some luck at last!" he thought. "Now I can get back to a Bastion, even if the Garden is gone I can carry on the good work I did there in another place. It is unfortunate it must be that way, but I can make a better life for myself yet, and be happy once more as I once was."

With that thought in mind, he gathered the Cabbage into a bundle again and tied it with the string. He then looked at the papers that were also delivered to him. Most of them did not mean anything to the Rabbit-Man, but the third one did – to his surprise, the sheet of paper was a Pass! Now the Rabbit-Man's enthusiasm reached a whole new level. Not only did he just receive a large amount of Coveted Cabbage, unexpectedly delivered to him, but now he also had the much-desired Pass he hoped to gain ever since coming to Main City. This all seemed too good to be true, but the Rabbit-Man also understood he had to act quickly and intelligently if he hoped to get what he desired. He was, after all, friends with Mr. One, and he did not know who else may have seen them together. He also considered if it was possible one of the flying worms had captured any images of them together and brought it along to the TeleWeb broadcasters. Beyond this, he had already come to the attention of the Guard Dogs, and even though his name was officially clear with them there was still a chance it could be soiled. The Rabbit-Man knew that time was of the essence and his freedom now depended on using the resources he had to escape to a Bastion in a timely manner without drawing any more unneeded attention to himself. After moving the Pass aside, he looked at the two photographs that were in the bundle he was given. The first was a blurry picture of a vehicle similar to the one the fly-man took Perthro away in. The one in the photo had slightly different details, but it was similar enough. The second picture roused more thought from the Rabbit-Man. The photo showed a slimmer and younger Marvin Pinkbelly smiling along with a woman in a lamb costume beside him. They both had joyful expressions on their faces. On the back of the photo was written "Me and Dolly." When the Rabbit-Man looked at this image of Marvin, it did not even seem like the same person. The lively young pig-man in the photo seemed like a stark contrast to the staggering, woeful, fat man that pointed an accusing finger at him the day before. "What happened to you Marvin?" the Rabbit-Man found himself whispering aloud as he peered at the photo. He felt like he was doing something wrong by holding it and possessing it. He did not mind accepting the Cabbage; he desperately needed that, and Marvin did go out of his way to try to harm the Rabbit-Man for his own gain. He could accept the Cabbage and the Pass easily enough. This photo, however, was a personal possession of Marvin's and should not have been taken from him. He looked at it with sorrow, because as he did so he knew the answer to the question he just softly asked: he knew precisely what happened to Marvin that changed him. Life in Main City was what happened to him. A long, painful life of shattered hope and growing fear under the grim shadow of the Guard Dogs transformed this happy-looking young man in a pig suit to a desperate fat old man with dung on his face. The thought of this made the Rabbit-Man very uneasy, so he stowed the picture away in his pocket and decided not to think of it anymore.

The only place he could think to ask of where he could get a Pass was the Registration Office he went to on his first day in Main City. Because he had no work he would have had to go there anyway if he had not received the Cabbage and the Pass. Out he went, tucking the Pass into his pocket before he left his container. As he walked toward the office, however, an idea occurred to him that he had not considered before: if he presented his Pass to the office in the hope of leaving Main City he had no idea where he was going to go when he left. His home was destroyed by the flames of the Blue Demon, and he did not know of any other specific Bastions he could travel to. Others existed, he was aware, but what if he tried to gain entrance into one of them and they turned him away? What if they disliked rabbit-suited men in the other Bastions? These questions troubled him, and he longed to see his friend Mr. One again. He missed having friends close by. He also pondered where Lady Easter was and hoped she was alright. A mixture of grief and anger welled inside the Rabbit-Man's mind as he thought of the hardships so suddenly brought upon his friends and himself. Despite having a large amount of Cabbage and a Pass, his situation still disturbed him in such a way that he had to consciously prevent despair from overtaking his mind. He walked on, not looking back, and firmly hoped that he would not encounter the Blue Demon again anytime soon. As he thought of this, the unsettling notion that the Blue Demon was still lurking about somewhere troubled him. Where was this strange antagonizing demon? How could such a thing even be real?

"Well, my only hope is to get out of here as quickly as I can," he thought. "If I see Mr. One and meet with him again soon, we would both be much better off. I wonder if the other Bastions know about this Blue Demon? That's it! That's how I can earn access into another Bastion – I can share my story and tell them what happened in my home, so that they may be better prepared to guard their own. I'm sure their Protectorates would be grateful for the information. And then, if I can somehow get in contact with Mr. One again, he could meet me in the other Bastion and we could help defend it from aggressive foes. That's an excellent plan. I just need to find where another Bastion is located that I may travel to. Perhaps the Registration Office can tell me that." Although the Rabbit-Man was very mistrustful of the offices in Main City, he had no idea where Peace Shadow or any of his other friends were and thus could not ask them. "If I see that man in the suit that was at the office, perhaps I could ask him about getting to a Bastion. He seemed approachable."

When the Rabbit-Man came to the Registration Office, there was a line of seven people waiting to speak to the woman in the bonnet at the desk. Knowing he would have to wait, he thought more of how he could implement his plan to escape to a Bastion and create a better life for himself once more. Even if he managed to achieve this, he knew that nothing could ever truly replace the life he once knew in the Garden. The friends he knew in the Garden he might never see again, with the possible exception of Mr. One, and it was unclear what his fate would be. As he reminisced, the Rabbit-Man thought about the little duckling-children he rescued from the Grandie bird on his last day in the Garden. He did not know what happened to their mother, Madame Duckly, but hoped that the little duckling-children were alright. He had no idea how close he was to one of them.

It was very unfortunate that the Rabbit-Man did not enter the registration office sooner, because only moments before he arrived, a woman left with one of the little ducklings he saved that day. The woman was named Sally Wonder and she wore the suit of a white dove. This little duckling-child fell from the Garden not long after the Rabbit-Man did, but he was fortunate enough to be closer to Main City. As Mr. One turned to face the Blue Demon, the child left the others who were taken by Christie Starlight to help Mr. One. The arms dealer was so focused on the demon he did not realize the duckling-boy's presence, and was attacked by the Blue Demon before he could notice. The boy also fell from the Garden but also survived. When the frightened toddler wandered into the streets of the Metroscape, he was spotted by Sally, who brought him home to her son and adopted him. Sally's husband was dead, and she feared for her only son, who she suspected was secretly meeting with members of the Mad Dog Tribe. If her suspicions were confirmed, she would be obligated by law to report her son to the Guard Dogs or the Main Patrol – something she was not sure she could do. She simply did not ask what her son was doing and hoped she would not find out. When she saw the frightened little boy in the duckling suit and took him in, she hoped that in raising him she could regain some of the joy she felt in raising her older son before life in Main City drove the teenage boy to affiliate himself with an outlawed gang.

The duckling-boy's name was Twig Duckly, and he remembered the man in the rabbit-suit that had helped him. If the boy had seen the Rabbit-Man while leaving the office with his mother he would have called to him, but they left too soon. Sally also worked in the Main City Mine and was seeking a new work assignment that day. She waited in the office for over two hours before being told they had no assignments for her. She left the office distraught, but tried not to show it to avoid upsetting Twig. Back to her small container they went. Their building was located only two blocks away from the Rabbit-Man's. Sally Wonder did not know what she was going to do, but she truly hoped she would not have to go to Mr. Spiderhat for aid. Doing so was what led to the demise of her late husband, and she was very resentful toward the owner of the Grand Coliseum because of it. She hated his show that was broadcast on the T-Web, but her adopted boy enjoyed watching it. His young mind was enthralled by the excitement and drama on the program. He did not understand what had happened to Mr. Wonder in the Coliseum, and Sally did not mention it to him. Almost all the children in Main City enjoyed watching the contests in the Coliseum, usually because their parents did. Most of the Main City youth idolized the Grand Coliseum Champion Eagle Top. Twig was different in this, however. He actually greatly disliked Eagle Top and could not understand why others were so fond of him. Twig knew his older brother wished to compete in the Coliseum one day (a notion that made Sally very nervous) and hoped he could watch him when he did. When Sally arrived home her older son was not there. Twig went and sat on the sofa of their apartment and turned on the T-Web screen. The program currently being broadcast interested but also frightened Sally very much – the narrator was providing a list of suspected affiliates to Sig Calcium, and acknowledged these individuals as people who may have helped him achieve his theft of the Coveted Cabbage. Images of the suspects were displayed on the screen as the narrator stated their names. Sally's heart sank when she heard that Try Wonder – her older son – was among the suspects. She broke down in tears as her worst fears were confirmed – her boy had gotten himself into trouble at last. Twig understood his mother's reaction and tried to console her. Although he tried to make his mother feel better, he could not help but weep himself. The young duckling-boy was very afraid. He lost one mother and home already … and he did not wish to lose another.

The Rabbit-Man also saw this same broadcast as he was waiting in the registration office, which had a screen on the wall of its main lobby. Another one of the suspects mentioned was his friend Peace Shadow who he worked with in the mine. The Rabbit-Man felt saddened that his acquaintance was named, because he guessed that everyone on the list would meet with great trouble whether they were guilty of anything or not. He was correct and he knew why – an institution with as much power, influence, and control over a place as the Caretaking Body had over Main City always needed to exhibit that power – especially when it was challenged. The only way this was done was by punishing people. If they could punish people for the crimes they committed, as they intended to do to Sig Calcium, this was best for them. If they could not, they would punish people for crimes they convinced the majority of the populace the condemned had committed. The Rabbit-Man knew this was the case with some of these individuals named, and Peace Shadow was probably one of them. Again he was overcome with ire and his desperation to get out of Main City was only enhanced. Still, he was glad he did not hear any bad news regarding Mr. One, and hoped his friend made it out of Main City by now.

When the Rabbit-Man's turn came to go to the front desk, he presented his newly acquired Pass to the woman with the bonnet. She looked at it and told him, "Wait one moment." and then typed something into a keypad on her desk. "Have a seat and someone will be with you."

The Rabbit-Man sat down in the front office and looked at the screen on the wall. Before long a man in a brown suit, not the one he met on his first day, came into the main office and greeted him. "Hello, Rabbit-Man," he said. "I understand you have a Pass you would like to use."

"Yes, please," the Rabbit-Man replied, and the suited man asked him to follow him back into his office. The room was very plain and had a brown wooden desk in the center. A plaque that read "Stud Stackman" was on the desk along with a framed photograph facing away from the Rabbit-Man and various papers. "Please sit down." said Stackman as he went to his chair behind the desk. "Well now, Rabbit-Man, based on the information taken from your card it seems you have recently been out of work when the Main City Mine closed. I'm sorry to hear about that. But you have a Pass with you now, and that should be able to help you. Please show it to me so I can determine how I can best assist you." The Rabbit-Man showed Stud Stackman the Pass he gained along with Marvin Pinkbelly's other valuables. The man behind the desk observed this for a moment, then set it down and looked at him. "Tell me, Rabbit-Man, what would you like to do with this?"

"I am hoping to go to the nearest Bastion, wherever that may be," the Rabbit-Man told him. "I come from Lady Easter's Garden, but my home has had much trouble and been destroyed recently. I cannot return there, so I am hoping to establish a home in another Bastion. I was hoping you might be able to give me more information on where I can go to."

"I would be happy to help you," Stackman said with a smile. "However, in this office we do not have any business with any of the Bastions. A person must get there on their own if they wish to do that. The best we can do is transfer you to another Metroscape. This Pass that you have cannot get you into a Bastion, anyway. You see, this is a Bronze-valued Pass. You must have at least a Silver-valued, but preferably a Gold-valued Pass, to even hope to gain entrance into a Bastion. Most are very particular about who they let in. I really would like to help you Rabbit Man, so I would suggest trying to use the Pass you have to get a better ranking work assignment here in Main City. I think that would suit you much better."

The Rabbit-Man was disappointed, but not very surprised, at this news. It seemed predictable that a Pass given to him in such a manner would not aid him much. Stud Stackman seemed friendly enough, but his suggestion that the Rabbit-Man would do better for himself remaining in Main City made him very mistrustful of the man behind the desk. "What kind of better ranking work assignment can I obtain?" the Rabbit-Man asked.

"I'll have to look into that and get back to you," Stackman replied. "I'll send a message to your T-Web screen when I learn of any positions better suited to you. For now, just hold on to that Pass... that Pass....that Passsssss...." Stackman's voice slurred and something strange started happening to his face as he said this last statement to the Rabbit-Man. It looked as if light grey steam started emerging from his ears, and two bright lights began twinkling and flashing before each of his eyes.

"The Pass is only a Bronze-valued Passssss...." Stackman's voice changed into a low, slurring drawl. "No Bastion, no Garden, because it's only a Bronze-valued Passss..... Rabbit-Man..... little rabbit, little rabbit... They are very particular about who... who..." now Stackman's voice lowered to a strange soft whisper. "... who they let in Rabbit-Man.... no, Rabbit-Man, not you..... not with your Bronze valued.... Bronze valued Passsss...." The Rabbit-Man then noticed, to his bewilderment and dismay, that the smoke coming from Stackman's ears was not grey but was now deep blue.

"Oh no! Not that!" The Rabbit-Man leapt up from his chair and made his way toward Stackman's door. The suited man's eyes were still flashing, and this time the twinkling lights before each eye socket were blue. "Stay away from me!" the Rabbit-Man said in desperation, unsure what was happening.

"I just want to help you, Rabbit-Man," Stackman said, this time in his normal voice. And then his voice suddenly changed back to the whisper again. "I just want to help... only a Bronze-valued Passsss..."

The Rabbit-Man went out the door and hastily fled from the Registration Office. When he exited the building and walked back onto the streets of Main City, he noticed that the same sickly blue aura – not quite a mist and not quite a light either – permeated the entire city the same way it had done in the Garden his final day there. Occasionally he would see flashes of the twinkling blue light in various places. Not knowing what to do, the frightened Rabbit-Man did the only thing he could think of and headed back to his container. As he hurried along, walking briskly but not running (even now he did not wish to draw any unneeded attention to himself), the flashing blue lights became brighter and more frequent until at last there came a screeching wind accompanied by a swirl of blue lights. The wind knocked the Rabbit-Man off his feet, and he heard a loud snap. He looked around him and noticed that the blue aura was gone after the snap. No more lights, no more aura; everything seemed to be normal enough. Still, the Rabbit-Man was very nervous and wanted to get his container as quickly as possible.

He made it to his building and walked up the staircase to his room and then used his card to enter. To his dismay, he found that somebody was sitting in the chair of his room. The person wore a dark grey cloak with a hood. The body beneath seemed very frail, like that of a very old person. The stranger looked up, and the Rabbit-Man instantly recognized the curved horns and bright yellow eyes upon the blue skeletal face. The Blue Demon was sitting before him in the chair of his container.

"How did you get in here?" the Rabbit-Man asked. "What do you want with me?"

The Blue Demon's face contorted into a hideous grin beneath the curved ram horns on its forehead. The demon's face was like a blue shrunken skull, except it had those glaring yellow eyes and sharp teeth lining its mouth beneath very thin lips which stretched far back when he smiled. The hideous grin the demon now wore on his face startled the Rabbit-Man. He also had a stringy grey beard growing off his chin, and pointed ears on the sides of its head that could hardly be seen beneath the hood. If he was not wearing the hood, his mangy grey hair would have shown. The head was large and did not seem to fit the frail body encased in the grey cloak in the Rabbit-Man's chair. The blue skin covering the skull-like head was thin and sickly, and the demon had no nose but only two small holes in the center of his devilish face.

"Hello, Rabbit-Man," the Blue Demon said. "I've been waiting for you. What took you so long to get here? I really couldn't wait to meet you again."

"What do you want?" the Rabbit-Man insisted. "Why have you been waiting for me? Haven't you caused me enough trouble already? Tell me what you're after!"

"I want to help you, Rabbit Man," the Blue Demon said in the same soft whisper he heard coming from Stackman earlier. "I know you Rabbit Man; I know you even better than you know yourself. I can help you achieve what you're after. I can help you become the lead Protectorate of your own Bastion."

"What do you mean?" the Rabbit-Man asked. "You destroyed my Bastion, my home. Lady Easter was a fine Protectorate of the Garden. You destroyed everything she created and made good. You destroyed everything we in the Garden worked so hard to maintain. Just what *are* you, anyway?"

"I don't know who told you I destroyed your Garden, but that isn't true." the Blue Demon answered. "It was that great bird and the other Grandies that destroyed your home. I actually killed some of them myself. I could have helped Lady Easter defend the Garden if I arrived there sooner. Unfortunately, the Grandies had already laid waste to the Garden by the time I was there. It's a shame really; that Garden had so much potential."

"Mr. One told me your fire burnt most of the Garden away. I don't believe you – I think you let the Grandies into the Garden!"

"You are quite mistaken, Rabbit-Man. It was actually Mr. One that led the Grandies into the Garden. If he wasn't always travelling in and out of your home he would not have shown them the way in. You know he wasn't supposed to be doing that anyway. Folks such as Mr. One are not supposed to be travelling in and out of Bastions at a whim. With someone like him around, it is no surprise your home met the fate it did. If you accept my offer for help you may be able to prevent such a thing from occurring to another Bastion."

"Why do you want to help a Bastion, anyway, Blue Demon?"

"Because I want to live in peace as well," the demon replied. "If you and I work together, we can gain our access into a Bastion and live there happily. What do you say?" For a moment the Rabbit-Man considered what the demon said, but the story did not make much sense to him. This entity was present on the worst day of his life, and he had difficulty believing it wanted to help him.

"I still don't believe you," the Rabbit-Man said. "I don't understand why you wish to prey upon me, but I don't intend to make it easy for you. Go away and leave me alone. I want nothing to do with you!" The Rabbit-Man then swiftly grabbed his bundle of Cabbage from his bed and ran out of his container, slamming the door shut on the Blue Demon behind him. As he ran out of the building, the blue aura appeared once more along with the passing flashes of blue light. He heard the demon's laughter once more and heard his voice echoing around him.

"You want nothing to do with me now, Rabbit-Man," the disembodied voice said among the laughter, "but I want much to do with you. You cannot escape me. I can get to you anytime I want." The Rabbit-Man went back through the streets of Main City in his haste to escape the demon. As he ran, however, the ground before him melted away, and he ran forward into a hole in the ground that closed up above him. He fell into water, and struggled for a moment to make his way onto a platform beside him. When he stood up on the platform, he looked around and realized where he was. It was the sewer of Main City. The Blue Demon created the hole he fell into, and now he was trapped underground. "What does that monster have planned for me now?"

the Rabbit-Man thought. There was no sign of the demon's presence anywhere – no aura or flashes or laughter or voice. The Rabbit-Man walked forward, and was surprised to discover the light source in the sewer. Even beneath Main City there was a T-Web screen on the side of the sewer wall lighting up the area. The Rabbit-Man looked up at it. He knew someone must have been using it before him, because it was showing one of the private stations which could only be accessed by someone seeking it out.

That was when he heard it. A private program was about to begin, and the Rabbit-Man heard the strumming of musical notes before a folk singer began the introductory song to whatever this independent program was. Various imagery of mountainous terrain streamed on the underground T-Web screen as the song played, and then finally this gave way to the image of a man with thick glasses, a mostly white suit, and a thick beard and immense eyebrows on his face.

"Greetings ladies and gentlemen from the Home Base!" the man said. "I am the White Owl-man Howler Highhorse, and I'm here with another segment of my program *Freedom for the Homeplace*! As many of you are fully aware by now, the Caretaking Body has been keeping the best and brightest of all people out of the Bastions for far too long. That is why I have chosen to endorse The Great White Calling, a collective goal for all like-minded individuals to escape the mundane and deprecating life of the Metroscapes in search of the finest Bastion of all, the Homeplace!

"I have shared the details of my plans in the various books I have published, and most viewers of my program have read them already. If you have not done so by now, make sure you read my books as they are the key to our entrance into the Homeplace. I know, better than anyone else, that if the boulder here at the Base Pad is removed, it will reveal the stairway that leads into the great Homeplace, the best of all Bastions. I know this because I was there once, and I wish to return there with only the highest quality folks who wish to free themselves of the vile Caretaking Body."

The Rabbit-Man was instantly intrigued by the speech of White Owl-man. He wished he had discovered his program sooner. He never imagined there was somebody out there that dared to openly oppose the Caretaking Body on an independent station. Furthermore, this old man claimed to know of a Bastion that could be accessed without any kind of Pass. The Rabbit-Man needed to know more, and his new goal immediately became obtaining the books Howler Highhorse had mentioned.

"In order to be successful I need all others who wish for freedom to meet me here at the Home Base. With enough of us, we can move this boulder and gain the freedom we have always desired. It can only be done if there are enough of us, and I am simply not getting the results I need. Only those courageous and dedicated enough can hope to make it here and remove the boulder. Who will come to me first? Who will answer the Great White Calling and establish a better future for the generations that will be damned under the Caretaking Body that has suppressed us so long? I hope that some of you watching this will do your duty and come to me. Come to me! Come to me, and together we will establish a life in a Bastion better than any that has existed before. Come to me! Freedom and fulfillment await those with the courage to answer my call! Come to me!"

Chapter Eight

Trouble in Main City

From the moment he saw Howler Highhorse's *Freedom for the Homeplace* show broadcast over the T-Web screen installed on the wall of the sewer, the Rabbit-Man's mind was ablaze with enthusiasm. He had to know more about it – it became his one overwhelming desire. All else seemed unimportant compared to the Great White Calling; all troubles could be dealt with if doing so helped him get to the Base Pad. The Great White Calling – there seemed nothing more to life. The Rabbit-Man's main goal, his obsession, was to get the books that Howler Highhorse had written and published. He immediately went back to his container – ready to fight the Blue Demon hand-to-hand if necessary. He believed he would smash the demon's skeletal face if it dared to hinder his quest for those books, which to him were equivalent to sacred scriptures that led the reader to freedom and salvation.

He eventually found a ladder in the sewer that led to a way out. When he returned to his container, there was no trace of the Blue Demon. Oddly, the Rabbit-Man's fear of the entity subsided; such was his vigor for the Great White Calling. After washing himself he immediately went to his screen and searched for information – about Howler Highhorse (sometimes referred to as the Great White Owl-Man due to the cause he espoused), The Great White Calling, and the Calling Books written by Highhorse that he mentioned on *Freedom for the Homeplace*. The Rabbit-Man absorbed all of this information like a sponge does water. There were various articles posted on the Calling's station that he read (most of them written by Howler Highhorse) about the Homeplace Bastion and the imperative of the Great White Calling. The owl-man had many detractors as well, some calling him a fraud, some claiming that his goal was unrealistic. The Rabbit-Man found other installments of *Freedom for the Homeplace*, and in many of these installments Highhorse made every effort to contradict or refute the criticisms of his detractors. The more the Rabbit-Man listened to him, the more impressed he became. There was even an installment of *Freedom for the Homeplace* in which the subject of demons was mentioned, and this only furthered the Rabbit-Man's trust and hope in the Calling.

"Demons are loathsome entities in the service of the Caretaking Body," the owl-Man said on his program. "They have fooled so many fine Companions into destroying their lives in the hope of gaining access into a Bastion or possession of some of that damn Cabbage that everybody goes insane for. To me, it is obvious what these demons really are – and they do not fool me one bit. The answer to the troubles facing people entrapped in the Metroscapes are not to be found with demons or any of this grotesque Cabbage, which actually has no nutritional value if eaten anyway. Believe me, I tried it. It is a completely artificial substance that the Caretaking Body has produced to keep its citizens enslaved, and it works damn well! It will not keep me enslaved, however, nor will it do so to all of the tried and true Companions out there who have heard the Calling! We will not give in to their awful plans, or be swayed from our duty to establish the greatest Bastion of all time! Tomorrow is ours, my dear Companions!"

"Indeed it is!" answered the Rabbit-Man as he watched the installment of *Freedom for the Homeplace*. "I know exactly what he means – I know what those demons really are, as well. That Blue Demon couldn't fool me, and they can't fool the great Howler Highhorse either. I simply can't wait until I make it into the Base Pad to help him move that boulder. I need to get there; it's only a matter of time."

The matter of time the Rabbit-Man imagined would be longer than he liked, but his dedication to the Great White Calling did not waver. It consumed his mind, and became his overwhelming passion. This benefitted him in a way nothing else was able to since he arrived in Main City – his fervent support of Howler Highhorse's idea replaced the sorrow and torment he felt since losing his home and being stranded in a place he greatly disliked and living a life he hated. Something that did this for a person in the Rabbit-Man's situation would have had such an effect on anybody. Furthermore, since Mr.

One's departure the Rabbit-Man did not have any close friends or confidantes he could share his passions with. Discussing the Great White Owl-Man and his ideals regarding the Homeplace Bastion would be considered a severe offense in Main City, and the Rabbit-Man was fully aware that mentioning such business to a stranger would be dangerous.

Thus, he kept his ideas and ambitions to himself and carried on his business as usual. All of his spare time was spent researching as much information as he could about The Great White Calling on the T-Web screen in his container. He even discovered a station that allowed him to have the Calling Books delivered discreetly to his container from the Base Pad. He did this, and waited with ardent anticipation for them to arrive.

"These books will give me everything I need to be successful as a Companion in the Great White Calling," the Rabbit-Man thought. "When I read them I'll know all I need to get back to a Bastion, once and for all. Not just any Bastion either; under the guidance of the Great White Owl-Man it will be the greatest Bastion that ever was. If I lend a hand in the establishment of the Homeplace, perhaps Lady Easter will find out about it and we can invite her to live there with us. The other Companions and I will create a Bastion so impressive that Lady Easter would love to live in it. I can look after her in the Great White Homeplace just as she once looked after me in the Garden. That would be amazing; a dream come true. That would be..." The Rabbit-Man's eyes filled with tears in the privacy of his container. He was overcome with emotions as he contemplated his beloved Lady Easter joining him in a Bastion he created. He knew the likelihood of such a scenario was very small, but nevertheless, he dared to hope; and having hope again was a feeling so good he wished he would never, ever lose it. That was what the Great White Calling meant to him. He fell asleep in his chair before the screen in his container. He dreamed of the ominous aura of the Blue Demon and was uncomfortable when he woke.

A few days later, the Rabbit-Man received a message from Stud Stackman from the registration office telling him he had discovered a new work assignment for him. The message appeared on his screen, and Stackman advised him to head to the Main City Committee Building the following day. The new work involved establishing a plan to better the education of the children in Main City, and Stackman suggested the Rabbit-Man as a prime candidate to the Committee. There was actually a list of candidates, according to Stackman, but all of them either denied the position or were unavailable. The Rabbit-Man was glad to have a work assignment to earn more Cabbage until he was able to relocate to Highhorse's Base Pad, but the message from Stackman was unclear as to what the work actually was. In his previous assignment he was digging holes. This new work sounded important enough, but he did not know what he would be doing to complete it.

"I wish I knew what education in Main City is even like," he thought. "I guess I'll find out soon enough. Tomorrow I'll begin and then see how it is."

That night he received a delivery at his container – it was a nondescript box containing the Calling books, and the Rabbit-Man was thrilled when he received them. He opened the box and began reading that night. His mind was entranced for the rest of the evening. No worries of the Blue Demon troubled him, no remorse for his lost home, and no fear of losing what little he already had. The story was everything he expected it to be. Howler Highhorse created an image so vibrant of what the ideal Bastion was that the Rabbit-Man had a hard time putting the book down when it was time to sleep. The following day he woke, washed himself, and set out for his new work assignment in the Main City Committee Building. His desire to get to the Base Pad was constantly in his mind and remained there like a constant buzz that one always hears, but because of its consistency forgets he is hearing it. The Committee Building appeared similar to most of the others in Main City, and there was a slot for the Rabbit-Man to place his card; He did so and entered the building. A man in a black suit wearing black shades greeted him.

"Greetings Rabbit-Man, please follow me," the man said before leading the Rabbit-Man down a hallway to a large dark room. "Please go inside with the other panel members." The Rabbit-Man stepped into the room where he saw a long elevated table on his right at the back of the room. Behind this were seats filled with various individuals. He saw a sign that read "Panel members this way" and an arrow pointing toward the long table. He walked along the table until he found an empty seat between a man in a chicken suit and another in a regular suit. He sat at the panel and noticed two empty chairs in the center of the room. The Rabbit-Man wondered what this had to do with education but assumed he would find out soon. The door to the room was closed and a light was turned on, illuminating the two chairs. The Rabbit-Man thought this looked like a kind of interrogation rather than a meeting about education. He had an uneasy feeling and wondered what was going to happen.

"Bring forth the citizens," said a man in a rhinoceros suit that was at the center of the long table. A woman in a dove suit and a child in a duckling suit were then led toward the chairs and instructed to sit before two black-suited men like the one the Rabbit-Man just met. The two that sat before the panel were Sally Wonder and Twig Duckly. The Rabbit-Man noticed the duckling suit that the boy wore, and recognized him as a boy from Lady Easter's Garden. "How did he get here?" the Rabbit-Man thought. "Did the others come here from the Garden as well? The woman he is with must have taken him in; the poor boy must have been even more confused than I was."

"Mrs. Wonder, you have been summoned before the Educational Committee to answer for the recent actions of your son, Try Wonder, and his suspected involvement with the loathsome thief Sig Calcium. Try Wonder has been found by the Main Patrol and turned over to the Guard Dogs for interrogation. You have said in your statement to the Main Patrol that the news of your son's suspected involvement with Sig Calcium came as a surprise to you. Still, it is the duty of the Committee to inquire as to what kind of home-life Try Wonder had in your container, and also what kind of upbringing your other adopted son will have in your care." Sally Wonder looked obviously distraught at the statements of the rhino-man, but she kept her resolve while answering his questions. The Rabbit-Man was overcome with admiration for her, and suddenly he felt angered that the panel was even questioning her at all. "What does this have to do with education?" he thought to himself. He knew essentially what was going on; this "committee" was formed with the intention of feeding individuals to the Guard Dogs for alleged involvement with outlaws. The Rabbit-Man knew that most accusations would be bogus, and the entire ordeal sickened him.

"I have been answering questions since the incident at the Guard Post occurred," Sally told the panel. "I don't know how my son could have been involved, and I knew nothing about Sig Calcium's plans to steal the Cabbage. I really don't know what else to say or do to convince everyone that I had nothing to do with any of this, and I am still convinced my son had nothing to do with it."

"We understand what you're saying, Mrs. Wonder," said a woman in a silky poodle suit. Her tone was snide, and the Rabbit-Man hated hearing her even more than the rhino-man. "But when things like this occur, we need answers. We need them because the Caretaking Body needs answers. We shall keep asking questions of you and anyone else connected to the suspects until we find the answers we need. Tell us, did Try Wonder ever mention Sig Calcium before this incident?"

The Rabbit-Man was very uncomfortable being on the panel. He looked around at the others seated near him. They gazed down at Sally Wonder, some with disinterest and some with a glare. What the poodle-woman said about asking questions until they received the answers they needed made him even more restless. He felt sympathy for Sally Wonder, and this was enhanced by the presence of the young duckling-boy. The Rabbit-Man resolved to not let this sad display of Main City nastiness continue, and he knew he was going to speak up on behalf of the woman and the boy. His inner passion for the Great White Calling made him bold, and he did not fear any negative reaction he would incur from the rest of the panel, even if it meant bringing attention to himself. He believed Howler Highhorse would be proud to see him do such a thing, and this idea made him glad.

"Now wait just a moment!" the Rabbit-Man said as he stood up and looked down the long table at the poodle-woman. "The lady said she doesn't know anything, didn't she? Unless anyone here has some proof that she had previous knowledge of Sig Calcium's scheme, then it is clear she is telling the truth. I know of a man who was heavily penalized for wrongly accusing someone of a crime, and I do not want the same penalties to befall us." The Rabbit-Man was of course referring to Marvin Pinkbelly's accusation, but did not mention that he himself was the recipient of the accusation. The Rabbit-Man had a clever idea in using the crime of false accusation as a means to discreetly help Sally Wonder. But he could not contain his indignation, and his composure soon gave way to his passion. "Why does everyone in this city need to be so aggressive toward one another?" He went on. "Didn't any of you ever hear of living in harmony with one another? How about helping people, for a change, rather than just preying on one another all the time? Did that idea ever occur to any of you? No, I bet it didn't! It didn't because that's the way of life in Main City – take as much as you can from others to benefit yourself. I see it happening all the time, and I'm really sick and tired of it!"

"Well, *excuse* me sir," the rhino-man said, "but I do not believe you have the right to criticize –"

"Well, excuse me horn-face, but I wasn't finished yet!" the Rabbit-Man shouted back. The rest of the panel was looking at him in shock and bewilderment. They had never seen one of their peers speak out on such a tirade before. "What you're doing to this woman is wrong, and all of you wretched fools should know it! The most pathetic thing is that you don't know – you just accept it as common practice in this place. Well, I say this place sucks and so do its warped standards of justice!"

"Mr. Rabbit-Man, you are quite mistaken," the rhino-man replied with a grin. "You see, there would be harmonious living in Main City if everyone followed the rules of the Caretaking Body. Unfortunately, people like Sig Calcium do not, and it disrupts the order that would be in place –"

"Order! I don't think so!" retorted the Rabbit-Man. "If Sig Calcium committed a crime, then get him in here and grill him instead. Intimidation by Grandie dogs and miserable snitches is not order, that's just... that just sucks, and that's all there is to it. You know what I say? I say screw the damned Coveted Cabbage and all the monsters that want to kill each other for it, screw Sig Calcium and his little stunt, screw the Caretaking Body, and screw these good-for-nothing Metroscapes! What? You don't like me saying it, rhino-man? Poodle-lady? Then I say screw all of you too!" The other panel members gasped when they heard this, and the Rabbit-Man pushed over the long table and leaped into the center of the room near Sally Wonder and Twig. The little duckling-boy had already recognized the Rabbit-Man as soon as he started speaking, and he was thrilled when he saw his hero once again. "That's the one that saved us from the scary bird!" Twig thought as he viewed the Rabbit-Man, gazing up at the familiar friend with wide eyes brimming with love and admiration that only a child could possess.

"Guards, please let Mrs. Wonder and the boy go home," the rhino-man called. "We have something much more severe to look into now. Mr. Rabbit-Man, you were entrusted to serve the Caretaking Body by being enrolled in this panel, and your words have mocked us and our masters! You shall pay for your insubordination and crude insults. We shall see to it that the Guard Dogs investigate you thoroughly!"

"You mean the way they're investigating numerous people who are most likely innocent, just because they cannot find the person who committed the actual crime? I'm not afraid of your threats or even the Guard Dogs for that matter. I'm fed up with this place!" By now two of the men in black suits had escorted Sally Wonder and Twig out of the room. Two Patrolmen arrived and turned their attention to the Rabbit-Man. They produced batons and brandished them at him, and he knew that he was in severe trouble now. He tried to think quickly how he could escape from the situation he was in. He was so aggravated at what he saw during his time at the long table that he simply he decided he was going to take his bundle of Cabbage, leave Main City, and set out for the Base Pad on his own. He knew this would be dangerous, but he did not care anymore. He was too weary of the negativity and wrongness that prevailed in Main City that he could not even tolerate being in it anymore. His plan might have worked out well if not for the trouble he just got himself into. If he was reported to the Guard Dogs he knew he would encounter a grim fate.

Nevertheless, he meant what he said, and he decided that he would make it to the Base Pad or die trying, for nothing else seemed to matter to him anymore. The Patrolmen and the men in the black outfits came upon him with their clubs; one of them hit him in the gut and the other on the back of his head. He fell to the ground where they continued to beat on him with the batons. Those sitting at the long table viewed this beating with pleasure. The poodle-woman and a small man in a snail suit walked out from behind the table toward the Rabbit-Man who was now prone on the ground. The two black-clad men lifted the Rabbit-Man by his arms until he was kneeling before the poodle-woman and the little snail-man. The woman slapped the Rabbit-Man's face several times with her gloved hand, shouting taunts and calling him a vile traitor.

"Mr. Squirms, come and give him your slime treatment," the poodle-woman commanded the snail-man. "I think that will do this little wretch some good." The snail-man called Mr. Squirms then walked over to the Rabbit-Man and started squeezing the torso of his snail suit, causing slime to ooze out of it. He then gathered the slime up into his hand and prepared to shove it in the Rabbit-Man's face. As he drew his hand back to send the slime flying onto the defenseless Rabbit-Man, a loud bang sounded in the room which then quickly permeated with a thick blue mist. The poodle-woman, the snail-man, and all of the guards looked around bewildered. A murmur of confusion sounded among those seated at the long table. The flashes of blue light then twinkled in and out in a manner the Rabbit-Man had come to know well. Out from the mist stepped a tall but thin figure clad in a grey robe. Two large bat-like wings protruded from its back, and this time the hood was not covering the head. The guards dropped the Rabbit-Man, but he could still clearly see the head above the grey robe. The curved ram-horns were unmistakable, and the skeletal face was the same as it appeared when the Blue Demon visited his container. Now the fiend had returned. The Rabbit-Man noticed that the Blue Demon's body seemed much more substantial beneath the grey robe than when the creature was in his container recently. It seemed like the demon could enhance his body size at will.

The others in the room seemed to not notice the tall figure at all, but were quite concerned with the mists and the twinkling lights. These seemed to be the only aspects of the demon they could see. At last the demon spoke; the two guards dropped to the floor unconscious, and the poodle-woman and snail-man fell to the ground with their hands over their ears. The deep, whispering voice of the Blue Demon sounded in the room. "Leave my little Rabbit-Man be," he said. "I have other uses for him that do not involve the Guard Dogs or the likes of you people. He has potential beyond anything any of you could imagine." The Blue Demon then turned his head and fixed his glowing yellow eyes upon the Rabbit-Man. "Come with me Rabbit-Man; I will help you be free of this city you despise. I can help you even make it to the Base Pad. That is, after all, your ultimate goal is it not? You wish to help Howler Highhorse move that boulder. I wish to see it moved as well, Rabbit-Man. I also would like that boulder moved. I have a keen interest in your success at the Base Pad. You have been reading the owl-man's books with much enthusiasm, and I like that. I wish to help you Rabbit-Man, I really do. Let me help you achieve what you desire."

"No, you stay away from me!" the Rabbit-Man answered as he got to his feet. "I will seek out the Base Pad and meet the great owl-man myself. I will help fulfill the Great White Calling on my own, and I will help to form the greatest Bastion ever known! It shall be a place where vile creatures like you don't exist! The owl-man was clear in stating his disdain for your kind. I have heard the voice of righteousness, I have heard the Great White Calling, and I will follow it until my duty is fulfilled. You will not hinder me, Blue Demon. Away with you! Leave me alone!" The Rabbit-Man then ran away from the tall figure of the demon and out the door. He ran back to his container as fast as he could. Once there, he gathered together his bundle of Cabbage, his bronze-valued Pass, and his Calling books. This he put in a backpack he had purchased previously and placed it onto his back. He knew he would need to leave his container and get out of Main City quickly if he was reported to the Guard Dogs. He left the building and ran along the streets of Main City until he came to a location where vehicles were rented and sold. These were usually considered either a luxury item or something used by those with an important purpose in the Metroscape. Still, the Rabbit-Man understood he needed to make a fast getaway and knew he could not do so on foot. He had experience driving a vehicle in the Garden and knew he would be able to. The vehicles were located at a lot sealed off by a tall fence with barbed wire at the top. A small booth stood outside of the fence, and inside it sat a fat man with a yellow t-shirt and no animal suit.

The Rabbit-Man went to the booth and showed the man his bundle of Cabbage. "Please let me in to purchase one of your vehicles, kind sir."

"Let me see your card first," the fat man answered. The Rabbit-Man did not want to do this because he was in a hurry and also because he did not know if the Guard Dogs and the Main Patrol would be looking for him yet. When it was clear he had no other choice, he handed his card to the man who slipped it into a small machine. "Wait here a moment," the man said as he handed the card back. He then disappeared through a door in the back of the booth and walked into the lot out of the Rabbit-Man's sight. The Rabbit-Man waited in nervous anticipation for the man to return. As he was waiting, he heard a voice call out "There he is! That's him!" he turned and saw the poodle-woman pointing her finger at him. Two Patrolmen in their red shirts were running after him with batons. The Rabbit-Man ran from them in the opposite direction through the streets of Main City. He was nervous but still determined to get out of the Metroscape as soon as he could. As he was running he turned through several alleyways and other streets to get the Patrolmen off his trail. Just when it seemed he had evaded them, his luck changed for the worse as he heard the roaring bark of a Guard Dog. The one pursuing him was one of the smaller Guard Dogs, but even still it was very huge and had a mouth disproportionally large to the rest of its body. It had mangy hair and looked more like a massive ball of fur with beady eyes and hideous fangs. He knew the likelihood of outrunning a Guard Dog was slim, but he would try anyway. He ran out into a street and was nearly struck by a vehicle. The Rabbit-Man narrowly dodged it, and it swerved and drove directly into the Guard Dog chasing him. He continued to run away.

He knew he was not far from the gate to Main City that he had entered when he first arrived, and guessed that his best hope was to simply try and get out the same way. He ran on until the gate was distant but at least in his sight. It was then that he heard even more thunderous barking, even louder this time. He took a brief glance over his shoulder, and to his dismay he saw the largest Guard Dog along with two others pursuing him. "Damn, this really might be it for me," the Rabbit-Man thought. "Well, if they get me, I'll just resist until they have no choice but to kill me. At least I'll die in the service of the Great White Calling, even if nobody knows or cares" As the Rabbit-Man ran on, he heard a change in the sound of the immense barking. Another glance over his shoulder showed him that a wall of blue flames had formed before the Guard Dogs, making them very angry. The Rabbit-Man suspected the flames came from the Blue Demon, but tried not to concern himself with it. He simply ran forward hoping to reach the gate and get out. He would decide his next move from there. The flames allowed him to put much distance between himself and the Guard Dogs, but eventually their leader leaped through the flames, searing much of his coat as he did so. None of the others followed him though. At last the Rabbit-Man made it to the gate, but they were shut before him and would not open. When the largest Guard Dog caught up to him, he slammed his captive to the ground and pinned him with his giant paw. The Rabbit-Man was almost crushed beneath the pressure. The Guard Dog opened his mouth, fully intending to tear the Rabbit-Man asunder, until a series of fireballs flew into the eyes of the great hound. The Guard Dog cried out in pain, lifting his paws to his eyes and freeing the Rabbit-Man, who looked over and saw the Blue Demon once more. The demon lifted his hand as black flames emanated from it and formed the shape of a grey, skeletal ghost-horse.

"Here is your chance to flee Main City at last, Rabbit-Man," the Blue Demon said with a grin. "I am offering you my horse to get you to the Base Pad. You will be awestruck at how fast he could carry you there. Accept my help now, or be doomed forever Rabbit-Man. The choice is yours. Your life is on the line now. You must act quickly, or die." The Guard Dog seemed to have cleared his eyes and made ready to pounce on his prey once more. Seeing there was no other choice, the Rabbit-Man ran to the Blue Demon's frightful-look-ing horse and leapt onto its back. He was immediately pulled forward by the steed as he heard the demon laughing behind him. The horse ran forward and busted through the Gates of Main City. The Guard Dog was barking furiously behind him, and the Rabbit-Man looked back to see that the Blue Demon had somehow shut the gates on the Grandie. The Rabbit-Man was able to grab his backpack before jumping onto the horse and he had it with him. Off he rode away from Main City and toward the Base Pad. The Blue Demon was right – the horse was incredibly fast.

As he rode away from Main City, however, the Rabbit-Man experienced one last feeling of overwhelming sorrow – for he knew that Sally Wonder and the little duckling-boy were still in the Metroscape he was leaving behind. How many of the other duckling-children might have been there too? He soon forced the notions from his mind, and focused on where he was heading. He was on his way to the Base Pad and Howler Highhorse. "At last I shall fulfill my duty as a Companion in the Great White Calling. At last I'll be free once more." thought the Rabbit-Man as he rode onward at incredible speed. He told himself this because doing so helped ease the troubles on his mind. He understood that many challenges awaited him in the future, and his troubles were far from over. For as he rode steadily onward to the Base Pad, the Blue Demon travelled after him.

Chapter Nine

Homeplace Bound

As passionate as he was, the Rabbit-Man was not the only person who had enough of the Caretaking Body's corruption. Before the fallen Rabbit-Man had even entered Main City the young and determined Sig Calcium had formed a bond with Try Wonder that was strengthened by their hatred of the power structure in Main City. Sig had obtained a bird suit that gave him enhanced powers which allowed him to compete even with Grandies. Try Wonder, only slightly younger than Sig, was impressed with this when his friend showed it to him. Sig managed to get Try a similar suit, fashioned to look like a raven. The two young men practiced flying in their bird suits together, and their skills were astounding. Unfortunately for them, the recorder worms that floated throughout the Metroscape spotted the antics of the brave but reckless duo. The footage the worms recorded were never shown on the TeleWeb but were reported to the Caretaking Body. Sig Calcium and Try Wonder became immediate threats to the Caretaking Body in Main City and thus the Main Patrol were assigned to capture them. When the Patrolmen tried to take the friends in for questioning, they easily evaded them by using their incredible suits. It was this activity that concerned Try's mother Sally Wonder, and she even suspected the two friends were up to something risky. However, she restrained herself from asking Try any questions for fear that the Caretaking Body would force her to betray her son. She wondered if Try and Sig Calcium had associated with the Mad Dog Tribe, but did not dare to ask her son.

"One day we are going to fly away from this place," Sig Calcium said to Try as they finished a flying session and relaxed on the outskirts of Main City. Sig Calcium lost his family because they went into debt and could not pay it off with enough Cabbage leaves. Try observed the way his beloved mother suffered to earn Cabbage, and was also angry at losing his father in Mr. Spiderhat's Grand Coliseum. The inner rage felt by the two friends was channeled into improving their situation, and when Sig managed to secure their fine suits from a secret benefactor, the two were given a feeling of freedom they had never known before as they flew through the air. It wasn't long before they planned an escape plan of their own. Try Wonder was determined to get his mother and newly adopted brother to a safer place. He loved them very much, and his determination made him feel like he had replaced his father as guardian of his family. This idea gave him motivation and resolve, and as Sig Calcium observed this he became just as dedicated to helping his younger friend. Sig Calcium had no one left in the entire Metroscape except Try Wonder and his beautiful family.

The friends' evasion of the Patrolmen was taken very badly by the Caretaking Body, and it was soon after that a greater force of Patrolmen was sent to capture the two suspects. The Patrolmen developed a clever strategy in which they attacked both Sig Calcium and Try Wonder separately. Sig was the more experienced fighter of the two and managed to defeat the Patrolmen that came after him with the abilities his suit gave him, but Try was unable to escape. Sig checked on Try's home and made sure Sally Wonder and Twig Duckly were safe before he flew away. He remembered in agony the last conversation he had with Try before his beloved friend was caught. "You're like a Protectorate sent to me and my family Sig," Try had said to him. "I can't say enough how glad I am that I met you. I can never repay all you have done for me and taught me since we met each other."

"Just keep being the brave and incredible person you are," Sig answered, and tears welled up in his eyes as he recalled the memory. He could not stand to lose another loved one, and the thought of his best friend being in danger finally made Sig Calcium snap. It was then he decided to bring the attention of the Caretaking Body upon him and steal Cabbage from the Guard Dogs. He went and did this, and to his own surprise and that of everyone else in Main City he succeeded. He was glad of the uproar and consternation he caused in Main City, but he was determined to find his friend and save him. After stealing the Cabbage he went into hiding, but his feud with the Caretaking Body was far from over.

"Just hang in their Try," Sig thought to himself. "I'll find you somehow. Just hang in their buddy- I'll save you," thought Sig. Although the sentiment was sincere and Sig Calcium's passion was strong, he had no idea how he would help his captured friend. He simply hoped he would find a way, and despite the confidence he gained after obtaining his exceptional suit, his faith in himself wavered. This only fueled his rage and hatred for the Caretaking Body and the pain they put him through. After stealing the Cabbage the conflicted young man not only wanted revenge on the Caretaking Body, but also made a silent vow to himself that he would help any victim of Caretaking Body in any way he could. Before long he would make good on that promise- but whether or not the person he helped would be his best friend remained to be seen.

•   •   •

Main City became a steadily shrinking Metroscape full of its tall grey buildings behind the Rabbit-Man as he rode on the demon's steed. He did not know exactly where the Base Pad was located, but during his research he discovered that it was to the northwest of Main City. He assumed that the spectral horse he was given by the Blue Demon knew the way there. Howler Highhorse's books referred to the Companions that made their way to the Base Pad first as A-list Companions, and the Rabbit-Man was eager to become one of them. Highhorse also described The Great White Calling as something that would begin as a powerful idea that would have few, but very determined, followers. These initial A-list Companions would set an example by their unflinching support of the Great White Calling that would awaken many other people in various Metroscapes to relocate to the Base Pad and help move the boulder, the only thing blocking entrance to the Homeplace. Those who manage to move the boulder would then establish the greatest Bastion that ever was, and all detrimental forces would be barred entrance. The owl-man made it clear in his books that a vast deposit of firearms would also be found beneath the boulder along with the stairway that would lead to their Bastion. "This is how the Companions of the Calling shall defend our sacred Homeplace from the terrible forces that have corrupted the Metroscapes." Highhorse said in one of his *Freedom for the Homeplace* programs. "Once the boulder is moved, our lives shall be our own to defend. This can only be done if I have enough Companions out here willing to fulfill their duty and their destiny. Their children and further descendants shall live in the greatest Bastion that ever was; but I need more bodies out here! This shall all begin with the A-list Companions who will set the example of what a true Companion must be. I need you out here, and I need you now!"

"I'm on my way, great owl-man," the Rabbit-Man thought to himself with fiery emotions blazing in his heart, contemplating how he was finally setting out to accomplish what he dreamed of doing for so many weeks. He had managed to evade the Guard Dogs, and even though he also had to accept the assistance of the Blue Demon, he knew it was all for the best in the end – it was for the Homeplace, a Bastion where children like the little ducklings he saved could live in peace and happiness as they were once able to in Lady Easter's Garden. "It will be because of me. I will help make it happen."

As the demon's horse galloped onward, however, the Rabbit-Man thought he heard something behind them. He was unsure of this, so he glanced over his shoulder and was frightened by what he saw. Very stealthily, seemingly out of nowhere, Wolfsnare the Terrible was following behind them. Although he was not as large as the Guard Dogs, the Grandie wolf looked fiercer and more insane and vicious than they did. His leering eyes and massive jaws were drooling as he watched the Rabbit-Man, and he remembered the scent of his prey. When he saw that the Rabbit-Man noticed him, he growled loudly and leaped forward.

"I knew I would find you again, little rabbit!" Wolfsnare called. "I said I would, didn't I? I don't know how you made it out of Main City, but it doesn't matter. You would have been better off staying there. Now I'll have you once and for all. Your horse can't outrun me; there are none who can!"

"Dammit!" the Rabbit-Man thought; he had no idea how to control the horse he was riding, and he feared Wolfsnare might possibly be able to overtake the steed even at the rate he was galloping. He did not have any weapons on him; his only hope was to get away from the Grandie wolf. He could not think of any way to throw it off his trail. He figured he at least needed to try communicating with the steed he was riding. "If we don't speed up, that wolf is going to devour us both. If there is any way you can run faster, please do it now!"

The horse must have understood the Rabbit-Man and heard the desperation in his voice. To the Rabbit-Man's surprise, the horse turned its head completely around and looked directly at him while still galloping full speed. "I can take care of him," the horse said in a raspy voice. "But then you'll be on your own from here. He is after you, not me. If you want me to get him off your trail I can, but then that is the end of my job."

The Rabbit-Man did not have much time to think about this. "Yes, please just get him away from me however you can."

"As you wish," the ghostly horse answered. The Rabbit-Man was then flung forward from the horse's back and the steed changed into a large mass of misty grey flames. This ghostly inferno engulfed Wolfsnare, who struggled greatly inside of it. The smoky flames then turned into a tight rope and wrapped itself around the wolf's neck and limbs. The rope then floated into the air and carried away the massive wolf, as he howled and growled with rage. The Rabbit-Man ran away from the wolf and the strange horse-turned-rope that bore it away. He imagined his journey to the Base Pad would be more difficult now, but he was very glad to have Wolfsnare away from him and relieved that he no longer had the demon's horse to concern himself with. The land around him was as bland and desolate as when he first fell from the large tree, but to his surprise the Rabbit-Man saw some smaller trees in the distance. He thought there might be people he could speak to in this location. With his backpack still strapped to him he started forward toward the trees in the hope of getting a better idea where he was, and how close to the Base Pad he had come.

He walked along with caution, and by the time he made it to the trees, which turned out to be a small grove, he was quite tired. Luckily for him, the occupants of the grove were very hospitable folk. As the Rabbit-Man walked among the trees with his backpack he was met by two very small people, each carrying small nuts along in a basket. He was astonished as he observed the appearance of these little creatures. They both appeared to be small fairy-like little women, but one had a suit that resembled a strawberry atop a plant-like green body and the other wore one which looked like a little yellow flower. The miniscule women were speaking cheerfully to one another and they both exhibited a very sanguine demeanor. This was quite a stark contrast to what the Rabbit-Man observed in Main City, and he wondered if he had come to a small Bastion filled with tiny plant-people amid the dismal land he was just travelling through.

"Hello, stranger," one of the women said to the Rabbit-Man. "What brings you out this way?"

At first the Rabbit-Man was unsure how to respond. These young ladies both seemed quite nice. As he observed them further the Rabbit-Man noticed they had long hair that was tied in braids down their backs. The strawberry-girl had a long green ponytail while the flower-girl had a brown one. He had not been addressed by women as friendly as these since his time in the Garden, but he was sure to keep his manners despite feeling surprised and a little shy.

"Hello," he answered after a brief awkward pause. "I'm the Rabbit-Man. It's a pleasure to meet you both. I've come here from Main City and I'm heading toward the Base Pad. I believe it is located northwest of here."

"Well met Rabbit-Man," answered the strawberry-girl in a high-pitched but friendly voice. Both smiled kindly at him. "I'm Heart, and this is my sister Sprout. You seem like a nice fellow, Rabbit-Man, why not have lunch with us while you're travelling along? I'm sure my parents would be happy to meet you. They are always fond of meeting new folk, so long as they don't bring any trouble with them."

"That is very considerate, Heart, thank you," said the Rabbit-Man. "I certainly don't intend to bring any trouble to this pleasant place. After lunch I really must be on my way though. I have to meet someone on very important business. I hope you understand."

"Certainly," Heart replied with a smile. She and Sprout led the Rabbit-Man though the grove to a very large oak tree with a door on the side of its trunk. The Rabbit-Man never saw anything like this before, not even in the Garden, and he was very curious as to how these people defended themselves from the Grandies outside their little grove, especially considering they were small and resembled plants. Heart and Sprout carried their baskets through the door and into the tree as the Rabbit-Man followed them. He actually managed to fit through the door, though he had to squeeze. If he was larger than he was he would not have fit. It was surprising that these small people had such a large door to their home. The inside was alarmingly spacious, with a little round table in the center of the room. Seven tiny children even smaller than Heart and Sprout were bustling about the room. They all resembled some type of fruit, vegetable, or flower in their appearance also. They all seemed happy and content and the Rabbit-Man could not tell if they were playing or completing chores. The Rabbit-Man could tell they were children because of their smaller size and more rounded appearance. He could not help but wonder what these small people were. They seemed to be the polar opposite of Grandies. Whatever they were, the Rabbit-Man was just glad they were friendly. A woman taller than the children was also in the room, and she greeted the young ladies warmly when they walked inside. She had the appearance of a pineapple, as her body was encased in the shell of the fruit while her hair grew off her head like the leaves. All these people were an amazing sight to see.

"Hello, Ma," said Heart as she placed her basket of nuts down beside the woman. "This is the Rabbit-Man; we just met him outside. Sprout and I have made sure he isn't dangerous, and so we invited him to lunch with us. We thought you and Pa might like to meet him."

"That's very nice Heart," the woman said to her daughter before turning to the Rabbit-Man. "Welcome, Rabbit-Man. My name is Sweetberry, and we are glad you could join us for a meal. I notice your pack; are you travelling somewhere?"

"I am," he answered. "I am meeting someone at the Base Pad. I don't suppose you would know where that is, would you?"

"I don't, but perhaps my husband would know. He is aware of many places around here that we have never heard of. He will be here shortly. Until then, please take off your pack and make yourself comfortable. Lunch will be ready soon." The Rabbit-Man did as Sweetberry instructed. He offered to help the ladies with preparation, but they declined so he sat himself in a cozy corner of the room and watched the young children play. He was very surprised at how they all accepted his statement of bringing no trouble without question. He knew he did not have a threatening appearance or demeanor, but they did not know him, after all. The door to the inside of the tree opened and in stepped a little man with a green shirt, brown pants, and a wide cap on his head that looked like a mushroom top. He kissed Sweetberry and greeted the children and the young women after setting down a tiny briefcase as soon as he walked into the house. The Rabbit-Man noticed there was a large blackbird that came in behind him and fluttered up into a corner of the room when the man stepped inside. The bird seemed massive compared to the small, exotic little people. For a moment the Rabbit-Man was sure it was the same blackbird he saw after he fell out of the Garden; the one that saved him from Wolfsnare the Terrible. He did not have much time to think about it though, because in a moment he was being introduced to the newly arrived father of the household.

"Rabbit-Man, please meet my husband Dag," Sweetberry said. "The Rabbit-Man is travelling to meet somebody and will be our guest for lunch today."

"It's a pleasure to meet you, Rabbit-Man." Dag said in a cheerful voice as he shook the Rabbit-Man's hand. "We're happy to have you. I'm glad to see you're in fairly good condition; most people that make it to our little sanctuary are in bad shape sometimes because of the beasties outside. If they make it here at all, that is. But you're here now and that's great!"

Heart and Sprout then brought bowls of nut-filled yogurt and a hot loaf of bread to the table while the children ate porridge at a smaller table of their own. The food was delicious – the Rabbit-Man never remembered having better. The entire atmosphere was serene and pleasant, and the Rabbit-Man felt comfortable for the first time since his departure from the Garden. "How can this be?" he thought. "These small plant-people are living in happiness and comfort right in the middle of this dangerous and rundown world around them. They are aware of the dangers outside this place, but seem unaffected by it." The Rabbit-Man did not want to appear rude and overly inquisitive to his hospitable hosts, but in the end his curiosity got the better of him. He had to know how Sweetberry and Dag and their family remained safe. If there was some secret they knew, it could be very beneficial information for him to bring to Howler Highhorse when he reached the Base Pad.

"Dag, this is a very nice home you have," the Rabbit-Man said. "Your family is very kind and hospitable, and I appreciate the excellent meal you provided. I can't help but wonder, though, how you keep yourselves safe from the dangers outside. I only narrowly made it here in one piece today. How can you be so sure none of the predators outside will trouble you? I have encountered a Grandie, Wolfsnare the Terrible, who is very vicious."

"I understand what you are asking, Rabbit-Man," said Dag with a grin. "And indeed Wolfsnare is one of the foulest beasts roaming the lands. I have ways of keeping him and other creatures at bay, though. Let me show you." Dag stood up from his seat and walked toward the back of the room where a brown curtain was hanging. He pulled a key from his pocket, pushed the curtain aside, and opened a door behind it with the key. He then took a long, hard stick with a wooden handle and a pointer at the top from the door he just opened. "Here is one of my methods of guarding my place." he said as he held it up. The Rabbit-Man concluded this was a type of firearm different than the ones Mr. One was known to distribute. "This is my power wand. The Caretaking Body has outlawed all individuals from having them, but they have a hard enough time enforcing the edict in their precious Metroscapes. I have plenty of these in here that I will not hesitate to use if necessary. Luckily for me, most of the monsters around here know that I am not one to disturb. That wretched Wolfsnare and I have a mutual agreement. As much as I hate him, he has not breached it so neither will I. We have agreed that he will not enter my grove under any circumstances whatsoever, and likewise I shall not do any harm to him outside of my grove. I wish I could save more of his helpless victims, but unless they can make it into the grove they are beyond my aid. That is why I was so glad to see you enter my domain safely. I'm always happy when people make it here. I can protect them while they are in my grove. The Caretaking Body would destroy this place if they could, but we Bitties make it our life's work to avoid those fiends."

"Bitties!" the Rabbit-Man blurted out before he could stifle himself. He did not want to appear impolite, but he was overwhelmed by curiosity. He had never seen Bitties before.

"Yes, we are the Bitties," answered Dag. "I'm not surprised you never heard of us. We avoid the Metroscapes and most of the Bastions. Some of our kind live in Bastions, but unfortunately even many of them have become dangerous in recent times. So we stick to ourselves. My family and I are happy here. We live in peace away from any predators."

"But how could you be sure I wasn't an enemy?" the Rabbit-Man asked.

"You did not have that feel about you," Heart told him. "My family and I have become very good at recognizing the nature of others. Our initial instincts are rarely ever wrong."

"Thank you Heart," said the Rabbit-Man. "I do appreciate that. Dag, I also noticed a blackbird enter with you. It was either he or one like him that helped me escape my first encounter with that dreadful Wolfsnare. How can he do such things?" The Rabbit-Man looked at the corner the blackbird flew into, but it was now gone. In fact, it was nowhere to be seen in the room.

"Oh yes," said Dag with a laugh. "We call him Brayne. He always comes and goes as he pleases. A very special bird he is, as you have seen. I'm very glad I met him, because even though I cannot harm Wolfsnare outside my grove, as per our agreement, Brayne flies around and helps the luckless stragglers outside whenever he can. I don't know where he's gone off to now, but I'm glad to hear he helped you."

"Please tell me, Dag and Sweetberry, is there anything I can do to repay your kindness to me?" the Rabbit-Man asked. "And Brayne too, for that matter; he saved my life when I was in danger."

"That's a very kind offer, Rabbit-Man," said Dag as he put his power wand away and replaced the curtain before the door. He walked to the Rabbit-Man and placed a hand on his knee. "But there is nothing any of us need. We have it all here. You can stay with us for a while if you like before moving on. You are nice company."

"Thank you for that offer Dag, and again I appreciate it deeply. I really must be on my way though. I need to make it to the Base Pad as soon as I can, for I am needed there. It was good to meet you all, and thank you again."

"Are you sure?" asked Dag. "You have made it out of Main City, which I'm sure was not easy. You can remain here with us indefinitely if you like. I can use a human to assist in maintaining my grove, and I'm sure Heart and Sprout would appreciate your company. They are very lonely girls, you know, and kind young fellows such as yourself are difficult to come by these days." Heart and Sprout smiled, and for the first time since the Rabbit-Man heard of the Great White Calling he was tempted to abandon the cause and accept Dag's offer. He never would have believed he could feel a desire to do anything but pursue the Great White Calling. He longed to be with this warm and kind family, but his resolve won out in the end. As much as he liked Dag and his family, he knew Howler Highhorse desperately needed help. "The Homeplace will not establish itself," he thought. He was determined to help found the greatest Bastion at all costs. Thus, he sincerely thanked Dag but declined the offer.

"You are welcome here anytime, Rabbit-Man," Sweetberry told him. She gave him a hug, and then Heart and Sprout did the same. They gave him some food to carry along in his backpack before he left. He offered them some of the Cabbage he carried, but they simply laughed and told him they had no use for it. Dag warned him to be careful, and gave him a little power wand to bring with him for defense, as the rest of his trip would be dangerous. This defense weapon was a brown stick with a multi-pointed star at its tip. The Rabbit-Man was nervous about taking this, because he was never properly trained to use one. Dag gave him basic instructions of how the device worked. The user simply had to squeeze the handle and a shower of sparks emerged that would harm an opponent. If the user squeezed very hard, it could blast a small fireball from the tip. This was one of Dag's weaker weapons, but the Rabbit-Man greatly appreciated it. Dag also gave him directions to the Base Pad. The entire family wished him well before he left, and he was sorry to go. Despite his enthusiasm for the Great White Calling, his brief time in Dag and Sweetberry's home was refreshing and part of him truly longed to stay there. It was the best experience he had since falling from the Garden, and it felt very good to feel genuine warmth and goodwill.

He had only passing moments of this in Main City; most people there were hostile and unfriendly. As he walked off into the grey landscape, leaving the strange grove behind, he was overcome by a feeling of amazement. The entire grove seemed so out of place in this desolate and miserable land. Still, he was happy for Dag and Sweetberry and their family. "A home like theirs is what I'll be creating for countless others in the Homeplace," he thought as he walked along. "That is my destiny, and when that's done I will have achieved something I can be proud of." As he was thinking this, the blackbird Brayne flew down and landed on the ground before him, looking up at him with suspicious white eyes.

"Brayne, it's nice to see you!" the Rabbit-Man said to the bird. "Thank you for helping me against Wolfsnare that day. I sure hope I don't encounter him again. Is there anything I can do for you to thank you? I do have some Coveted Cabbage on me."

"Thank you Rabbit-Man, but there is nothing I need," said the bird. It still surprised the Rabbit-Man that he could talk; he seemed too regular to be a Morphie and far too small to be a Grandie, though he was larger than other blackbirds. "I will leave you with a bit of advice though. If you enter the Base Pad I cannot follow you there. You will be on your own. I know that Dag and Sweetberry did not ask you about it, but I know what you are going there for. It's a bad idea, Rabbit-Man. Turn back while you can. Dag can employ you until you find a better road into a Bastion. It would be wise to abandon this Great White Calling; nothing good can come from it."

"I appreciate your concern for my well-being, Brayne," the Rabbit-Man answered, "but I really must be moving along. I have a mission to accomplish, and I will not be content until I have done my duty. Thank you again for helping me, but my interest lies solely in the Calling."

"What a waste," said Brayne mournfully. "Well, if I cannot persuade you to turn back, I can at least make your trip there a safe one. Once you get to the Base Pad, however, I cannot be with you any longer." The blackbird then plucked a feather from one of his wings. "Here, take this. It will help you get to the Base Pad faster and unseen. Best of luck to you, Rabbit-Man."

"Thank you Brayne." the Rabbit-Man said, taking the feather. The blackbird then flew off. The feather then changed in the Rabbit-Man's hand. It grew much larger and swept itself under the Rabbit-Man. He fell inside the enlarged feather and it wrapped itself around him. He was somehow able to see through its black strands, as though it were transparent on his side. It then glided forward with the Rabbit-Man inside. As he travelled along, he used this time to read the remainder of the Calling books that he had not finished yet. He eventually helped himself to a dinner from the food Dag and Sweetberry gave him. As the sun set and night arrived, he grew tired and fell asleep. When he woke, the feather was gone and he was before the entrance to the Base Pad. He made it there at last.

Chapter Ten
The Movement That Never Was

The joy and determination that rushed through the Rabbit-Man was unlike any he ever felt before. The entrance to the Base Pad was rather nondescript, but he guessed that it would be like that. Despite trying to locate other A-list Companions, Howler Highhorse was careful to keep his plans and ideas limited to those who were willing to assist him. There were large double-doors surrounded by a silver-grey lining and a tall white barrier surrounding it. This was on the outskirts of another Metroscape the Rabbit-Man did not care to enter. He saw a button on the door and pushed it.

A buzz sounded, and then he heard the voice of Highhorse, very familiar to him from the programs he viewed on his T-Web station, ask: "Who is it? Are you interested in renting any books or vehicles?" The Rabbit-Man knew what this meant; the owl-man asked this to anyone who rang, because the Base Pad had a book and vehicle rental service as a cover-up for his Calling activities. This was addressed in the Calling books, and the Rabbit-Man knew the password he was expected to provide.

"I wish to advance to a higher place," the Rabbit-Man said. The doors opened and he stepped inside. There he was greeted by the fabled owl-man that he dreamed of meeting. He was of average height and only slightly taller than the Rabbit-Man. He wore a white suit with a brown cap and thick black-tinted glasses with dark red rims that curved at the corners, giving his face the look of a wise and mysterious owl.

"Hello, my fine Companion and welcome to the Base Pad," he said as he shook the Rabbit-Man's hand. "So you have come by yourself? I'm not surprised, there are too few – far too few – willing to do their duty and answer the Great White Calling. I am very pleased to see you made it here though. I hope there are many others that follow your fine example Mister –?"

"S.T. Ranger is my name. I'm the Rabbit-Man, and it's an honor and a pleasure to meet you, Mr. Highhorse. I've read your Calling books and have seen your program. I can't wait to begin working on creating the Homeplace. Please tell me; do I qualify as an A-list Companion? I know there must be others helping you. Where do I stand?"

"Indeed you are an A-list, Rabbit-Man," the Howler Highhorse answered. "Because you're the first to arrive here. Yes indeed, no one else has done what you have, and I truly hope that your example will be an inspiration to others out there." At this last statement the Rabbit-Man's heart sunk. He knew he would be one of the earlier arrivals because of the great owl-man's desperate tone on his programs, but he also thought surely at least *some* other people made the trip he did. Still, he was glad he made it and was still eager to assist in the plan. The owl-man wasted no time in getting down to business with his newly arrived Companion. He provided the Rabbit-Man a fine breakfast in his home and then led him through the Base Pad.

Howler Highhorse lived in a small hut with basic necessities and a TeleWeb screen, but not much else besides. After their breakfast he and the Rabbit-Man went down a dirt road flanked by some trees and shanty buildings. The Rabbit-Man was pleased to see there were trees in this area, which were noticeably absent in Main City. Howler pointed out a small blue building to the Rabbit-Man. "This is where I deliver my mail from. Anyone interested in the Calling may contact me through my private underground T-Web station. After I have done a background check on them, which I have the means to do, I send them an introductory letter. Once they have read that, if they are still interested, they may order the Calling books. I am careful who I send those to, but I am sure it is only a matter of time before the enemy finds them and reads them, if they haven't already done so."

"Aren't you afraid the Caretaking Body will come after you?" the Rabbit-Man asked. "I understand your agenda, and I know it is for the best, but they have Guard Dogs and other powerful beings under their command. They have destroyed many people for very small offenses, let alone direct opposition to their authority."

The Rabbit-Man

"Fear is for the weak and foolish," the owl-man replied. "I have never known it in all my days. Would you believe I have been in stark opposition to the Caretaking Body for almost fifty years? They have never found me, and I have never feared them. If a day comes when I am confronted with their Grandies and whatever other means of intimidation they use on the general population, I'll meet it with outright defiance. Only those who are truly courageous may answer the Calling, nothing less will do. We cannot have our Companions afraid of being harmed by the enemy. It is inevitable that some of us will be. My only hope is that if it happens to me, there will be others to pick up with the Calling where I left off. Besides, the Caretaking Body will have little chance of overcoming us if we gain the weapons we need, and I'll show you where those are to be found."

Howler then led the Rabbit-Man to the great boulder he wished to move in order to reveal the stairway to the Bastion and access the store of firearms beneath. It seemed more like a small mountain to the Rabbit-Man – though an oddly round-shaped mountain – and he wondered at how such a thing could ever be moved. Even a Grandie gorilla would have great difficulty getting the freakishly enormous rock to even budge.

"So this is it?" asked the Rabbit-Man, in a tone of enthusiasm that masked the inner doubt he was feeling. He consciously suppressed these feelings of unease, fearing they might be signs of weakness that the owl-man admonished. "It will be quite a task to get this moved. Are you sure it can really be done."

"It must be done!" Howler answered him. "It is the only way to provide hope for a better future for both ourselves and future generations of Companions. But before we can do anything like that, we must first recruit more like-minded persons to join us here at the Base Pad. That is what I will need you to start with, Rabbit-Man. Come back to my hut with me and I'll show you what you can do to fulfill the Great White Calling." They both returned to the hut of the owl-man, and he brought the Rabbit-Man before his screen. He used his controller to show the Rabbit-Man all the messages he received from other people living in Metroscapes, inquiring about the Calling and what they could do to assist.

"You will find that many people contact me saying they want to help our most sacred cause," Highhorse told the Rabbit-Man, "but they will make every excuse possible for not leaving wherever they are. I get this very often. What I need you to do is go through these messages and give a polite and tactful answer to these people. Give them encouragement where you think they might

117

need it. But be sure not to give away too much information. If folks want that, they will need to read the Calling books." The rest of the day continued with the Rabbit-Man learning the process of answering the inquiries the owl-man received. He provided the Rabbit-Man with a meal of spaghetti and meatballs at the end of the day, and then led his new Companion to a hut similar to his own. The Rabbit-Man had his own screen in this hut and could answer messages from there. Several months passed this way – the Rabbit-Man doing business on the T-Web and reporting back to Howler on a weekly basis; often he did this several times in a week. They did not receive any results for their efforts.

Occasionally that small seed of doubt that grew in the Rabbit-Man's mind on the first day he arrived at the Base Pad threatened to bud. In those moments the Rabbit-Man had to make a serious effort to reaffirm his commitment to the Great White Calling in his mind. He told himself all of the rhetorical marks he learned in the Calling books, and also recalled the anger and humiliation he felt while he worked in the Main City Mine – especially Archo's terrible insult and injury. Further, and worse yet, he always remembered the loss of his beloved home in the Garden and the days he spent there in happiness until it was destroyed. After pondering these things, he usually found the strength to continue with his work. Howler Highhorse was correct in stating that the correspondences did not seem to yield many results in the way of more Companions relocating to the Base Pad.

On one particular day – when the weather was foul and dreary, full of rain pouring from a hazy sky – the Rabbit-Man took a break from his work and took time to reflect. He thought back on the Garden and how much his life changed since he left there. He never thought he would be assisting someone such as the great owl-man. He lost track of how much time had passed since his terrible fall, but he knew it was a while. He remembered Lady Easter and how he spent time with her in those better days. Her attitude toward life was always positive, and her happiness was contagious. She dedicated herself to nurturing life in the Garden, and those who interacted with her were always inspired to do the same. The Rabbit-Man was no exception to this. As he reflected, he remembered the most valuable instruction Lady Easter had ever given him: "Be content in who you are and always strive to do well, Rabbit-Man." she told him once. "Help those who need it, and try to be as kind as you can in all situations. There is an unhappy world beyond our kind Garden, and there are many out there who are suffering. If trouble should ever overtake us, do not let it overcome you. Remember yourself and what you wish to do, pursue what is right and you will flourish always."

The memory of those words was very bittersweet for the Rabbit-Man when he remembered them. They made him feel good because he believed (or at least had convinced himself) that he was quite content in who he was, and that he was pursuing what was right. He had come to believe that the Great White Calling was the only truly righteous cause that remained in the dreadful world he was now immersed in. Although remembering Lady Easter's words was encouraging to him, it also reminded him of how much he missed her, and a burning sensation of longing welled up inside him that he could not suppress. He wept tears of anguish and discontent in the privacy of his hut at the Base Pad. He eventually went to bed and had an uneasy sleep that night. The following day, he would report to the Great White Owl-Man again and continue their usual business.

When the Rabbit-Man woke the next day he did not feel well. He did not remember his dreams, but suspected they may have been nightmares. The reality and direness of his situation always resonated most clearly with him in the moments before he fell asleep and immediately after he woke up in the morning. He was not sure which was worse – the nightmares or the feeling of weary discontent he felt in those brief moments. After he fully came to and got out of his small bed, the foul feeling passed and he continued his day normally. After fixing himself a quick breakfast he set out for Howler's hut, which was not far away. He was greeted by the mastermind behind the Calling and welcomed into the hut. He noticed something strange in the structure, but could not quite tell what it was. It almost seemed to the Rabbit-Man like a faint smoke permeated the entire place, but the owl-man seemed not to notice anything unusual. The Rabbit-Man figured it might just be his imagination and said nothing about this oddity he noticed.

"We have had some developments regarding movement of the boulder that I have not discovered before," Howler told him. "There are arcane machines that were once used for such things, but have been outlawed by the damn Caretaking Body long ago for 'safety concerns' as they put it. If we could find any of these in functional condition, however, it might make our task much easier. I've tried contacting some acquaintances of mine who may know of such things. These machines are very specific, and they require sophisticated…." the owl-man continued with his discussion of the machines, but as he talked the Rabbit-Man was distracted by the smoke getting thicker. Howler may have noticed his reaction, because he commented on it. "You don't look very good, Rabbit-Man. You should go outside and get some fresh air. It may help you clear your mind; you seem distracted."

"Have you ever encountered any demons, Howler?" the Rabbit-Man asked. Howler's face immediately grew dark and he gave the Rabbit-Man a scowl. "Many times, and I would rather not discuss it now. Suffice it to say there will be no demons in the Homeplace. Go and get a breather; it will do you good." As it turned out, some fresh air did do the Rabbit-Man some good. The weather had improved that day and the dreary, rainy weather had passed. It seemed like a fine day for a walk, and the Rabbit-Man decided he would take a stroll through the Base Pad and enjoy the newly arrived sunshine. He went back into Howler's hut and told him he would be walking about for a short while. The owl-man was before the screen in his hut and answered the Rabbit-Man in a dreamy voice. As he walked along, the Rabbit-Man made an effort to clear his mind. It did not work, because as he walked, he felt an urge to return to his hut and check his own T-Web station. After his walk he did this, and to his surprise there was a personal message on his screen from Mr. One. The Rabbit-Man wondered what may have happened to his old friend and was delighted to receive the message. It read:

Dear Rabbit-Man,

I hope this message finds you well. I had to make a hasty escape from Main City, but I am safe at the moment. I heard about Sig Calcium's theft of the Cabbage and was very surprised by it. I have never met him before, but I would be very glad to learn where he got such a fine bird suit from. I hope I can reconnect with you soon, but it would be very dangerous for me to return to Main City. I have learned more information I would like to share with you next time we meet. Until then, take care of yourself Rabbit-Man and stay true.

Your friend,
Mr. One

The Rabbit-Man sent a message back to Mr. One telling him of his own flight from Main City but avoided mentioning his current location at the Base Pad.

He did, however, suggest that Mr. One look into the Calling books. The screen allowed people to exchange messages that only the deliverers and receivers could view. There were ways the Caretaking Body and others could view classified and personal information on other peoples' stations, but their agents were usually too busy to discover everything that was done and said over the system. Every screen was connected to the TeleWeb, but the information contained therein was so vast not even the Caretaking Body could regulate it all. Thus, the Rabbit-Man knew there was a slight risk corresponding with Mr. One through the screen, but he had no other choice and knew it would most likely be safe.

After he sent his message to Mr. One the Rabbit-Man made his way back to Howler's hut, eager to tell him about the news of his friend. Mr. One would make a very valuable Companion if he learned of the Great White Calling, and the Rabbit-Man had every intention of suggesting his longtime friend to the owl-man. When he knocked on the door of the hut there was no answer, so he went inside. It was there he saw Howler slumped over onto his desk before the screen. He was sleeping, but the aggravated expression on his face gave the impression he was having very bad dreams. He was mumbling words the Rabbit-Man could not make out, and upon looking closer the Rabbit-Man noticed strands of stringy grey hair floating up from an unseen head behind Howler's slumped body. The head then rose up and revealed two glowing yellow eyes the Rabbit-Man knew all too well. The Blue Demon's dreadful face emerged from behind the Rabbit-Man's Companion and leered at him. A long dark tongue extended from the mouth and went into the owl-man's right ear. The blue aura pervaded the hut, and the Rabbit-Man now understood that the Blue Demon was most likely the cause of the smoke he noticed earlier. The Blue Demon grinned hideously at the Rabbit-Man through his skeletal face as he rose higher; his freakishly long tongue remained in the owl-man's head. Again he wore the misty grey cloak around his body, and from the back of it the two great wings began to spread. While the demon levitated into the air he appeared larger and more ominous than ever before.

"No, it can't be!" the Rabbit-Man cried. "How did *you* get through the entrance? Nobody can get into the Base Pad without being let in by the great owl-man. How did you get in here?" The demon laughed in his dreadful manner when he heard this.

"You foolish little bunny," the demon said, able to talk despite his extended tongue. "A simple locked gate cannot keep me away. I told you I wanted to help you, and so I do. I can go anywhere I please, and appear to anyone I please. Your friend here is powerless to stop me, as are you Rabbit-Man. I know you think you were very clever in how you disposed of my steed, which I kindly lent to you, but you will not keep me away. I am here now, and I will offer you my aid once more. If you refuse this time, Rabbit-Man, I am afraid I will have to resort to more extreme measures to persuade you."

"You should know I don't want anything to do with you!" the Rabbit-Man shouted. "Howler, wake up! Get that demon's tongue out of your ear!" the Rabbit-Man ran over and shook his Companion, but it was no use. The Blue Demon's tongue remained where it was, and this seemed to have no affect on the monster's ability to speak. Try as he did, the Rabbit-Man was unable to wake Howler, and so he ran out of the hut as quickly as he could. He intended to go back to his own hut and retrieve the small power wand he received from Dag. Once he got there, he heard the demon's laughter outside. It seemed like it sounded throughout the entire Base Pad. The Rabbit-Man had retrieved his power wand and ran back outside with it ready for action. He could not see the demon anywhere, though he still heard the laughter. He went back to the owl-man's hut and barged in. This time Howler was awake and there was no sign of the demon.

"Quick, get your firearm!" The Rabbit-Man said to the confused-looking owl-man. "A demon has made its way inside the Base Pad; we have to destroy him or he'll ruin everything. For the sake of the Calling, Howler, hurry!" The owl-man retrieved his firearm and together he and the Rabbit-Man made their way out of the hut and into the streets of the Base Pad. "We need to check the gate and see how he got in." Howler said. "If our gate is breached then we may be in trouble." They headed to the gate and found that it was wide open, as if it had been smashed open with a large battering ram. There was no sign of any explosives used. Even worse for them, as the demon's laughter sounded around them (though Howler seemed not to notice it), into the entryway of the gate stepped Wolfsnare the Terrible. He looked ghastly, and much more horrific than before. The Rabbit-Man guessed it was his struggle with the ghostly horse that did this to him. The Grandie's eyes were wide and bulging, his fur was even more disheveled than before, and long strands of misty grey matter hung about his body – which the Rabbit-Man recognized as the remains of the strange horse that morphed itself and engulfed the giant wolf. The Grandie leered at the Rabbit-Man and Howler with his murderous eyes, and they both opened fire on the massive beast with their weapons. Howler fired missiles from his firearm as the Rabbit-Man blasted small fireballs from his power wand. Wolfsnare snarled and shrieked, but the shots only seemed to make him angrier. Neither of the Companions caused any serious harm to the Grandie wolf.

"It's now or never, Rabbit-Man!" said Howler. "We must move the boulder now. Let's go!" They ran away from Wolfsnare back into the Base Pad toward the great boulder. Once they were there, the owl-man produced a wooden branch. "This is all we have so far. We have to try to pry the boulder out with this." The Rabbit-Man thought this a completely absurd idea, as he knew the branch would never move the boulder. Still, he helped Howler try to pry the boulder with it, and the great rock did not budge the slightest bit. Blue flames formed behind them and the boulder; from among these rose the Blue Demon. This time Howler saw the demon, and he and the Rabbit-Man both shot at him with their weapons. The sparks and missiles passed through the demon and he laughed at them.

"Last chance!" he screamed at the Rabbit-Man. "Join me or forever regret it!"

"Never!" the Rabbit-Man shouted back. Then the flames parted down the center and the demon floated into the air. Wolfsnare, bloody and angry, stepped into the clearing among the flames. He was shaking with rage and hatred for the two small men that pierced his body with fire and missiles, although none of his injuries were fatal. In a fleeting instant, the Grandie wolf's long purple tongue shot from its mouth and wrapped around the torso of Howler, pulling him into the wolf's jaws quickly. The wolf's chomping and the Blue Demon's laughter drowned the screams of the owl-man out as the hideous fiend swiftly devoured him. The Rabbit-Man fired sparks repeatedly at the wolf, but with no effect this time. The Blue Demon had cast a spell of protection on the Grandie. In a flash of realization more sudden than Wolfsnare's tongue, the Rabbit-Man understood all at once how futile the idea of moving the boulder and forming the greatest of all Bastions really was. No such thing could ever possibly happen in a world such as this – and now it seemed as obvious to him as raindrops falling from clouds during a storm.

After Wolfsnare swallowed the last remains of his victim, the Rabbit-Man stood in a state of numbed agony and disbelief. It was then that the Blue Demon held out his hand, and five streams of dark black matter emanated from his fingers. These then engulfed Wolfsnare and submerged the Grandie in blackness for a moment until the black substance was absorbed into the wolf's body. After this occurred Wolfsnare began to change, and he became even more hideous to look at. His fur stood out on end and his color became pitch black. His eyes were the same glowing yellow as those of the Blue Demon, and his already gruesome teeth became even more long, sharp, and deadly. This fearsome Grandie was now under the influence of the Blue Demon, but the Rabbit-Man's chief tormentor did not stop there.

"This is a new nemesis for you, Rabbit-Man," the Blue demon said. "Because you will not accept my aid, I have crafted this Grandie into a tool of coercion. He is no longer Wolfsnare the Terrible – now he is Hungry Hayt, a bloodthirsty demon controlled by me. He will feed off of the negative emotions of others – for it was his consumption of that foolish owl-man, eating him and absorbing all the bitterness that festered in his pathetic person, that allowed me to transform this wolf so. I suspect you will have a great deal more negative feelings as time goes by, Rabbit-Man, and after that you will make a fine meal for Hayt the Hungry. I changed my mind about you, Rabbit-Man. I thought I could use you in my plans, but since you refused, this demon-wolf will serve my purposes instead. But that is not all Rabbit-Man. No indeed; you see, Hayt will devour your carcass after your soul has been corrupted and twisted to resemble my own, but until that happens you will have yet another foe to contend with."

The Blue Demon raised his hand again and produced the foul black substance once more. This time it changed into a deep dark bluish-black and formed into a robe floating in the air beside the Blue Demon. The hood of the robe fell back and revealed a dreadful grey skull with two red orbs as eyes. Strands of yellow hair grew from the sides of the skull and curved upward like horns. Two sickly purple hands with long nails emerged from the sleeves. "This is a very old friend of mine." said the demon. "He is an ancient ghost that has allowed me to capture the minds of numerous people beyond counting. He is known by very many names, but for you Rabbit-Man, I think he will be best known as Despair. He and I have overcome countless individuals together, and you shall soon be among them. It is now your inescapable fate"

"Get away from my friend, you hellish fiends!" called a voice from behind Hayt the Hungry, the demon, and the ghost. Suddenly there came a loud bang and a flash of bright yellow light. Hayt yelped in pain and ran off. The Blue Demon called after him but it was too late; the mutated wolf Grandie had run away. This revealed another individual standing in the clearing of the black flames; it was the person that called out to the demon. The Rabbit-Man recognized him, and was incredibly happy to see Mr. One holding a massive firearm aimed at the Blue Demon and the Ghost of Despair. The Rabbit-Man's longtime friend set out to meet him after he received the Rabbit-Man's reply message on the T-Web. For the first time ever, the Rabbit-Man was not alone when confronting the Blue Demon.

Chapter Eleven
The Old Wicked Ghost

As the Rabbit-Man and Mr. One were left to confront the Blue Demon and the horrific Ghost of Despair he summoned, Main City was in more turmoil than when the Rabbit-Man had left. On the day he disturbed the inquisition of Sally Wonder and escaped the Guard Dogs, there was a message sent throughout the T-Web stations that he was wanted. The importance of this news was quickly diminished, however, as even more pressing concerns flooded the stations of the T-Web. Even Sig Calcium started to become an afterthought in the mainstream media of Main City. The reason for this was the increased activity and notoriety of the Mad Dog Tribe. After Sig Calcium's theft of the Coveted Cabbage, many more rebellious individuals became more open in their defiance of the Caretaking Body, and within a matter of weeks there were too many offenders of the CTB's law for the Main Patrol and the Guard Dogs to keep track of. Most of the infractions were minor, such as people speaking out against the CTB or openly mentioning ideas that were part of the Old Focus. The Mad Dogs, however, were not to be taken lightly – and both the agents of the CTB and the populace of Main City knew it. The notorious group became more active than ever before.

When Sally Wonder's questioning was through after being disrupted by the Rabbit-Man, she and her son Twig were led away by a Patrolman and directed to go back home. For several weeks after that she had only heard from the authorities once, but the news they delivered was very grim. Her son, Try

Wonder, had been found guilty of subversive activity. This was all that the Patrolman delivering the message told Mrs. Wonder, but it was also all she needed to hear. She knew her son would be dead soon. Anyone accused of subversion was put to death by the Guard Dogs. Sometimes on occasion, a person would be given the chance to compete for their life in the Grand Coliseum owned by Mr. Spiderhat, and these were always popular spectacles. This was all just a show, however, because the convicted subversives would inevitably be placed in a match against a foe they could never hope to defeat. It was very rare when one such accused person would find a way to win their competition and thus go free, winning a small degree of fame in the process. Even still, Sally Wonder knew that no such chance would be given to her condemned son because of the recent activity in the Grand Coliseum. In the past week, the Mad Dogs hijacked some of the spectacles in the Grand Coliseum and threatened Mr. Spiderhat, telling him they planned to invade the Coliseum and run it themselves. At first the Caretaking Body intended to swarm the Coliseum with their Patrolmen and Grandies, but Mr. Spiderhat persuaded them not to. He always had a special rapport with the Caretaking Body, and they surprisingly agreed to the Grandie spider's request. Instead, Mr. Spiderhat capitalized on this scenario and offered the Mad Dogs a chance to compete in the Grand Coliseum to win what they wanted. The already high popularity of Mr. Spiderhat's show increased drastically after this. Mr. Spiderhat made a deal that if any member of the Mad Dogs could win the Grand Coliseum Championship from Eagle Top in a one-on-one competition, he would relinquish control of the Coliseum to them. The Mad Dogs eagerly agreed to this, but their members had to earn this chance by winning in various contests before they could challenge the champion Eagle Top. A majority of the viewers of the Grand Coliseum were firmly behind Eagle Top as their favorite, and Mr. Spiderhat supported his champion as well – or at least so it seemed.

Entirely unknown to the public was an agreement made between The Caretaking Body, Mr. Spiderhat, and the Mad Dogs' leader Rip A. Sunder. The entire scenario of the alleged invasion of the Mad Dogs was just a show orchestrated by the three parties. The Mad Dogs were a subversive group at first, but they were so effective that the Caretaking Body eventually brought them into their employ. Mr. Spiderhat was secretly planning to betray his champion Eagle Top and allow the Mad Dogs to "win" the Coliseum as he went into a comfortable retirement. Eagle Top was oblivious to the treachery of his employer Mr. Spiderhat, and even most of the Mad Dogs were unaware of the deal their leader made behind their backs. Nobody in Main City knew of the deal, but watched the Grand Coliseum show on their screens with eager anticipation of what would occur next.

Young Twig Duckly also watched these developments in awe. In his young mind, however, he did not favor the Mad Dogs or Eagle Top, as he greatly disliked them both. When he was not watching the competitions on the screen the little duckling-boy's time was spent with his grief-stricken mother. Caring for Twig was the last thing Sally Wonder had to keep herself motivated, and often the boy spoke to her about his new hero – the Rabbit-Man that saved him on two separate occasions. Although the Rabbit-Man did not have much chance to interact directly with Sally or Twig when he disturbed their questioning, he hoped his actions aided the little duckling he recognized from his home and the kind woman who took him in. Twig also remembered the Rabbit-Man and recognized him. He hoped the Rabbit-Man was still out there, and that he could possibly see him again sometime soon.

Young Twig's hope of the Rabbit-Man still being abroad was true, though he was in a difficult situation when he and Mr. One stood in opposition to the Blue Demon and the Ghost of Despair that he summoned. Although the Rabbit-Man's small power wand had no effect on the Blue Demon, Mr. One possessed much more advanced weaponry. It could not destroy the demon or the ghost, but it could at least hinder them enough to give the two friends a chance to escape. "Stand back, Rabbit-Man!" Mr. One called to his friend, lifting his huge firearm that had a large metal barrel at the end. The Rabbit-Man did so, and Mr. One aimed the barrel at the demon and the ghost and blasted them both with fierce blazing fireballs that shot out of it. The ghost shrieked and was knocked far backward and the demon fell to the ground temporarily stunned. This was their chance to escape.

"Follow me, Rabbit-Man!" Mr. One called and they both set off away from the boulder. The blue flames produced by the demon vanished when he was hit, and so the two ran off and came to the vehicle Mr. One arrived at the Base Pad with. Mr. One pulled a remote controller from one of his pockets and the doors of the vehicle opened on both sides. He leaped in the driver's seat and put the large firearm behind it. The Rabbit-Man hopped into the other side and both doors closed. Mr. One then drove the vehicle away, leaving the demon and ghost behind.

"Thank you Mr. One!" the Rabbit-Man said. "If you hadn't arrived I would be a goner. What was that firearm you used against them? I never saw anything like that before."

"I just built it recently." Mr. One replied as they drove through the gate of the Base Pad, forever leaving it behind. "I wanted to get here as soon as I got your message. I found out more about the Blue Demon. I still don't know where he comes from, but I know what he's trying to do. You're his next target. He finds people that he thinks he can feed off of and follows them until he destroys them. Doing this makes him stronger, but he's growing weak now. He needs to eat you or something like that, and then he'll gain more power until he finds his next victim. When I heard you were working with Howler Highhorse, I figured you were at his Base Pad. I knew I had to get there, knowing the demon would probably not leave you alone. Luckily I knew where the Base Pad was, though I bet Highhorse didn't know it."

"I'm very glad you got there when you did," the Rabbit-Man answered. "I'm glad to see you're alright. That demon destroyed the owl-man. I don't know if you're familiar with his plan, but he wanted to create a better life for people. At least that's what he claimed. Thinking back on it, I don't even see how that could have possibly worked, but I was desperate to try something. I feel like a fool now."

"Don't let it trouble you," said Mr. One as they drove through the grey landscape. "You meant well in trying that. I heard of Howler Highhorse and his Great White Calling before, but I agree with you. I don't think there was ever any real chance of success. Someone like him is so immersed in his delusional ideas he cannot think of anything else, and it didn't get him very far. That beast that devoured him was hideous. We really need to avoid it if possible."

"You're right. After it ate Howler The Blue Demon changed it into something even more awful. The demon called it Hayt the Hungry. It seemed like the Blue Demon can control the monster after placing a spell on it, as if Wolfsnare wasn't bad enough as he was. It would definitely be best to avoid all of these enemies. Unfortunately, I don't see how that will be possible."

"Why do you say that?" Mr. One asked.

"Because I need to return to Main City. I don't really want to, but I have to."

"Are you crazy? Why would you want to do that? You came to the Base Pad and pursued this Calling idea to get away from all the misery that exists there; what in the world would make you want to go back there now?"

"I found one of the duckling-boys there – one of those in Madame Duckly's care. I'm sure you remember; I sent them along with you before I fell from the Garden."

"Yes I remember. That's interesting. I wondered what happened to them after I got caught up in the trouble there as well. Was there only one, or were some of the others with him?"

"I think it was only one," the Rabbit-Man said. "A woman from Main City must have adopted him. They were being questioned by a committee I ended up being part of. I took a stand in their defense and that's what set the Guard Dogs after me before I fled. I know it's dangerous and probably close to suicidal, but I need to return to Main City and make sure they're alright. I'll never be able to live with myself if I didn't at least try. I felt awful leaving them behind the first time. I have to go back and set it right if I can. If you don't want to come along I can understand and I surely won't hold it against you. But if you could please leave me at the entrance to Main City I would appreciate it."

"Well, if you intend to go back there I'll go back with you. Besides, I've been keeping up with the news in Main City and we might be safer there now than we were before. With all the trouble and havoc the Mad Dogs have been causing there, we're probably much farther down on the CTB's wanted list. If we make an effort to be as discreet as we possibly can, we might get through this unharmed. If we could get the duckling-child and the woman looking after him out of Main City and to a Bastion somewhere, that would be the best thing we can do."

"It would, and after the failure I just encountered at the Base Pad I would feel much better if we did. I still can't believe I fell for that!"

"That's it then, our next stop is Main city – come whatever may." Mr. One then drove his vehicle along the dusty grey land until Main City with all its tall nondescript buildings was in sight. On the way there, the two friends saw in the distance two of the demon-headed vehicles the Mad Dogs rode passing by. "I imagine they're up to no good." Mr. One said casually as the vehicles sped on by with their riders. The Rabbit-Man was surprised to see anyone, even the Mad Dog Tribe, coming and going from Main City so freely. He instantly recognized their attire. The Mad Dogs dressed with spiked caps and wore a dog's snout strapped to their faces. Their clothes were often cut leather, and they wore gloves with claws on their hands and large black boots. They were the most fearsome-looking of all animal-suited people. When the Rabbit-Man and Mr. One came to the entrance of Main City they discovered why the Mad Dogs they saw were able to exit the City so easily – the Main Gate was busted open. It appeared that explosives were used for this, and they both correctly guessed it was the Mad Dogs that caused this. The Rabbit-Man was surprised at how quickly the CTB seemed to be losing its monopoly of control on Main City, but then he also wondered if this was permanent, or if it was only a matter of time until the CTB reorganized its forces, suppressed the Mad Dog Tribe, and regained control of their Metroscape once more. Either way he did not believe it would end well for Main City's common populace.

Mr. One rode the vehicle through the busted gates and into the streets of the city. It looked even more hostile to the Rabbit-Man now than when he first arrived. As they rode along, the Rabbit-Man saw something that made him call out for Mr. One to stop the vehicle. It was a young man hanging from two parallel posts jutting up from the ground. They both stepped outside the vehicle to examine this further. To their surprise and disgust, they noticed the victim was still a boy, though approaching adulthood. He was impaled upon the two poles through his armpits and left to hang there as a grim message to all present in the Metroscape. The Rabbit-Man read a sign beneath the boy's dangling feet. It read: "Beware those who wish to upset the peace in Main City. The Caretaking Body will remove all such problems." Then on a smaller sign beneath this was a label which read: "Try Wonder." The Rabbit-Man remembered where he heard the name and his heart sank. This was the last name of Sally Wonder, the duckling-boy's adopted mother. The Rabbit-Man desperately hoped that Try's mother and adopted brother did not suffer a similar fate to his.

"This is how the Caretaking Body promotes peace," Mr. One said with disgust. The Rabbit-Man explained the relationship of the victim to the boy they were there to help. "Well, this doesn't necessarily mean they have been harmed." he told the Rabbit-Man. "From what I understand, the CTB is very hesitant to do this to just anybody like they used to. Now they focus more on people who committed actual crimes. Their hold is slipping, and though it's still strong, I doubt they would torment a mother and her child – well, besides the mental torment of doing this to a loved one. Do you think this boy did something serious? If so, that may explain it."

"I'm sure he did nothing to deserve this treatment," the Rabbit-Man answered. "Maybe he had an affiliation with the Mad Dogs. Before I left, I know there were many young people getting involved with them because of their understandable resentment of the CTB. I don't know if this guy did that or not, but I just hope the rest of his family is okay."

"I know the Mad Dogs offer similar treatment, or worse, to their enemies too," said Mr. One. "The poor citizens of this wretched city are now being terrorized by two foes. They must be scared out of their wits."

"I think we should move along," the Rabbit-Man suggested. So they did, and cruised slowly through the streets of Main City in their vehicle. The Rabbit-Man remembered Main City as a dismal and unpleasant place, but in the weeks he was away from it the city's condition worsened. Between the agents of the Caretaking Body and the vagabonds associated with the Mad Dog Tribe, Main City now had a completely hostile appearance. Before, dismal though it was, its hostility was still slightly masked in its outward appearance and had only shown through during interaction with its citizens and institutions. Now, however, the grey buildings were riddled with black scorches – the aftereffect of explosives used during the outbursts of violence that occurred between the CTB's forces and the Mad Dogs and their affiliates. The streets, never in pristine condition to begin with, were now busted up and had many cracks and holes making them difficult to travel in. Mr. One was driving his vehicle slowly through the roads, and the ride was still rough. They passed the building where the container that was the Rabbit-Man's former home was located. Eventually the road became so rough and severely damaged that Mr. One's vehicle could no longer safely travel over it. He pulled it aside, removed the key, and locked the doors.

"We'll have to walk from here," he told the Rabbit-Man after locking the vehicle. "It may be safer that way. We didn't see many other vehicles coming in, so they are much sparser. Driving in this one might only bring more attention onto us." The Rabbit-Man agreed with this, and so they continued along with caution. Mr. One did not like the idea of leaving his large firearm behind in the vehicle even though it was locked. He and the Rabbit-Man both had small weapons concealed on them, which was better than nothing, but Mr. One knew carrying such a large firearm would bring immediate suspicion and may ruin their plans. He wanted to help the duckling-boy the Rabbit-Man was after and move on from Main City as soon as possible. It would have interested both of them to know that the thing which brought an end to the violence in the streets was Mr. Spiderhat's agreement to let the Mad Dogs compete in the Grand Coliseum. Now most of the violence was restricted to his great arena. However, it still flared up in Main City occasionally.

The Rabbit-Man did not know it when they entered the Metroscape, but Sally Wonder's container was in a building not far from the one he previously lived in. He and Mr. One were close to it, but neither of them was aware of it. The Rabbit-Man hoped he might find Peace Shadow or another acquaintance of his that he was on friendly terms with, but he knew he could not rely on such a lucky chance meeting. At last his only idea was to try and find Sally Wonder's address by looking at a T-Web screen. The only one he could think of to view was in the underground sewer tunnels, where he first discovered Howler Highhorse's *Freedom for the Homeplace* program. He and Mr. One located a manhole cover, and they were very lucky to find it considering the poor condition of the roads. They lifted it, found the ladder, and down they climbed. To the Rabbit-Man's disappointment, the first screen they came upon was heavily cracked and beyond any hope of working. "Damn this rotten luck!" said the Rabbit-Man. "How will we ever find them?"

Before Mr. One could offer any kind of response, they heard footsteps coming toward them. Both were quickly on their guard, and on either side of them they saw people coming toward them in the dark sewer. The first person the Rabbit-Man spotted was a man in a crocodile suit followed by two other men, one in a skunk suit and the other in a dog suit, but not like the ones the Mad Dogs wore. On the other side came two women not dressed in animal suits but with patched and frayed clothes and leather jackets. They had poorly applied make-up smeared over their faces, giving them a spooky look. With them was a short man in a strange red and dark purple suit and a helmet on his head with a long spike at the top.

"Who could you fellows be looking for down here?" the short man asked. "Most folks know not to come down here." He grinned at the two friends, neither of whom liked the look of the newcomers nor trusted them. The skunk-man who came alongside the crocodile-man sniffed at the Rabbit-Man's suit.

"We don't want any trouble," said Mr. One. "We were simply looking for a screen to use. If you know where one is we will be glad to hear it. Otherwise we'll be on our way."

"These guys must be new!" said one of the women with the short man as she giggled at them. "They don't seem to know much."

"Sorry pal, but the CTB's goons destroyed every single screen that existed down here," the short man said. "We eventually drove them out with the help of the Mad Dogs, but it wasn't easy." The man's grin widened. "But we don't let folks come down here without paying a toll. What have you got on you? Give it to us and we'll consider letting you go." Mr. One produced his small firearm and the entire group took a step back. It seemed evident none of them expected the newcomers to be armed. "Leave us alone, and I'll consider letting you live." he told the short man.

"You messed with the wrong gang down here, pal," said the crocodile-man as he went to produce something – probably a weapon – from a pocket in his suit. Mr. One was too quick for him and in an instant he blasted a fireball the crocodile-man. The reptilian man flew backwards and into the sewer water. "Get away from us, or you'll all be goners."

The rest of the sewer gang got the message and backed away. "Let's get out of here," Mr. One said to the Rabbit-Man, who went back to the ladder and climbed out of the sewer. Mr. One followed cautiously, keeping his firearm drawn until he exited the sewer and covered the manhole again. They returned to their vehicle and Mr. One decided he would carry his large firearm regardless of the risk it might cause. They walked further down the streets, and the Rabbit-Man had an idea. He told Mr. One to follow him but stay behind and keep a lookout. He decided to return to Snoop's eatery he visited occasionally when he was working in the mine and try to get more information there. To his surprise, Snoop was still in the building and his business seemed unaffected by the carnage that plagued Main City recently. Snoop greeted him kindly and allowed him to use the T-Web screen that was located in the eatery. The owner of the eatery ignored the wanted status of both the Rabbit-Man and Mr. One. It was here the Rabbit-Man discovered Sally Wonder's address. He and Mr. One then set out on foot to find the building where she lived. The Rabbit-Man no longer had his old registration card from Main City, and to his surprise they didn't need it to access the building. They went to the container of Sally and knocked on the door. When she opened it, she looked surprised and relieved to see the Rabbit-Man.

"Hello, Mrs. Wonder," said the Rabbit-Man. "I hope you do not mind that I looked up your address on the T-Web screen. I was away from Main City for a while, but I wanted to make sure you and the young boy who was with you during your questioning are alright."

"Oh, yes, that's very kind of you." Sally replied. "We are just fine. I'm sure Twig would like to see you again. Please come in." The Rabbit-Man introduced himself and Mr. One to Sally and as they entered her home young Twig Duckly greeted the Rabbit-Man very enthusiastically. He embraced the duckling-boy when he saw him, and it was a very cheerful meeting that uplifted the morale of all present. Sally brought drinks for the guests and they sat in the main room of her small container. Here they discussed the occurrences in Main City. Sally told them of how the rioting subsided after the Mad Dogs got their chance to compete in the Grand Coliseum. She said that many individuals could prospect for them and earn entry into the gang by winning a match on their behalf in the arena. She also described how the spectacle became much more violent in recent weeks as a result.

"I was afraid my son Try would end up in there," she told them, "but his own fate turned out much worse." The Rabbit-Man and Mr. One offered sincere condolences to Sally for her loss. She would never be able to get over it, but she was comforted by these two strangers arriving to check on her well-being and that of little Twig. She offered the Rabbit-Man and Mr. One her container to sleep in for the evening, which they gratefully accepted. Twig then entertained the guests as he brought out his toys made in the likeness of the Grand Coliseum competitors. He had a miniature model to play with them in, and between his enthusiasm at having guests and his active mind, he amused the three adults who watched him go. It was the first time Sally Wonder genuinely laughed since her son's demise, and it was a much-needed lighthearted activity for the Rabbit-Man and Mr. One, who narrowly escaped a conflict with a demon, a wraith, and a possessed Grandie wolf. As the three adults laughed and watched little Twig Duckly playing, the Rabbit-Man noticed a familiar comforting glow emanate from everyone in the room. He immediately recalled how this sensation came to him just after his fall and protected him from the Blue Demon. It was beautiful, the greatest sensation he ever felt, and the Rabbit-Man was overwhelmed by warm feelings, among them being gratitude for the reappearance of the glow. Before he could think of it much, the glowing light was gone but its effects remained. The Rabbit-Man did not know if any of the others saw this the way he did, but it strengthened his resolve and increased his morale. He would need this spiritual boost he received for the coming trials that lay ahead of him, and especially after his failure at the Base Pad. But for that moment, he simply enjoyed good time with his friends as the recollection of the soothing glow receded once more into his mind, but remained in his heart.

As the day grew later, Mr. One thought it best to retrieve his vehicle and park it behind the building where Sally lived. The Rabbit-Man followed him outside to the location. They got inside and as Mr. One turned the vehicle around they were immediately stopped by someone standing before them in the road. The person was very tall and wore a dark purple cloak with a hood. The Rabbit-Man saw the face in the hood and recognized it – it was the Ghost of Despair who the Blue Demon had conjured to follow them when they left the Base Pad. Mr. One grabbed his large firearm and leaped out of the vehicle.

The Rabbit-Man readied his power wand and did the same. The wraith pulled back its hood and revealed its terrible skull-head. Then it spread out its arms and floated high into the air. Mr. One fired at the creature, but it dodged the large bright missiles produced from the barrel. The ghost then spit a strange purple fireball at Mr. One's vehicle and caused it to explode. The wraith cackled at the two friends and then said in a screeching voice that sounded like grinding metal. "You two will not get what you want! I will make sure you achieve nothing you set out to do. The woman and the boy you wish to save shall be mine to devour, and you will do nothing to stop me. Turn yourselves over to the Blue Demon now or your friends are doomed!" The ghost then turned around and flew toward Sally's building. The Rabbit-Man and Mr. One ran after him as quickly as they could. By the time they reached the building, the Ghost of Despair had Sally and Twig laid out on the ground before him unconscious. He floated overtop them and the Rabbit-Man ran at the ghost, knowing that the missiles from his wand would do little good against the fiend. Mr. One thought differently, and tried to call a warning out to his friend, "Rabbit-Man, wait! Don't do that!" But it was too late, and as the Rabbit-Man approached the ghost it spread out its arms and its purple cloak opened. The Rabbit-Man ran straight into the cloak, and was engulfed inside it in an instant. Mr. One could not believe what he saw; the Rabbit-Man seemed to be absorbed into the wraith's flowing robe. It then descended upon Sally and Twig and then they too were sucked into the folds of the cloak just like the Rabbit-Man was. Mr. One would have fired at the ghost with his weapon, but now he was afraid he would destroy his friends. Before he could act, he heard a voice call behind him.

"Halt! Stop right there and lower your weapon!" He turned and saw a two Patrolmen running toward him. As they did, the ghost cackled and glided up into the air. It then flew off and Mr. One could not see it anymore. One of the Patrolmen seized him and the other grabbed the large firearm from his hands. They beat him with their clubs and placed cuffs on his wrists behind his back. One of the Patrolmen lifted him and carried him off. Mr. One knew he was in dire trouble now, but he feared for the Rabbit-Man, Sally, and Twig. What had that ghost done to them, and where were they, he wondered. He could not think of it for long, though, because as he was led away by the Patrolmen he knew he would have plenty of troubles of his own. He was arrested by agents of the CTB, but the Rabbit-Man was gone. He was unsure if it was he or his longtime friend that had the worst of it. Because of the direness of both situations it didn't matter which was worse – both were very bad.

Chapter Twelve
The Nightmare Country

The fate of Mr. One was far from pleasant, but at least he soon discovered what it would be. When the Patrolmen lifted him to his feet they jabbed him in the back with their clubs and marched him forward. They recognized who he was, and both men were elated when they discovered they captured the much-wanted Mr. One. They led him onward as other Patrolmen joined them. Soon residents of Main City filtered into the streets from the building as the pair of Patrolmen moved onward. They wished to walk him through the city rather than force him into a vehicle to display their success. The tiny little image-recording worms that floated through the air caught many images of Mr. One to supply to the T-Web stations. The two Patrolmen that made the catch exchanged comments with their peers such as "This catch will certainly earn us a promotion!" and "Who would have thought we could find the dreaded Mr. One right here in the middle of the street!"

These comments were met by ones such as, "You will be notorious by the day's end," and "Excellent job! It's about time the Main Patrol can save face!" All the while Mr. One walked along as a captive of the Patrolmen, he said nothing and paid little attention to their comments. He was too busy wondering what had happened to the Rabbit-Man, Sally Wonder, and Twig Duckly in the robes of the terrible ghost that came upon them. His attention was directed elsewhere soon, because he recognized the massive structure the Patrolmen were leading him toward. A command must have come down to the Patrolmen

139

from the Caretaking Body amid the commotion after he was captured. They led Mr. One to the Grand Coliseum. He knew why they were doing this: it was the recent trend in Main City to place all captured individuals that were wanted into the Coliseum and have them compete for their lives in a competition.

Mr. One was very familiar with this process, and he did not fear it. He did, however, wonder if they would allow him to use any of his weapons. He knew they most likely would not, and in such a case his chances of survival were very small. Still, he marched on resolutely, not at all happy with his situation but taking care not to show it. He accepted that the CTB may get hold of him sooner or later, and would not show how much it upset him. If only these sleazy Patrolmen did not take him by surprise he could easily have defeated them both with his massive firearm. It was in their possession now, and he was left with nothing except a small knife he kept strapped to his lower calf under his pants. Maybe that would do him good in the Grand Coliseum. They led him through the large gates of the structure – there was sure to be a popular spectacle on Mr. Spiderhat's show tonight with Mr. One featured in a competition. The Patrolmen led him onward before the Grandie spider, the spectators in the Coliseum, and before the viewers that would be watching on their screens.

As Mr. One was brought into the Grand Coliseum the Rabbit-Man was in an altogether different situation. After running into the cloak of the Ghost of Despair, everything went black around him. He became disoriented for a moment, and when he regained his senses, he was surprised to see he was in Lady Easter's Garden again. He knew, however, that this must be a dream. He remembered everything that happened to him since his fall and that it was not possible to return to his old home. Nevertheless, the place he was in seemed to be a very accurate replica of the Garden he once knew, and not far in front of him was beautiful Lady Easter herself sitting on a fallen tree in the lush green grass. At this the Rabbit-Man forgot himself and ran over to her. Though he knew it was too good to be true, he had to see Lady Easter again if he could. When he got to her, she stared onward with a blank and expressionless face he never saw her wear before.

"Lady Easter, is it really you?" he asked, and she made no reaction. "What's wrong? Why is this ghost showing me this," he asked himself, growing nervous. Lady Easter simply raised her hand and pointed upward to the sky. The Rabbit-Man looked up, and to his horror he saw something that resembled a big, pale-yellow slimy tube that was bundled up and wound about itself. The worst feature to this disturbing image was a grotesque face formed at the front of the bundle. It had large, wet eyes that were dripping with a kind of red ooze similar to blood and its purple-lipped mouth had sharp teeth and it spit up a foul green liquid. As the Rabbit-Man saw this nasty sight the sky above him darkened, he looked down, and Lady Easter was not on the fallen tree anymore. The grass on the ground withered and died until the ground looked like the grey substance outside of and throughout Main City. The Rabbit-Man then heard the cackling of the ghost far above him and out of sight. He looked up again and saw that the sickly thing was hanging from something so far above him that he could not see where it was attached to. The tube extended up into the darkness. He then heard pained cries and screams in the distance, but again could not see where they came from.

"Who are you Rabbit-Man?" he heard the ghost ask him. "Who are you really, without your precious little Garden of blissful seclusion? What has your life come to? Can you answer that question for me, Rabbit-Man? Can you please? I will let you go if you can." The Rabbit-Man was unsure how to reply to this. His gaze was fixed on that disgusting thing and he realized as he observed it further that looked like intestines. The voice did not come from it. The foul face just kept spewing the green liquid. But the voice of the ghost repeated its questions to the Rabbit-Man. To his great dismay, he found he could not come up with any answer. This troubled him greatly. Then, in the distance, he saw something else coming fast toward him. It was a bed, and upon it was Lady Easter. Now she appeared to be weeping, and as she did so, the head of the Blue Demon rose from behind the bed and laughed menacingly at the Rabbit-Man. He could not stand to see this. He produced his small power wand and aimed it at the demon's face, but as he tried to shoot his weapon would not fire. The demon's head continued to laugh until the image of Lady Easter sunk into the bed, which then morphed into a smaller version of the Rabbit-Man. It was him as a child; still in the same rabbit suit, only smaller. The Blue Demon's head then moved forward, and the Rabbit-Boy was swept up in his mouth and devoured before blue flames poured from the mouth. As it continued to laugh the head disappeared, and the next image the Rabbit-Man saw was Mr. One. He was tied up in a spider's web. Before he could do anything, this image faded away, and so did the nasty intestines with a face. The Rabbit-Man was left alone with just the fallen tree nearby. Then another image appeared – this time it was Pertho, the woman he met after he fell from the Garden, holding her infant son in her arms. The fly-man Buzzy

Hopedasher who took her away that day then buzzed down and landed beside her, only this time the fly-man was unnaturally large. He picked Pertho up and flew away with her, but then they too were captured in a spider-web, and then this image also faded.

The Rabbit-Man began to understand this was the ghost playing tricks on him, and he heard its voice again, taunting him cruelly. "Do you remember her Rabbit-Man? That was Pertho, the woman you wished to help. She preferred a wretched man in a fly suit over you. Do you know why that is, Rabbit-Man? Do you? I do...." The ghost's voice trailed off and then another image appeared before him. This time it was the not-so-great owl-man Howler Highhorse standing before the boulder he longed so desperately to move. Again the image of the child Rabbit-Man appeared, and he walked up to Howler, who produced the branch he tried to move the boulder with before he was devoured by the Grandie wolf. Instead of forcing the boulder back with the branch, the great rock rolled forward and crushed both of them. The Blue Demon then rose from behind the boulder, still wearing the grey robe and laughing at the Rabbit-Man. From each side of the demon emerged the Ghost of Despair and Hayt the Hungry. The three of them howled laughter at the confused and frightened Rabbit-Man until he was blown back by a strong and piercing cold wind. He fell onto his back, looking up as the images of his three dreaded enemies faded. Now the disgusting intestines with a face returned and hovered above him as the green liquid dripped from its mouth down onto him. The Rabbit-Man got up and moved away from the dripping green substance.

He looked up and saw hovering behind the intestines another nasty organ with a distorted face. This second was a heart, deep red and riddled with bulging black veins which gave it a very unsavory look. Then the Ghost of Despair appeared behind him and grabbed his arms, clutching him so firmly he was unable to move. The intestines floated down before him and hovered toward him. The ghost held the Rabbit-Man's arms tight, but he kicked the intestines away from him. To his surprise, he was able to break himself free from the grip of the ghost and run away.

He still heard the ghost's voice taunting him. "You have achieved nothing since leaving the Garden – it would have been better for you if you died then, because you have no hope of surviving in a Metroscape – in the real world, and you know it, you fool! You could not save the woman and her son, you invested your fullest efforts into a ridiculous plan that never had any hope of success, and then you allied yourself with Mr. One – a good-for-nothing know-it-all who thinks he can just drift his way through life without fear of consequence or outcome. Well, your old friend's luck has run out and he is soon going to die. He is in the Grand Coliseum as we speak, and he will receive no mercy there. You cannot help him or anyone else, Rabbit-Man! You cannot even help yourself! You are pathetic and not worth anything to anyone. You can change that, however. Let me bring you to the Blue Demon and you can merge with him – become one with a being as powerful as he, and you will never feel the pain and shame these last several months have brought you ever again. It would be a very wise thing for you to do."

The Rabbit-Man simply did not know what to do or say. Everything around him was black again, and all he could see was the fallen tree once more. He walked over to it, very tired and upset, and sat down on it. The intestines and the heart reappeared and hovered above him once more. The green liquid dripped down onto his rabbit cap, but he was too disheartened to care. The mutated heart started to beat, and it made a gurgling, belching sound as it did. There sat the Rabbit-Man, in disgust and misery. The old wicked ghost's words affected him very badly. Then the intestines lowered and slowly began to absorb the Rabbit-Man's person into its slimy intertwined tubes. The heart also descended and hovered close to the Rabbit-Man. This was how the ghost intended to capture him and deliver him to the Blue Demon. They were both very old beings, and had formed an alliance long ago to capture and subdue men and women as they were about to do to the Rabbit-Man. Innumerable people fell to their power this way. But just before the intestines were able to completely engulf the man in the rabbit suit, something happened the arcane Ghost of Despair did not expect. The Rabbit-Man looked up and believed he saw Lady Easter lying before him once more. In a final moment of misery, he said a last goodbye to her in his own mind and began to weep. Before the intestines closed in around his face and completely immersed him in their filth, he noticed the image he saw was not Lady Easter. It was a woman wearing a white dove suit, which Lady Easter never did. It was Sally Wonder. Suddenly the Rabbit-Man remembered what he was doing before he ran into the cloak of the ghost. He remembered he was trying to save Sally and Twig. He began struggling within the intestines that held him tight. As he struggled more, they became increasingly loose until he was able to rip himself free and tear the nasty tubes apart. He then grabbed the hideous heart that beat and belched before him and ripped it to shreds also. He heard the voice of the ghost wailing in anger. He ran toward Sally Wonder, who was laying asleep in the darkness.

Before he reached her, the ghost appeared before him with its large purple hands outstretched. It grasped the Rabbit-Man's neck and strangled him. He fought his way out of the intestines easily enough once he regained his motivation, but now he was completely defenseless. His vision blurred and he felt himself growing weaker. Luckily for him, little Twig Duckly was nearby and saw what was happening. Frightened though he was, the boy in the duckling suit ran forward and with the dull tiny beak on his cap he pecked the hand of the old wicked ghost.

This had no effect, but then Twig grabbed the Rabbit-Man's power wand which had fallen to the ground. He aimed the wand at the ghost and shouted "Leave my friend alone! Get away from him now!" With an intense concentration of energy, Twig squeezed the wand and sent out a great blast of sparks that shot forward at the wraith. This made the ghost shriek and drop the Rabbit-Man, who fell down unconscious. The ghost was now angrier than before, and the frightened young duckling-boy was unsure what to do. In an instant he then recalled the day the Rabbit-Man saved him from the Grandie bird. He recalled the predatory hunger that burned in the predator's eyes before the Rabbit-Man arrived and gave him and his siblings a chance to escape. Twig thought of all this as he raised the power wand once more. As he did so, the soothing glowing light surrounded the boy, which empowered him and frightened the ghost. This was the same benevolent light that had comforted the Rabbit-Man earlier, and now Twig felt it and was empowered by it. The duckling-boy blasted sparks once more at the face of the looming ghost, and the wraith wailed again and shrank back. This time the ghost flew away and left the Rabbit-Man. Sally Wonder woke and saw Twig standing over the Rabbit-Man. She reached out and embraced both of them, and when she made contact with them the ground beneath them gave way and the darkness cleared. They landed with a thump onto the grey dusty ground. They were not in the same location as when they were absorbed into the ghost's cloak. They could see Main City in the distance, but they were outside its parameters.

"Are we going to be okay, Mommy?" asked Twig.

"Yes, we will be fine," she answered. They both looked at the Rabbit-Man who was still unconscious. They shook him, but it took a few moments for him to wake up. He gave a slight jump before he realized he was no longer in the Ghost of Despair's fabricated Nightmare Country. He looked around after the relief of realization set in and saw it was still daylight, but fading into twilight. None of them had any idea how long they were in the Nightmare Country inside the cloak of the ghost, but they were all relived to be free of it.

"Twig, Sally…" the Rabbit-Man said after waking. "You saved me. That ghost almost had me, and I would be a goner if not for you."

"We were only returning the favor," Sally answered him.

"What's that noise?" asked Twig. There was a commotion not far from where they were. The Rabbit-Man looked around and noticed one of the sporadic outcrops of rock that riddled the land outside Main City. He and the others went and hid behind it. They peaked out from behind and saw a group of Patrolmen off in the distance. They were carrying a large man among them, who must have been a prisoner. The Rabbit-Man feared it was Mr. One, but then realized it could not be because the prisoner was too large. They brought their captive to a tree that was far off but still in sight of their location. After a good deal of commotion the Patrolmen left the tree, and the Rabbit-Man and his friends saw a body dangling from it. He was reminded of Try Wonder hanging from the two posts, and feared the worst for the current victim of the Patrolmen. After the Patrolmen were gone back toward Main City and out of sight, the Rabbit-Man stepped out from behind the rock.

"Wait here while I see what happened." Sally and Twig did as the Rabbit-Man suggested as he went onward to the tree where the prisoner was dangling from. He was nervous, but sure the Patrolmen were out of sight. As he got closer, he was assured that the figure on the tree was not Mr. One. When he approached it he could see that it was an old man, though a very large old man. He was hanging by the neck from the tree, and the brim of a large black hat hung over his face. From beneath the brim the Rabbit-Man could see two strands of a long and braided silvery beard. His hands were also bound by rope. The tree was knotted and gnarly, so the Rabbit-Man was able to climb the side of it, though he had difficulty. When he was above the stranger, he reached out to the rope and grabbed it. When he had well enough balance he brought his head to the rope and used the rabbit snout strapped to his face to nibble through it. The stranger fell onto the ground with a thud, and then groaned. To the Rabbit-Man's surprise, the bound old man was not dead.

Chapter Thirteen
The Old Stranger

The Rabbit-Man was wary of the man even though he just saved him from what would surely have been a slow and painful death. He also bit through the rope binding the man's hands with the teeth strapped on his face. The old man then stood up, and the Rabbit-Man was surprised at how tall he was. The broad brimmed black hat cast a shadow over most of his face, but the Rabbit-Man could tell he wore glasses with very dark lenses over his eyes. In a strange way he slightly resembled Howler Highhorse, though only in his face. He wore a tattered black overcoat with cut off sleeves, and his wrists had large leather cuffs on them the use of which the Rabbit-Man did not know. The tall man stood up and let out a deep sigh. Then Rabbit-Man was sure Sally and Twig were watching from a distance, but he was not yet sure if he should bring this stranger near them.

"Thank you, kind fellow," the man said in a deep voice. "Those wretched folk from the Metroscapes are always tormenting me these days. Would you believe that I used to be able to pass through places completely unnoticed if I wished? Some of the other places I visited were far more hostile than Main City." The Rabbit-Man was unsure how to answer this. The stranger was rather big, and the idea that he could pass through a Metroscape unnoticed did not seem likely. Still he refrained from saying anything because he was not entirely sure if he trusted this old man or not. Despite these feelings, he was drawn to this mysterious man by some sense of desire he could not control or understand. He somehow instinctively knew that this was no ordinary old man and wondered what kind of secrets the odd stranger knew. He appeared to be quite an experienced person to the Rabbit-Man. Beneath his black hat grew a large mass of matted silvery hair that hung down past his broad shoulders. Some strands of the hair were woven into braids, but most of it was hanging freely. With both the parted beard and the hair it looked like the old man had a silvery mane, which gave him the look of someone powerful but mystical. Such people were not common to come by in that time and place, and this is why the Rabbit-Man was wary of the stranger. Nevertheless, curiosity grew in the Rabbit-Man's mind, and his recent traumatic experience in the nightmare country of the Ghost of Despair had made him less wary of negative consequences from other humans. Although he was still feeling troubled by the insults of the cruel spirit, he felt good about this old man. He asked the stranger his identity without any formal introduction as he would usually give.

"Who are you?" he asked the tall old man.

"I am Arman Tier," the old man answered, "and I have been around a good while. But even I have difficulty surviving in this strange and deranged world, as most of the others like me do. And who are you, kind fellow?"

"I'm the Rabbit-Man S.T. Ranger; it's a pleasure to meet you Mr. Tier," the Rabbit-Man said as he began to feel more comfortable with the old man. "I can tell you don't have a high opinion of this place, and I certainly understand. Did you come from a Bastion as well?"

"In a manner of speaking I suppose you could say that," Arman Tier replied. "My old homeland was not really a Bastion, but compared to a place like Main City it could qualify as one. I was once a great leader among men – stout and able men, but time went by and things changed. My influence wavered and all of my followers either died or drifted away. I used to have a wonderful time with them. My story is a long one, but I am sure you have other things to do so I will not tell it all. Instead, tell me about yourself and I will do what I can to help you. You just helped me, and I would be glad to repay the favor you have just given me."

The Rabbit-Man felt that Arman's offer was genuine, so he told him about his home in Lady Easter's Garden and his fall, as well as his travels through Main City and the Base Pad and finally of his return to the Metroscape and recent confrontation with the Ghost of Despair. Arman listened with keen interest, and after the Rabbit-Man explained all this he led Arman back to where Sally and Twig were and introduced them.

"Sally, Twig, please meet Arman Tier," the Rabbit-Man said. "He is an enemy of the Caretaking Body as well. It's lucky we spotted the Patrolmen stringing him up to that gnarly old tree, otherwise he might be a goner." Sally and Twig greeted Arman kindly, but the Rabbit-Man could tell by the look in Sally's eye that the dove-suited woman did not favor the stranger. He had no idea why, as Arman did not seem threatening to him after he spoke. He was unable to tell what Arman thought because of the dark glasses over his eyes, which were mostly shadowed by his hat anyway. The Rabbit-Man had already told Arman of his desire to help Sally and Twig and also shared his concern for Mr. One, of whom they found no trace. Arman believed he could help the Rabbit-Man find his friend.

"I have heard of Mr. One before," Arman said. "I am surprised he survived as long as he did without being subdued by the Caretaking Body. Folk like him are usually destroyed sooner or later. Unfortunately if he is not here now some terrible fate might have befallen him."

"I surely hope not," answered the Rabbit-Man. "Besides Twig he is the only friend I have left from the Garden, and I have been through much with him by now. After I get Sally and Twig to safety, I must return to Main City yet again to see if I can learn where he is."

"It's not always good to assume the worst," Sally said, with a very brief dark glance toward Arman. "Mr. One is very skilled. He may have gotten away once more. It's possible he is just as concerned for us as we are for him. I'm sure we'll meet him again, hopefully sooner rather than later."

"I know of a place somewhere nearby that might serve as a good refuge for you and Twig," the Rabbit-Man said to Sally. "I met a family of Bitties headed by a couple named Dag and Sweetberry. They have a small grove that they defend from the dangers of the outside world, and I'm sure you will both be safe there. I would be happy to stay there with you, but I can't leave Mr. One without trying to find him. I just don't recall the exact location of where that grove was."

"You will have difficulty finding it," Arman said. "I am surprised you entered that place at all. I know Dag and Sweetberry, and you're right about them knowing how to defend themselves, but nobody ever enters their place without them first consenting to it. I'm sure they recognized you as being harmless, Rabbit-Man, but if you left them I doubt you will be able to return even if you did know the location."

"Have you been there before?" the Rabbit-Man asked.

"I have, though it was a long time ago. Dag and I are actually old friends, and I helped him establish that home he has in the grove. I have not seen him in a long while, though. I have a suggestion; we should find a relatively safe place to stay and I can offer you some personal advice. You can decide what to do with yourselves after that. I know of a path that leads underground to an abandoned shelter I have been using when I needed to. There is a T-Web screen there in which I will try to contact some friends of mine – of the few I have left."

The Rabbit-Man and Sally agreed to this and so Arman Tier led them away until they came to a hill among the dry grey landscape. It bulged from the ground and was black like some of the other rocks riddled throughout the area. Arman led them around to a side where there was a crack in this exceptionally large rock. At first it looked to the Rabbit-Man like the old man could hardly fit through it, but he slipped through quickly and easily. Before the Rabbit-Man's friends followed him inside, Sally touched his arm. "How can we be sure it's safe in there?" she asked him. "I don't trust this man. He has a dark presence about him I don't like. I'll follow you inside if you are sure he's alright, but just be careful."

"I think we'll be okay," the Rabbit-Man answered, and then he led them inside. The crack led to a dark underground tunnel, which eventually opened into a wide and vast hall with a long table in the center. There were glowing orbs on the walls that lit the room, and the Rabbit-Man saw a large screen on the far wall that resembled a window. The room was old and dusty, but to his surprise the screen worked very well. Arman had entered a message into the screen and then turned and sat down at the table. The others also took seats near him.

"I have just sent a message to some of my contacts regarding Dag's grove," he told them as he sat at the front of the table before the screen. "Now Rabbit-Man, I will be glad to offer you what assistance I can. As you may be aware, I have travelled to various places and have been around a long time. I know a great deal about the world and the changes it has gone through. I know much more than most people even believe there is *to* know. So here is my offer: because you helped me, I will answer any three questions you have. If I cannot answer something you ask of me, you can ask about something else. I will tell you now, however, I do not know the whereabouts of your friend Mr. One, so you will have to ask something besides that. Now ask me whatever you like."

"Okay," said the Rabbit-Man, slightly bewildered but also intrigued. "What actually happened to the Garden I came from? Please tell me as much about this as you can."

"The Garden of Lady Easter was always one of the most esteemed and secluded Bastions," Arman answered. "Because of this, the Caretaking Body despised it, as they disliked all Bastions because they could not control them. For years now, the Caretaking Body has secretly been sabotaging the borders of the Bastions and slowly erasing them one by one. Once the borders became weak enough, outsiders could access the Bastions. This is what happened to Lady Easter's Garden. The destructive elements in the service of the CTB wore down the protective barriers outside her Bastion, and thus the Blue Demon crept inside. He opened the Bastion and left it susceptible to the Grandies that entered and invaded your home. It was in his dark magical fire that the Garden burned, and one of the finest of all Bastions was destroyed. It is a very sad tale and I am very sorry for your loss. But at least you and young Twig here escaped with your lives. Many did not."

"Thank you," said the Rabbit-Man. "My next question is about the great owl-man Howler Highhorse and the ideology he espoused known as the Great White Calling. He wished to move a boulder to gain access to one of the greatest Bastion known. What was really beneath this boulder?"

"That is a good question. The Great White Calling was theoretically a good idea, but it would have been disastrous if that boulder had been moved. Beneath it is not a staircase, as had been rumored and as the not-so-great owl-man believed. He was a man who became so disgusted with the current order of things he was willing to try anything just to upset the current established way. His attitude is understandable considering the condition of the modern world and his personal experiences therein, but his solution was not a good one. No staircase lies beneath the boulder. The rock was placed there a very long time ago to cover the tunnel leading to the home of the great demon Warface. If the boulder was removed and he was freed once more, such pain and chaos would ravage the world that its present condition would seem blissful by comparison. It is good that you left the Base Pad."

The Rabbit-Man considered his last question carefully. He wished to ask about the Blue Demon, and maybe he should have done so, but in the end he could not help but ask the question that had been troubling him since his confrontation with the Ghost of Despair. At last, he asked, "Who am I really?"

Arman simply sat and looked at him grimly when he asked this. "Again, that is a very good question, but the answer may be difficult for you to hear. I will answer you though, because I promised I would. I understand why this question troubles you so much, as it does so many others in these times. You see Rabbit-Man, all your life you were led to believe that the rabbit suit you wear is an intrinsic part of yourself, and the animal suits that other people wore were the same to them. That is not true, however; not really. Such suits are only costumes, outer garments that people wear to replace the identity that all humans were robbed of in the Metroscapes."

"I don't understand what you mean, Arman," the Rabbit-Man said. "Of course, my Rabbit outfit is part of who I am. I was born with it, and it has grown with me since I was a child. I know there are people in the Metroscapes who lack suits, but they aren't like me. We who were born with outfits have always lived with them. How can it be any other way?"

"I would not trust him, Rabbit-Man," Sally said. She sat in uncomfortable silence as Arman Tier answered the first two questions. It was obvious she did not like him, but the Rabbit-Man was intrigued by what he said and had to hear the end of it.

"Indeed, this is always an uncomfortable revelation for those who wear the animal suits," Arman said in response to Sally's comment. "Most remain resistant to the truth of the matter. But you asked me Rabbit-Man, and I will tell you. Since you arrived in Main City I have no doubt you believed that the people that lacked animals suits were a separate species from you, because they appeared strange to you without an outfit that resembled a kind of animal. They are the same as you, and you are like them. The tradition of the animal suit is very old and a vast majority of humanity does not remember any history before its formation. That is because of the Caretaking Body, which outlawed mention of anything before their rise to power by making it part of the Old Focus. As you have already noticed, outlawing ideas and occurrences cannot suppress people from discussing them altogether; but when they attached a strong stigma to older history and anything else they did not approve of, most people eventually came to disregard the matters in order to avoid trouble. In addition to this, the Caretaking Body established all communities they controlled in such a way that people had to work long and hard hours for many days at a time. While working so hard and long, people did not even bother to think of things listed in the Old Focus.

"But there are some who still know of what happened in the days before the Caretaking Body took control of all civilization, and the history is not a pleasant one. A small group of individuals came to control all sects of government and all major businesses in the known world. When the governments and the major businesses formed into a single entity, the Caretaking Body had its beginning. With seemingly absolute control over the world, they established the Old Focus – and listed within it everything that was important to people and had given them an identity. For example, there were sets of traditions and rituals that various peoples practiced as their religions. These gave many people a set of values and principles to live by, and also provided an answer for difficult questions such as what the purpose to life involves. People have always had the same questions about the world that you are considering now Rabbit-Man, and religions helped provide answers to those.

"There was a serious drawback to the existence of religions, however. Different groups of people held different religious beliefs. Many people were very passionate about their worldviews and ideas, and when these clashed with those of other peoples, serious wars were fought and many were slaughtered in the process. Because religions were so divisive among people, the Caretaking Body outlawed them all and forbade people from mentioning anything they considered a superstition."

"I don't understand – what do you mean by 'different groups of people?'" asked the Rabbit-Man. "Does that mean people with different suits?"

"This is what I am trying to explain." said Arman. "You are so unaware of the differences among humanity that you can hardly fathom people being as different and separate as they once were. There are many kinds of people, and they all lived in different regions of the world. They not only looked different physically in different regions, but they spoke different languages and practiced different traditions and had different beliefs – religions among them. This was a beautiful thing, but as with most things human, it was also a basis for conflict. Thus the Caretaking Body also outlawed any mention of cultural heritage or individual identity. With people having different values and beliefs, and identifying themselves as separate from each other, they would fight among themselves and be very difficult to control. By establishing the Old Focus, everybody had one set of beliefs, one collective identity, and nothing to distinguish themselves from one another.

"The next part you are aware of. The Caretaking Body allowed two separate types of locations for people to live in – Bastions and Metroscapes. People that did not seem harmful or threatening were allowed to live in the peaceful Bastions, and everyone else lived in the congested and dangerous Metroscapes.

Now this brings me back to the animal suits. People began wearing animal suits to give themselves a sense of identity once more. The Caretaking Body saw that this did not threaten them, and they used it to their advantage by making it law that everyone who lived in a Bastion be required to wear a suit at all times. Suits were voluntary in the Metroscapes, but most of the citizens of those places were so overworked that it did not matter there. The tradition of the suits became so integrated with the lives of people over the generations; it simply was not questioned anymore. You are not really a "Rabbit-Man," just a man in a rabbit suit. Only the Grandies and Morphies are separate beings – all humans are humans, with or without an artificial suit."

The Rabbit-Man was surprised to hear this. He was nervous about asking Arman his final question, and he now understood why. But after hearing all of this his entire perception of everything shifted. He looked back on his life in the Garden and Main City, and everything he once cared about now seemed meaningless and futile to him. With the Caretaking Body having such over-whelming control over everything – even the Bastions which he thought were independent of their rule – there seemed no real point to life anymore. All activity seemed to just play into their power. But to the Rabbit-Man's dismay, Arman Tier was not finished delivering his answer to the final question.

Chapter Fourteen

A Difficult Decision

"What does it matter if the animal suits are really just wardrobes?" asked Sally, who was distraught at how downcast the Rabbit-Man appeared after hearing Arman Tier's explanation. "There are still important things the Caretaking Body can never replace or subdue. As long as we have contact with people we love, we will be okay. That's what is most important. We don't necessarily need one codified form of living or a specific way to identify ourselves. Friendship and love are what is necessary. Anything that enhances those things is good. They can never be truly suppressed or taken away, so long as we are near our loved ones." Twig held his mother's hand tightly as she said this, and she embraced the little boy and held him close to her.

"I believe you are referring to the concept of the family," Arman replied, "Another idea listed in the Old Focus, although it is a rare exception in which its ban is not often enforced. It is common knowledge that people reproduce themselves, but it is illegal to mention it aloud in a public place. In the ancient days, people used to live with their birthmothers and birthfathers for their early years, rather than being given a suit and then being raised by a caregiver appointed by the CTB, as is done these days and has been for a long time. That little boy in the Duckling suit is not your biological son, Mrs. Wonder. You were able to circumvent the Caretaking Body's law and keep your firstborn child, but they took him away from you anyway. I know that is difficult for you, and I am truly sorry for your loss. However, this also brings me to the

Michael Babbish

last part of my answer to the Rabbit-Man's question. Just as Madame Duckly was not young Twig's biological mother – the people in rabbit suits that raised you and the other rabbit-suited children were not your parents either S.T. Ranger. You always knew this though never spoke it as you knew it to be against the law, which you always obeyed until you came to Main City.

"To fully answer your question I will tell you about your real origin, Rabbit-Man, though you will not like it. I know what else you wanted to asked about – this character known as the Blue Demon that pursues you. The question you asked is best though, because you will learn more about him anyway. He is a very old spirit, and the CTB is very adamant to not allow any mention of the existence of demons like him. Still, he has been present for a long time. He factors into your story in an interesting way. As you know, Lady Easter ruled over the Bastion known as her Garden for as long as you have known. There was a period in the history of that lovely place known as the Dark Spell."

"Yes, and I don't know much about what it entailed." said the Rabbit-Man. "Now I think I might be afraid to find out."

"Do not be afraid of anything Rabbit-Man," said Arman, "Least of all knowledge. Many believe it is worth dying for. Anyway, the Dark Spell occurred when the Blue Demon asked permission to enter the Bastion of Lady Easter. He appeared in the form of a ram-man, and the kind lady thought he was harmless. After he was inside, though, he took advantage of her and forced himself upon her. He raped the kind lady and then fled. Nine months later she gave birth, and that is how you were born Rabbit-Man. I know you are not happy to learn this, but you asked me of your identity and I have provided an answer. Do not let it trouble you. Even though the Blue Demon is a fierce and powerful adversary, there may be more potential within you than you fully realize."

The Rabbit-Man was horrified at this discovery. This wretched creature that was pursuing him had also fathered him. He was greatly distraught, but Sally Wonder and Twig Duckly did what they could to comfort him. "Don't let that bother you, Rabbit-Man," Sally said to him. "That does not determine who you are. How do we know that this man is even telling the truth anyway?"

"If you have any proof to contradict what I have just said, Mrs. Wonder, please produce it," said Arman Tier.

"This seems so unreal," said the Rabbit-Man. "How can I ever overcome this monster that has been pestering me if his essence is within me?"

"I can help you with that," Arman Tier said. "I know the secret to defeating the Blue Demon, and all demons for that matter. I used to teach such skills to people when they still bothered to listen to me. I have been made an outlaw by the Caretaking Body, so that did not help, but I am certain many would get by well with my help. If you follow my advice Rabbit-Man, you may have a chance of overcoming the demon, but I cannot guarantee it."

"The Blue Demon aside," said the Rabbit-Man. "I wish to bring Sally and Twig to safety. And besides, I still don't know where Mr. One is. If he is in danger, I mean to help him."

There came a call from outside the entrance of the underground hall. "Father, are you down there?"

"Yes, please come inside," Arman answered. Another man entered who was wearing a hood and a scarlet cloak. In physical appearance, he resembled a much younger Arman Tier. "Hello, Father. I received your message and came as soon as I can. What can I help you with?"

"Please meet my eldest son Herman Longhorn," Arman said to the others in the hall. He then addressed his newly arrived son, "Herman, my new acquaintance here the Rabbit-Man wishes to bring this young woman and her boy to the home of Dag and Sweetberry in their grove. I must ask that you escort them safely there. It is up to the Rabbit-Man what he will do next – he has a decision to make."

"I'll help you anyway I can," said the man with the hood and cloak. To the Rabbit-Man he seemed like he came out of a distant time and place.

"What do you mean, I have a decision to make?" asked the Rabbit-Man.

"You can do one of two things," Arman answered. "You can either go with Herman Longhorn here to guide Mrs. Wonder and Twig to the Bittie family's refuge, or you can return to Main City with the hope of finding your friend Mr. One and fulfilling your own destiny in the process. If you entered Dag's home once before, I am sure he will welcome you back though his grove is difficult to find. Herman will help you find it again. You have a choice between living in comfort and peace or facing an enormous risk that may either turn out quite well for you or be your doom. The choice is yours, Rabbit-Man, but you do not have much time to choose. I must also add that it is uncertain how long Dag's home will remain a safe haven even for himself and his family. The world grows ever more dangerous as the Bastions are being corrupted and overrun. You went to the Base Pad in hope of finding a solution to the troubles you have seen in the Metroscapes. That has failed, and I cannot guarantee that you will discover it by returning to Main City. You will at least have a chance of doing so, and you might better yourself in the process. Think of what you would like to do."

Sally and Twig walked over to the Rabbit-Man and she placed her hand gently on his shoulder. "Come with us to the home of your friend," she said. "You do not need to return to Main City – you will only find trouble there. You have no idea where Mr. One is, and he can take care of himself as he has proved many times already. You have suffered enough from that place. Come with me and Twig and be safe. Let go of the worries that trouble you and be safe at last." The Rabbit-Man was just about to agree with her when Arman Tier walked to him and stood at his other shoulder, towering above him.

"Let me remind you that you have not destroyed the Blue Demon," Arman said as he gazed down at him. "Nor the other foes he has summoned to pursue you. Dag is a well-armed and capable Bittie for sure, and there are none more resourceful than him. But entering his home once more might only bring danger upon him and his kind family. Why not just return to Main City and end this trouble once and for all, or at least go down trying? You must overcome the demon that torments you. You cannot run from him, as I am sure you already know."

"He's right Sally," the Rabbit-Man said. "I can't go with you and Twig. I'll be happy knowing you both are safe. That was what I wanted to accomplish, but I really need to resolve this issue with the demon once and for all. He will never leave me be. I don't care what kind of relation he is to me, I must put a stop to him at last, or there's no telling what other kind of damage and harm he'll cause to others. Please be safe and take care of yourself and Twig. I need to go back to Main City though."

"That's okay," Sally replied. "You must do what you believe is best. Thank you for helping us."

"Thank you both for saving me from that awful ghost," the Rabbit-Man answered. He hugged both Sally and Twig.

"Good-bye, Rabbit-Man," said Twig. "I'll miss you, but maybe we'll see you again sometime" They both turned and followed Herman Longhorn out of Arman's underground hall. Twig turned and waved to the Rabbit-Man before he and Sally left. It took all of the Rabbit-Man's self-control to hold back his tears, as he did not wish to appear weak before Arman. Herman Longhorn brought them into his vehicle and drove away. When they were gone the large old man patted the Rabbit-Man on the back. "Good choice! Off we go then." The Rabbit-Man followed him outside until they emerged from the crack in the rock they had entered. Herman's vehicle had already driven off and was out of sight.

"What am I going to do once I get to Main City?" the Rabbit-Man asked. "You are going to do whatever you need to," Arman replied. "Survival and advancement must be your only goals and concerns now. First off, I would recommend discarding that old rabbit suit. You need to be a real man now, not some wayward fool parading around in an animal's outfit. Then when you return to Main City nobody will recognize you. They will believe you come from another Metroscape and will give you a better work assignment. I cannot go with you there. You will be on your own after this, but I wish you all the best."

Arman then brought the Rabbit-Man to the tree where he was hung upon from which the Rabbit-Man saved him. It was there that the Rabbit-Man stripped himself of the floppy brown suit he wore all his life. The irony of Arman suggesting the Rabbit-Man discard the suit he used to save the old man escaped him altogether as he hung the suit upon the point of a broken branch on the side of the tree. He hated giving the suit up – after Twig left with Sally and Herman Longhorn it was the only connection he had left to the better times in his life. With a heavy heart he turned and walked away from the tree and headed toward Main City. He still had the Pass and some of the Coveted Cabbage he gained in Main City because he had them in his suit pocket when Mr. One rescued him at the Base Pad. He still possessed his power wand which was the only weapon he had, but was still better than nothing. Arman only accompanied him part of the way before offering him a final farewell.

"Arman, can I ask you one more thing before I go back?" asked the now suit-less Rabbit-Man, who now wore a blue shirt with a yellow tie, light brown pants, and dark shoes that he previously wore beneath his customary rabbit suit.

"Yes," said Arman. "I'll answer it if I can."

"If I – I guess I should say when I – see the Blue Demon again, will I be able to overcome him or will he get me once and for all."

"I don't know that for sure, Mr. Ranger," said Arman, intentionally using the Rabbit-Man's birth name. "If you remain courageous and keep your own well-being in mind you may come out of all your trials and tribulations well. I don't know if you will overcome the Blue Demon or not. You are not alone in your struggle against one such as him though. No indeed, everyone has a demon of their own that they must overcome. You are actually fortunate to see yours – believe me, your struggle would be far more difficult if you could not. I will give you my best guess of how it will turn out, though my intention is not to frighten you. In the end you may fall to the power of your enemy and he may get you at last. Most demons and foes and creatures that mean to do us harm …. well, most of the time, they get us all in the end."

With that final grim notion in mind the Rabbit-Man left Arman Tier and continued to the blasted open gates of Main City yet again. For the first time, despite being somewhat disillusioned by Arman's words, he did not feel frightened as he walked into the Metroscape. Instead he felt a strange empty apathy that dominated his mind. He knew what he intended to do, but in the back of his mind it all seemed like going through motions just to come to the same egregious outcome. This would be a disquieting thought, but it lodged itself into the Rabbit-Man's mind in a way that he simply accepted it as something that was unchangeable and immutable. Onward to the registration building he went, and went through the same process as when he first arrived in Main City. When the worker in the office took his name and blood sample she did not bother to match it with any others on their database, so nobody discovered he already had a different identity in Main City. He was surprised the Caretaking Body was even able to enforce their own oppressive laws at all – having so many resources available to them that they lost track of them all. He registered under his real name S. T. Ranger, which was listed on his old registration card, but this no longer seemed to matter. S.T. Ranger left the registration office, and was led by a man in a groundhog suit to his next workplace. He had not yet seen a T-Web screen during this next entrance to Main City. If he did, he would have been startled to see that Mr. One was in the Grand Coliseum with his fate to be determined.

•　　•　　•

After being taken by the Patrolmen, Mr. One was led into the Grand Coliseum and brought before Mr. Spiderhat himself. The structure was a massive and impressive sight to see, but Mr. One could not enjoy the view as the Patrolmen marched him along. He was not even given any trial or hearing because his notoriety was so widespread. Besides this, being brought into the Coliseum was never an official punishment – it was just something the Patrolmen did. Mr. Spiderhat took advantage of this to sustain his show, especially since his recent "struggle" with the Mad Dog Tribe. The Grandie spider had an agreement with the CTB that allowed him to proceed with this habit. Mr. One would soon be the Main Attraction of the Grand Coliseum show, but not immediately. Mr. Spiderhat was an exceptionally intelligent entrepreneur. He knew how to break his victims down and build them up into a marketable showpiece. No matter who they were, anyone brought before the great spider who owned the Coliseum would first be imprisoned in his lair until they were so desperate for freedom they would be willing to rip any opponent they faced to shreds. This never failed to produce an entertaining spectacle, and Mr. Spiderhat had the entire process down to an exact science. However, Mr. One was no ordinary individual. His resolve was firm and Mr. Spiderhat would discover that the arms dealer was not as easy to break down as the other victims brought into his arena.

At last Mr. One was brought into Mr. Spiderhat's guest chamber, which was also a very large room. He had seen the owner of the Grand Coliseum on the T-Web screens before, but nothing compared to seeing Mr. Spiderhat in person. He was even more massive than one might have thought from an image on the T-Web screens. He had a huge brown body and very long spider legs that were striped with black and white. They were very hairy, and as he sat with them coiled up beside him, few could imagine a more treacherous-looking thing. His dark blue head had a few long strands of hair emerging from the sides, and an array of eyes shown on his head, though two large yellow ones were larger than the rest. His mouth was lined by sharp teeth and flanked with pincers. A long grey, sharp tongue sometimes slithered from his mouth as he spoke to people in private.

"Ahh, this is a most special prize!" said Mr. Spiderhat as the Patrolmen led Mr. One into his guest chamber. His voice sounded cracked and wispy. It was not very soft, but cunning and sly – a stark contrast to the way he sounded when he addressed his audience over a megaphone in the Grand Coliseum. Mr. One was not impressed with what he saw. To him the large spider looked more disgusting than ever, and he would have liked nothing more than to see it squashed. The arms dealer longed for a chance to blast the hideous monstrosity away with one of his most powerful firearms. An inner rage burned in him to do this, and he fully intended to make Mr. Spiderhat history the moment he got his hands on a firearm weapon again.

"Tell me, Mr. One, would you like to compete for a chance to be liberated from the very many charges leveled against you by the Caretaking Body?" Mr. Spiderhat asked. The question was rhetorical, and asked only to maintain a façade of courtesy. The recorder worms were floating throughout the chamber, so the scene was being broadcast over the T-Web to enhance the drama of the

Grand Coliseum show. Mr. One did not answer immediately, but only glared at the Grandie spider.

"Will I even have a chance at all, or is what you call a competition really a public execution?" asked Mr. One, who was not afraid of the spider as most were. Mr. Spiderhat simply laughed. "No, no Mr. One, you have it all wrong. Of course you will have a chance. In fact, I think your first competition will be quite easy for you. It will be like a warm up. If you try very hard to win, I'm sure you will manage somehow." He then addressed the two Patrolmen. "Gentlemen, please remove Mr. One's cuffs and bring in his opponents." The Patrolmen hesitated for a moment, but then did as they were asked. They then moved to a door at the far end of the visitor's chamber and opened it. In stepped a man in one of the worst lizard outfits Mr. One had ever seen, and he could not help but laugh at the sight. The man leaped at Mr. One and pounced on him. Mr. One grappled with the man for a brief instant before throwing him off and getting back to his feet. The man leaped again, but this time Mr. One dodged the attack and wrestled the man to the ground. He then pulled a knife from his boot and put it up to the man's throat.

"Quite impressive, Mr. One," said Mr. Spiderhat with glee. The two Patrolmen came and took the lizard-man away. Just then another door opened and two black Grandie red-eyed mice emerged and attacked Mr. One. He grabbed one of the Patrolmen's clubs from his belt and used it against the enemies. It was not long before he destroyed them both. After he did this he threw the club at Mr. Spiderhat, who let out a shriek and, with a swiftness that was surprising for his size, changed his position and sprayed Mr. One with his web. Mr. One was caught up in the sticky substance and unable to move. Mr. Spiderhat then outstretched his horrendous long legs and hovered above Mr. One laughing. He gazed down at him and said, "You are a feisty fellow Mr. One, and I hope for your sake you keep that energy for your competition. Your life will depend on it." He then lifted an end of Mr. One's web binding with one of his claws and dragged him off. Two large double-doors at the back of the room swung open and revealed a very dark room – which was more like a cave contained within the massive structure of the Grand Coliseum arena. It was unlike anything Mr. One had seen before. The hard ground was riddled with bones and various scraps of clothing, and hanging from the unseen ceiling were bundles of web with victims inside. Mr. One could not tell if those inside were alive or dead, but it was not long before Mr. Spiderhat strung him up and hung him from the ceiling as well. The Grandie spider then left Mr. One hanging in the darkness of this room until his time to participate in the competition had arrived.

Chapter Fifteen
The Triumph of Inhumanity

The Rabbit-Man, now officially under his full name S.T. Ranger, was given work at a location he had never been to before. It was a simple one-story building, and he was greeted by a small and emaciated man when he entered. He was brought to a desk which had a screen on it. "What we will need you to do is search through as much information in the Main City registration as you can. Research the account of each citizen and see if there is any Cabbage credit they owe to the CTB. If they do, forward their information to T-Web station labeled "STOP." If they are owed any Cabbage value to their card by an agency of any kind, then forward their information to T-Web station labeled "GO." You may receive messages from citizens throughout the day. Answer their questions and concerns if you can, call on one of our staff if you cannot. Do you have any questions?"

"No, I understand," he told the frail man. He sat at a desk with a screen before him in a room with about one hundred other desks like his. The job was very simple and monotonous, but still not nearly as bad as working in the Main City Mine (which had reopened since his previous departure). He received many messages throughout the day and could not answer any of them. The staff consisted of people walking through the room and answering questions that all of the workers had. Because there were so many desks, the staff were usually overwhelmed and in a bad mood. The person S.T. most often asked for assistance from was a man in a goldfish suit. Most times he received a message from a citizen on the screen he did not know what to do and had to call the staff. The goldfish-man would come to his screen, type in information on the keyboard at the desk, and then walk off to answer another question. The former Rabbit-Man spent the next month working at this assignment. His new container in Main City was a small building with a single room inside. It was nicer than his last container, so he did not complain. There was a T-Web screen in this container as well, but he did not watch it often. In fact, when he was not at his work assignment, he did not have much interest in anything else. He even lacked interest in his work – it was simply something he did to pass the time it took him to earn more Cabbage and "better himself," as Arman Tier suggested. He was not even sure what entailed bettering himself, but he hardly felt like he was. He did not feel the same without his rabbit suit. He felt naked, empty and formless. He saw no sign of the Blue Demon, the Ghost of Despair, or Hayt the Hungry. It seemed even his enemies no longer had an interest in him while he lacked his former identity. He was lost in a trap of stagnation and indifference to everything, and did not know how to get himself out. Arman Tier, who suggested this path to him, was not even in Main City with him. Nobody was with him now. So he simply went on like this for several weeks, until one fateful day his life had changed again.

He went into work, and the day was exceptionally difficult. He received more messages from citizens with issues he could not resolve, and the goldfish-man that usually helped him was not there that day. After about two hours into the day his screen stopped working altogether, and went completely black. He got up from his desk and tried to find help, but all of the staff in the room was busy. Seeing there was nothing else to do, he wandered off into a hallway that led to the back offices of other staff members in the building. At the end of the hallway was a large unmarked door. He stepped inside this door, and was disturbed by what he saw. The room was dark, but in the center of it was a massive Morphie pig-man. The body oddly resembled a human, but it was unnaturally obese and its skin was pink with bulging blue, red, and purple veins throughout it. The head was similar to that of a pig, but its eyes were human-like and they were large and bloodshot. Its hands and feet had hooves like a pig's, and various chords and tubes were connected to this creature's head, with a very large tube going into its stomach. S.T. was unsure if he should be disgusted by what he saw or if he should feel pity for this Morphie. He felt a mixture of both. It was only a brief moment before several people in long white coats surrounded him and asked him what he was doing there.

"My screen is broken and I needed help to fix it." he told them "I was not sure where to go, so I came here. What is that thing, and what are you doing to it?" The people in the coats were obviously unhappy with his arrival, but one of them pulled him farther into the room and shut the door behind him. It was a tall man with a mop of raggedy brown hair and spectacles over his eyes.

"You and the other workers are not supposed to see this," that man told him. "That door is almost always locked, and we will look into why it was not locked and sealed just now. I will explain to you what this is if you promise not to share the information with anyone. Do you swear to keep all information confidential?"

"Yes," answered Rabbit Man.

"Well, this Morphie that you see here is one of the most important individuals in all of Main City. He is an All-Consuming Animal, and he is among those who power the TeleWeb throughout the entire city. Without him, much of Main City would be disconnected from the T-Web. There are other All-Consuming Animals in Main City, but none are as important as this one. And that is why you must never ever enter this room again. Not ever!" then the spectacled man suddenly started shouting loudly in S.T.'s face. "Not ever again! And if you wander in here again, I'll see to it that you are delivered directly to the Guard Dogs in an instant! Now get your ass out of here before you ruin something very important!" At this instant something stirred inside Rabbit-Man. After the several weeks of apathetic existence in Main City after his return, he wanted to do something again. Something that would bring excitement and break the monotony of his existence would have pleased him much. When the man shouted at him, it startled him and woke the old spark of discontent that existed in him since he entered the Metroscape for the first time. At last he was shaken free from his apathy and was filled with enthusiasm once more.

In a single moment, an idea passed through his mind. "None of my friends are here with me, and I really hate everything I am doing here right now. It's time for something to change," he thought to himself. He felt like he did when he interrupted the interrogation of Sally Wonder. As if destiny itself had observed this sudden spark within S.T. Ranger, the former Rabbit-Man then observed something that stirred his passion once more and ignited a righteous fury inside him. It was feeding time for the All-Consuming Animal. Two other people with long white coats and dark masks over their faces approached the Morphie carrying a large box. They opened the box, and to his horror and consternation S.T. heard cries from small voices in the box. He then watched in terror and rage as the two masked individuals each took live Bitties from the box and placed them into the mouth of the All-Consuming Animal. The frightened Bitties cried for help before they were mutilated and then swallowed by the chomping of the hideous Morphie pig-man. A carrot-shaped and plum-shaped Bittie were shoved into the creature's mouth and devoured as they screamed.

The former Rabbit-Man could not believe what he saw. These Bitties might have looked much different than anyone else, but they were still people. They could have been distant relatives of Dag's family. He could not stand to see this happen to any more of these small innocent little people, the likes of whom once helped him when he was in need. To set his rage into a whole new level after it had already escalated, the spectacled man said to him, "Hey asshole, I said get out of here!"

Then S.T. shouted back at the man, "You know, you're right, sir! You're absolutely right! I should never ever come in here again, and I'm not going to. But first, I'd like to extend a sincere thanks to your kind self and all of Main City. Here's to you, cheers!" He then punched the man in the face and stomped on him repeatedly when he was on the ground. The other people in white coats stopped what they were doing immediately and then stood and did nothing – they were utterly petrified. No one ever got violent in that particular building, but the former Rabbit-Man snapped and now he was pummeling on one of their colleagues mercilessly. He then walked up to the All-Consuming Animal and ripped the tube from its stomach. The pig Morphie let out a squeal but did nothing else. A nasty green sludge poured from the end of the tube, and the Rabbit-Man turned and pointed the gushing tube at the other people in the white coats and masks. It covered them and they slipped and fell onto the ground after dropping the box filled with terrified Bitties. He then turned the tube up at the All-Consuming Animal's face and sprayed it with the green sludge. He then threw the tube aside and crawled up onto the Morphie's seat. He ripped the chords from its head and then punched it in the face many times. The Morphie fell backwards and slipped off its seat. It rolled on the ground until it rolled on top of the tall man with the spectacles and crushed him beneath its incredible weight.

The Rabbit-Man grabbed the box of Bitties and then ran out of the room and left the building. "I guess that will count as my official resignation," he said, then he opened the lid of the box and addressed the Bitties inside. "Don't worry my little friends, I'm going to get you out of here. You don't need to be afraid of these monsters anymore." The Bitties looked at him with expressions of confused relief. Small, living, breathing apples, bananas, broccoli stalks, and other various plants shuffled around in the box as S.T. Ranger ran along the street of Main City, not entirely sure where he was going but too hyped on adrenaline to care. There was uproar in the main room of the work building when every screen in the place stopped working. The former Rabbit-Man left feeling quite content with himself. He knew he would be in serious trouble when his actions were discovered by the Guard Dogs and the Main Patrol, but he no longer cared. It would be better than sitting in that awful place for another day.

By evening the Main Patrol was already looking for him and it was not long before they caught him. The man that yelled at him about the All-Consuming Animal being the source of power for the entire TeleWeb in Main City was wrong; the pig Morphie actually only supplied power to that particular building, and the remaining T-Web screens still worked throughout the city. The CTB told the workers that the All-Consuming Animal powered all of the TeleWeb to enhance their performance in feeding the beast, but because the Bitties were hard to find and S.T. Ranger just stole all the ones they had left, the Morphie would soon starve and be put out if its extensive misery. S.T. had no idea what to do with the Bitties, so he asked one of them were he should bring them.

"Oh, thank you so much for helping us, Mr. Saviour!" cried an apple-shaped Bittie from the box.

"Actually it's Mr. Ranger, and you're quite welcome." he answered. "How can I get all of you to safety?" The Bitties then told him about a spot behind the registration building where fugitive Bitties could escape underground and make their way back to the Vegetable Patch where they came from. S.T. Ranger brought them to the specified place and they all ran away through a hole in the ground after thanking him profusely. Feeling much better but still unsure what to do with himself, the former Rabbit-Man simply returned to his container and waited for the authorities to come get him as he knew they certainly would. Before long a group of ten Patrolmen busted down his door, beat him with their clubs, and carried him away. The former Rabbit-Man laughed as they carried him off. He did not know at the time that they were not taking him to the Guard Dogs, but rather to the Grand Coliseum.

With his hands in cuffs behind him he was led into the Grand Coliseum and brought into the guest chamber of Mr. Spiderhat. It was a few weeks after Mr. One had been taken to the Coliseum, but the Grandie Spider offered the

Rabbit-Man the same opportunity he offered Mr. One – to compete in a competition for his freedom. The Rabbit-Man eagerly agreed, thinking that if he did not win in the Grand Coliseum he would simply die anyway. As with Mr. One, the recorder worms were floating through the room to broadcast the meeting across the T-Web. Mr. Spiderhat had announced earlier that month that the infamous Mr. One would eventually compete, but he withheld having the featured competition until he needed something to boost the rates of his show again. The Rabbit-Man was tossed onto the floor of the chamber before the Grandie spider and his cuffs were removed per Mr. Spiderhat's request. He had not watched Mr. Spiderhat's show recently and thus did not even know that Mr. One was also currently a captive of the Grandie Spider.

In a voice very different from the jovial, announcer-like one with which he spoke to his audience watching the show, the giant spider spoke to S.T. Ranger. "You have made a terrible error little man. I don't know who you think you are to attack one of our precious All-Consuming Animals, but I should eat you alive for doing so. But because I am such a kind person I will allow you a chance to compete for your life and freedom in the Grand Coliseum."

"Screw you and this foul city!" answered S.T. Ranger. "You're all a bunch of murdering scumbags, and you're one of the worst of them!" Before the former Rabbit-Man could say much more, Mr. Spiderhat gestured for the Patrolmen to bind him again, and then he ordered them to bring S.T. down into the arena floor before the audience. As S.T. Ranger was brought before the crowd, Mr. Spiderhat addressed the audience in his loud, announcer voice through his megaphone as he ascended onto his perch in the rafters of the arena.

"Good evening ladies and gentlemen!" the Grandie bellowed as his voice echoed through the arena. "On today's episode of the Grand Coliseum, we have a competitor making his first appearance in the Battle Zone. May I introduce Mr. S.T. Ranger. The Main Patrol recently brought him in for attacking an All-Consuming Animal of the Citizen Control Building. Such an offense is usually taken care of by the Guard Dogs, but as you know I have been granted permission from the Caretaking Body to allow offenders to clear their name right here in the Grand Coliseum!" There was uproar of cheers as Mr. Spiderhat said the title of his arena and show. When he announced the former Rabbit-Man's crime to the audience, they booed and hissed at him and shouted their wishes that he suffer for his heinous actions. S.T. observed with disgust how sheep-like the audience of the Grand Coliseum behaved.

"As most of you know," Mr. Spiderhat continued, "an offense as severe as Mr. Ranger's cannot go unrecognized here in Main City. As always, I know the perfect match for who his opponent shall be tonight. You are all in for a very special treat tonight, my friends, because S.T. Ranger's opponent shall be none other than the Grand Coliseum Champion himself – Eagle Top!" There was an even louder outburst from the audience when Mr. Spiderhat announced this. The Rabbit-Man looked around and noted the glee in the faces of the audience. He was disgusted that he ever endorsed the Grand Coliseum show by viewing it. Now that he stood in the center of the Battle Zone facing an enemy he could never defeat, the concept seemed more unappealing to him than ever. He was led away by the Patrolmen until his match with Eagle Top would commence later that evening.

In the meantime S.T. Ranger was led to a room where other competitors were waiting to compete. There were four others inside. Their faces were all grim and downcast. They were various individuals with stories of their own, but none of which anybody would remember. The only thing they all had in common was that they had crossed the Caretaking Body at some time. The former Rabbit-Man was alarmed when he recognized one of them – lying on the ground was Marvin Pinkbelly, the man in the pig suit that accused him at the Guard Post. His once-pink suit was now so stained and dirty he almost did not even realize who it was. Not far from the pig-man was a tall man with orange hair that wore a green robe and a brown hat. His name was Daryl Fair; S.T. heard of him on the T-Web, but could not recall where and in connection to what. Also in the room was a young man with a curly mop of brown hair that made his head appear very large and disproportionate to the rest of his lean body. He was Ed Barren, and his reason for being in the chamber was because he pursued a relationship with the girlfriend of Eagle Top, Diva Sweetbud.

The Grand Coliseum's champion was intent on making a public display of Ed Barren's destruction because of it. Ed Barren made his advances to Diva before she was Eagle Top's girlfriend, but this didn't matter. The last captive was a little girl with orange hair wearing a large cap with a star on the pointed end. She had a small pair of wings strapped to her back. From the look of her she could have been Daryl Fair's sister or daughter, but there was no relation between them. The chamber had a view from which the battleground of the Coliseum could be seen, but none of the captives bothered to watch the competition going on below. The little girl with the star cap looked most upset of all in the room. The former Rabbit-Man walked to her and tried to comfort her.

"I'm sorry to see you in here, little girl," he said. "How did you get caught in this awful place?"

"I don't know," the girl replied, and then curled herself up in the corner of the room.

"It's kind of you to ask," said Daryl as he stood up. "But that is all any of us could get out of her. I don't know who she is or why she is here. Believe me, I tried to console her as well, and so did Ed Barren here." He gestured to the young man, who waved at S.T. "There was a time when I could brighten the mood of anyone I encountered, but then I came to Main City and all that changed." Before Daryl Fair could finish his story, a door opened and in stepped Eagle Top with a woman and two Patrolmen. S.T. saw images of him on the screen before, but he was still impressed with the Morphie's appearance. Mr. Spiderhat looked foul in person when viewed up close, but Eagle Top appeared very strong and majestic. His head was that of an eagle, and he had two great wings on his back. His torso was like a man's, only larger and very muscular, while his legs were those of an eagle and he had long tail-feathers that trailed behind him. He towered over the other captives, and they all seemed very small and pitiful before him.

"Well well, it looks like my competition will be easy tonight," he said. "I can't wait to please my crowd by picking this lot apart." Grinning, the eagle Morphie walked over to Marvin, who was the only one that made no reaction to the former Rabbit-Man's entrance. He nudged the pig-man with the fearsome talons of his foot. The pig-man whined and squirmed at the feel of it, which made Eagle Top laugh gaily. The woman, Eagle Top's girlfriend Diva, laughed loudly as well. Seeing Marvin's misery evidently amused them greatly, and Daryl Fair simply stood and scowled at them.

"Leave me alone," squealed Marvin. S.T. could not recall ever seeing a more wretched-looking person, and despite Marvin's attempt to get him in trouble many months ago, he could not help but feel overwhelming sorrow for him. Then he remembered the old picture he found in the bundle he received from Marvin's belongings – how the young pig-man looked happy and had a woman with him. Now he was being tormented for pleasure by Eagle Top. The Rabbit-Man really wanted to comfort the poor pig-man, and seeing Eagle Top's antagonizing angered him greatly. There was no reason for one as large and strong as Eagle Top to prey upon such a weak and helpless person. To him, Eagle Top was no different than the Blue Demon, and did to Marvin and these other people what the Blue Demon and the Ghost of Despair had done to him – tormented them in an effort to break their spirit. That result already seemed accomplished with poor Marvin, and yet Eagle Top continued anyway.

"Is that really necessary?" S.T. asked. "To do that to him? I would expect more from the champion of the Grand Coliseum, or I would have at one time. Now that I see what this foul place is really all about, I am disgusted with all you people – you especially Eagle Top. You and Spiderhat are two loathsome creeps, and I really hope that you both suffer the consequences of your awful behavior one day. What have any of these people done to you?"

Eagle Top stood and smirked for a moment, and then brought his foot down onto Marvin's back, causing him to shriek in pain. "It is necessary if I say it's necessary!" the Morphie said to the S.T. "I don't know who you are, and I don't care. All I know is that I do whatever I want to whoever I want. I'm the champion and I'm in charge of this place. I'm sure there are many like you that would love to see something bad happen to me, but it's not going to happen! Do you know why?" The ex-Rabbit-Man did not answer the question; he just stood and stared with contempt at Eagle Top. The eagle-man then swiftly kicked S.T. to the ground and pinned him down by pressing his huge talon foot onto his head. "I'll tell you why – because Mr. Spiderhat and I control this place, and whatever we want to happen is what happens. That crowd out there thinks what we want them to think. Nobody is ever going to change that. You, little man, will live or die as we see fit – in any manner we see fit. You are the property of the Grand Coliseum now. If you don't like it, you should have thought of that before you got yourself in here!"

In a movement so sudden S.T. did not even perceive it at first, Eagle Top sent his knee into his stomach. He groaned on the ground in severe pain. Eagle Top laughed and ordered the Patrolmen to take the ex-Rabbit-Man to the Dark Room. He and Diva Sweetbud both laughed as S.T. was dragged off. They left the room and the two guards did as Eagle Top commanded. S.T. was dragged from the room and left the others behind. He was brought through a corridor until two great doors opened and they brought him into a room that was indeed very dark. There were bundles wrapped in a web hanging from the ceilings that the Rabbit-Man could see. Mr. Spiderhat was in the room feeding on one of these bundles. He let it drop to the ground to see what the guards were bringing him. The ex-Rabbit-Man saw the victim that was in the bundle and recognized who it was – it was Buzzy Hopedasher, the man in the fly suit that had taken Pertho on his first day after he fell from the Garden. He was surprised at this, but it affected him little because of the rage he felt at Eagle Top's insult. He felt like he was reliving the moment when the rodent-man Archo insulted him over again. Unbeknownst to S.T. was the reason why Buzzy was Spiderhat's current meal. The fly-man was an old friend of Eagle Top who learned of Mr. Spiderhat's plot to betray the champion. He never was able to warn his friend however, and the fate of Pertho would remain a mystery to S.T., though he did not have much time to contemplate it at the moment.

"What's this?" asked Mr. Spiderhat after he turned away from his meal.

"Eagle Top suggested that we bring this one here to hang, sir," said the Patrolman.

"Very well," said Mr. Spiderhat, who then wrapped S.T. in a web and hung him with the others before he resumed eating Buzzy. It was there that the former Rabbit-Man remained until he received some unexpected help.

Chapter Sixteen
A New Beginning

Mr. One was also in the Dark Room of Mr. Spiderhat, but he was re-moved from that place a short time before his old friend the former Rabbit-Man was brought there. After Spiderhat let him hang in the web for some time, the firearms dealer was very weary and weakened by the experi-ence as S.T. Ranger would soon be. Such was the effect the web of Spiderhat had on its victims – it drained their energy and warped their mind, and their perception was greatly altered after their experience for a good while after-ward. Sometimes Spiderhat would eat the victims if he had no further use for them or if he wanted them gone (as in the case of Buzzy Hopedasher), but he was very eager to use Mr. One for his show, and he needed it. Re-cently the air-worms that gathered images for the T-Web were steadily dis-appearing. The death of one of the All-Consuming Animals by starvation had an effect on this, but it was not the root cause. He was careful not to show it, but Mr. Spiderhat was becoming increasingly fearful of Main City slipping from the control he held over it. He answered to the Caretaking Body, of course, but they were located in another Metroscape. It was his job, along with the Guard Dogs, to enforce their rule in Main City, and he could only do so by maintaining absolute control over the Metroscape him-self. Now it was time for him to make an example of Mr. One, and remind everybody that he was in fact the effective ruler of Main City as the chief agent of the CTB.

Michael Babbish

Mr. One was delirious and hardly even knew where he was when he was cut free from the web. He was given a meal and then led away by Patrolmen into the Battle Zone of the arena. The audience booed and hissed as he walked out, but they cheered fervently as his opponent entered. This was a man called Prince Bacon, who wore a white blood-stained apron and wielded a large knife. Mr. One was equipped with a knife of his own, though it was not as huge as his opponent's. Mr. Spiderhat instructed Prince Bacon before the bout not to end it too quickly, and make a spectacle of Mr. One's demise. To this the butcher eagerly agreed, but it would be his downfall. Mr. One would have easily defeated Prince Bacon, but because of his wearied condition from being trapped in the web Prince Bacon dominated most of the match. It was interrupted, however, by an unexpected individual. Nobody knew how he managed to sneak into the Grand Coliseum, but he did. Before Prince Bacon could end the contest by slaying Mr. One, down from the rafters of the arena swooped Sig Calcium, the bird-man that stole the Coveted Cabbage. He kicked Prince Bacon to the ground and killed him with his own knife. The crowd was in uproar, but Sig acted fast. He grabbed Mr. One and very swiftly flew away from the Battle Zone with him firmly in his grasp. Two massive Guard Dogs leaped into the Battle Zone to catch their much-detested foe. The cunning Sig Calcium was too quick for them, however, and he and Mr. One exited the Grand Coliseum as sig punched a hole through the roof in the top of the building. Mr. Spiderhat was furious after this, and wanted nothing more than the heads of both Mr. One and Sig Calcium displayed in his arena for all to see. He sent the Guard Dogs and many Patrolmen away after them.

The ex-Rabbit-Man was completely oblivious to his friend's rescue, however, because he was hanging in Mr. Spiderhat's web and growing weaker each moment he did. He was not kept there as long as Mr. One though. After only several hours of remaining in the foul web, a small and inconspicuous person gained access to the Dark Room in an effort to complete a rescue of her own. Very subtly and stealthily the little girl with the star cap snuck into the Dark Room as the Patrolmen were bringing another victim inside. Once she was there, she waited until the guards were gone. She was so impressed with the way S.T. Ranger defied Eagle Top that she wanted to help him. She found the web he was bound inside. She took a little power wand that she secretly kept with her from her pocket and cut him free with a small flame emitted by the wand. She was brought to the Grand Coliseum for a debt to Mr. Spiderhat she could not repay. The guards did not even bother to search her and thus

176

never found the power wand. She would not have been expected to compete in a match, but instead they intended to use her as a servant to Eagle Top and his friends, which some might have considered an even worse fate. The little girl was being punished by Diva Sweetbud when she was in the waiting room with the others.

When S.T. Ranger was freed, he blinked and looked around. "I know a way out of here." she told him in a soft voice. "It was nice of you to try to stand up for that poor pig-man. I have seen too many others like you get killed, and I don't want to see it happen to you. I'll show you the way out. Come back with help if you can. If not, good luck to you."

"Why are you doing this?" asked S.T. "Who are you?"

"My name is Twinklette," said the little girl with the winged suit. "Eagle Top owns me now, but I have a friend working to win my freedom for me. You need to get out of here quick."

She then led him to an exit at the back of the Dark Room. While working as a servant to Eagle Top she learned of many secret passages in the arena. There was a chute where the bones of Spiderhat's victims were disposed of. Twinklette showed this to the ex-Rabbit-Man. He thanked her heartily and embraced her. She refused his insistence that she go with him to safety. She knew she would get caught, but there was a chance S.T. might not. He thanked her again and then slid down the chute. Once he was on the other side, it was daytime and he regained his senses. He continued along as quickly as he could, leaving the Grand Coliseum behind. He now travelled through backstreets in Main City he never saw before, and the ground turned from the dusty grey to black. The ground was more hard and barren than before, but he moved on because there was nothing else he could do.

For the whole day he travelled that way. He no longer had any Cabbage because it was left in his container, and he did not dare to go back and get it. He fell to the ground, hopeless and unhappy. None of his friends were near, and he was close to succumbing to despair. If the Blue Demon and the Ghost of Despair had found him then, they would surely have destroyed him once and for all. But they did not, and the former Rabbit-Man had another chance to make things better for himself. As he lay on the ground in misery, he saw a small rabbit hop along by him. He did not see any stray rabbits or any animals in Main City before, except the rats when he was in the sewer. As curiosity grew inside him, he got up and followed the rabbit. He really needed to see where it was going. He had difficulty believing any wild animals could survive in the hostile environment of Main City, but surely this rabbit had to live somewhere. He followed it along until the black ground changed brown, and the brown land eventually had patches of green grass growing on it.

"How could this be?" he wondered as he followed the rabbit along. It led him to a small brown house amid a pasture of green grass. The scene was so pleasant he hardly believed it was real. The rabbit joined several others in the grass, and then they all hopped away and disappeared through their rabbit holes. Then S.T. saw something that surprised him greatly. A man was working in a vegetable patch beside the house. To his surprise, the man was wearing a grey rabbit suit. It looked different than the suit he used to wear, but nevertheless he went forward to meet this stranger. He was overcome with grief at the loss of his old suit, and wished very much to have it again. He approached the rabbit-suited man and greeted him.

"Hello sir, what brings you here?" the man asked. "You don't look so well, and if you just came here from the rest of this terrible Metroscape, that is surely understandable."

"I am the Rabbit-Man… actually, I used to be," he answered. "My name is S.T. Ranger. And yes, I just came from the Grand Coliseum. I was captured in Mr. Spiderhat's web, but a kind young girl freed me. I saw a rabbit and could hardly believe my eyes. I followed it and so here I am. I really like your suit; I used to wear one similar to it. What is your name?'

"I am Geb Growth," said the new rabbit-suited man. "And thank you for that. I would have liked to see your suit, but maybe I can help you get another one. Yes, this is the last place anything nice can still exist in Main City. The metal giant has been very good to us, and has kept the Guard Dogs away from these parts for a long time. Come inside and have a bite to eat, I'd really like to learn more about you."

S.T. thanked Geb Growth and went into the house with him. He was pleasantly surprised to see there were Bitties living inside the house. They helped Geb work in the vegetable patch nearby. The two Bitties in the room were shaped like an eggplant and a sunflower. S.T. explained his history up to his most recent experiences. Geb and the Bitties listened with keen interest and Geb said afterward, "After all that I'm glad to see you made it here alive. I don't blame you for wanting to try the owl-man's idea – I heard his show and considered doing it myself – but things like that never work out. I discovered this place not long ago, and have been happy here ever since. You mentioned Sig Calcium – would you believe I know him? He's a good friend of mine!"

"Really?" exclaimed the ex-Rabbit-Man. "That's exciting. How did he manage to get away with his theft of the Cabbage?"

"He came here for refuge at first," said Geb, "but if the Caretaking Body sent reinforcement to help the Guard Dogs catch him, even the efforts of the metal giant would not stop them. So Sig moved on, but I have no idea where he is now. It was a dangerous move on his part to steal that, and I won't hide my concern for him. Still, he made his decision and it worked out well enough for him. He wished to make a statement against the Caretaking Body, which he did quite effectively. Ever since his dear friend Try Wonder died he hasn't been the same. He always did love risks, but after Try's death by the CTB Sig has been downright reckless. If he's not careful he'll come to a very bad end. That excellent suit the metal giant made him really seems to be working out though."

"Yes, he did have an excellent bird suit!" said S.T. "He could actually fly like a bird with it on. Who is this metal giant that could make such fine suits? Is your suit made by him too?"

"It is. The metal giant was here long before I arrived, and nobody is sure where he comes from. He is very friendly and nice to talk to, and his skills are incredible. He made my suit as well as Sig's, and he did so for many others as well. You see, he can make a suit that actually enhances the abilities of the person wearing it – that's why Sig can fly like a bird when he wears his bird suit. The metal giant has even made suits to allow people to breath under water. Let's go back outside and I'll show you what I can do with my suit." Geb led S.T. outside. He ran around his house so quickly it seemed like a flash to the former Rabbit-Man. Then he leaped up and must have soared about twenty feet into the air before landing neatly on his own two feet again. "How about that!" he exclaimed. S.T. was very impressed by what he saw and eager to learn more about these enhanced animal suits.

"It sounds like you still have trouble in Main City, and with that Blue Demon and his minions after you, you sure could use a suit like mine. How about it? I'll take you to the metal giant and see if he can make you a new rabbit suit, and you can become The Rabbit-Man with an appropriate outfit once more, rather than just a plain, regular-clothes-wearing man like you are now."

"That would be fantastic!" S.T. answered. "Thank you very much! Please tell me more about this giant before we meet him."

"Like I already said, I don't know where he comes from, and he can change his size at will. He used to be an average-sized person when he first came to

Main City, but he can make himself grow. He has a very special suit that allows him to do this, and his entire body is covered with a metallic substance. I say 'metallic' because he can move and flex inside it with ease. It might not even be metal as we know it, but it looks that way from the outside, and because he is now very large everyone I know that met him calls him the metal giant. His real name is Cyber Wurko. I have no idea what that means, but it was his name in the strange place he came from. He can read people very well, and knows when somebody is a friend or enemy. Despite his generosity and eagerness to assist those that come by him, he has never left the spot in the woods where he sits. He just stays there, and even though he's very polite to those that speak to him, he never eats or drinks. To me, he seems very sad. I think something bad happened in his former home that he does not like to talk about. Still, he dislikes the Caretaking Body and will be glad to help those who are at odds with them. He'll be glad to make you a new rabbit suit to replace the old one you lost."

When Geb led S.T. before the metal giant once known as Cyber Wurko, he appeared to be a very large metal outgrowth in the ground. Upon closer observation, S.T. noticed that he was sitting with his legs curled before him and his knees to his chin. He sat among trees in a grassy place, and his arms wrapped around the legs. He must not have moved for some time, because moss and dirt caked his entire body. Strange buttons and designs were on his surface, but these were also covered. He looked like an old machine that was abandoned. His head was the only lively part of him. It was a shiny metallic color with a very wide shape. A few wires stood out on it, and it had a small little antenna on his right side, and a longer one pointing upward on his left side. His eyes were surrounded by black circles on his metallic face which gave them a mystical look. There was no mouth that the Rabbit-Man could see except a very thin line near the bottom of his head about where a mouth should be on such a bizarre-looking face. In a strange way, the metal giant had a friendly feel and look to him. The Rabbit-Man thought he looked like a massive children's toy.

"Hello friend," said Geb as they approached the metal giant. "I have a newcomer here with me that ran into some trouble at the Grand Coliseum and just barely escaped. He is the Rabbit-Man S.T. Ranger, formerly *the* Rabbit-Man from Lady Easter's Garden. He lost his old rabbit suit, and I was wondering if you could make him a new one that can help him get back at Main City for the troubles they put him through. He's also being pursued by an enemy called the Blue Demon and two of his goons. Can we help him, metal giant?"

"We can," replied Cyber Wurko. His voice was very clear and welcoming, and even youthful. "Welcome, Mr. Rabbit-Man. I'm sorry to hear of your difficulties, but the suits I can produce have helped others tremendously before. Please come forward and let me get some information from you. Then I will begin work on the suit right away." The Rabbit-Man stepped forward. The metal giant asked him to hold out his hand. He did so, and the antenna on the right side of his head extended and touched Rabbit's palm. It then went back to the giant's head. "Thank you." he said, and then started producing a strange humming noise.

"It will take him a little while to finish that," said Geb. "Let's go work in the vegetable patch and have dinner. After that he should be done and you will be ready with your new rabbit suit!" They went off and the Rabbit-Man, now more comfortable with his traditional identity and very eager to gain a new rabbit suit, worked the soil with Geb and the Bitties. He really enjoyed doing so. It felt good to him to do meaningful work for a change, rather than the pointless, monotonous, and tiresome jobs of Main City. Several other Bitties came and helped them. The Rabbit-Man was delighted when he met the same Bitties he saved from the All-Consuming Animal, and they shared a joyful reunion. As they were working a vehicle came into view and stopped not far from them. Out of it stepped a beautiful woman with a light blue dress and sandals. She approached Geb and greeted him.

"Selene, it is great to see you as always!" exclaimed Geb and he hugged the newly arrived woman. "Let me introduce the Rabbit-Man. He came from a Bastion and ran into trouble in Main City. He lost his suit in the process, so Cyber Wurko is making him a new one now. It's almost time for dinner. We'd love for you to join us."

"Yes, thank you," she said to him, and then said to the Rabbit-Man. "It's nice to meet you, Rabbit-Man. I understand your difficulties with Main City. I've been having trouble there recently too. Well, actually it is a friend of mine who is in trouble there, not me."

"Oh no, what has Christie gotten herself into now?" asked Geb. Selene sighed and put her head down. "I'll tell you during dinner if you want. She is going into the Grand Coliseum with the suit the metal giant made for her. I know it is a spectacular creation and all, but I think that arena might be more than she, or anyone, can handle."

"I am familiar with that place," said the Rabbit-Man. "I only narrowly escaped it myself. I'm lucky to even be alive." They all went into Geb's house.

The Rabbit-Man and Selene sat at the table with Geb as the Bitties enthusiastically prepared a hearty stew for dinner. Selene told them of her friend's involvement in the Grand Coliseum and her fears for her. The Rabbit-Man learned that her friend was Christie Starlight, also known as "The Dream Queen" and the very same Protectorate that helped Mr. One rescue the duckling-children in the Garden. The Rabbit-Man knew The Dream Queen was a popular entertainer in Main City, but did not know much else about her. He was eager to learn more.

"You know Christie's young friend Twinklette," Selene said, and Geb nodded. "The poor girl was caught with counterfeit Cabbage, though of course she didn't know it at the time. The Mad Dogs were circulating it in their attempt to cause trouble, and some of it still exists. Of course the Caretaking Body takes this very seriously and wishes to prosecute anyone found using it. Twinklette can take care of herself well despite her young age, but even she could not spot the counterfeit. She was taken immediately to the Guard Dogs. I have no idea what her punishment would have been, but Mr. Spiderhat got wind of the affair, and he paid off the Guard Dogs and refunded the counterfeit Cabbage. Twinklette has then been in debt to him and was made a servant to his competitors – chiefly the champion Eagle Top. Oh my goodness Geb, if you heard what that young girl had to endure there, the punishment of the Guard Dogs might have been better for her! I don't think they harmed her physically, but their personalities are dreadful. Diva Sweetbud, the girlfriend of Eagle Top, is the worst of them. Christie has had limited contact with Twinklette since the girl's captivity to Eagle Top, but from what she has gathered so far they have not physically harmed her. They treat her terribly – always making her clean up the messes they make, and Eagle Top's girlfriend delights in tormenting the poor girl."

"That damn spider Grandie will never miss an opportunity to take advantage and exploit somebody, will he?" said Geb in disgust.

"That's what his business thrives on," answered Selene. "Now my friend Christie is entering the Grand Coliseum to fight for her friend's freedom. With the metal giant's suit I know she is capable of incredible things, and I hope her popularity as a musician gets people to support her, but Mr. Spiderhat could choose anybody as her opponent. What if it's a Grandie? I'm very worried for her. She believes she can win with her abilities, but I'm doubtful. I love Christie, but I feel like she's being led into a trap." The Rabbit-Man and Geb were both troubled by this news. The Grand Coliseum was a very nasty business when one had the awareness to acknowledge it for what it truly was – a public show that capitalized on the misfortunes of others for a gross profit. The three in the room realized this. Unfortunately, the multitudes of Main City did not. Twinklette had helped the Rabbit-Man escape Mr. Spiderhat's Dark Room in the arena, and he felt very indebted to the courageous girl as well as to Christie Starlight who helped the duckling children when the Garden was destroyed.

"She helped me escape," said the Rabbit-Man. "Geb, when the metal giant is finished producing my suit, I must return to the Coliseum at once to help this poor child. I can't let this go. Besides, I'm looking for as many reasons as I can find to cause trouble for Eagle Top and Spiderhat. I can't stand either of them!"

"That is very risky, Rabbit-Man," said Geb. "But if that's what you want to do, then go for it. Just be very careful."

"That's very kind of you to do that," said Selene. "I wish you all the best." They had a pleasant dinner that evening, and when it was finished the three of them went back to the metal giant.

"Hello, my friends," he said to them. "I have your suit finished, Rabbit-Man. I hope it serves you well." The metal giant then extended his hand that had a square package in it. The Rabbit-Man opened this package and found a suit even more delightful than the one he had before. It had a white cap with a rabbit's face at the front of it. Two teeth came down onto his forehead and the rabbit ears pointed into the air. The torso of the suit was a golden-yellow vest that stretched overtop a long-sleeved light blue undershirt, and protective grey elbow pads and gloves came with it. The lower part of the suit's body was possibly even better. It included brown pants that were large in the hips and thighs (which would give the Rabbit-Man enhanced speed and allow him to jump very high and land safely). It also had knee-high boots, the feet of which were shaped like a rabbit's feet and would also help his speed and agility. Protective kneepads were also included. The back of the pants had a puffy white rabbit tail. The entire suit had a protective power instilled by the metal giant that would allow it to be very flexible but also serve as protective armor. Even the Rabbit-Man's face would be protected from harmful elements despite being exposed. Such was the mysterious power of Cyber Wurko.

The Rabbit-Man wasted no time putting the suit on, and he looked much better than he did in his old one. He felt like himself once more, and felt better than he ever had since his fall from the Garden. Then Cyber Wurko told him

"This may be of some use also." He then produced a long smooth power rod (similar to a power wand, but more powerful) with an orange carrot-like piece at the top of it and a green stump at the bottom. This was an incredible weapon that could be used as a striking weapon with the carrot piece at the top, which was much harder than one would expect. The tip of the carrot piece could also fire sparks or missiles as many firearms and power wands did. This new weapon was a significant upgrade to the power wand the Rabbit-Man still possessed.

"That weapon is more dangerous than it appears," said the metal giant. "It can deal powerful blows and can shoot powerful energy blasts at enemies. So it serves as club or a firearm. Give it a try, but do not shoot at anybody, of course." The Rabbit-Man did this. The carrot at the tip could pound as hard as a hammer if he intended it to do so. The energy blasts emitted from the weapon were comparable with the best of Mr. One's firearms. They could emit soft or devastating projectiles depending on his need, and always hit their mark. Perhaps the best aspect of the weapon was how light it was to carry and wield. The Rabbit-Man had no idea how the metal giant could produce such advanced weaponry, but he was certainly glad Cyber Wurko was on their side. He then aimed the tip of the carrot at a distant large rock and squeezed the power rod. It sent out an energy beam that disintegrated the rock upon contact. The Rabbit-Man and his friends were impressed.

The Rabbit-Man was overwhelmed with gratitude, and after leaping into the air several times in ecstasy he fell onto his knees and bowed on the ground before the metal giant. "Is there anything I can do to repay you for this, great metal giant?" he asked. "You are like a savior to me for providing me this incredible gear. All my life I've been powerless and weak, but now I feel like I can actually accomplish something good!"

"Thank you for your offer, Rabbit-Man," said the metal giant. "Just use the suit well and take care of yourself. One last thing you should know is that the suit is powered by your intentions. I can tell you have a pure heart and that's why I agreed to help you. Maintain good intentions and your suit will assist you well. The suit is only a tool, it is your intentions and desire that are your real power now."

The Rabbit-Man thanked Cyber Wurko again and then ran around the area. He could hardly believe his own speed. He then jumped high into the air again and again. He leaped up to twenty feet as Geb had done before. He was exhilarated, and had not felt so good in all the time since he had fallen from the Garden. In fact, even most of the time he was there he did not feel quite as good as he did then. He felt like a brand new person. He made up his mind that he could proudly be both the Rabbit-Man and S.T. Ranger, and he fully intended to use his newfound abilities to help Twinklette and Mr. One.

He stayed at Geb's house that night and had a fresh start and a wholesome breakfast the next morning. His focus now was to return to the Grand Coliseum and free Twinklette whatever way he could. Selene thanked him again for his efforts and hugged him, and he shook hands with Geb before he departed. They both warned him not to get overconfident in his abilities, as the Caretaking Body and the Mad Dog Tribe both had very powerful beings under their control too. The Rabbit-Man understood and assured them he would be careful. Then he was off. It was a new dawning day for the Rabbit-Man – for the first time in his unhappy existence in the Metroscape he felt empowered and in control of his life and destiny. Not only did he have a new suit, but also his meeting with Geb, Selene, the metal giant Cyber Wurko, and the Bitties was very uplifting. He made new friends and was shown great kindness by them for no other reason than because he went to them in need. This quick encounter with goodness in a bad world was all it took to give him new motivation like he never had before. He set out once more with his sights set intently on the Grand Coliseum, and bringing justice to those who needed it there.

Chapter Seventeen

The Flight of the Dream Queen

The Rabbit-Man, now redefined and possessing a new sense of confidence, could not have found a better day to enter the Grand Coliseum. It was another of those influential days that had a great and permanent impact on him. It was also the day that "The Dream Queen" Christie Starlight would make her first appearance in the Grand Coliseum. Known and loved throughout Main City as a dancer, musician, and entertainer, she would now enter the Grand Coliseum to compete on behalf of her friend Twinklette.

The Rabbit-Man was eager to enter the arena, but he knew tickets to such a place could be very costly, and he no longer had his bundle of Cabbage. Then a wild idea occurred to him. He wondered what would happen if he went back to his old container before entering the Coliseum. With his enhanced speed and agility, he figured he would give it a try. The suit also helped him to be very nimble, so he was able to avoid being seen by any Patrolmen or Guard Dogs in the streets. When he came to the old building where his most recent container was he found it deserted. The door was open so he went inside. He could hardly believe what he saw – inside his container was his old backpack untouched. It still contained the Cabbage and the Bronze Pass. The Rabbit-Man took this and quickly left the container building. He passed the building he worked at for the Citizen Control Office. This was deserted as well. It seemed that after his incident with the All-Consuming Animal, the place was immediately put out of operation. He was glad. Then he went directly to the

Grand Coliseum. There was a ticket booth outside the arena, and so he purchased one with his Cabbage and went inside. He was early, and the next show
was not set to begin for another forty-five minutes. He went down a corridor
and then came to an opening where he had a choice of where to go – he could
go straight and be above the Battle Zone but still have a good view of what
was going on. He could go down a flight of stairs and be level with the Battle
Zone, or he can go upstairs and be on the higher balconies looking down at
the action. In the end, despite being the most crowded of the sections, he went
straight ahead. There he waited among a crowd of people he did not like or
care to be around. He maintained a low profile as if he were simply a common
observer of the spectacle to take place before him. Unknown to the Rabbit-
Man, though he would not have been surprised to learn of it, was the plot of
the conniving Mr. Spiderhat to undo the Dream Queen before the public eye.
The Grandie spider was fiercely resentful of the young Christie Starlight's
popularity and success. The fact that Christie genuinely enjoyed making people happy, rather than trying to only profit from their support as Spiderhat
did, made the owner of the Grand Coliseum despise her even more. His wrath-
ful envy drove him to capture the innocent Twinklette, and the sly spider now
intended to capitalize on the situation and undo The Dream Queen. Mr. Spiderhat would soon learn that the Dream Queen had more strength and resilience in her person than he anticipated. However, the Grandie spider was a
cunning creature, and he had an especially formidable opponent in store for
the Dream Queen that she would surely have great difficulty overcoming. The
opponent would be a surprise to all in attendance at the Coliseum, including
the Rabbit-Man.

When the show finally began it was midday and Mr. Spiderhat's "show"
voice echoed through the arena. He announced the first match of the day as
he sat on his web above the higher balcony overlooking the arena. The Rabbit-Man watched the match with growing disgust. He still could not turn away,
however, and kept scanning the vast audience for any glimpses he could catch
of Twinklette, Eagle Top, or Eagle Top's girlfriend Diva Sweetbud. Both Daryl
Fair and Ed Barren each participated in a match, but they were both defeated.
Ed Barren was pitted against one of the Mad Dogs fighting on behalf of his
team as they still pursued the G.C. Championship. Ed was beaten severely by
the Mad Dog member, and after his match Mr. Spiderhat announced the arrival of Diva Sweetbud, who received an applause from the audience. As the
beaten and desecrated Ed Barren lay prone on the floor of the battleground,

Diva kicked him and shouted insults at him through a megaphone as the crowd cheered on with delight. Eventually Ed was carried from the battleground by the red-shirted officials of the arena (to the Rabbit-Man they slightly resembled the Patrolmen), and then Diva addressed the Mad Dog that had just defeated Ed Barren.

"I hope you enjoyed that victory over that pathetic loser," said Diva. "Because you and your foul gang will never defeat my man Eagle Top! He is in a league of his own, and has never been defeated since he became the champion of the Coliseum. He will never lose his title, and the Mad Dogs will eventually be crushed once and for all." To this statement the crowd burst out in cheers again. Diva seemed to be as popular as her boyfriend Eagle Top in the Coliseum. The Mad Dog member that was in the Battle Zone was laughing and he received a megaphone of his own from an official.

"That's very cute," he said in a gruff voice, still grinning. "But I think you and your little boyfriend Eagle Top are in for a very big surprise. We Mad Dogs have a prospective member in a competition here later tonight. All of Main City will be amazed when they see who we have as a possible contender for the championship. And when we win that crown from your lover boy Eagle Top – as we sure will – the Mad Dogs will be in charge, and the Grand Coliseum will never be the same again!" The Mad Dog member then dropped his megaphone and walked off laughing. He was met with boos from the audience as he walked away. When Diva left the battleground, Mr. Spiderhat announced a short break for the show. It took every ounce of self control the Rabbit-Man had to prevent himself from leaping onto the arena floor and stopping Diva from tormenting the defeated Ed Barren. He hated the Mad Dog Tribe because he knew they caused trouble for the citizens of Main City, but when he saw Diva's behavior and recalled Eagle Top's mannerisms he almost wished they would win the championship and do away with him and Spiderhat after they had control of the Coliseum. He had a strong urge to simply call out Eagle Top then and there, but resisted the temptation. His intuition told him to wait, as he still needed to learn of the situation of Twinklette and Selene's friend Christie Starlight.

He bought some food and a drink at the refreshment stand and then returned to his place. It was a good thing he kept his wits and did not interrupt Diva, because he would have his chance to confront Eagle Top soon enough. There were two other matches in the Grand Coliseum after the break, but neither involved anybody the Rabbit-Man knew. As he was milling through the crowd, he overheard a conversation between two people that Mr. One had escaped from the Coliseum with the aid of Sig Calcium. The Rabbit-Man did not see this, but he was glad to hear his old friend made an escape and hoped he and Sig Calcium were alright.

Then the moment came when Mr. Spiderhat, still sitting in his web in the rafters of the arena and speaking through his megaphone, announced that The Dream Queen Christie Starlight would be competing next. Christie entered the battleground with a grand entrance, full of music that entranced and energized the listener. She put on a very impressive dance routine as she made her entrance and was cheered by the audience. As if her dance was not impressive enough, her costume that the metal giant made for her was also visually striking and gave her a very mystical and captivating look. This undoubtedly added to the sensationalism of The Dream Queen's persona and the current Grand Coliseum match. She wore a large blue cap with three long tassels and small yellow balls at the end. Her hair floated around her head as the ends of several strands were lifted by little shining orbs at the ends. Her outfit was mostly blue and silver, with stars and other celestial shapes worked onto the fabric. She also wore a silky cape that could help her fly if she intended to. The arena grew dark and shimmering stars glittered throughout the entire structure while the ambient dance music played. The orbs in Christie's hair shined along with the twinkling stars. Her blue shirt and a glittering cape that also had sparkling stars, and her pants with celestial shapes to decorate them enhanced her performance. One thing was certain – The Dream Queen knew how to make an entrance.

When Christie Starlight's entrance was finished and she stood in the battleground she produced a power wand with a large shining star at the end. The Rabbit-Man was glad to see she had a weapon produced by the metal giant, because he was familiar with how potent they were.

Mr. Spiderhat announced Christie Starlight's reason for competing, "The Dream Queen is here for a specific purpose. A young friend of hers was caught circulating counterfeit Cabbage, which of course is a dire offense." There were moans from the crowd. "But I gave the little girl a job instead of leaving her to the wrath of the Guard Dogs." On cue the crowd cheered. "Young Twinklette has served us well here in the Grand Coliseum, but the Dream Queen wishes to have her excused of her offenses because of the girl's young age. As you know, we offer such a chance here at the Grand Coliseum. Please bring forth the girl in question." Two officials then led Twinklette out to a balcony across from where the Rabbit-Man was standing and watching. She was frightened at first, but her face brightened when she saw Christie.

"I will have everyone here know that little Twinklette is not in danger," Mr. Spiderhat said. "If The Dream Queen wins, Twinklette leaves with her. If Christie Starlight loses, Twinklette continues her assignment, and the Dream Queen will be brought to my web. And now... to introduce the opponent of The Dream Queen..." Before Spiderhat could finish, however, the grinding music of the Mad Dog Tribe sounded once more. It was unclear to the Rabbit-Man if Mr. Spiderhat intended for this to happen or not, but two of the Mad Dogs entered the battleground. One of them was their leader Rip A. Sunder.

He had a megaphone in his hand and addressed Spiderhat, "It's time for us to introduce our new prospective member of the Mad Dog Tribe..." Now everyone in the arena was in anticipation, including the Rabbit-Man. He wondered who the Mad Dogs could have recruited. At first he became nervous that it might be Mr. One or Sig Calcium, but he soon dismissed those notions. Then he thought perhaps Arman Tier returned to Main City and aligned himself with the Mad Dogs, but he dismissed this notion as well. Then Rip A. Sunder continued, "Making a long-awaited return to the Grand Coliseum, please welcome – Kroscar Hunderbar!" There was gasp among the entire audience. Kroscar had not been seen in the Grand Coliseum since his infamous match with Eagle Top several years ago, but today he had returned, and his first opponent was the Dream Queen Christie Starlight. Twinklette looked distraught in her lonesome spot on the balcony.

If Christie Starlight was afraid, she did not show it. Kroscar stepped forward and stood beside Rip A. Sunder and the other Mad Dog flunky. He looked different now than when the Rabbit-Man saw him on the screen. He had the same jaws and snout of a dog strapped over his face, though the teeth were larger and sharper. He wore the spiked cap of the Mad Dogs on his head, and large leather boots with spiked bottoms. His shorts were held up by red suspenders, and he had clawed gloves over his hands. He looked fearsome and dangerous, not least of all because of the glint in his eye that burned with bitterness and resentment that the Rabbit-Man instantly recognized, and it made him shiver. Kroscar stepped forward with a large battle-axe in hand to meet his opponent. The Mad Dog members left the Battle Zone, and then Mr. Spiderhat announced the beginning of the competition. Christie Starlight was not the least bit intimidated by fierce Kroscar, though many would have been. She had confidence in herself and determination to help Twinklette. Kroscar had a severe ferocity that would enable him to defeat many foes, but he knew the Dream Queen was no ordinary opponent, and had his own treacherous plan to win.

The Rabbit-Man had a very bad feeling about the contest. He was aware that Christie Starlight had a suit made by the metal giant and she wielded a power wand as her weapon, but he wondered if the Mad Dogs were somehow able to gain similar suits themselves. If the metal giant could make such things, maybe there were others who could too. Even if he did not have an enhanced suit, Kroscar appeared vicious enough without one. As the competition began, the Rabbit-Man saw the powers that Christie's suit gave her. She could levitate in the air for a long period, and she used the power wand to produce a fine mist. When she sprayed Kroscar with this, he staggered and she kicked him backward. The wand she had could also deal heavy strikes, as Kroscar soon learned when she hit him with it and sent him sailing across the Battle Zone. The audience was delighted with the spectacle. Christie's attack had only enraged the dog-man, however, and he very quickly became wise to her methods. After the Dream Queen evaded several attacks from his battle-axe, Kroscar tossed his weapon aside and decided to fight with his clawed hands. He grabbed Christie's right arm and twisted it until she dropped her wand. He could have broken her arm if he wanted to, but was distracted by the wand. He threw her aside and kicked the wand beyond her grasp. Christie was at a slight disadvantage without her weapon, but could still defend herself well. She tried attacking Kroscar with a series of swift strikes and kicks, most of which he blocked or dodged until she landed a powerful kick to the head that knocked the dog-man down.

The enraged Kroscar leaped up immediately. Christie used the abilities of her suit once more to quickly fly out of the way as he leaped at her. She was very quick, and evaded many of Kroscar's attacks while landing several strikes of her own. Her suit gave her incredible strength, but Kroscar was very resistant to her strikes, and only became angrier with each blow the Dream Queen landed.

It was at this point that small bombs landed into the Battle Zone and exploded, emitting a strange grey smoke. Nobody saw where these came from, but several Mad Dogs surrounded the Battle Zone and threw them in. This was technically against the rules, but Mr. Spiderhat ignored the interference and let the match continue. He knew what the Mad Dogs were up to, but he wanted Christie to lose the match. Mr. Spiderhat secretly hated women and this made his ire for Christie even greater. One of the bombs struck Christie and disoriented the Dream Queen temporarily. This foul turn was enough to allow Kroscar to gain a distinct advantage, and he kicked Christie hard in the stomach. Although her suit protected her from taking extremely harmful damage, Kroscar followed up with several strikes that subdued his opponent.

Soon Kroscar caught Christie and had her on the ground. Although Mr. Spiderhat was against the Mad Dogs in the public eye, he was secretly delighted that Kroscar had her down. She was on her stomach as the prospective Mad Dog member sat on her back. He placed his clawed hands on her neck and pulled her head back. The position appeared very painful, but Christie held on as long as she could. Her suit would normally have allowed her to easily escape this hold, but the smoke that she breathed in hindered her mind and she could not concentrate. In fact, the effect of the destructive smoke enhanced the pain of Kroscar's hold. Kroscar pulled harder and further, and soon the Dream Queen was nearly bent in half. She then lifted her open palm and tapped on the ground in the gesture of submission, thus ending the contest. Kroscar was declared the winner despite the cheating that occurred.

The crowd was still stunned at Kroscar's return, but nobody cheered him when he won the match. The Dream Queen was too popular and the Mad Dogs too detested in Main City for Kroscar to get a positive reaction. The Rabbit-Man's fury was now at an all-time high and he could no longer bear to watch such a spectacle. He refrained from interfering even when he saw the bombs entering the Battle Zone because it seemed like Christie might still win, and he did not wish to disrespect her or get her disqualified by getting involved. Now he was as disgusted as ever. Before the officials came to pull the defeated Dream Queen away and send her to Mr. Spiderhat's web (which the Rabbit-Man was familiar with), he decided he could not tolerate the injustice any more. The Rabbit-Man ran forward, leaped over the balcony, and directly into the Battle Zone. He stood near the prone Dream Queen and helped her to her feet. The effect of the poison smoke wore off and Christie's strength returned. She walked off to the side of the Battle Zone feeling disappointed and angry. She feared she had failed her dear friend Twinklette. The Rabbit-Man called to an official to get him a megaphone. Once he had one, he addressed Mr. Spiderhat and everyone in the arena.

"I've seen enough of this damn show and I'm tired of it!" he shouted, and then turned to Mr. Spiderhat, "You disgusting creep! You just sit there on your web and watch people tear one another apart, just so you can profit from their misery! That has gone on too long! You have grown fat from the pain of luckless people for too long and I won't let it go on anymore!" The Rabbit-Man then addressed the audience, "And all of you good-for-nothing cretins just sit here and endorse such things the whole time! You are just as much to blame for the agony that occurs in here as this nasty, fat old spider! I'm going to tell you all something right now, and let me make myself perfectly clear – This show and the Grand Coliseum that hosts it both really suck! There is no such thing as genuine entertainment in this rotten place, except from people like the Dream Queen who was just cheated. You all saw it! Main City is nothing but a festering dump that is ruled by soulless monsters that will destroy other people for sport and think nothing of it. I once saw a place where life was valued, and I would give anything to be there again, but I can't. And because I can't get back to where I was, I'll do what I can where I am now!" With this said the Rabbit-Man put his megaphone aside and picked up Kroscar's battle-axe from the ground. Kroscar looked on with amusement as the Rabbit-Man spun around with the axe in his hand before letting it go and sending it flying up toward Mr. Spiderhat's perch. The Grandie spider evaded the attack, but was obviously distraught by it. The Rabbit-Man then picked up his megaphone again.

"I want the wretched Morphie that calls itself a champion to come out here now!" he shouted. "Where are you Eagle Top? Come on out and face the Rabbit-Man! Come on champion! You're not afraid of me, are you? Bring that nasty little girlfriend of yours too if you want. I don't care about your stupid championship and your crown and whatever other little decorations you have. I just want to rip those tail feathers from your butt and shove them down your foul throat!" Now the audience was utterly flabbergasted. The Grand Coliseum show was usually interesting when drama was stirred up, but nothing quite like this ever occurred before. Kroscar was quite amused by this spectacle, and very much enjoyed watching the Rabbit-Man go on his tirade; the prospective Mad Dog agreed with most of it himself. Of course Kroscar was unaware of Rip A. Sunder's behind-the-scenes deal with Spiderhat, but this did not matter at the moment. For now he watched the Rabbit-Man call the G.C. Champion out.

Soon a symphonic melody was heard throughout the arena and Eagle Top emerged. He did not come through one of the two main doors that opened onto the Battle Zone, but rather emerged from just beneath Spiderhat's perch. He spread his wings and glided down into the Battle Zone. His girlfriend Diva

Sweetbud was not with him as he descended. Eagle Top held the Championship Crown in his hand and walked up to the Rabbit-Man. He towered above him, but the Rabbit-Man was not intimidated by him as he was the last time they met. He did not know if Eagle Top recognized him from before, but he did not care. All he was concerned about was making an impression, and also securing an opportunity for Christie Starlight and Twinklette to escape the Coliseum. This partly worked, because as Eagle Top was making his entrance, Twinklette snuck down to the Battle Zone unnoticed. As the Rabbit-Man went on his rant, Christie moved away near the door on the side of the battleground she entered from. She was still in some pain and was aching from her match, but Twinklette met her there, and she held the girl close to her as they had a tearful reunion.

Eagle Top now had a megaphone of his own and addressed the Rabbit-Man's taunts. He was performing now, and he moved and spoke with a very dignified manner. This contrasted with how he acted backstage, but that did not matter. As long as the audience perceived him as a righteous hero, that was all that mattered to him and Spiderhat. "Your audacity will be your downfall, little Rabbit-Man," said Eagle Top. "I don't know who you are or why you are doing something so stupid, but I assure you that I can defeat you easily. It is well that you do not desire my championship because you don't have a hope of gaining it. Nevertheless, I will not ignore your challenge. It has been a while since I squashed an enemy like you and showed off my true strength, and I feel like doing so now."

"Hold it right there!" shouted Kroscar, who moved to the side and watched how events would unfold. But by now he decided he watched long enough. He said with a megaphone of his own, "I see what the two of you are doing. Don't think I'm going to stand by and let the attention be turned away from the Mad Dogs – who will soon own this Coliseum! If anyone wins the crown from Eagle Top it will be a member of the Mad Dogs. Let me give you a glimpse of what we are capable of." He then turned to the door on his side of the Battle Zone and called to two of his friends that were waiting behind it. "Hey Turnoff and Abbo, let the folks here in the Grand Coliseum see the Blackwind Train!" The door busted open and a long black metal snake-like miniature train shot into the Battle Zone. Atop the train was a grungy man dressed similar to the Mad Dogs and a woman wearing black face paint. The train busted into the Battle Zone so quickly that the Rabbit-Man and Eagle Top both had to leap out of the way before being run down by it. Kroscar then jumped onto the train as it circled the Battle Zone. It then shot into the air and up onto the balcony and ran among the audience. The frightened viewers either leapt from its path or were run down. There was now mass panic in the Coliseum, and all order was disrupted. Spiderhat was livid when this occurred and called to Eagle Top to get control of Kroscar and his allies. The Rabbit-Man did not like the audience in the arena, but he was still troubled by how mercilessly the train operators ran over some of the viewers without a care. The friends of Kroscar called Turnoff and Abbo seemed to be enjoying themselves very much.

The Rabbit-Man saw his opportunity and took it. He ran over to Christie and Twinklette and introduced himself quickly. "I know Selene and Geb, and I know you both need to get back to them. Let's get out of here while we have the chance!" They then ran back through the door Christie entered in and away from the Battle Zone while all of the commotion ensued on the balconies and throughout the Coliseum. They came to the exit and ran away quickly without being noticed. Such uproar was made at the event that several Guard Dogs were running to the Coliseum, but none of them noticed the Rabbit-Man or his friends fleeing.

Meanwhile Eagle Top pursued Kroscar and the others, trying to get hold of the train and stop the chaos. The Blackwind Train was too swift even for him, and it soon busted through a window in the Coliseum's side and went downward. Kroscar, Turnoff, and Abbo all managed to get inside one of the cars of the wormlike train as it hit the ground outside the arena and burrowed a hole into it. The vehicle then somehow covered the ground behind it and was gone. The Guard Dogs, the Patrolmen, and Eagle Top could not pursue them. Order was then restored in the Coliseum after some time, though Spiderhat's reputation suffered greatly after the scene. He did not forgive the intruders and swore he would take revenge upon them all. An idea began to blossom in his mind of how he could defeat his enemies and regain control of Main City once and for all. This scene with the Blackwind Train was not something the Grandie spider had agreed on with Rip A. Sunder, and Mr. Spiderhat was enraged when he eventually discovered Twinklette and Christie Starlight escaped the Grand Coliseum. The Grandie who owned the Coliseum intended to make sure his authority would never be challenged again, and even began to rethink his deal with the Mad Dogs.

Chapter Eighteen
The Hall of the Elite

It was clear that the success of the Mad Dogs as a force of opposition was firmly established in Main City when Kroscar and his friends used the Blackwind Train in the Grand Coliseum. The Rabbit-Man was as surprised as everyone else when he saw it, and how it swarmed over any surface like a large snake. He did not see it burrow into the ground and cover its hole behind it. He was too busy escaping the Grand Coliseum with Christie Starlight and Twinklette. This they managed to do effectively, and the Rabbit-Man swiftly brought his friends to Geb's Vegetable Patch, which was kept safe by the presence of the metal giant. The Rabbit-Man ran remarkably fast in his suit as Christie held Twinklette in her arms and glided along. Because they both had suits from the metal giant Cyber Wurko Christie was able to keep up with him easily.

Geb and Selene were pleased at their arrival, and Selene embraced her longtime friend Christie. The Rabbit-Man could not help but wonder where his old friend Mr. One had gone to. He was sure the commotion that was caused by the Mad Dogs would overshadow Mr. One's escape and Sig Calcium's second offense to the power structure in Main City. It was becoming clear in the entire Metroscape that the power of Mr. Spiderhat and the Guard Dogs was weakening. Everyone in Main City noticed it, though nobody dared to say it aloud. It seemed like the Mad Dogs were truly invading Main City, although it only appeared this way because nearly everyone was unaware of Mr. Spiderhat's secret deal with Rip A. Sunder. The Rabbit-Man was also oblivious to the deal and believed Mr. Spiderhat and the Mag Dogs were truly at odds with one another. He thought the rising influence of the Mad Dogs was a good thing overall, though he questioned whether they would be a good replacement for the Caretaking Body. It was a grim thought, and neither the CTB nor the gang seemed desirable as rulers.

After the Rabbit-Man exchanged greetings with Geb and Selene, they were met with another visitor in the vegetable patch. To their collective surprise, it was Kroscar Hunderbar. He walked up and extended his hand to the Rabbit-Man. After a moment of hesitation, the Rabbit-Man shook it. Although he detested Kroscar's cheating methods in his match with the Dream Queen, the Rabbit-Man did not want to cause commotion in the Vegetable Patch if he could help it.

"That was a pretty impressive display you made earlier," Kroscar said. "I can tell you're no friend of the Caretaking Body yourself. You can come with me to a hideout of the Mad Dogs if you like. We can use the efforts of someone like you." He grinned as he said this. Christie Starlight glared at Kroscar and was ready to confront him, but Twinklette held her back. For the sake of her friend she resisted her urge to fight Kroscar again, though she was sure she would defeat him in a fair duel.

"Look Kroscar, I understand your grudge with Eagle Top," the Rabbit-Man said. "And I hate him and Spiderhat and the Caretaking Body, but I have no intention of joining the Mad Dogs."

"You don't have to join if you don't want to," Kroscar said. "I just happen to see a common interest among us. I'm coming to you here because I want to see if you're interested in bringing down the power structure in Main City once and for all. I can tell by the way you shouted at those slugs in the Coliseum that you have been wronged by this place – very severely wronged, as so many others have. I've had enough of it and I want to get back at them. Why don't you at least come and meet with us and hear what we have to say? Some of your friends can come if they like." The Rabbit-Man turned to the others. Christie and Twinklette viewed Kroscar with understandable displeasure, and Selene's expression showed the same. The Dream Queen had not forgotten the ferocity and underhanded methods Kroscar fought with.

"Rabbit-Man, you seem like a good guy, but you would have to be crazy to trust him," said Christie, still holding Twinklette close to her.

"I don't like the sound of that either, Rabbit-Man," said Geb. "You can do whatever you like, but I'm not going to affiliate myself with anything the

Mad Dogs are doing. The choice is yours." The Rabbit-Man thought about this. He would very much have liked to stay with Geb and the others. He even might have considered making a home in the Vegetable Patch if there was room for him. However, his grudge with Main City was too strong, and Kroscar's offer got his attention. If the Mad Dogs had a plan of attack against the Caretaking Body he would at least like to hear it. After all the pain and hardship they caused him and his friends, he longed to take revenge on them. He did not like the way Kroscar fought against Christie Starlight, but he also remembered the impaled corpse of Try Wonder due to the actions of the Caretaking Body. Although he felt remorse, he decided he should at least hear Kroscar's proposal.

"There is another reason aside from helping Twinklette why I went back to the Grand Coliseum, after all," he told Geb and the others. "I have to finish what I started. I still believe it is my duty to get back at the Caretaking Body in some way. Thank you for all your help Geb, I really appreciate it. Christie, Twinklette, Selene- it was a pleasure meeting you all, and I truly wish you all the best. I'm going to go with Kroscar for now though, and see what he has to say."

"I wish you all the best too, Rabbit-Man," said Geb. The Rabbit-Man embraced Geb and then Selene.

"Thank you for helping us." Christie told him before he hugged her and Twinklette. "Thank you for saving me!" he told the girl. " I might not even be here if not for your bravery.

"You might be small Twinklette, but you have a strong spirit. It's encouraging to see that in someone as young as you. I'm glad I could return the favor." He then turned and followed Kroscar out of the Vegetable Patch. They walked on until they came to the area with blackened ground between the Patch and the rest of Main City. Here Turnoff and Abbo were waiting with the long worm-like Blackwind Train close behind them. Although the Rabbit-Man knew his own intentions were pure, he could not shake the feeling that he was affiliating with villains by joining this crew. His resolve remained firm despite this.

"Good t'meet ya," said Turnoff in a very low, grumbling voice as he shook hands with the Rabbit-Man.

"Are ya ready for a ride?" Abbo asked him. He noticed the black designs of her face paint more distinctly when he met her up close, but he had no idea what it meant, if anything.

"Hop aboard the train, Rabbit-Man!" said Kroscar. "You are about to meet the Mad Dogs!" He then leapt into one of the cars of the train as the roof closed above him. Turnoff went into the front car along with Abbo, so the Rabbit-Man went into the one behind Kroscar. As the roof to the car closed above him, he felt like he was being trapped in the vehicle. It was too late to leave, however, when the train started moving and darted down into the ground. It tunneled deep and moved far until it stopped. There the roofs of the cars were removed and the Rabbit-Man saw he was underground. Kroscar and the others led him though a dark tunnel beside the train in an underground cavern where the vehicle stopped. After walking some distance they came to an opening. Inside was lined with lights and it reminded the Rabbit-Man of a more furnished version of Arman Tier's underground hall. There was a large picture of a black demon holding a sword with outstretched wings. Beneath this image the words "Hall of the Elite" were written. Inside was a long table where several members of the Mad Dog Tribe were seated. At the head of the table was Rip A. Sunder their leader.

"It's about time you showed up!" Rip said to Kroscar and the others as they entered. There were not many Mad Dogs in the room, but there were more than the Rabbit-Man expected.

"Allow me to welcome our three newest members – Kroscar Hunderbar and Turnoff and Abbo!" There were cheers in the room as the three of them entered. The Rabbit-Man felt more and more uncomfortable as this went on. He disliked the Caretaking Body, but was not fond of the Mad Dogs either. Still, he agreed to hear their plans and he would do so. Kroscar then introduced him to the group.

"This is the Rabbit-Man," said Kroscar. "He called out Eagle Top in the Grand Coliseum and expressed an interest in bringing down the power structure of Main City."

"I'm glad to hear it," Rip said to the Rabbit-Man. "I don't blame you for wanting to be on the winning side. We will indeed be taking over the Grand Coliseum once and for all, and a new age will dawn in Main City." Again the Mad Dogs that were present cheered. "All hail the new dawn!" they cried in unison. "The power of the Caretaking Body is finally beginning to weaken in all of the Metroscapes." Rip continued. "I have spoken with Tribe members in other Metroscapes, and similar things are happening there. I've even heard there is much internal dissent among the Caretaking Body itself, and that's why it's collapsing. We'll capitalize on this to seize control of Main City, and then we'll exterminate everybody from the old regime."

Now the Rabbit-Man felt more uncomfortable than ever before. He wondered just who the Mad Dogs would regard as members of the "old regime" and also how many people this would entail. What good would it be, thought the Rabbit-Man, if the terrible reign of the Caretaking Body ended only to be replaced by a bloodbath of more terror and pain? He did not like the idea, and then Kroscar said something that made him even more ill at ease in the underground room.

"If only we could summon the powers of the legendary Warface to help us," Kroscar said to the gathering. "He would help us tremendously. In fact, we would be essentially unbeatable with his aid." The Rabbit-Man recalled his conversation with Arman Tier, and remembered how the old man mentioned Warface and his uncontrollable rage. "He would have the potential to destroy the entire world, and would do so if he could" was one thing Arman Tier said about him. The Rabbit-Man then discovered that Warface was the black demon pictured in the image at the back side of the Hall of the Elite. He then spoke up.

"I think that would be a very bad idea," he said to them all. "I know of someone who tried doing something like that before. The owl-man Howler Highhorse claimed he would create a new beginning in the greatest Bastion of all. He said the key to this would be to remove the giant boulder located at the Base Pad. I was there, and I know firsthand that it cannot be moved – nor should it be. Supposedly Warface dwells under that great rock. But he is an uncontrollable monster, and he would have ruined everything in existence. To free him would be disastrous."

"How do you know that for sure?" asked Rip. "You don't even know who Warface really is. Maybe he would destroy people like you, who come from a Bastion, but we would flourish with him in our ranks. I believe he would value a tribe like the Mad Dogs, as we would deliver him a steady supply of weaklings to feast upon."

"I have heard of the Great White Calling before," said Kroscar. "I'm surprised that you made it to the Base Pad, Rabbit-Man. I would have done so myself if I had not met the Mad Dog Tribe and found my place among them. I still think moving the boulder is a good idea, and if it would assist Warface in resurfacing again I think it would be even better yet. If you and the owl-man couldn't do it, that's too bad, but I think me and the Mad Dogs definitely could."

"Howler Highhorse is destroyed," the Rabbit-Man told him. "He was devoured by a monster called Hayt the Hungry, who was summoned forth by a demon similar to this Warface that you are so fond of. Perhaps you are right, Mr. Sunder, I don't know much of Warface and who he really is. I don't want to. I want nothing to do with the likes of him."

"Then I don't know why you're even here!" said Turnoff with a scowl in his grumbling voice. "The Hall of the Elite is for the strong and ruthless only. We want to kill those who deserve it. If you don't have what it takes to remain with us, go back to some little Bastion with other fuzzy little friends and stupid Bitties and don't bother with us."

"You're right, I don't belong with you," the Rabbit-Man said. "And for that, I am quite glad. Your obstinate and hollow pride will be you ultimate downfall. The Caretaking Body may be wrong, but none of you are right."

"Then leave and go about your business," said Rip. "It's not a problem for us. If you ain't a Mad Dog, you ain't a Mad Dog, and that's all there is too it." The Rabbit-Man then turned to leave, and was given a final dark look by Turnoff as he left. He went hastily out of the tunnel and passed the Blackwind Train again. Behind it a tunnel went on. He continued along this in darkness until he finally came to a slope. He used his carrot-tipped power rod to blast a hole out of the top which he then leaped through to the surface. Once he did so, he was on the black ground on the outskirts of Main City once more. He was glad to be away from the Hall of the Elite and never intended to re-turn. He wished to go back to the Vegetable Patch of Geb and meet the others once more. He was sickened by the ideas of the Mad Dogs. "They really *are* mad." he thought to himself, and wondered how there could be any hope for the future. It was another difficult moment for him, and as he walked along he was met by an old enemy once more. It was twilight, and the sky above him was darkening, and as he moved along he heard a familiar cackling behind him. It was the Ghost of Despair – who had recovered since their last encounter. The Rabbit-Man turned and saw his foe. The ghost was hovering in the air with his dark blue cloak floating around and beneath him. The Rabbit-Man knew the wraith would try to trap him in the cloak once more, but with his new suit he was sure he would be able to outrun it. He did not want to return to the Vegetable Patch just then, however, because he did not want to lead the ghost to it. Instead he turned and confronted the ghost.

"What do you want?" he asked. "If you think I'm going to join the Blue Demon – or whatever it is you want me to do – the answer is still no. I might as well just align myself with the Mad Dogs if I was going to do something like that!"

"That would be a good idea if you did," the ghost replied. "You would be in a much better situation than you are now. You have a new outfit, but your friends are not with you now, and the entire world is in more danger than it was when you first arrived in the Metroscape." The ghost then floated to the ground until he hovered just before the Rabbit-Man. "Your Bastion is not the only one that was destroyed – it is steadily happening to many others. The Bastion that the foolish owl-man believed a staircase led to does not even exist anymore, and the staircase beneath the great boulder was destroyed by War-face and his minions. The only choice facing Main City now is whether the Caretaking Body defeats the Mad Dogs, restores itself to its full power, and instills an even stricter rule over its miserable citizens; or if the Mad Dogs do indeed manage to overcome the CTB, they will enforce a militant rule over the city that will cause just as much, if not more, pain and chaos than the CTB ever did. You know this, Rabbit-Man, and I'm sure by now you realize there is nothing at all you can do to prevent the disaster."

"You are trying to overwhelm me with distress and sorrow," the Rabbit-Man answered. "You've been doing this to people for a very long time, and the Blue Demon named you well, Ghost of Despair. I'm not going to let you control my mind. I know what is important, and if I cannot help this wretched world that is far beyond redemption, I can at least help myself and the few people I care about as best I can. The Base Pad is not the place for me, nor is the Hall of the Elite. Main City is not where I belong either. I have no place in this world, and that is a difficult thing. But many others have gotten by with even less than that. Arman Tier has been an outlaw in every Metroscape he has ever been to, and still he pushes on. I am no Arman Tier, and I don't wish to be. I am the Rabbit-Man; I am me. I don't need much more than that. In fact, I don't need anything beside that."

The Rabbit-Man then swung his carrot rod and struck the ghost's sickly head with it. The wraith shrunk back with a shriek, but then he flew forward and stuck his long pointed fingers into the Rabbit-Man's stomach intending to impale him. The suit was resilient to the attack. The Rabbit-Man kicked the ghost away and beat him onto the ground with his carrot rod. He took the opportunity to practice some moves he was eager to try and hoped he could have used on Eagle Top in the Grand Coliseum. He was happy to settle with using them on the Ghost of Despair instead. Fist he plunged his carrot rod into the ground and pummeled the ghost's head with a series of rapid blows he called the Pounding Punch. He then took up his carrot rod again to use its firearm capabilities and riddled the ghost with missiles. His foe was driven backward, but then flew forward again with intimidating speed. The Rabbit-Man was too quick, however, and he executed a move in which he quickly spun himself around as his opponent headed toward him. He then began striking his enemy in the abdomen with his right elbow, then in the face, and then in the abdomen twice again. The Rabbit-Man then spun around once more and delivered a punch to the wraith's face. He called this move the Rhythmic Elbow Beat, and it sent the Ghost of Despair reeling. The dreadful spirit then flew off.

The Rabbit-Man's stomach began to sear with pain, and he fell to the ground clutching it. It was an aftereffect of the dark magic used in the ghost's first attack. The Rabbit-Man laid there hurting into the night, and heard the cackling of the ghost in his mind. "I infected you with my seed of sorrow using my infectious powers." the ghost said. "It will grow within you, and soon your guts will look like mine did. There is no more hope for you Rabbit-Man. The only choice before you is this: let yourself deteriorate into a ghost even more wretched than I am, or kill yourself now before such a thing can happen. The choice is yours, either way you are defeated, so just accept it. No fine suit can help you now. You are on your own and beyond rescue."

The Rabbit-Man then forced the voice of the ghost out of his mind, but his stomach still troubled him severely. He lay on the ground in agony for some time before an incredible bout of fatigue overwhelmed him and caused him to fall asleep. He was oblivious to the rest of the world as he slept. As he lay unconscious the ghost descended upon him and the Rabbit-Man was engulfed in the Ghost of Despair's cloak once again. This time he was troubled by dark dreams of his enemy's foul heart and intestines, and he dreamed they took up residence inside him and destroyed him. Through these bad dreams the Rabbit-Man returned to the nightmare country once more, this time with no friends to help him in his struggle in that dark territory.

Chapter Nineteen
Return to the Nightmare Country

The Rabbit-Man's second experience in the nightmare country was much different than his first one. Before when he was absorbed into the Ghost of Despair's cloak he had two friends to help him get out of it. Now the ghost was troubling his mind and he was alone. This second struggle was the more difficult. In this dark dream world he was again standing in a flat and desolate landscape similar to that surrounding Main City. Only the land in the nightmare country was darker – the sky was covered with thick black clouds and red lightning shot through them. The ground was black and grey with patches of red, as if there were spots beneath in which burning magma was close to the surface. Before him, amid the lightning, the ground rose up in a large mound that stood high above him. It morphed itself into the head of the owl-man Howler Highhorse, and the eyes glowed red from behind the curved glasses.

"Why didn't you help me move the boulder, Rabbit-Man? It was your duty!" The head then began to shake rapidly until it exploded and rock pieces flew off in all directions. Then, where the giant head was, he saw Pertho standing before him. She was holding her baby in her arms once more, and the Rabbit-Man noticed that the severed head of the fly-man was lying by her feet. As Pertho stood there the Rabbit-Man tried to call out to her, but he could not. His voice did not seem to work in the nightmare world. He was then frozen in the spot where he stood. Pertho grew larger and larger and walked forward.

She stepped on the Rabbit-Man and squashed him into the ground. He remained alive as a pile of visceral mass and was still able to see.

Then a giant Diva Sweetbud appeared and approached Pertho. Diva held out her hands and demanded that Pertho hand over the infant. Pertho reluctantly did so, but then fell onto the ground in front of Diva and begged her not to harm the child. Diva laughed and then, to the Rabbit-Man's horror, her head changed into that of Mr. Spiderhat. The infant began to cry before it was consumed by Spiderhat's head on Diva's body. Pertho wept on the ground and shrunk back to her normal size. Then a crack split in the ground's surface and widened until she and the spider-headed giant Diva fell into it. After this Arman Tier climbed out from the crack, and he was holding a carrot stick identical to the Rabbit-Man's. Then Hayt the Hungry appeared and leaped after Arman Tier. The old man tried to fight the monster but was overcome. Hayt the Hungry held him in his jaws and then threw him back down into the crack in the ground. The monster then looked at the Rabbit-Man and laughed. The Rabbit-Man then realized his body was back to normal and not squashed anymore, but he was trapped in a web like Mr. Spiderhat's and could not move. He also noticed he was now completely naked in this nightmare – no rabbit suit of any kind nor any clothes.

Hayt the Hungry then stood over him, and morphed into the intestines with a face that the Rabbit-Man encountered when he was previously inside the cloak of the ghost. The face in the intestines then changed into his own face, and it spit its green fluid onto the trapped naked Rabbit-Man. This was a terrible nightmare, and the Rabbit-Man was determined to find a way out of it. He was still dreaming within the ghost's cloak. He had to somehow find a way to wake himself up and fight back against the enemy, because knowledge that he was in a dream was not enough to do so. He struggled inside the web but it only became tighter. He then spit back at the intestines. To his surprise, he produced clear water from his mouth when he spit and the intestines shrank away. He then spit water onto himself and freed himself from the web. He stood up and walked forward. He saw something coming toward him in the distance. It was the Blackwind Train, with Turnoff and Abbo and Kroscar at the head of it. The Rabbit-Man then decided, since this was a dream, to change himself into a massive rabbit Grandie. He did this, and then kicked the Blackwind Train out of his way as if it were a toy. Then before him was the metal giant Cyber Wurko, only now he was even larger than in the Vegetable Patch, and he was standing upright. Then the face of the metal giant fell away, and beneath it was a face the Rabbit-Man never saw before. It had bushy grey eyebrows and a beard similar to the owl-man's but somehow the Rabbit-Man knew in the dream that this was the face of an aged Kroscar Hunderbar. This metal giant with old man Kroscar's face came after him swiftly, but he moved out of the way. The Rabbit-Man, in his Grandie dream-form, saw that many black spikes rose from the ground around him. The giant with Kroscar's face tripped and fell face-first onto one of these spikes. The Rabbit-Man then turned and saw a staircase extending into the sky. The thick dark clouds parted where the stairs went and a beautiful white light shined down. "That's where I need to be." the Rabbit-Man said to himself and headed toward the staircase. Before he could reach it the Blue Demon appeared before him.

"Don't go that way, it's bad for you," said the Blue Demon grinning. He wore a black robe around himself and his wings spread ominously behind him. He raised his hand and a black fireball formed in its palm. He made ready to blast the Grandie rabbit with the fire and destroy him, when an idea occurred to the Rabbit-Man in his dream-state. He imagined the fireball turning into a big ball of flower Bitties with smiling faces. This happened, and the flower-Bitties scattered on the ground. They danced around the Blue Demon and started singing a song. The Blue Demon shrieked in horror as the tiny little flower-people did this. They then hopped onto his body and started dancing on him. The Blue Demon began to shrink as this happened, and now it was the Rabbit-Man's turn to laugh at him. He realized his own thoughts and imagination also had an effect in this dream world, and that it was his best defense against the ghost's tricks. The Rabbit-Man laughed at the Blue Demon's comical predicament in the dream and the demon became smaller and smaller as the flowers danced upon him. Finally the Rabbit-Man in Grandie form leaped over the whole scene and went toward the stairway and the light above it. A large, friendly-looking squirrel Grandie with a ribbon on her head peeped out from behind the staircase. "Great Job!" she called to the Rabbit-Man, and then she went up the stairway into the light. The Rabbit-Man leaped up the steps toward the light. He almost made it there before he woke.

He sat up on the ground. It was morning; he must have slept a long time. The memory of the dream quickly faded from his mind, but he felt very refreshed and the pain in his stomach was gone. He looked around and saw no sign of the old wicked ghost anywhere. He did not see the Blue Demon or Hayt the Hungry, or any of the Mad Dogs either, and for this he was quite relieved but also confused. He got up, and decided to go back to the Vegetable

Patch and see how everyone was doing there. Although he was not consciously aware of it at the time, he had temporarily defeated the Nightmare Country as the Ghost of Despair let him go due to his resilience in the dream-state. But the Rabbit-Man would meet the ghost called Despair once more.

Chapter Twenty
The Fury of the Mad Dogs

The Rabbit-Man was welcomed enthusiastically at the Vegetable Patch. He was very happy to be there, and he felt like a terrible burden was lifted from his shoulders. The Dream Queen Christie Starlight and Twinklette stayed with Selene in a home near Geb's house, but they were all working in the Vegetable Patch with the Bitties when the Rabbit-Man returned. "We were very worried about you." Geb said as he sat down with the others in his house for lunch. "Those Mad Dogs are crazy; they think they will overcome the Caretaking Body by gaining control of the Grand Coliseum, but I think Mr. Spiderhat will beat them in the end. Despite the numerous setbacks he encountered, he's very cunning and he'll find a way to defeat them once and for all."

"I think so too," the Rabbit-Man said. "The Mad Dogs are too arrogant and are becoming overconfident in themselves. Of course, they really have given Spiderhat a run for all he's worth, but they think too highly of their gang – especially Kroscar, who is now officially one of their members."

"That doesn't surprise me," said Christie with a frown; she and Twinklette remembered her match with Kroscar vividly and had not forgiven him. "To be honest with you, I hope they are defeated by Spiderhat." said Christie, "I hate that spider and Eagle Top very much, but at least you know what to expect from them. They are terrible, but in my opinion the Mad Dogs are even worse. I think most people prefer the Caretaking Body to rule Main City simply because they are the lesser of two evils."

"The lesser of two evils is still an evil," the Rabbit-Man said. "The best scenario will be for both sides to destroy one another, but even that might result in unimaginable chaos. This does not seem like a good situation, no matter how one looks at it. Did any of you hear any news on the T-Web screen?"

"I have been checking mine, and Spiderhat is really livid from both Sig Calcium's rescue of Mr. One, and especially the recent episode with the Mad Dogs," said Geb. "He will not let any of them have a match against Eagle Top, though. It's starting to become obvious that he fears the Mad Dogs, and is very nervous that they may have a better chance of conquering the Coliseum than anyone originally thought. Kroscar is scheduled to have a match tonight, though I did not hear who his opponent is supposed to be. It might be worthwhile to watch and see."

The Rabbit-Man assisted the Bitties with work in the Vegetable Patch, and that night he and the others did as Geb suggested. Geb's screen was located in the front room of his home, and he had enough wooden chairs with cushions for everyone to sit on. Twinklette still shuddered when she saw or heard mention of Kroscar Hunderbar or Eagle Top, and Christie's distaste for both of them was obvious. The competitions had become very gruesome, and they did not watch most of the matches, but rather paid more attention to the announcements in between that told them news of what was occurring. It turned out that Mr. Spiderhat told Kroscar he had recruited a new competitor among his ranks – somebody that had much to gain from winning a match in the Grand Coliseum. Kroscar replied that he was eager to face anybody that Spiderhat would give him. Everyone watching in Geb's house was very interested to see who Kroscar's opponent would be, as was all of Main City.

That evening the time came for Kroscar to compete. To the surprise of everyone, his opponent was Sig Calcium. Mr. Spiderhat did something very clever when he introduced Sig Calcium into the Battle Zone: he claimed that he arranged a deal with the wanted bird-suited outlaw to compete in the Grand Coliseum for a pardeon of his severe offences. He knew Sig had gained much silent popularity along with his notoriety in recent weeks, and thus arranged the competition to make him into a celebrated hero rather than a suspicious villain as Sig was previously portrayed on the T-Web stations. This tactic made Kroscar even more hated among the audience in the Grand Coliseum. In reality, unknown to the general public, Sig was eventually captured by the Guard Dogs, and was given a chance to compete in the Coliseum for Mr. Spiderhat's purposes. The Rabbit-Man would later learn that Sig Calcium had a battle with the Guard Dogs that he narrowly escaped, and in a very injured state he crawled to Dag's grove for help. The Bittie family of Dag and Sweetberry helped the brave bird-suited rebel recover his strength, and when Sig was in good condition again, he returned to the Grand Coliseum and saved Mr. One. He brought the Rabbit-Man's old friend back to the grove, where they lived with Sally Wonder and Twig Duckly. Mr. One and Sig both intended to move on soon, but Dag insisted they stay because his place was well guarded. In the end it did not matter. The tiny recorder worms that floated through the air followed Sig to Dag's grove and reported the secret location to the Main Patrol. The Patrolmen and Guard Dogs received reinforcements from the Caretaking Body and Dag's grove was raided. Sally Wonder and Twig, who were also staying there, were captured along with Dag and Sweetberry and their entire family. Arman Tier's son Herman Longhorn tried to resist the raid and defend those present in the grove, but he was overcome and beaten to death by Boss Barns, Chief of the Patrolmen. Mr. Spiderhat heard of this and began setting up competitions for his show. He said he would allow Sig Calcium and Mr. One to compete against the Mad Dogs on behalf of everyone captured in the grove for their freedom. They had no choice but to agree. Now, as those gathered in Geb's house watched on the screen, Mr. Spiderhat revealed one of his new "token competitors" that he mentioned to Kroscar and the Mad Dogs. This was Sig Calcium.

"I don't believe it!" the Rabbit-Man shouted as they watched the show. "Why would Sig Calcium return and join with Spiderhat?"

"Probably because he didn't have a choice," said Christie Starlight, and the Rabbit-Man understood what she meant. He knew Sig must have been caught and was now competing to save his own life. "I wonder if Mr. One is with him." said the Rabbit-Man. "They were last seen together. Maybe he is part of Mr. Spiderhat's team also." When this occurred to the Rabbit-Man, he felt compelled to rush to the aid of his longtime friend. He knew Mr. One was most likely in the Grand Coliseum as well, and was therefore in great danger.

"Look everyone, I have to go," said the Rabbit-Man. "If Mr. One is there, I cannot leave him and Sig Calcium to be destroyed by any of these wretched foes – Mad Dogs or Guards Dogs or Grandies or whatever they may be. Mr. One helped me in my hour of need after I left the Base Pad, and he and Sig Calcium are going to need as much help as they can get. I'm off to the Grand Coliseum before it's too late. I'll crash Mr. Spiderhat's show again if I have to!" At first the others tried to persuade him not to go because of the danger, but they saw his resolve to help his friend and admired it. Christie Starlight and Geb even agreed to go with him, while Selene would stay behind and look after Twinklette, the Vegetable Patch, and the Bitties. They would be safe, as they still were in the presence of the metal giant. Twinklette was sad to see Christie go, but she understood the direness of the situation. Christie kissed her several times on the cheeks and assured the little girl she would return to her.

"Thank you both so much!" the Rabbit-Man said to Christie and Geb. "It is very kind of you to come with me, but you must understand this could possibly end very badly."

"Yes, but it needs to be done," said Geb. "We understand why you're going there, and we won't let you walk into something like that alone. I hope we can help Mr. One, and even though all likelihood is against it, I hope something good can eventually come of all this disruption." So they said farewell to Selene and Twinklette and the Bitties and then went on their way. They eventually came to the Grand Coliseum, walked past the ticket booth, and presented themselves to a guard. When they expressed interest in competing in the arena, the guard led them inside. It seemed Mr. Spiderhat was becoming very desperate to get help, and the Rabbit-Man and Christie Starlight were already known in the Coliseum from the Dream Queen's match with Kroscar. They had arrived not a moment too soon.

As they were being led to the waiting room for the competitors, the match between Kroscar and Sig Calcium had already begun and took a very strange turn. From one of the doors the Blackwind Train rode into the Battle Zone and pursued Sig Calcium. He flew away from it, but with the arrival of Turnoff and Abbo he was outnumbered. They used the same bombs against Sig as they had used in Kroscar's match against the Dream Queen. This was technically against the rules, but the non-interference rule was often overlooked. This time Mr. Spiderhat was very upset with the interference, however, and sent in several Patrolmen to stop the Blackwind Train and get Turnoff and Abbo out of the match. But the Patrolmen were all run down or attacked with smoke bombs. It was then that both Mr. One and the mushroom Bittie Dag appeared in the Battle Zone. Mr. One wielded a large firearm and Dag had two power wands. Mr. One blasted the Blackwind Train with a fireball before it could ride into the balconies among the audience again, and the front of the massive train shattered, sending debris in all direction. The train crashed into the sidewall of the Battle Zone and was destroyed. Turnoff and Abbo were enraged at this. They narrowly escaped injuries because they leaped off the train as it crashed. Mr.

One and Dag kept their weapons ready. It was not unheard of to see such a variety of weapons in the Grand Coliseum. The Rabbit-Man, Christie, Geb and the guard with them all heard the commotion and rushed to the nearest door leading to a balcony. They saw what was happening, and Mr. Spiderhat was screaming into his megaphone, cheering on Dag and Mr. One.

"So Dag is here too!" exclaimed the Rabbit-Man, who had a very bad feeling about what was happening. He could not wait to help his friends. He and his two companions, using the abilities granted by their custom suits, leaped over the balcony and into the Battle Zone. Mr. One, Sig Calcium, and Dag were glad to see them, but they were busy fighting off the Mad Dogs. The Rabbit-Man was not aware of it at the time, but Sally Wonder and Twig Duckly were both in the audience along with Sweetberry and Dag's children. Twig was thrilled when he saw the Rabbit-Man, and heartily cheered him on. Despite the new arrivals, Kroscar seemed undaunted, though Turnoff and Abbo were both still very angry at the destruction of their Blackwind Train. Mr. One fired more explosive missiles at them, but they hid behind a large piece of their train that shielded them. Kroscar laughed and called at Mr. Spiderhat, "I know you think you're clever, Spiderhat, but you aren't the only one that has a team in this match! The rest of the Mad Dogs are with me, and I'm glad you're sending forth all your recruits now, because we intend to take over the Grand Coliseum by force this very night!"

Then several other Mad Dogs ran out onto the Battle Zone to attack Kroscar's enemies. After them, other allies of the gang also ran onto the Battle Zone. Mr. Spiderhat was not pleased at this declaration, but it seemed like he was expecting it. He gave a gesture and then Eagle Top's symphonic theme music sounded as the audience erupted in cheers.

Eagle Top entered the Battle Zone along with several other competitors on Mr. Spiderhat's team. The esteemed champion called to Kroscar, "You idiot, you know the championship can only be won in a one-one-one competition! Even if you win this, the title will never be yours! You know I can beat you, and that's why you are trying to invade the Coliseum rather than win it properly. All the better for us, though, because now we will wipe out all of your stupid Tribe!" Mass fighting broke out then between the Mad Dogs and all other competitors. In all the history of the Grand Coliseum a battle like this was never seen before. Eagle Top flew throughout the Battle Zone and quickly defeated one of the Mad Dogs. The Rabbit-Man with his carrot rod and Geb with a one-handed firearm fought against the allies of the Mad Dogs that filtered onto the Battle Zone. These allies of the Mad Dogs had various animal suits and weapons, but could not compete with the suits made by the metal giant. As the Rabbit-Man and Geb fended off these other intruders, Christie Starlight tried to attack Kroscar before two other Mad Dogs intercepted her. She was able to fight both of them on her own, and neither of them dealt a single blow to the Dream Queen, though they were very resilient in the fight. Mr. One, Sig Calcium, and Dag all held their own ground, though none of them came into contact with Kroscar or any other leaders of the gang. Eagle Top and Kroscar began fighting hand-to-hand and were very evenly matched.

Amid this riotous melee, the leader of the Mad Dog Tribe Rip A. Sunder rode into the Battle Zone on one of his steel demon-headed vehicles. He nearly ran down the Rabbit-Man, who leaped out of the way just in time. He lifted a single-handed but powerful firearm and shot at the roof of the arena. He then laughed, and grabbing a megaphone, he called to Mr. Spiderhat. "Now the Coliseum is ours, with or without winning the championship! We have an ally that you cannot possibly defeat!" After Rip said this, the entire Coliseum began to shake and rumble. Before anyone knew what was happening, a large portion of the arena's roof was blown away, exposing it to the black, star-speckled night sky. Then a very large creature with black wings flew into the Battle Zone from the sky above. He held a long sword in his claws, and he landed on the ground so hard it caused another rumble throughout the arena. The Rabbit-Man recognized who it was, though he hardly believed it. He had no idea how the Mad Dogs released him, but the new entrant in the Coliseum was Warface, the black demon that Arman Tier had warned him about.

This newly-arrived menace was able to send flames spurting from the tip of his sword, and the first thing he did upon entering the Coliseum was turn and blast a flame at Mr. Spiderhat on his perch in the rafters. The Grandie spider fell far down into the arena floor with a thud. The massive spider was shouting and cursing in his naturally raspy voice as he tried to shoot his web at Warface. The demon countered and incinerated the web with his flames before it even touched him. Warface swung his sword and severed off half of the Grandie spider's legs. Mr. Spiderhat called to Eagle Top for help, but Kroscar was grappling with the champion and did not let him get away. Mr. Spiderhat quivered before the vicious black demon and begged for mercy. He offered the demon anything, and even admitted defeat and said the Mad Dogs could take the Coliseum as their own. This did not matter to Warface, who simply scowled at his prey. The demon then sliced off Spiderhat's head with the large blade of his sword and held it above him laughing.

"No!" Eagle Top shouted in despair. He could not believe what he was seeing, and neither could anyone else. Silence took the crowd as they stared on in awe. Warface then blasted flames into the audience, scorching many spectators where they stood as the Mad Dogs cheered him on. Their cheers sounded like gargling growls that served as a hellish theme song for the black demon. The Mad Dogs had double-crossed Mr. Spiderhat after all, abandoning their deal with him in favor of absolute chaos – the only environment where they and Warface could truly prevail.

Eagle Top fought with renewed intensity against Kroscar, but he still could not overcome his foe. The champion did not know Mr. Spiderhat planned to betray him, but he understood the severity of the threat of the Mad Dogs and began doubting his ability to defeat them. Screams where heard as Warface's flames singed and burnt spectators in the balconies.

"My family is in those balconies, you bastard!" cried Dag as he leaped forward with his power wands. He fought against Warface, who towered high over every other person in the Battle Zone. The Bittie was very nimble and seemed to match the demon well in the duel using his power wands. No other Bittie could have hoped to challenge a demon, least of all Warface, but Dag was exceptional and fought with amazing speed and intense passion. The Bittie used his power wands well and fought with vigor, but he could not do any harm to the fierce demon.

The fighting continued among everyone in the Battle Zone as tiny Dag and the gigantic Warface fought in the center. Luckily Dag's family and their friends remained unharmed as the flames did not scorch their section, and Sally and Twig still hoped for the Rabbit-Man and his friends to make it through this horrid spectacle that had turned into an all-out war. Eagle Top proved a fearsome foe to Kroscar and started gaining the upper hand in their duel. However, Rip A. Sunder made his way into their fight, causing the eagle Morphie to fight against both Kroscar and Rip A. Sunder at the same time. The Rabbit-Man was troubled by this, and though he detested Eagle Top's character, he still did not think he should face two skilled opponents alone. He would have made his way to the eagle Morphie if he could, but allies of the Mad Dogs blocked his path. He fought these enemies with his carrot rod and used several of his new moves such as the Pounding Punch and the Rhythmic Elbow Beat. These moves and the attacks from the power rod were very effective, and left many of his enemies unconscious. Unfortunately for the Rabbit-Man, more allies of the Mad Dogs attacked him and Geb.

Mr. One used his large firearm against Turnoff and Abbo, who remained behind wreckage from their train and attacked their opponent with their smoke bombs. Mr. One blasted many of these away as they sailed through the air, destroying the bombs and preventing them from affecting any others in the Battle Zone. Meanwhile the Dream Queen was steadily overcoming several Mad Dogs, but she was still unable to reach Kroscar and gain her much desired revenge on him for cheating her and nearly keeping Twinklette trapped in the Grand Coliseum.

Unbeknownst to those fighting in the battle Zone, one of the victims of Warface's searing flames was Eagle Top's girlfriend Diva Sweetbud, who was burnt beyond recognition by the demon's fire. It would have been a more merciful fate for her to have died. She lay on the ground wailing, but was approached by Ed Barren, who went to her side and comforted her in their final moments. He was ravaged by the flames and injured himself, but his feelings for Diva remained unchanged despite her previous insults to him. He placed a cloth on her face and held her close to him before piece of debris from the arena fell onto them and crushed them both.

In the Battle Zone the Rabbit-Man saw Daryl Fair, whom he met backstage in his first visit to the Coliseum. The orange-haired man in the green tunic was struck down and crushed by one of the Mad Dogs and the Rabbit-Man was greatly pained that he was unable to get to Daryl's aid in time to save him. Several of the Mad Dog allies began overtaking him and Geb until Sig Calcium swopped onto the scene and evened the odds. As this was occurring, the Rabbit-Man glanced over to the center of the Battle Zone and saw Dag held tightly in the grip of Warface. He tried all he could to make it to the mushroom Bittie, but he could not get past his enemies, several of whom leapt onto him and forced him to the ground. As he struggled he glanced at the duel between the Bittie and the demon. Warface mercilessly squeezed Dag's tiny body in his massive black hand and then spit fire onto his small but valiant opponent, incinerating the bravest of all Bitties. This was an awful sight, and the Rabbit-Man was overcome with grief and rage. In an adrenaline rush the Rabbit-Man leaped up from beneath the enemies huddled on top of him. He struck them all forcefully with his carrot rod and sent them flying off in all directions.

Enraged by the death of his Bittie friend the Rabbit-Man attacked Warface head-on and landed several blows on the demon with his carrot rod.

These attacks did not harm Warface severely, and he struck the Rabbit-Man down with his fist. The demon swung his blade with the intention to kill the Rabbit-Man, but S.T. Ranger evaded the strike. Warface then blasted the Rabbit-Man with flames from his sword. This greatly weakened the Rabbit-Man, but the special suit of the metal giant prevented him from being killed or severely burnt by the flames. Warface lifted the Rabbit-Man by his ankles with one hand and swung him hard into the wall of the Battle Zone with such force it left a large crack in the wall. The Rabbit-Man fell prone onto the ground. Warface turned and blasted flames that destroyed several other competitors of Mr. Spiderhat in the Battle Zone. Several Mad Dogs surrounded the weakened Rabbit-Man and might have killed him if Christie Starlight had not intervened. She fended off the Mad Dogs and quickly cast a healing spell on the Rabbit-Man that allowed him to recover enough to fight on. He clutched his carrot rod for fear of losing it as several allies of the Mad Dogs surrounded and attacked him. The Mad Dogs and their allies swarmed into the Battle Zone until they outnumbered their foes by many, and with Warface on their side defeat for their opponents appeared inevitable. It was the day Main City truly felt the fury of the Mad Dogs, and it seemed like the fate of the Metroscape would be for life to continue beneath the spiked boots of the gang, but the battle was far from over.

Chapter Twenty-One
Doom of the Powers

The Rabbit-Man could not see any sign of Geb, Christie, Mr. One or any of his other friends. He was being kicked and struck by various enemies and could not get to his feet. He clutched desperately to his carrot rod for fear of losing his weapon, when suddenly an unexpected ally came to his aid. His foes were knocked aside and over him stood Arman Tier, now wearing a metal helmet decorated with wings and a leather vest. He held two large battle-axes in his hands as he gazed at the Rabbit-Man. "Well S.T. Ranger, I suppose the rabbit suit is a staple to your character after all." said the tall old man. "Not many people confront Warface and live to tell about it. I'm impressed by your development." And as quickly as he appeared Arman Tier then went off into the fray. The Rabbit-Man meant to thank him, but the old stranger was already lost in the commotion. Mr. One then appeared by the Rabbit-Man's side when he got to his feet. They fought together after a brief but happy greeting, but both were starting to wonder if they would make it out of the Coliseum alive. It was then that the tide of the battle turned.

From outside the hole in the Coliseum's roof and into the Battle Zone leaped the Guard Dogs, who were sent by the Caretaking Body after they heard of Mr. Spiderhat's death. Boss Barns and many Patrolmen accompanied them. The Grandie dogs of the CTB caught many of the Mad Dogs up into their jaws and devoured them. This lessened the numbers of the Mad Dogs and their allies, but it really only evened the odds. When Warface confronted the Guard Dogs he was able to destroy many of them with his flame-spouting sword and breath, and he left many of them dead. He simply seemed unde-featable, and watching the Guard Dogs fall so easily really hurt the morale of everybody fighting against the Mad Dog Tribe. Again, even though the odds were more even with the presence of the Guard Dogs, the seeming invincibil-ity of Warface made the loss of the Grand Coliseum to the Mad Dogs appear likely. But an array of shiny stars emitted by the Dream Queen's power wand lit up and sparkled throughout the arena. The stars made the Mad Dogs they touched fall into a dreamy daze. She could no longer bear to see her friends among such danger, so she conjured up this powerful attack from her power wand. Her trance-inducing stars had no effect on Warface, but it did affect many of the Mad Dogs, who were then struck down and defeated by their op-ponents. Now their numbers began to dwindle, and there were few of them left. Still, Warface could not be overcome, and his trail of death continued.

Things continued this way until Arman Tier confronted Boss Barns, the Chief of the Patrolmen. Barns had slain Arman Tier's oldest son Herman Longhorn during the raid on Dag's grove and the old man longed to avenge the loss. Just like Sally Wonder, Arman Tier now lost his eldest child to the Caretaking Body, and thus his wise and experienced mind had become fixated on vengeance. In a furious rage the old man leaped at the Chief Patrolman and beheaded him with his powerful battle-axes. Eagle Top, having knocked Rip A. Sunder and Kroscar aside, flew toward Arman Tier outraged at what the old man had just done. "What are you doing?" shouted Eagle Top, "Whose side are you on?"

"I am not on any side except that of righteousness," replied Arman Tier, "which neither the Caretaking Body nor the Mad Dogs are. That bastard I just killed murdered my son. I intend to make both of these factions suffer for their atrocities." The bewildering, starry spell of the Dream Queen actually saved Eagle Top's life, because her array of stars touched Kroscar and Rip and made them dizzy for a moment. This gave Arman Tier the opportunity to ap-proach Eagle Top and speak to him. His words had an effect on the Grand Coliseum Champion that nobody would have predicted. "You are fighting very bravely Eagle Top," Arman said to the Morphie. "I remember when your fa-ther held the championship that you hold now. He defended his title with courage and dignity. He was a true hero. The people of Main City adored him, and rightfully so. They look to you as their hero now Eagle Top, but you have become vain and cruel during your time as champion. You must regain the valor your father White Top had. Look around at the people in these balconies. Even after all the chaos and destruction that has occurred in this battle, still they stay and cheer you on. They believe in you- they are here for you. They are now under threat, and they need you to do something about it! Now is your chance to be the champion they need you to be."

Arman Tier then stepped aside as Eagle Top looked around into the balconies and saw the terrified and confused people in the audience. These were the people that erupted in cheers the moment his theme music hit. These were the ones who gave him the support he needed to ascend to the top of the Grand Coliseum. He understood what Arman Tier had said, and as he gazed at the crowd the vanity and pride that characterized him for so long instantly vanished and was replaced by devotion to his adoring audience. The spectators of the Grand Coliseum were usually unruly and cruel, but in this dark moment they looked to their beloved champion, and in a single instant of intense carnage, nearly an entire arena of normally wicked people become good again for a moment. The genuine care Eagle Top and the audience of the Coliseum had for each other superseded any previous nastiness that had defined them. Eagle Top grabbed a megaphone and addressed the audience, "Don't be afraid! Mr. Spiderhat might be dead, but I'm not. I said I'll defend this Coliseum from these disgusting fiends and I intend to do so! I am the champion of the Grand Coliseum, and I'm here for you all! Thank you for giving me your support. Each and every one of you- thank you all for believing in me!" He then threw down the megaphone. By now the Dream Queen's spell wore off of Kroscar and Rip A. Sunder. After Kroscar regained his senses, he decided to leave Eagle Top to Rip and went to find the Dream Queen. As the remaining crowd chanted Eagle Top's name, Rip dashed at Eagle Top and they engaged in a brawl once more. Now encouraged and empowered by the chants of his audience, Eagle Top grabbed hold of the leader of the Mad Dogs and soared into the air. He then threw Rip to the ground with incredible force, and then plunged down onto his opponent as he drove his knee into Rip's neck and broke it, slaying the leader of the Mad Dog Tribe.

Kroscar would have stopped Eagle Top's defeat of the Mad Dog Tribe's leader if he were not so fixated on finding and destroying the Dream Queen. He desperately wanted to kill her since their previous match. He saw her as a threat and feared she would tarnish his reputation if she defeated him. When Kroscar found her The Dream Queen gladly engaged him in the rematch they both wanted. Christie was undaunted by her previous defeat to Kroscar though she had not forgotten the pain she felt in his cruel hold, nor had she forgotten the torment she felt at the prospect of letting Twinklette down. Rage grew in the usually jovial Dream Queen as she recalled Kroscar's cheating methods in their previous duel. They engaged one another in an intense fight.

The Rabbit-Man longed to assist his friends in the Battle Zone, but he was still overwhelmed by his numerous foes. He had yet to slay any of his enemies but he was able to consistently defend himself with his powerful carrot rod. The Rabbit-Man knocked a weasel-suited opponent to the ground. He then leapt on the enemy and battered him into the ground with his rabbit-booties. He then jumped upon his foe with both feet four times, soaring higher and higher into the air with each successive jump. On the fifth jump the curled himself into a ball and came down upon the weasel-man with such force it drove his opponent into the ground of the Battle Zone and left him completely unconscious. This attack the Rabbit-Man called the Hop-and-Drop, and he repeated it with the same result on one of the Mad Dogs that attacked him, leaving this enemy also unconscious in a small hole left by the force of the final drop.

Arman Tier remained unscathed in the battle to that point, and nobody had any idea how he got there in the first place. Next he appeared to Sig Calcium, who was isolated from his allies and fighting two Mad Dogs. Arman Tier destroyed these Mad Dogs with his axes and addressed Sig Calcium. "I know why you were wanted by the Caretaking Body." The old man told Sig. "It wasn't because of an affiliation with the Mad Dogs as some believed. You and your friend Try Wonder were plotting an attempt to steal the Coveted Cabbage and get his family to a better place than Main City. He was caught, but you still achieved the goal you both shared. This was a most impressive feat, and you are a talented young man. Now is your chance to gain the ultimate vengeance for your murdered friend. Bring down the foes around you in your friend's honor. Help destroy these monsters and realize the dream you and he shared!" Just like Eagle Top, Sig Calcium was moved by the words of the old man and fought with renewed vigor against all who stood in his way.

Arman Tier again resumed fighting in the battle until he was confronted by the demon Warface. Arman Tier was powerful, but Warface seemed virtually unstoppable. The old man attacked Warface with his axes, and the giant black demon fell backward, though he was far from defeated. Warface got back to his feet and engaged Arman Tier in an intense duel. Arman was able to evade the demonic fire that had destroyed so many, and he was the only warrior in the Coliseum that was able to stand a chance against Warface up to that point.

As Arman Tier battled Warface the Rabbit-Man continued fighting various Mad Dogs and their allies until Turnoff and Abbo attacked him. Turnoff attacked him from behind and caught him off guard. He knocked the Rabbit-Man to the ground as he and Abbo kicked their foe repeatedly.

"I wanted to beat your ass ever since I first saw you in our hall," Turnoff said in his grumbling voice, and he and Abbo continued to stomp on the fallen Rabbit-Man. "Let's finish him off Abbo! This runt isn't worth the space he takes up." Mr. One intervened and sent Turnoff and Abbo reeling. Once they where faced with an even number of opponents they ran off and left their fight with the Rabbit-Man. As this occurred, another series of blinking lights began to appear throughout the Battle Zone. These were not the stars of the Dream Queen however, because these flickers of light had a more ominous look – a *blue* ominous look, and not the pale light blue of the Dream Queen's outfit. The Rabbit-Man and Mr. One exchanged uneasy glances, because they both knew these lights preceded the arrival of the Blue Demon. They knew this, but nobody else did, and the Blue Demon did not show himself immediately. Rather, the first obvious enemy that made his appearance on the Battle Zone was Hayt the Hungry, who peered through the hole of the arena's roof and down onto its occupants with his glowing yellow eyes. His black fur was standing on end, and his jaws were larger and more horrid than ever before.

The Hayt monster lunged down into the Battle Zone and tore apart both the Mad Dogs and their opponents indiscriminately. By now most allies of the Mad Dog Tribe and most Guard Dogs were destroyed. Hayt the Hungry was there for one purpose: to destroy and devour, exactly as the Blue Demon wished. He killed the few remaining allies of the Mad Dogs that were still on the Battle Zone ground, and also tore one of the remaining Guard Dogs asunder. He stalked through the arena amidst the fighting.

As Kroscar and Christie Starlight continued their heated duel, the Dream Queen hit Kroscar with a particularly powerful blast from her power wand. As Kroscar flew backward Hayt the Hungry leaped behind him and swept the Mad Dog member up into his jaws. He devoured Kroscar to the dismay of the remaining Mad Dog Tribe. Turnoff and Abbo were angered when they saw this. They charged head-first at the Grandie monster and threw pieces of debris from their ruined Blackwind train at the beast, which bounced off of Hayt as he lunged forward and swallowed both of them as well.

The Rabbit-Man and Mr. One found Christie and Geb, and the four of them stayed near each other, fending off any enemies that approached them.

Michael Babbish

They made their way to a corner of the Battle Zone in an effort to stay away from Hayt the Hungry and Warface. In the center of the Battle Zone Arman Tier was fighting the demon Warface. The old stranger's helmet was knocked off and most of his vest was burnt away, but he still held his ground against the fearsome demon. It was then that the Blue Demon physically appeared and descended into the Battle Zone. He no longer wore the robe and had a very muscular human body, though his head and wings looked the same. He was now visible to all in the Coliseum, and the long blue tail the Rabbit-Man recognized waved behind the longtime enemy. The Blue Demon blasted a fireball at Arman Tier, who deflected it with one of his powerful axes. In the same instant Warface kicked him, and Arman Tier fell backwards. Behind him was Hayt the Hungry, who swallowed the old fighter up in his jaws and devoured him as he did Kroscar and several others. The Rabbit-Man could not believe his eyes when he saw Arman Tier devoured by the Grandie wolf and his heart sank. The Blue Demon then destroyed many of the remaining Mad Dogs with his blue fire as Warface viewed this spectacle and laughed. The Mad Dog Tribe had summoned the black war demon to their aid, and he betrayed them, watching them burn in the Blue Demon's fire with amusement. The remaining Patrolmen of the Caretaking Body were devoured by Hayt the Hungry.

Eagle Top, with a renewed sense of purpose and newfound principles, was also now able to see the Blue demon as everyone else in the Grand Coliseum could. The eagle Morphie leaped forward to attack this newly arrived foe, still with every intention of defending the people in the Coliseum from any oppressors. He bravely attacked the Blue Demon, but the ram-horned demon scorched the champion of the Grand Coliseum with his blue flames until the mighty champion was totally incinerated. This was a terrible loss, because Eagle Top could have been a great force for reform in Main City if he had survived.

Sig Calcium tried to take a final heroic stand and attacked Warface. The young and determined bird-man flew into the air as he called, "Try, this one's for you my friend!" he thought as he landed onto Warface's head and grabbed a large curved horn protruding from the demon's skull. In an incredible feat of strength Sig broke the demon's horn off and rammed it into one of Warface's eyes. Sig was the first person in the entire Coliseum to deal any severe damage to Warface, but this only enraged the demon. Insane with rage Warface swung his sword wildly at Sig. The bird-man evaded as many of the slashing swipes as he could but the angered demon was just too fast. A final swipe from the blade of Warface severed the heroic Sig Calcium in two at the waist. Even the enhanced suit of the metal giant could not protect him from such a potent blow as the one Warface dealt in his peak of rage. Also, the anger that festered in Sig's heart, though understandable, made him more susceptible to Warface's attack. The sword of Warface was an exceptional weapon, like the power wands and power rods the metal giant could produce. Sig Calcium was brave, but ultimately he was far outmatched by Warface. His life of sorrows ended with a final act of defiance against evil, which had troubled him for so long.

At last it was only the Rabbit-Man and his three friends on the Battle Zone ground. They quickly made for the door, hoping to exit the Battle Zone. But before they got to it blue flames shot up in front of the exit and cut them off. The Blue Demon laughed as they all turned and faced him. Warface and Hayt the Hungry loomed behind him. The Demon hovered into the sky and Hayt the Hungry stood aside as they both made way for Warface, who they both greatly feared though they tried not to show it. The black demon made ready to send spurts of flame forward to engulf the four friends, but he did not do so. Before he could manage his shot, a blast of fire hit him on the side of the head and sent him sailing sideways across the decimated and corpse-riddled Battle Zone floor.

A figure then floated down into the Battle Zone from the night sky above. The four friends recognized it – Cyber Wurko, the metal giant that made their suits, removed from his spot in the Vegetable Patch for the first time in recent memory, made his way into the Grand Coliseum to help his friends. Warface leaped up in a fit of rage, and shot multiple blasts of fire at the large metal figure. Cyber Wurko deflected these and they had no effect on him. As Warface tried to attack him with his massive sword, the metal giant stopped the blow by grabbing the demon's wrist and then grabbed him by the neck with his other hand. The metal giant pried the sword from Warface's hand and impaled the black demon with it. He then sent spurts of the horrid flames out onto its owner and consumed Warface in his own fire until he was singed into a large, fearsome skeleton that crumbled onto the ground. The Blue Demon gasped in dismay, and hastily flew away without looking back. Now only Hayt remained, and though he feared Warface, he impulsively attacked the metal giant. Cyber Wurko caught the beast in midair as it leaped at him and he tore his jaws in two, thus destroying the Grandie monster once and for all. He then turned to the others behind him. "Shall we go home now?" he asked in a casual voice.

Cyber Wurko shrunk down into his normal human size (he was actually somewhat small) and glided out of the Battle Zone with the others following closely. The flames of the Blue Demon vanished when he fled and they were able to exit safely despite the commotion from the audience. The remaining spectators fled the arena after the demise of Eagle Top. Once outside the Coliseum, they located Sally Wonder, Twig Duckly, and Dag's family amid mass panic in the streets of Main City. The friends all left Main City for the Vegetable Patch as quickly as they could. Behind them the Grand Coliseum was burning away in the fires left by the demon Warface. It was now deserted. The iconic structure of Main City would be no more. It was completely devoured by flames by the night's end, and the bodies of all who fell there were cremated. The following morning only ashes would remain as the souls of the fallen left the Grand Coliseum through the smoke that filled the nighttime air.

Chapter Twenty-Two
The Lesser of Evils?

The flames near the door died away when the Blue Demon left, and the four friends and Cyber Wurko went through it. They eventually met Sweetberry and her children along with Sally Wonder and Twig Duckly on the way out. They left the Grand Coliseum, which by now was burning away in the remainder of Warface's fire. They all went back to the Vegetable Patch in the hope of recuperating after the very terrible battle they just experienced. Dag's family was grief-stricken, and the others were very wearied by the ordeal. Unfortunately for them, an enemy awaited them when they arrived at Geb's home at the Vegetable Patch.

Sitting square in the middle of the Vegetable Patch when they arrived was the Blue Demon. He had Selene and Twinklette along with the Bitties lying asleep behind him. He had cast a spell on them when he arrived and waited for the others to return. Cyber Wurko left Selene and Twinklette with weapons when he left them, but they were unable to overcome the Blue Demon. Then they saw the old wicked Ghost of Despair descend and hover over both of the captives of the demon, and from his dark blue robe came the nasty-looking intestines with an ugly face that the Rabbit-Man saw in the nightmare country. "My demand is simple," the Blue Demon said to them all. "I want the Rabbit-Man. Let me take him, and the others go free. Otherwise Despair will put such dreadful nightmares in the minds of your slumbering friends that they will go insane and never be the same again."

"Never!" shouted Mr. One as he stepped forward. "You have caused the Rabbit-Man and all of us enough trouble already. I'll face you one-on-one for their safety if that's what you want Blue Demon! Mr. One is not afraid of the likes of you!"

"This is not the Grand Coliseum, Mr. One," answered the Blue Demon. "As you have just seen, there is not much of it left. All I want is the Rabbit-Man. He must come with me and my ghost here, and you will never hear from us again."

"Fine!" said the Rabbit-Man as he stepped forward. "Have it your way. But I'm only going to go with you if I know for sure that the others will be alright."

"You're the only one I have an interest in now, Rabbit-Man," answered the Blue Demon. "Come with me and these other people will never see me again. You are the only one I've ever had an interest in, and if you do as I ask I will explain why."

"Lead on then," said the Rabbit-Man, "But don't harm anybody else."

"No Rabbit-Man," said Mr. One. "Don't do this; he can't be trusted. He destroyed Lady Easter's Garden. Don't go with him. You have no idea where he'll take you, and you may never come back."

"I appreciate your concern Mr. One," answered the Rabbit-Man. "But this has to end. I cannot keep running from this demon forever. He will just follow me wherever I go. I'm not afraid of him anymore, really. After all we've been through in Main City and witnessing the destruction of the Grand Coliseum, it's time to finish my feud with this enemy once and for all. I really hope something good can come out of all that happened during this dreadful night. Several of our friends are gone, but I'm glad the rest of you are okay. It's not over for me though, and it never will be so long as this Blue Demon is on the prowl."

"Come then," said the Blue Demon, and then he lifted his hand and a grey mist came from it. It formed into a large skeletal face with curved ram horns on the forehead like those of the Blue Demon. The mouth of this apparition opened wide. The Blue demon stepped inside the mouth of the face he just conjured. "Follow me," he said to the Rabbit-Man, who then followed him inside. He walked down into the face until the mouth closed behind him, and it vanished. Sally Wonder and Twig Duckly wept as the jaws of the demon face closed behind their friend, and all the others were made uneasy at the sight. After the demon face vanished, the Ghost of Despair floated into the air and also vanished; Selene, Twinklette, and the Bitties were now safe, and the others never saw the old wicked ghost again.

The Rabbit-Man was calm and resolved when he entered the mouth of the demon face and followed his nemesis inside. He knew the entrance had closed behind him, but he did not look back because he knew seeing his friends would be too difficult for him. The only thing he could see was the Blue Demon before him standing on a long grey slope that seemed to be floating arbitrarily in the surrounding darkness. The demon had already shed his dark grey robe as he appeared in the Grand Coliseum. This revealed the demon's true form to the Rabbit-Man – his face was the same with glowing yellow eyes and the ram horns, but his body which once appeared small beneath the robe was now large and muscular. His skin was deep blue and he wore short brown trunks around his waist and black boots. His wings were still large and wide, giving him the ominous look the Rabbit-Man was familiar with, and his pointed tail floated behind him. He was a fearsome sight, and the Rabbit-Man was loath to look at him. Still, he was glad he still wore his new rabbit suit that the metal giant gave to him, and he still had the powerful carrot rod with which he defended himself in the Grand Coliseum as well as Dag's small power wand if he needed them.

He followed the Blue Demon up the strange slope, as all around him the darkness gave way to the demon's trademark hazy blue aura. His enemy then led him up toward a large fortress with a high peak in the center. It was here that the Blue Demon turned and gazed at him. "I have something to show you," he said to the Rabbit-Man. The atmosphere around them changed and the part of the slope they stood on seemed to float forward and went into the fortress before the tower in the center. The Blue Demon then held out his hand and touched the Rabbit-Man on the shoulder. They floated above the ground, and the demon then pulled the Rabbit-Man forward. He brought him through the walls of the tower, and then down through the ground beneath it. They came to an underground chamber at the bottom of the fortress. The Rabbit-Man did not know how any of this had happened, but the power of the demon was strange, and it seemed like he had control over material substances that other things did not. Not even the wise Arman Tier seemed to possess abilities such as his. The room they were in had many tools and various weapons on shelves along the wall. In the center was a large chair, and seated upon it was a dusty skeleton. The Rabbit-Man noticed that the skeleton's head had ram horns on the forehead of the skull. It seemed for a moment like it could have been the Blue Demon's skeleton, though the Rabbit-Man did not know how that was possible.

Michael Babbish

"Do you know who this is?" the Blue Demon asked, referring to the skeleton in the chair.

"I don't," the Rabbit-Man answered.

"These are the remains of a Morphie who was a laborer for one of the men that founded the Caretaking Body. These are the remains of that large and fearsome man, and those who lived inside the walls of the fortress you just saw knew him well. His name was Vulgar Squalor. Being a large Morphie with much strength, his skills were valuable to those who financed construction of the fortress, and he helped them build it in ancient days to protect them from the dangers of the outside world – like Grandies and other such things. Vulgar Squalor built most of the walls around the fortress himself, but near the end the owners brought along others to assist him. When the wall was finished, and it came time for Vulgar's payment, the masters of the fortress gave him much less than they promised – telling him that he had not earned the full amount because he received assistance during his work assignment. Vulgar felt betrayed and was overcome with rage. He wanted more than anything to take vengeance upon the masters of the fortress. He could not do so, however, because in the process of the fortress's building the masters confiscated all firearms and weaponry from those who lived inside, and the high chambers in the tower where they lived were the most protected parts of the entire structure.

"They then invited Grandies into their fortress to protect them from the others that lived inside. This was something they promised their subjects they would never ever do, but by the time they did so their power was absolute, and their subjects had no way of resisting anything they did. Thus the Grandies were in the fortress to stay. Most simply accepted that this was their fate and surrendered to the masters of the fortress, but Vulgar Squalor never forgot the wrongs he endured, and his hatred and bitterness only grew with time. That was when I appeared to him, and offered to help him get the revenge he wanted so intensely. Of course he agreed right away, and I aligned myself with him, entering his body and making him the most powerful Morphie in the world at the time. He fought and defeated many of the Grandies that guarded the masters, and eventually got his hands on several of them. The others escaped, however, and both Vulgar Squalor and I – now unified as one – intended to pursue them. For centuries we searched and could not find them, until we recognized some of the old masters of the fortress in what is now the Caretaking Body. Vulgar's search continued for centuries and I went along with him the entire time.

"Just as we seemed ready to destroy our old enemies at last, Vulgar came upon a Bastion – it was Lady Easter's Garden. Vulgar saw the fair lady that ruled the Bastion and fell in love with her. He wished to abandon his quest for revenge that he pursued so long. I would not let him, and because I now dwelled within him I took control of his body. Lady Easter was horrified at the change that had come over her lover when I acted through him, and she tried to kill us. She failed and I raped her, thus you were conceived. After I did this, Vulgar tried to take control again and commit suicide. After many failed attempts he drank poison, and then I had complete control of his powerful body. Now, however, my time in his body is dwindling and I need a new host. Because you are the son of Vulgar Squalor, I could continue in your body with the same power I already acquired from him. So this is my proposal to you: let me into your body. When I have destroyed those that Vulgar Squalor intended to, I will then return to your friends and protect them. We will both benefit – I will have finished Vulgar's deeds that he aligned himself with me for, and you can be sure your friends will be safe from any new enemies that might surface in their world. It will benefit both of us. If you are concerned about frightening your friends, I can protect them while remaining invisible. You have much to gain and nothing to lose."

"I have already lost enough thanks to you," answered the Rabbit-Man. "My answer to you is still no. I will not join with you, or let you invade my body and mind and destroy me like you destroyed this Vulgar Squalor. What you have done was terrible, but I am curious: why do you wish to destroy these members of the Caretaking Body? If you were searching in Vulgar's body so long, I am sure you prolonged his life, but how did these people survive so long? And why are you so eager to destroy them? It seems strange to me that a powerful demon like you would have such a determined grudge against greedy humans – unless those in the Caretaking Body are demons themselves"

"Asking good questions as always, Rabbit-Man," answered the demon. "You are a clever little fellow. The people Vulgar sought to destroy have been possessed by demons of their own. Those demons are rivals of mine, one of them especially, and I have never been powerful enough to challenge them until I possessed Vulgar. I thought for sure I could finally defeat them while inside of him, even if it took me a very long time. They eluded me for a while, but then Vulgar fell in love with Lady Easter and that ruined my plans completely. Now I can only vanquish them if I maintain Vulgar's essence. You are his only child, and because his essence is inside you I must possess you if I am ever to defeat my rivals. Let me add one other thing to all this: the demons that possess the Caretaking Body are much more terrible than me. Yes Rabbit-Man, I have destroyed your beloved home and I know that it has caused you great misery. That was unfortunate, but I only attacked the Bastion in order to pass into Main City and get to my foes. You see, Vulgar's love for Lady Easter hindered me and kept me bound in outer space outside the Garden – a special barrier formed by their union that I could not pass through without Vulgar's death and the destruction of the Garden. I could not pass through Easter's Bastion without destroying it, and there was no other way for me to get to Main City except through it. By betraying me, Vulgar inadvertently protected the foes he was after. I was stuck outside Lady Easter's Garden, until I saw you and saw my only means of defeating the other demons. You have witnessed the misery they have put so many people through in Main City. They are far worse than me. Will you let such atrocities continue, or will you help me defeat them and literally save the world at last?

"I do not wish to be evil, Rabbit-Man, but it is the only way I can overcome greater evil. I can actually become a very good demon with the help of someone like you – the best there ever was, in fact. Together we can make the world a peaceful place once more. But that can only be done with the destruction of the other demons that I am against. Please understand they are actually the ones that caused the destruction of your home, by giving me no other option but to destroy it to get to them. They are afraid of me, as they should be, because they know I can right the wrongs they have done when I destroy them. Help me to do it Rabbit-Man. You can stop their evil."

This final revelation of the Blue Demon really got the Rabbit-Man thinking. If the demon really could destroy the Caretaking Body and bring about a more peaceful existence in the world, he thought this was something to consider, even if it meant aligning himself with the demon he truly did not like. He thought long and hard about the demon's offer, and then gave his answer.

"I really would like nothing more than to see the Caretaking Body overthrown and a better way of life to exist." he said to the demon. "But there is a right and wrong way to do things. Overthrowing the Caretaking Body is beyond my skill, and if I cannot accomplish it with my own skill then I shall not be the one to do it. Aligning myself with you to destroy them would not be a righteous thing to do, because I see what you are, Blue Demon. You are not much different than the Mad Dog Tribe. You are simply envious of the other demons that control the Caretaking Body because they are influencing the world with their wickedness and you are not. You simply want the power they have, and demons like you take possession of far too many people. You will not take possession of me. You say that you will undo their wrongs and restore a better situation to the world, but I don't believe you. I think your way will be just as bad as theirs, perhaps with some minor differences in the details. The lesser of two evils is still an evil, and I don't support such things. I don't trust you, and Vulgar Squalor should never have trusted you. I will not do what you want. Do to me what you will, demon. I'm not afraid. My fall from the Garden was terrible, but I met many good friends along the way and I would not give that up for anything. I've seen the resilience to evil that people are capable of. I saw the famous and talented Dream Queen be beaten down by detestable enemies. Yet she was unbroken by the ordeal, and still returned to the scene of her torment and helped my friends and I in our struggle. I saw Sig Calcium rise up and steal the Coveted Cabbage, defying immediate danger as he did so. He was overwhelmed by grief and sorrow at losing the only friend he had in the world, but he still helped my friends and I in the Grand Coliseum, confronting a demon even stronger than you. They are proof that people don't have to be like you to achieve good ends. There is true goodness out there in the world, even in Main City – the likes of which even you cannot touch. I don't know or understand what it really is, but I've felt the soothing glow of love's goodness. I know it is out there, and that's enough for me. You can't do anything to me"

The Blue Demon shouted in fierce rage. "I'll show you what I can do to you, little fool! You arrogant little runt – you are a disgrace to humanity, and you are unworthy of your powerful father's legacy. He was a strong individual in every way, and you're nothing but a puny little soft-hearted misfit! If you won't join with me I'll kill you! I have nothing left to lose."

The Blue Demon then attacked the Rabbit-Man. They became engaged in a very heated duel, and the demon did not expect the Rabbit-Man to be as skilled within the metal giant's suit as he was. The Rabbit-Man landed several powerful blows on the demon with his carrot rod, and knocked his enemy back. The demon regrouped and flew forward at the Rabbit-Man, who countered by spinning around and attacking the demon with his Rhythmic Elbow Beat. After another strike from the carrot rod that left the blue demon on his back, the Rabbit-man leaped into the air and delivered the Hop-and-Drop onto the Blue Demon. The Rabbit-Man's skill took his opponent by surprise, but the Blue Demon soon countered S.T. Ranger's offensive attacks with his blue fire. Although the Rabbit-Man's suit protected him from lethal harm from the flames, the demon's fire weakened him greatly when it hit him. The Rabbit-Man put forth a valiant effort against his longtime nemesis, but the fire of the demon eventually overwhelmed him. The demon landed several powerful strikes on the Rabbit-Man and knocked him to the ground. But S.T. Ranger was determined not to give up in his struggle.

The Rabbit-Man tried to defend himself with his carrot rod, but his enemy seized this and to his great distress the demon broke the power rod in half across his knee. The Blue Demon then grabbed the Rabbit-Man by the neck, lifted him high and slammed him onto the ground. He then grabbed the Rabbit-Man's head in one of his massive hands and beat it against the floor. Luckily the Rabbit-Man's cap protected him from the blows. He lifted his legs and kicked the demon off of him. With the enhanced strength of his suit, the demon fell backwards. The Rabbit-Man then grabbed the carrot-tipped half of his rod and used its firearms capabilities as the metal giant showed him how. Luckily for him the weapon still worked. He fired several missiles at the Blue Demon. They punctured the enemy's skin and drew black blood, but the demon still seemed mostly unhindered by the attack. He leaped forward at the Rabbit-Man and threw him against the wall, causing many of the weapons and tools on the shelves to fall to the ground. The Rabbit-Man dropped his weapon and fell. The demon then had the upper hand in the struggle and blasted his black fire onto the Rabbit-Man before beating him with his fists and kicking him with his large black boots. Even with his suit the Rabbit-Man was overcome by his enemy. The demon slammed the Rabbit-Man onto the ground once more, and then placed one of his massive boots onto the Rabbit-Man's head and pressed it into the hard ground. At last, as the Rabbit-Man lay prone on the ground beneath the Blue Demon's feet, the enemy made his final demand to his long sought after prey, "Surrender to me... or die."

The Rabbit-Man made a final effort and knocked the demon off of him. He struggled to get back to his feet but managed after some effort. His body ached, and he was wearied by the beating the demon gave him. He walked over to the chair in the center of the room and pushed the remains of Vulgar Squalor out of it. He sat in the chair and looked at the demon. "I'm not letting you have possession of me," he said. The demon stood and leered at him with hateful eyes. It was then that the Rabbit-Man saw something move behind the Blue Demon. He recognized the skull-face that appeared behind his opponent – it was the Ghost of Despair. He wrapped his purple hands around the demon's neck from behind and strangled him. The wraith then plunged the long fingernails of his left hand into the demon's torso. The demon struggled, but his body grew smaller and thinner and the ghost choked him. It seemed as though the musculature of the demon's body was gradually evaporating.

"What.. are you...doing?" gasped the demon. "We had... an... a...gree... ment."

"You have failed on your end of the bargain," answered the ghost.

The demon now sank onto his knees. His yellow eyes actually began to flicker. "Don't do this... please...." the demon said amid coughs. The Rabbit-Man observed how the old wicked ghost betrayed the Blue Demon. The Rabbit-Man had assumed the Blue Demon was the more powerful of the two foes, but unbeknownst to him the Ghost of Despair was actually much, much older than the Blue Demon, and had destroyed many other demons before. The Rabbit-Man was weakened by his fight with the demon, and he was unsure of what to do. Then the demon's eyes closed and he fell forward onto his face. The Rabbit-Man then saw that the intestines with the ugly face were upon the demon's back. Parts of the organ were submerged in the demon's spine, and one tube came from the nasty mouth and into the demon's body, sucking from it like a straw. The Rabbit-Man saw this and was very disturbed. He hated the look of Despair's terrible organs possibly even more than that of the Blue Demon. He also wondered what the ghost might do to him if he destroyed the demon. The Rabbit-Man then got up from the chair and lifted the top half of his carrot rod again. He fired a shot at the foul intestines, causing the ghost to shrink away in fright. He then fired another shot that hit the exposed heart inside the ghost's purple cloak. He fired a final time and hit the ghost in the forehead. It let out an awful, shrill cry and flew off through the wall and out of the room. The Rabbit-Man went to the Blue Demon, who was now in a very bad way. He turned over his enemy, who was now smaller and much lighter. The demon looked at him, and now his yellow eyes were small, barely glowing orbs in the hollows of his skull-like face.

"Thank you, Rabbit-Man," he said softly. "If he got me, it would have been the worst fate I could ever encounter. I thought he was on my side. He and I had an agreement. Now I know what Vulgar Squalor must have felt like. I am really sorry for what I did to him. I am very weak now, Rabbit-Man, but you helped me even though I hurt you severely. I'll do what I can to help you." The Blue Demon lifted his hand and a thin mist came from it. It formed a hole in the floor of the room. It actually resembled a rabbit-hole slightly. "Go ahead through there." he said to the Rabbit-Man. "It will bring you to a better place." The Rabbit-Man could not see anything else to do, so he did as the demon suggested and went into the hole. Before he knew it, he was falling once more. For a split second he thought the demon might have tricked him, but then he hit a surface and was out cold.

Chapter Twenty-Three
The Garden of Heartfelt

When the Rabbit-Man finally woke, he was at the base of a tree once more. A fresh scent was in the air, unlike any he remembered from Main City. He sat up; his head was aching severely. He noticed that he was lying beside a large root that was almost his size. He also observed green grass around him – something he never encountered in Main City except for in Geb's Vegetable Patch. As he looked up, he realized a fine-looking dog with a golden-brown coat was watching him. When he saw it he tried to stand up, but his body was too sore and he fell back down. The dog ran off, and he laid there on the ground which was surprisingly comfortable. He lied on his back and saw that the tree was very tall, and at the tips of its branches were green lush leaves. This was another contrast to the barren trees that were in the area surrounding Main City, with the only exception being Dag's grove which was eventually ruined anyway. He wondered where he was. For a brief moment he thought he might have returned to Lady Easter's Garden. This thought gave him pleasure for a moment until realization set in that such a scenario was impossible. Still, the place he was in seemed pleasant enough. He thought of the Blue Demon again.

"Could he have brought me here?" he wondered. He thought it very unlikely that his longtime nemesis would send him to such a fair place. Still, he did keep the demon from being destroyed, so maybe he helped him after all. He looked very weak and defeated when the Rabbit-Man last saw him, and he wondered if the Blue Demon had died after he left the strange twilight world where the fortress and the tower were. He heard birds singing somewhere, and was happy to hear it.

At last his body recovered a bit and he got up. The large root was to his left, and he noticed a small pool of clear water not far to his right. He went over to it to splash some water on his face, and he cringed when he saw his reflection. He was in very bad condition – his face was dirty and his rabbit cap was smeared with soot. He was covered in dirt and his suit was scuffed and smeared with dirt and blood in various spots. Despite the dirt on the surface the actual material of the suit remained intact well. The small fluffy tail on the back of his waist was scorched but not gone. He did not have time to think about his reflection for long. He heard voices behind him coming from beyond the tall thick tree he woke near. He crawled silently back to the root and crouched behind it, looking over to see what was happening beyond it.

To his surprise, he saw a very beautiful woman. He thought she was lovelier than Lady Easter herself, and certainly more so than anyone else he met in Main City. She was nicely clad in a light purple and pink dress, and had several small Bitties playing near her. The dog he saw before was sitting beside her as she talked happily to the Bitties. A squirrel was seated beside a little flower-shaped girl listening to what the kind woman was saying. Two other Bitties, each shaped like an apple and an ear of corn, were seated not far from them. There were squirrels and rabbits running around the area too. The Rabbit-Man was moved by the scene, and he wondered if the place he was now in was a Bastion. Unfortunately for him, this concept invoked fear inside him before anything else, because of the unpleasant memories he held of the destruction of his own Bastion. He wanted to approach the woman, Bitties, and small animals, but he could not get himself to move from behind the root where he crouched. He also did not want to frighten them with his appearance, because he was so ravaged from his fight with the Blue Demon. So he simply sat, waited, and watched.

His esteem for the people he observed only increased as he saw how they laughed and interacted. At first he was reminded of the children of Madame Duckly where Twig came from, but in retrospect even Madame Duckly's group of children went about their business in a more structured and rigid fashion. The scene he now observed seemed more welcoming and pleasant than any he had ever known, even in the Garden. He remembered his old rabbit suit, and wished that he had it now. Even though it lacked the abilities he now possessed it might have been more appropriate for this strange but pleasant new location.

At last one of the squirrels sat up and looked toward him. The woman noticed this and looked in the Rabbit-Man's direction. He became very nervous and ducked beneath the root, but she already spotted the rabbit ears of his cap behind the root. She walked over to him, followed by the three Bitties and the other animals. He sat nervous on the ground when she came to him. He did not wish to appear suspicious by running off, so he stayed where he was.

"Hello," the woman said to him. "What are you doing here? I don't think any of us have met you before. What's your name?"

"Hello ma'am," said the Rabbit-Man as he slowly got to his feet. "I'm S.T. Ranger, the Rabbit-Man, and I don't even know how I got here myself. I had an unpleasant experience with an enemy of mine, and somehow I ended up here. I have no idea where I am. Is this place a Bastion?" At this last question the woman laughed.

"No, this isn't a Bastion," she answered him. "I didn't think any of those even existed anymore. You are on the outskirts of Sleek City, one of the biggest Metroscapes. We are close to the Garden of Heartfelt, which is almost like a Bastion, some people say. I am Rose Allure, and these Bitties you see here are my friends Kinder, Carefront, and Fullwit." The flower-girl, then the apple-girl, and then the corncob-boy each stepped forward to greet themselves as Rose Allure said their respective names. "You look like you can use some supper and rest," she continued. "Come with us and we'll help get you cleaned up." The Rabbit-Man then followed Rose and her friends to a house not far from the large tree. There he took a bath as the Bitties cleaned and mended his rabbit suit. He had a very pleasant dinner with them, and came to fall in love with Rose. He enjoyed her company and that of her friends and pets very much. He was surprised that such a place as Rose's home could even be part of a Metroscape of any kind, let alone the largest of them. The world just got stranger and more unexpected as the Rabbit-Man went along. Rose invited him to stay with them for a while, and he eagerly accepted the invitation. He missed his friends, but had no idea how to get back to them. Rose was unfamiliar with Main City's location in relation to her home, though she heard of it before. As he spent time there he became happier than he felt in a long time. Still there were two things that troubled him: he wondered if his other friends from Main City were alright, and he wondered what became of the Blue Demon.

"If that miserable foe follows me to this wonderful place," the Rabbit-Man thought to himself, "I don't know how I could handle that. To think that such a foul monster could emerge and cause trouble to my beloved Rose and her wonderful friends is an idea too awful for me to think of for long." Although this was a very real concern for the Rabbit-Man, he also remembered how his final moment with the Blue Demon was not altogether bad. The creature had sent him away from the twilight world they drifted into, and that was how he ended up near the Garden of Heartfelt at all. He did not know if this was the demon's intention all along, or if he simply sent him off to a random location and he was lucky enough to meet as kind a person as Rose. Either way, the Rabbit-Man thanked his lucky stars that he ended up where he was.

Rose brought him to the Garden of Heartfelt, and the Rabbit-Man was impressed by its beauty. It had various fruit trees and vegetables growing, and many pleasant flowers inside it. They visited it regularly, and it was here that the Rabbit-Man finally shared his feelings for Rose. To his delight she told him that his love was wholly returned, and they had many sweets moments together.

"If my life could remain as it is now," the Rabbit-Man thought to himself one day as he watched the three Bitties play in the yard behind the house, "I believe I will be quite happy after all. I think I would even be more content than if I had lived my entire life in the Garden of Lady Easter."

The Rabbit-Man missed his old home still, but the goodness he encountered within Rose's home and the Garden of Heartfelt helped him to accept the reality that his former home was part of the past. All of the pain and misery he suffered in Main City still existed as bad memories in his mind, but this too he accepted as over and done, and it no longer troubled him much. His most recent experiences were good, and so his life was good. But fate was not to let the Rabbit-Man be well off so easily. After he was at Rose's abode for several months, dark dreams crept into his mind and disturbed his sleep. When he shared this with his lover Rose, she consoled him and made him feel better. But the nightmares did not go away. Soon the Rabbit-Man saw a shadow floating around the home where he stayed, and he did not like it one bit. He told Rose about this, and she was also concerned.

The Rabbit-Man soon discovered what the shadow was. One day the sky was overcast and the flower Bittie Kinder ran to Rose frightened and in tears. She was unharmed, but she said a strange thing scared her by the large tree. She did not know what it was. Rose consoled her small friend, and the

Rabbit-Man went to the tree to investigate. Anxiety crept into him once more, the likes of which he had not known since his earliest days in Main City.

"If that demon is here to cause trouble, I can't bear it," he thought to himself as he made his way to the tree. "I can't bear being unable to escape or conquer this foe of mine." When the Rabbit-Man looked behind the tree, it was not the Blue Demon that was there. He saw a figure wrapped in a dark cloak huddled against the trunk of the tree. It turned its head and the Rabbit-Man recognized the face beneath the hood – it was the old wicked Ghost of Despair. The Rabbit-Man was so concerned with the Blue Demon he almost forgot this enemy. The ghost cackled in his usual manner and the Rabbit-Man immediately tried to attack him. The ghost flew away and made for the house. The Rabbit-Man pursued him as fast as he could. The three Bitties were inside, but Rose came out and saw the ghost. She backed against the door as it cackled hideously.

"Not you again!" she called to the wraith. "I thought you were out of this place for good!"

"I was." the ghost replied. "But the Rabbit-Man was kind enough to show me the way back!" The Rabbit-Man saw this exchange and it was too much for him. In a fit of rage he leaped forward at the ghost. The wraith spread his arms and once again immersed the Rabbit-Man in his cloak. Rose cried out, but the ghost hovered into the air and flew away with the Rabbit-Man trapped inside his magic cloak. He was not transported back to the Nightmare Country, but he could not get free of the cloak however hard he struggled.

"Don't hurt him!" Rose called to the Ghost of Despair. "You are not supposed to be here! Go away! Leave the Rabbit-Man and go away from here!" After hearing this, the ghost dropped the Rabbit-Man onto the ground. He crawled toward Rose and noticed she now wielded a power rod.

"I'll give you a choice Rose Allure," the Ghost of Despair said. "If I take the Rabbit-Man, I will leave and never return. But if I leave him here, I can return to your home whenever I wish. If the Rabbit-man goes with me, our previous arrangement will still be in effect. But if he stays, I can come back at any time. Choose wisely Rose!"

The Rabbit-Man crawled forward before Rose. "Rose, dear, I can defend us from this ghost once I have a powerful weapon again. I'll send him away. Don't let him take me. I swear I'll protect you."

"I'm sorry Rabbit-Man," Rose said with tears in her eyes, "You can never protect me. I'm very sorry to do this to you, but I cannot have this ghost constantly threatening me and the Bitties I protect. That happened once be-fore and I swore it never would happen again. Good-bye Rabbit-Man!"

"Wait, no!" The Rabbit-man cried. "Rose, please-" but it was no use. The Ghost of Despair descended upon the Rabbit-Man and trapped him in the cloak once more. The wraith flew away, leaving the sorrowful but safe Rose Allure behind.

The ghost flew on and on, until finally it made its way into the midst of Sleek City. They were far past the outskirts and the Garden of Heartfelt, and made their way into the largest and nastiest Metroscape of all. Mr. Spiderhat's Grand Coliseum would appear to be child's play compared to some of the ac-tivities in Sleek City. The Rabbit-Man was somewhat fortunate in that he never had to experience most of the nastiness of the place. The ghost brought him into the largest structure in the entire Metroscape. The building was an incred-ible mansion that had undergone many changes throughout the centuries, but the Rabbit-Man would have recognized it if he was not wrapped in the wraith's cloak. It was the same fortress that Vulgar Squalor built very long ago, though it was renovated and remodeled many times. It was the most fortified building in the entire world, and it was also the home base of the Caretaking Body.

Onward the ghost went with the Rabbit-Man in his cloak. The Garden of Heartfelt was now behind him, and Rose and her friends were safe. But the Rab-bit-Man was brought by the Ghost of Despair into the fortress of Sleek City. It was called the Great Giver by the citizens of Sleek City, as it allegedly provided them with everything they needed. Little did the citizens of Sleek City know the ghost that carried the Rabbit-Man, though firmly fixed in the Old Focus as all ghosts were, was a good friend and valuable asset to the Caretaking Body and the demons that controlled them. The ancient ghost was happy to help them ruin their rival the Blue Demon, and the old wicked ghost also promised his longtime business partners that he would provide a special treat for them – that treat was to be the Rabbit-Man S.T. Ranger, the most coveted soul of the Blue Demon.

There was one thing the old ghost did not know, however, when he left the Blue Demon behind. The Ghost of Despair did not kill the demon, who was a very vengeful being. The Blue Demon, though weakened and nearly on the brink of death, was filled with hatred at the ghost's betrayal and would stop at nothing to get revenge upon him. He knew the ghost would go to Sleek City at some point, so the Blue Demon crawled his way into that Metroscape to head off his new enemy. He had time to recover, although he was still weak-ened and far from his full power. He was waiting for the old ghost there.

Chapter Twenty-Four
Struggle within the Great Blue Star

The fortress at Sleek City was an impressive structure despite the evil that dwelled within it, but the Rabbit-Man only saw the inside of the structure. The Ghost of Despair entered through the walls of the fortress, magically transporting the captive Rabbit-Man with him. The wraith travelled through the halls and into the highest rooms of the mansion, until he came at last to the meeting room of the Caretaking Body. It was a vast but dark room, and along its back was a panel lined with very high seats. These were the seats of the elite members of the CTB. They were expecting the ghost, who informed them he was planning to make his move beforehand. He now hovered into the room and dropped the Rabbit-Man onto the floor. He was nearly suffocated during the trip, and being within the robe of the wraith drained much of his energy. He could not tell how many people were seated on the high seats above him when he looked around. He did not even know where he was.

There was one figure that was central among those seated, however. He was actually a very small man, but he looked larger from his seat which was higher than the others. He wore a nondescript dark red suit and had a large cap on his head. The cap was black and appeared to be made of some kind of solid black metal, and two curved horns came from beneath it on either side of his head. His eyes were covered by very big glasses, the frames of which looked more like two square screens than lenses. The figure also had a tiny red cape that he wore, which actually made him look somewhat comical. The

Rabbit-Man was too disoriented and confused to think anything of the little man's bizarre appearance. He simply got to his feet and looked up at the row of seats.

"Here is the prey of the Blue Demon and one of your major enemies, Lord Red," said the Ghost of Despair. "He is yours for the taking now. I have saved him from being consumed by the Blue Demon, who he actually resisted. This plays well into our hands, because the Blue Demon is now crushed and his prey is here. As we all know, it matters not whether the Rabbit-Man resists the likes of you. You shall nourish yourself from him either way. As we agreed, I have brought him. I actually had a much easier time catching him than I thought."

"Thank you, old friend," said Lord Red in a soft voice. "I believe this is a former affiliate of our old rival Arman Tier, who was also recently destroyed. Yes indeed, things will be better for us than they ever were before." Lord Red then stepped from his high seat, levitated into the air, and gently floated down onto the floor before he walked over to the Rabbit-Man. He was shorter than S.T. and looked up at him with those blank, square screen-eyes and said nothing. He then turned away, keeping his back to the Rabbit-Man. "Strip him and take him to the Preparer. I should very much like to see how he tastes."

"Not if I could help it," said another voice in the room. They all looked over and saw a strange form lying on the floor. The Rabbit-Man recognized it as the Blue Demon. His muscular body was now shriveled and very thin. He was crawling along on his stomach, and his great wings now looked like two large deflated balloons that he dragged behind him like a big blanket. His head looked the same as it always did; it seemed to be the only part of him that had not changed. He crawled slowly forward on all fours, until he collapsed before Lord Red, who looked down on him with the same expressionless face. He then looked at the Ghost of Despair. "When you said you defeated the Blue Demon, I thought you meant you destroyed him," he said to Despair. "I am very disappointed."

"I am sorry, Lord Red," replied the ghost. "I will do away with the Blue Demon now." The ghost then made an effort to fly toward the Blue Demon, but before he could do anything the demon vanished and the familiar blue haze filled the room. There was an unsettled murmur among those in the high seats, and the ghost let out a shriek of dismay. Sparks and glimmers of blue lights flashed within the room, and then a bright white orb engulfed in transparent blue flames appeared in the center of the room.

"If I cannot surpass Lord Red and his ravenous horde as I long desired to," the voice of the Blue Demon said, "then I will at least destroy you, old ghost. You cannot survive in the Great Blue Star that I came from. Even though it may destroy me to conjure it once more, I will make sure you are taken there and be finally annihilated once and for all!" The Blue Demon's voice then began laughing as the ghost was sucked toward the orb of shining fire. The wraith grabbed the Rabbit-Man's arm, and they were both pulled into the orb. Lord Red still stood there expressionless for a moment, and then addressed those in the seats behind him. "What an inconvenience this Blue Demon is becoming," he said. "I suppose if I want something done I must do it myself. I will be back shortly." He then leaped into the shining orb and then it vanished, leaving no trace in the room.

The Rabbit-Man was pulled by the ghost through a swirling, winding maelstrom of various shades of blue color swarming about him with black and white occasionally appearing in the mix. The laughter of the Blue Demon surrounded them, until at last they left the strange whirlwind of color as if they were shot from a tube. Then nothing but blackness surrounded them and in the distance there was a shining blue star. In an instant, the star swelled until they were both flung forward into it, and Lord Red followed behind them. They all were thrown into the Great Blue Star.

•   •   •

Back in Main City, after the carnage and chaos that followed the destruction of the Grand Coliseum, the entire Metroscape was almost completely serene and silent for the first time since its formation. Most of the Guard Dogs were destroyed in the last battle in the Grand Coliseum, and with the death of Mr. Spiderhat and the Main Patrol the entire city was left leaderless and without structure or order. However, the Mad Dog Tribe and a majority of their allies were also destroyed, so the threat of violence was lessened. In fact, it was the most peaceful Main City had ever been. Those who remained in Geb's Vegetable Patch were very sorry to see their friend the Rabbit-Man go. The final image of dear S.T. Ranger passing through the skull-like gateway the Blue Demon conjured haunted them, but their spirits were lifted by Christie Starlight as she reminded them of the Rabbit-Man's resilient spirit and his skillful use of his suit. The metal giant Cyber Wurko would still protect them from any dangers nearby, but even he did not have any means of locating or assisting the Rabbit-Man.

Mr. One and Dag's family were invited to stay in the Vegetable Patch and they accepted gladly. Mr. One no longer had his old cache of firearms, but was working with the metal giant on creating a replacement. The arms dealer was fascinated by the power wands and rods the metal giant produced and was eager to learn more of these. Cyber Wurko created a hammer for Mr. One to use in addition to the few firearms he had left. Sally Wonder and Twig Duckly moved into a house located near Geb's. The Dream Queen Christie Starlight and Twinklette lived with Selene in another house near those. The family of Dag made a home in a tree similar to their old one near the Patch. Geb still tended his vegetables with the Bitties, and things seemed good for the small group of friends until one day Twig ran up to the other rabbit-suited man flustered.

"Geb, you have to see this!" said Twig. "I think it's that Blue Demon that took the Rabbit-Man away. I found him in the woods nearby!" Geb contacted Mr. One, the metal giant, and Christie Starlight before Twig led them to the spot in the woods where he saw the Blue Demon. The others hardly even recognized the creature except by his color and his face. By now his body had become so weakened and his spirit became so drained that he was mostly a skeletal head with curved horns – the tips of which were now chipped off – and a large messy mass of blue flesh he pulled along with withered arms. By now he crawled like a snail with his chin to the ground, and had great difficulty getting by. When he first came upon Twig, the boy lifted a rock and made ready to destroy the creature, but the Blue Demon asked him to find the others. He told the boy the Rabbit-Man was in danger, and they needed to help him. Twig was a bright boy and did not ask any further questions. He found the others and led them to the weakened demon.

The Blue Demon used much of his remaining vitality to open his fiery orb portal in the mansion of the Caretaking Body, leaving him with very little power. With what little power he had remaining he transported himself back to the Vegetable Patch as he flung the Ghost of Despair – inadvertently with the Rabbit-Man and Lord Red as well – into the Great Blue Star. He was now near the point of death. He realized that the Rabbit-Man had been sucked into the star with the ghost and that the leader member of the Caretaking Body followed them. He knew he had to act quick, so the Blue Demon appeared in the Vegetable Patch at Main City in a final desperate attempt to prevent Lord Red from consuming the Rabbit-Man.

With the metal giant, The Dream Queen, and Mr. One close behind Geb leaned forward and turned the limp body of the demon onto its back. He held the head of the demon in his hands. "What is going on?" Geb asked the demon. At this point Selene, Twinklette, and Sally Wonder joined the others. They were horrified at seeing the Blue Demon again, but eager to hear news of the Rabbit-Man.

"The Rabbit-Man…" the Blue Demon croaked. "The old ghost betrayed me. He took the Rabbit-Man. I sent them into my star, where I was created. Only I can open the portal, but you must help him. I am too weak. He would not let me possess him, but now he is facing an even more terrible fate. If I open the portal again, it may take the last bit of strength I have to do it. You must find the Rabbit-Man and bring him back, but leave the ghost and the other demon behind. They will not survive in my star. You must do this quick; I don't have much time left." Geb and Mr. One lifted the demon and brought him back to the Vegetable Patch and informed the others what was going on. The other women and the Bitties were frightened of him, but Sweetberry understood the severity of what the demon said. Together with her daughters and the Dream Queen, who possessed incredible restorative powers, they nursed the demon back to health until he had a bit more strength. He was still very weak, but was able to speak better. The Dream Queen then used the powers contained in her wand to aid the demon in conjuring his portal once more. It was more difficult than he expected, even with his slight rejuvenation and Christie Starlight's help. But the Blue Demon did manage to bring forth his portal.

"Those of you who wish to aid the Rabbit-Man and are brave enough to enter, do so quickly, but beware," the Blue Demon said, obviously growing weary as he exerted more effort. "The Ghost of Despair is very treacherous, and he will slay you all if he can."

Without hesitation Mr. One stepped forward and leaped into the portal as he called, "Don't worry, Rabbit-Man, Mr. One is on his way!" Twig Duckly was overcome with enthusiasm and desire to help his friend and ran in immediately after him. He was too quick for his mother Sally Wonder to stop him. It was just then that the Blue Demon lost consciousness and passed out, causing the portal to disappear and leaving the others behind. This trapped Mr. One and Twig within the Great Blue Star along with the Rabbit-Man, the Ghost of Despair, and Lord Red.

• • •

"The Blue Demon has tried to foil me to get revenge for my betrayal, no doubt," the Ghost of Despair said to the Rabbit-Man within the Great Blue

Star. They were now in a misty blue land under a black sky. The ghost was still unaware that Lord Red had followed them inside of it. "You will not escape this time. Very few have ever overcome the Nightmare Country once I brought them into it; I have no idea how you were able to do it twice. Even less have lived long after doing so, and now your end has come. I would have liked to feed you to Lord Red and his associates, but seeing as how your personal demon trapped us in this star of his, I will just kill you here and now. I will simply tell them that I could not bring you back."

"There is no need for that," said Lord Red, and the Ghost of Despair turned around in surprise.

"I did not know you followed us in here," said the ghost. "Are you sure that was wise? Places such as this are very dangerous."

"It is no more dangerous for me than it is for you," replied Lord Red. "Besides, I really wish to feed on this enemy of ours. No one shall ever challenge our power the way this fool did and get away with it. All the better for me if I am isolated from the others; now I have the little rodent to myself."

The Rabbit-Man did not know what Lord Red meant by "feeding on" him, but he knew it did not sound good. Whatever the meaning, he knew he was in trouble. It seemed the Blue Demon helped him once more, though he could hardly believe it. He no longer had his very handy carrot rod, but still intended to defend himself against the two enemies. He still had the power wand he received from Dag in a pocket of his suit. The ghost flew at him and wrapped his arms around the Rabbit-Man's throat and choked him. The Rabbit-Man struggled as much as he could, but his foe's grip was tight. Lord Red looked on, still with no noticeable expression on his face. At last the Rabbit-Man pulled the power wand from his pocket and blasted the ghost away from him. To his surprise, the wraith's grasp was broken. He knew the odds were against him, but he tried to run away from the ghost until he could think of a better plan. It was no use; the ghost grabbed his ankles and tripped him. He then raised the Rabbit-Man by his feet and slammed him hard onto the ground. He repeated this several times until the Rabbit-Man was significantly weakened. The ghost laid the Rabbit-Man on the ground flat on his back, his arms and legs were sprawled and he could not move. Then Lord Red walked over to him. The little man with the large screen-glasses stepped onto the Rabbit-Man's chest and looked down at him. "So much trouble caused by such a seemingly insignificant runt like this," said Lord Red as if to himself. It was then that the tunnel of swirling color reappeared and dropped Mr. One and

Twig Duckly into the star zone. It then vanished, as this was the same moment when the Blue Demon fell unconscious.

"You leave him alone you vile fiends!" called Mr. One. Twig stood close beside him, though he was not afraid of the enemies. They both recognized the Ghost of Despair. The wraith flew forward with its hands outstretched to grab Mr. One, but he had a firearm with him. He drew his weapon and blasted the ghost. Despair fell backward onto the strange translucent blue ground beneath them. Mr. One then took the special hammer from his belt that was produced by the metal giant. As the ghost was stunned on the ground, he shattered its skull with the hammer. A dreadful cry sounded as black steam issued forth from the remains of the skull, but then it faded away along with the wretched scream. It was the end of the Ghost of Despair, an old wicked soul that delighted in torment. Though others like him still existed, this one was destroyed at last.

Mr. One then turned and faced Lord Red, who now had stepped down from the Rabbit-Man's body and stared at the two arrivals. "That was impressive," he said to Mr. One. "I did not think you would be able to defeat that ghost, Mr. One, for he destroyed many souls I would have regarded as much greater than you."

"Who are you, and how do you know me?" asked Mr. One.

"I know all the enemies of the Caretaking Body," answered Lord Red. "And I get them all in the end – one way or another. I have been after you for some time, but I am glad you are here along with that little fellow. I will have more of a feast than I had anticipated."

"You aren't going to be feasting on any of us," said Mr. One. "I don't know who you are, but if you try to harm my friends I'll blow you away just like I did that ghost." He aimed his firearm at Lord Red, who was unaffected by the sight of it. By now the Rabbit-Man got to his feet. He was in pain, but still walked toward Mr. One and Twig. He fell to his knees beside the little duckling boy, who swung one of his arms over his shoulders and held him up. "Don't worry Rabbit-Man, I've got you!" he cried. "It is impossible to not love such a good boy as you Twig. Your mother must be proud." he said to the duckling-boy, grateful to be near two familiar friends once more.

"Let us out of here, or you'll never be feasting again!" said Mr. One with his firearm still aimed at Lord Red, "Let us out and nobody has to get hurt."

"You do not understand me, Mr. One," answered Lord Red. "You all will be hurt. You are enemies of the Caretaking Body. You may not believe it, but

Michael Babbish

I am one of its founders. You know, I actually somewhat appreciate individuals like you and the Rabbit-Man offering some resistance to my regime. It gives us the chance to exercise our immense power. The whole ordeal with the Grand Coliseum was a disaster, I grant you, but it is nothing we cannot amend. I have been in control of the Metroscapes for quite a long stretch of time, and I know how to handle such things. I did not accomplish all of my success alone, however. In fact, since it is only you and your friends here, I can let you in on a little secret. It is a shame you did not unite yourself with the Blue Demon, Rabbit-Man. If you did, you would not defeat the likes of me, but you would at least have had a standing chance…maybe."

"What are you talking about?" asked Mr. One.

"Let me reveal to you the secret to my success," replied Lord Red. "I shall let my own demon come forth, and then he will devour you all. Mr. One, Rabbit-Man, and duck-child… prepare to meet Ekthorn the Evallion!"

When he said this Lord Red began to grow much taller and large wings emerged from his back. The metal cap and glasses burst from his face as it turned a bright yellow. His eyes were red and glowing and grey horns grew from his forehead. The clothing ripped from his body and it became large and muscular. A tail swung behind him, and his nails grew long and sharp. He looked even more fearsome than the Blue Demon, which was appropriate because Ekthorn the Evallion was more powerful than him. As this demon emerged more completely his skin became scaly and developed a strange red glow. The Rabbit-Man and Twig were both frightened by the sight. Mr. One was alarmed, but he held his firearm and hammer and stood resolute before the emerging monstrosity. He then aimed his firearm and blasted at the great demon that had been possessing Lord Red for innumerable years. The demon backed up a few steps but was not knocked from his feet. He gave a deep and growling laugh.

"You are a fool if you think I will be destroyed that easily!" said Ekthorn the Evallion. He then held out his hand and red fire emerged from it, which then formed itself into a large black spear. The demon placed the tip of it on the ground and turned it red. He then took the spear and very suddenly attacked Mr. One. The demon struck his opponent with such force it sent Mr. One sailing high into the air. Ekthorn then flew up with his large wings. The demon struck Mr. One with such force it sent the former arms dealer crashing down onto the now red ground with a crash.

"Mr. One! No!" the Rabbit-Man called. He leaped to his feet in terror and dismay. Ekthorn grabbed Mr. One by the neck and held him up before

250

throwing him forcefully back onto the ground. Mr. One landed with a thud. He then slowly turned his head and looked at his longtime friend the Rabbit-Man with an expression of anguish. Ekthorn then raised his hand and a massive geyser of fire exploded beneath Mr. One's body and immersed him in flames that soared very high. Mr. One's screams resounded throughout the star zone. The demon continued his wretched laughter as he levitated into the air. The arms dealer had a spell from the Dream Queen upon him that prevented him from being killed by the fire, but Mr. One was still in bad condition after the attack. The Rabbit-Man leaped from the ground as Mr. One fell down unconscious. The new rabbit suit allowed him to jump very high, but he was only able to grasp the left ankle of the demon. He clung hard onto Ekthorn's leg, and then sank his teeth hard into his enemy's heel. Ekthorn was surprised at how much this hurt, and he screamed as he kicked the Rabbit-Man away from him. The Rabbit-Man fell onto the ground and hit it hard. Twig cried out and ran to him, but before he could reach him the demon threw his spear down onto the Rabbit-Man. The enhanced suit prevented the Rabbit-man from being impaled, but dark magic emerged from the spear's tip and pinned the Rabbit-Man to the ground. Twig went to the Rabbit-Man weeping and held him tight. The Rabbit-Man grasped the boy's arm firmly.

"I'm sorry, Twig," the Rabbit-Man sputtered before he started to cough blood. Ekthorn descended and kicked Twig aside. He then placed his injured heel over the Rabbit-Man's neck as he slowly removed his spear. It was then that the color-tunnel appeared within the star once more. From it the Blue Demon fell onto the ground close to Twig. He lifted Twig in his arms, not as frail as before, and tossed him through the portal, and then went and did the same to the knocked out Mr. One before the portal closed off. The Blue Demon then fell onto the ground motionless. Twig and Mr. One were safe, and the Rabbit-Man saw their departure before his vision blurred. He hoped they made it back to the Vegetable Patch safely. He laid there as his body went completely numb. Suddenly he felt very sorry that he could not remain with Twig and his other friends longer. In his mind he then cursed fate, that he should be put through so much misery only to be teased with a better existence before being robbed of it. But then, in his mind and heart, he refused to believe that this would be the end. He always believed since the moment he woke up and realized he was no longer in his Bastion that he would eventually come to a bad end. And yet there was something inside him that resisted this fatalistic belief.

The Rabbit-Man recalled what Lord Red told him regarding the Care-taking Body and the demons they foster – they get them all in the end. He was just a man in a rabbit suit in a world where he did not belong. Perhaps it was all really just a long, slow process of death since he fell from the Garden. He was overcome with hatred and bitterness, as Ekthorn would have been pleased to know, but it was not to last. In his final moments the Rabbit-Man thought back on his time in the Garden of Heartfelt and his most cherished moments with Rose Allure and her lovable Bittie friends. He remembered his happy visit to Dag and Sweetberry's home on his way to the Base Pad. He remembered the day he and Mr. One visited Sally Wonder's home and watched Twig Duckly playing. His anger and bitterness faded, and then he was overwhelmingly grateful for the time he was able to spend with such a kind and amazing group of people. Nothing could compare to the happiness he felt for that brief time, and he was glad to have known it.

If his life after the fall was his prolonged death, "What a beautiful death it was." he thought to himself as his eyes closed and he prepared to breath his last. But the pain faded, and soon he was surrounded by the same effulgent and soothing glow that had come to him before. In that moment the wounds from Ekthorn's attacks healed and the Rabbit-Man was no longer afraid. Immersed in this glow the Rabbit-Man was taken away from the Great Blue Star forever. With no more anger or fear he flew away, leaving the two demons behind.

Now only the Blue Demon and Ekthorn the Evallion remained in the Great Blue Star. Because the Blue Demon was born there only he could create the portal in and out. Both he and Ekthorn were confused by the Rabbit-Man's departure, but they soon turned their attention toward each other. The Blue Demon laid on the ground near death as his longtime rival stood over him. Ekthorn lifted his longtime nemesis by the neck and held his face close to his own.

"Open it up again," he said to the Blue Demon, "and I can restore you. You have my word on it." But then the Blue Demon simply laughed, and his body crumbled to the ground in ashes. Ekthorn understood what this meant, and for the first time since untold millennia Ekthorn the Evallion experienced genuine fear. The Blue Demon was gone, and thus there was no way in or out of the Great Blue Star, and it would begin contracting with Ekthorn inside. Not even the most powerful of all demons could survive the implosion of a demon-star while they were inside; he knew his time was at an end, though it would take very long to pass. He understood that shouting and raging would do him no good, and this only increased his frustration. Being unable to use force or coercion to solve his problems was not a feeling Ekthorn the Evallion was used to, and he despised it. He would have many long years to get used to it as the demon-star gradually imploded with him inside and would finally be destroyed. In anger that he could not channel anywhere the demon sat down, and before long he changed back into little Lord Red, and muttered as he sat awaiting his final doom, "All because of that fucking Vulgar Squalor!"

Chapter Twenty-Five
The Founding of Sproutland

Twig Duckly was frightened and upset when he fell through the portal and back into Geb's Vegetable Patch. Mr. One's unconscious body fell beside him. The boy was in hysterics, and his mother and all the others tried consoling him – all to no avail. He simply cried and cried, and the screams of agony chilled their spines and darkened their minds. They all remembered that dreadful day for the rest of their lives. However, it was the Dream Queen Christie Starlight that finally managed to calm the traumatized boy. She took him into her arms and held him tightly. The suit that the metal giant crafted for her sparkled and its array of stars glimmered as the boy began to doze in her arms. Once he was in a deep sleep, they laid him on a bed and the Dream Queen waved her wand over his head. She absorbed most of the traumatic memories from his mind, and then absorbed them through the wand into her own brain. Twig would always remember something bad happened that day, and he would be aware the Rabbit-Man did not make it out of the portal after him, but none of the details beyond that. These the benevolent Dream Queen took into her own mind as if she had experienced them in Twig's place.

This heroic gesture by Christie had its consequences, though they were not unbearable. Christie Starlight visibly aged about two years after absorbing all the memories, though she still looked beautiful. After the process was complete she broke down and wept for a good while herself, until she finally came to and explained everything that happened in the Great Blue Star. The others were horrified to hear of the events that unfolded there, but they were all very grateful for Christie's efforts, especially Sally Wonder. When Twig woke, he was fine and still very much the same boy they all had known.

Mr. One was cared for by Dag's widow Sweetberry and the other Bitties, and when he fully recovered he gave his account of the struggle in the Great Blue Star to the others as well. He wished Cyber Wurko, The Dream Queen, and Geb could have been there to help them, and his concern for the Rabbit-Man's well-being was shared by all in the Vegetable Patch. Although it seemed like their rabbit-suited friend S.T. Ranger met with a terrible fate, Mr. One maintained his confidence that the Rabbit-Man would be alright and would eventually return to them. He knew the Rabbit-Man for a long time and believed his friend would find a way to survive his ordeal in the demon-star. His attitude gave encouragement to the others.

In Main City, the power structure was decimated. The Caretaking Body had to use its resources to maintain control of Sleek City, and so the other Metroscapes were not a priority for them. The few remaining Guard Dogs destroyed one another, and eventually the citizens of Main City found a cache of firearms that Mr. One had hidden there a long while back. The people used these to defend themselves from any Grandies that wandered into the area. Geb still maintained his Vegetable Patch, and together with Cyber Wurko and the others they began a business of making suits and weaponry for the residents of Main City to supplement their defense against the Grandies outside. The Metroscape became a bustling, independent, and healthy series of towns, and the people living there were much happier than ever before. They were able to provide for themselves, defend themselves, and take care of themselves without fear. Perhaps the most famous customer of Geb and the metal giant was Valen Tier, the son of Arman Tier, who purchased many weapons and goods from the metal giant and went on to route and destroy the remaining members of the oppressive Caretaking Body.

One day Twig was in the woods and he found a pet that he brought home. It was a large rabbit with a strange blue coat. Nobody had seen anything like it before, but Twig was instantly attached to the little creature. He kept it at his home with his mother, and everybody who lived near the Vegetable Patch enjoyed the blue rabbit's presence. They even viewed him as a good luck charm. Some folks who heard the entire account of events afterward would theorize that perhaps the strange rabbit was the spirit of the Blue Demon – returning to the world as a demon no longer. Now that there was no more

Old Focus to be afraid of, people began discussing such things openly again. Most people who heard this theory did not believe it at all, but there were a few who believed that in his final moments the Blue Demon wished to be a kinder spirit than what he was through most of his existence. It seemed some intelligence that existed beyond the regular world sent the Blue Demon back; and in the Vegetable Patch he remained as a protective spirit as he once told the Rabbit-Man he would do.

The remaining members of the Caretaking Body had a very difficult time maintaining order after their leader Lord Red disappeared and never returned. Slowly but surely, things got ever worse in Sleek City, and soon the Caretaking Body became careless and apathetic toward everything going on in their primary Metroscape. It took many years for it to happen, but soon the Grandies they employed turned on them and most of them were devoured by their very own Guard Dogs. Valen Tier's assault on them also led to their eventual downfall. Many of the folks who obtained the advanced suits and weaponry from Main City made their way to Sleek City and overthrew the Grandies after assisting Valen, thus creating a similar situation to that of Main City. Some members of the Caretaking Body were still abroad, and so were the demons that possessed them. They still sometimes caused trouble to the now encouraged peoples who were establishing better lives for themselves, but usually they were overcome sooner or later.

In the Garden of Heartfelt, Rose Allure and her friends lamented the departure of the Rabbit-Man. Rose wished to have her lover back, but feared the worst. One day however, she was visited by an old woman that brought her a gift. She presented Rose with a basket that contained a beautiful rabbit with a golden coat. Rose accepted the gift with gratitude and asked the kind old woman who she was. Her guest identified herself as Lady Easter. Rose invited the woman to stay in Heartfelt, and Lady Easter gladly accepted. The golden rabbit was beloved in the Garden of Heartfelt, and he warded off evil from the area. It was a pet Lady Easter raised herself. Rose and her friends were very pleased. Some visitors to the Garden of Heartfelt even claimed this special rabbit could change itself into a human – just like the original Morphies used to do (which is how they got their name). Again, most folks did not believe these stories, but mused on how interesting such a thing would be. The Morhpies used to change between human and animal shapes until the scientists of the Caretaking Body hindered their abilities – leaving them with both human and animal traits, but unable to change.

Eventually more trees and plant life began to grow in the former Metroscapes and the areas around them. The world became beautiful once more. Between Main City and Sleek City there were many independent towns and states, but the entire land soon collectively became known as Sproutland, because it was the beginning of a new era for those places. As it had done innumerable times before, and would continue to do perhaps infinitely, the world had gone through changes, but luckily this time they were for the better. The Dream Queen, Mr. One, the metal giant Cyber Wurko, Geb Growth, and all the other friends of the Rabbit-Man were hailed as heroes throughout Sproutland and as saviors of the population. This was a pleasant and flourishing time for Spoutland, but the heroes still wondered what happened to the Rabbit-Man S.T. Ranger, and they wondered if Mr. One's intuition that he was still alive was correct. The Rabbit-Man would have quite a story to tell his friends if ever he met them again, because he did not meet his end in the Great Blue Star.

Chapter Twenty-Six
Eternal Love

The Rabbit-Man was carried off in the soothing, glowing light that had come to him several times before he was taken away from the Great Blue Star. He was carried far away, beyond the world of the Bastions and Metroscapes, even beyond space itself. He found himself seated upon a large cloud in a bright place. All of the wounds he received from the demons he had fought were now healed, and his rabbit suit was in fine condition once more. Immediately before him the effulgent light that carried him off now gathered itself in front of him. It formed into an elongated shape and appeared as a shining light ray that formed itself into a small human shape. A beautiful smiling face appeared on this light ray, and the Rabbit-Man was filled with joy when he looked at it. Despite all of the hardships he recently endured he felt confident that everything would be alright. All fear was dispelled as he looked at the kind face within the glowing body of light.

"Hello Rabbit-Man" said the ray of light.

"Who are you?" the Rabbit-Man asked.

"I'm the Light Beam. I've been with you this whole time, but you were so distracted with the troubles you were facing that I was only able to reach out to you every once in a while. I hoped I would be able see you and speak with you like I am now."

"I remember feeling your light shining around me before," said the Rabbit-Man. "I had no idea it was you. But now that I see you here in front of me, it makes sense. I feel like I've known you all my life. But I've never seen you before. How can this be?"

"Don't worry about it," said the Light Beam. "I reside inside everyone, and I shine brighter inside those who try to do well. You remained true to your values and overcame the adversity you faced. I am impressed, and wanted to tell you how well you've done."

"What do you mean?" asked the Rabbit-Man. "How have I done well? I didn't destroy any of the enemies I faced, and I couldn't defeat that last demon I fought against. All of my other friends did better than me in the battle at the Grand Coliseum. My performance was hardly impressive at all. I'm afraid I don't understand you, Light Beam. I appreciate all you've done for me – your presence has certainly helped me, but I don't feel like I've accomplished anything significant."

"Just because you didn't destroy your enemies doesn't mean you didn't overcome them." the Light Beam answered. "Numerous enemies and obstacles tried to subdue you and break your spirit, yet you carried on with firm resolve. Even if at times your idea of how to overcome your troubles was mistaken, as in your experience at the Base Pad, you still continued to do what was right and help the people you cared about. You saw a world in agony and wished to spread the goodness you felt deep inside you to help heal it. Only special people have such an attitude. But it is through efforts like yours, and also those of your friends, that have allowed me to shine through. I enjoyed shining through you, and hope to continue doing so.

"The reason I appear to you now, Rabbit-Man, is to remind you that there is much love and joy to be found in the world and in your own life. So do not let the snares of these ghosts and demons or the unjust actions of other people overshadow that for you. You have felt true joy in the presence of your loved ones, and you have helped them experience it too. That is why you noticed my serene glow consciously. I must tell you now that you are in a dream state and will not remember this meeting specifically upon waking. But you will still carry the inner tranquility that I provide to you upon waking. There will be other challenges for you and your friends, but fear not because I will be with you and all of them. Always remember what is truly important, Rabbit-Man, and you will be invincible. Remember there is much goodness everywhere – you have experienced that when you shared good times with Mr. One, Sally and Twig, Geb, the Dream Queen, and all the others. Do not let the darkness trouble you. Sometimes there can even be goodness in that too. Remember how Eagle Top relinquished his wicked ways and fought passionately for the audience that supported him in his final moments. Goodness is there, let my brightness that shines within you rekindle it wherever you go."

"I think I see what you mean," answered the Rabbit-Man. "All I wanted was to help those I love. I still want to do that, but I feel so powerless. These demons and ghosts and other entities are so strong, and their power is so vast. Even with the talents that my special suit offers me, I can hardly compete with them. What should I do, Light Beam? How can I counter the evil in the world?"

"Just talk about your own journey here," said the Light Beam. "That's what is important. It is great that you have come so far as to see me now, but your journey there was what is really important. The things you learned and the way you grew will help you be better than ever."

"But does that really help anything? There were so many other great personalities in the Grand Coliseum that would merit recognition. People like wise Arman Tier and brave Sig Calcium. Who would care to hear about a rabbit-suited man that fell out of a garden?"

"Many people would love to hear about it, and also about the others too. You have longed to find peace and struggled to obtain it. That is common to very many people. Tell your story, and you'll do just fine. May your tale reach out and touch all souls who long to find peace. May it find its way to those who have lost a home that was dear to them, or who have struggled to find an identity as you have, or who have struggled with demons of their own. Your tale will inspire those who hear it to help others, and value doing so. May your story spread truth and love to the hearts and minds to those who hear it, as your deeds and convictions have spread such things in your world. Share your story, dear Rabbit-Man, so that others may find their own Light Beam too."

"I understand now," answered the Rabbit-Man. "I am glad you appeared to me, Light Beam, and I'll do all I can to keep your vibrant glow alive. The work of S.T. Ranger is far from over. Anywhere demons or ghosts roam to prey upon the innocent, I will counter their influence by remembering you, kind Light Beam. I feel better than I ever have before. I can't wait to tell the others what I've learned! All we need to overcome are the difficulties we face is inside of us. Thank you, Light Beam!" The Light Beam then entered into the Rabbit-Man, and he set out with renewed vigor. From the cloud he was seated on a bridge appeared that he knew he must follow. He walked along this silvery bridge through a starry region of space. He could not wait to meet up with his friends again. He was more powerful than ever before, but also more calm and serene. If he faced any of the enemies he previously encountered he would have had little difficulty overcoming them. As he walked along and reflected, he believed his fall from the Garden turned out to be a good thing after all. It allowed him to discover himself and connect with the beloved Light Beam. His far fall from the Garden allowed him to ascend to greater heights than he even knew existed, and for that he was very glad.

CPSIA information can be obtained
at www.ICGtesting.com
Printed in the USA
BVOW03s2027261116
468971BV00016B/908/P